Praise for *The Secret L...*

"Witty, whimsical, and yet so wonderfully down-to-earth, Sharon Hinck's *The Secret Life of Becky Miller* is everything you'd want in an entertaining read. It's smart, funny, and real. A convincing cast of characters is headlined by the perfectly drawn wife and mother whose secret ambitions add punch and panache to every chapter."

—Susan Meissner, author of *Why the Sky is Blue*

"Rarely does an author possess the ability to merge good storytelling with good word flow and still touch deeply into the heart of the reader. Sharon Hinck has done all three at one time, and this is only her first novel! This book comes alive from the very first page. I very much look forward to reading many more works from this unusually talented author."

—Hannah Alexander, author of *Under Suspicion*

"Hinck's humorous portrayal of the insecurities and struggles of Becky Miller made me see my own life as a Christian mom with a fresh perspective. *The Secret Life of Becky Miller* cleverly illustrates the difference between being busy for God and finding a place of genuine purpose."

—Sharon Dunn, award-winning author of the Ruby Taylor Mystery series

"You'll love getting to know Becky Miller! She's just like you—smart, tender, and deliciously witty, with an I-can-SO-relate-to-that life."

—Meredith Efken, author of the mom-lit comedy *SAHM I Am*

"A delightful read! Sharon Hinck will have you laughing, crying—and anxiously awaiting the next book from this extremely talented author."

—Cyndy Salzmann, author of the Friday Afternoon Club Mystery series

"Wonderful! Clever and heartwarming. From Becky's wild adventures to her daily drama to her spiritual poignancy, Sharon Hinck draws a story that captures the heart of the Christian mother, and speaks to the wannabe superhero in all of us. I loved it!"

—Susan May Warren, award-winning author of *Everything's Coming up Josey*

"From page one, Becky Miller sneaks into your heart—she's every wife and mom who wants to do it all but discovers she's only human. Christian authors are giving the literary world a run for their money, and Sharon Hinck is at the front of the pack. *The Secret Life of Becky Miller*, written in James Thurber's Walter Mitty-style, packs an Emeril-sized BAM!"

—Ane Mulligan, Novel Reviews

"In the style of James Thurber's Walter Mitty, Sharon Hinck delivers an exceptional read that will touch your heart and your funny bone. By the end of the book, you'll feel like Becky Miller is your best friend."

—Tim Bete, author of *In the Beginning . . . There Were No Diapers* and director of the Erma Bombeck Writers' Workshop

Gilber✝ex Foundation
1209 West Indiana Ave.
Midland, Texas 79701
432-570-9023
www.gilbertexfoundation.org

Renovating Becky Miller

Renovating Becky Miller
Copyright © 2007
Sharon Hinck

Cover design by Zandrah Kurland
Cover photos by Roberto Adrian and Olya Telnova

Published by Bethany House Publishers
11400 Hampshire Avenue South
Bloomington, Minnesota 55438

Bethany House Publishers is a division of
Baker Publishing Group, Grand Rapids, Michigan.

Printed in the United States of America

ISBN-13: 978-0-7642-0130-1
ISBN-10: 0-7642-0130-1

Library of Congress Cataloging-in-Publication Data

Hinck, Sharon.
    Renovating Becky Miller / Sharon Hinck.
        p.   cm.
    ISBN-13: 978-0-7642-0130-1 (pbk.)
    ISBN-10: 0-7642-0130-1 (pbk.)
    I. Title.

    PS3608.I53R46   2007
    813'.6—dc22

                                                                    2006036989

To Malvine Alutis

Home with her Savior at ninety-nine

Granny, you didn't see this book in print,

but you were so joyful that it was contracted.

Thank you for your love and prayers.

Renovating Becky Miller

a novel
by SHARON HINCK

BETHANY HOUSE PUBLISHERS
Minneapolis Minnesota

Chapter One

The pulsing siren *of a French police car shattered my ability to reason. Pure instinct took over. I had to get away.*

With a sharp crank of my steering wheel, I reversed into a spin, nearly impaling a bus with my Mini Cooper. Gears ground as I tore away down the narrow streets of Paris.

My tires skidded on the cobblestones. Two motorcycles appeared in my rearview mirror, joining the chase. Ever since I'd woken, half drowned, on a fishing trawler, I'd been fighting to regain my memory. If they caught me now, I'd never find the clues I needed. Never find answers to the questions that tortured me. Why did I have a dozen passports? Why did I know how to fight off armed opponents? When did I learn to drive like this?

I rocketed around a corner. My car lifted onto two wheels as I dodged down an alley and burst out onto a busy street. Ahead, traffic bottled up my escape route. My pursuers were right on my tail.

Without thinking, I cranked the wheel and bounced onto the sidewalk. Tourists and Parisians jumped out of the way. Lampposts blurred past. The edge of a perfumery sign scraped along the side of the car. I nicked a phone booth door. An explosion of glass showered my car.

I'd lost the first police car, but others had joined the chase. Time for a surprise.

There. *An opening appeared up ahead.* I cut left across traffic and through a small park, aiming for a walkway. A narrow stairway led down toward the Seine.

Adrenaline surged through me and I shot over the edge. My car lurched and bounced, as out of control as my life. The shocks rattled with each step.

So did my bones. I reached the bottom with a scrape of the chassis and took off again. Burning oil stung my nose. The Mini couldn't hold together much longer.

More sirens sounded a condemning blare behind me. Up ahead, a vendor pushed his cart into my path. A flower cart.

Vibrant blue bouquets filled my vision. Forget-me-nots. What irony.

I slammed on the brakes.

Dust swirled as the minivan skidded to a sudden stop. "Mommy!" Kelsey screamed from the backseat.

My fingers loosened their death grip on the wheel. "Sorry, honey. There was a squirrel."

The furry beast scampered away, oblivious.

I waited for the adrenaline rush to calm and eased the car forward, steering around construction materials and earth-moving machinery. The whole congregation was excited about the building project, but navigating in and out of the complex was a hazard. Especially when daredevil squirrels launched sneak attacks.

A long line of cars inched into place, waiting their turn to make the dash onto Bailey Avenue. Faith Community Church's school program had mushroomed, and dozens of parents clogged the driveway when morning kindergarten and day care let out each day. Located in an expanding suburb of Minneapolis, the church struggled to keep up with rapid growth.

My toes hovered impatiently over the gas pedal. "So how was school?"

Kelsey drew a deep breath, but I waved my hand in the air. "Wait. Let Micah go first."

Kelsey blew out steam like a tiny blond teakettle. "Micah doesn't have anything to tell. All they do is play." The elder stateswoman of kindergarten sneered in her brother's direction, daring him to contradict.

I adjusted my rearview mirror so I could see directly behind me. My youngest bounced his chubby legs and beamed. Cheetos-orange stains circled his lips, and Kool-Aid streaks flecked his sweat shirt.

"Me did songs." He launched into a muddled version of a praise chorus, punctuating each line with a kick to the back of my seat.

When he stopped for breath, Kelsey cut in. "I learned that one when I was a baby."

His face wadded up like a gum wrapper. "Not a baby."

A few cars pulled out, but Dolores Krause's maroon wagon sat unmoving in front of us. I tapped the horn, and she closed the gap between the SUV in front of her. I smiled through the mirror at Micah. "Of course not. You're a big schoolboy now." Micah loved believing that his morning day care was on par with Kelsey's kindergarten.

Kelsey fluffed her curls with one hand. "He's only two and a half."

"And you're five, and Dylan is nine. And Mommy and Daddy are thirty-three. We're all the age God made us to be." There. I'd held off a conflagration and slipped in a teachable moment all at the same time. I nosed our blue Windstar up to the intersection. When a brief gap in traffic appeared, I gunned the engine and barreled out. "So what did you learn today, Kels?"

"Blue and yellow make green."

"I like gween," Micah said, his dark lashes swooping adoringly in his sister's direction.

She ignored the interruption. "Lots of words start with T but you don't always say *T-T-T*. Sometimes you say *Thhh*." She sprayed the sound. Micah giggled and chimed in. I tuned them out as they experimented with all the spittle-producing consonants they could create.

The left lane was moving faster and I cut over. I needed to get the Fall Retreat Guide to the printers and then get the kids home for lunch. The car in front of me slowed and then flicked on a left turn signal as an afterthought. *Thanks for bothering to warn me, bud.*

I huffed and cranked the wheel to the right as soon as I saw an opening. We blazed toward the next intersection. The light switched to yellow and I braked hard. I could have made it through, but ever since my car accident a couple years ago, I'd been nervous at busy cross streets. Impatience and caution squabbled inside me when I drove—like the other conflicts I lived with constantly.

I was a full-time mom. And I loved it. Except when it drove me crazy. My children were magnificent, bewildering creations gifted to me from the Almighty. Except when they were tormenting me like gleeful gargoyles wielding red-hot pokers.

"We're not having that for supper again, are we?"

"Mommy, she broke my Lego house."

"He stole the red piece. Tell him to give me back the red piece."

"Mom, I'm supposed to bring cookies today. Can you drive for the field trip?"

"Mommy, Micah put the gerbil in the toilet. Do something!"

I glanced into the backseat. At least when we were buzzing from place to place, they were buckled in and I could keep track of them. We turned into the strip mall, and I squeezed into a parking place near the print shop.

I shoved the car door open and reached across the seat for my cane. The kids had plastered it with stickers. Strawberry Shortcake, Snoopy, and rainbows overlapped their way up from the rubber-tipped foot to the coated-aluminum handle. Kelsey unlatched her buckle and helped Micah from his car seat.

My friend Lori often reminded me that having a mom with a disability would help my children learn independence and compassion. A comforting thought. I had added the notion to my mental jelly jar of encouraging words for the days when the pain and nuisance of my damaged leg overrode my ability to keep smiling. But I still hated moving like a senior citizen when I was in my early thirties. Some days I reminded God that He could have stopped the semi that had skidded through the intersection, totaling our car as well as my left knee and hip. Months of physical therapy had helped, but the last year there'd been no further improvement. The pain fluctuated—some days were better than others—but the total healing I'd prayed for hadn't come.

Today was better than most. Dry, late-September air stirred leaves into rowdy square dances in the corner of the parking lot. No storms moving in. No change in air pressure. The ache in my hip and knee was tolerable. "Micah, hold your sister's hand." I hefted my bag to my shoulder and hobbled up the sidewalk with the children skipping beside me.

Kelsey and Micah aimed for the candy dish on the service counter. A white-haired man in a mint green polo shirt popped up his head from behind a copy machine.

I rummaged in my bag for my program folder. "I need two hundred copies of this booklet, spiral-bound with a laminated cover. I'll pick them up on Friday."

He scribbled on an order sheet and nodded. Kelsey and Micah glanced around the shop, tempted by the buttons on the self-serve copiers. But they stayed close. Our rule was they always had to be able to touch the cane by the time I counted to three—one of my creative solutions, now that I couldn't chase them through grocery stores and malls at a full sprint.

The elderly clerk smiled at Kelsey. "Where do you get your pretty blond curls? Must be your daddy."

I handed him the church credit card and sighed at his implication. Kels didn't get her looks from me. My coarse brown layers refused to hold a curl.

"Nah." Kelsey pirouetted. "Daddy's hair is chocolate chip." She had a new set of sixty-four crayons and was precise about variations in shade. "I got my hair from Aunt JuJu."

"My sister is a blonde," I explained, signing the receipt. Blond, stylish, flawless. Judy had encouraged me to adopt a more professional look now that I was working. My blue sweater set over straight-leg khakis might not be a power suit, but it was a big step up from the mommy-sweats I used to wear. Of course, Judy would have added the perfect scarf and a sleek leather attaché case.

The only adornment around my throat was the macaroni and hot-pink yarn necklace that Micah had made in day care that morning. My tote had once served as Micah's diaper bag. Quilted fabric with teddy bears did a poor job of imitating a briefcase.

I never could get the hang of accessorizing. Those extra details were not for moms of three young children. I was lucky to run a comb through my hair and brush my teeth before hurrying out the door each morning.

My cell phone chittered from deep inside my bag. I reached for it, nodded good-bye to the clerk, and steered my kids toward the door. We paused on the sidewalk. "Hello, this is Becky."

"Oh, I'm glad I caught you." Teresa Vogt's ramped-up voice buzzed through the phone. "I've got a bunch of ladies from the decorating committee here, and they can't find the things—" Garbled voices in the background interrupted her. "Okay, I'll tell her. They need the silk-leaf runners and can't find the candles."

"They're in the closet by the kitchen."

"Um. Yeah. They said they already checked there. Look, can you swing by for a few minutes to sort this out?" Her good-natured energy sounded a bit frayed around the edges. Teresa was terrific in her role as Adult Ministries Director. She was a visionary. But I knew she had little patience for details like votives or floral arrangements.

Her recommendation had led to my job at Faith, and I remained grateful to her, even when she roped me into more work than I could manage. "Okay. I'll be right there."

Kelsey's shoulders slumped. "But, Mom, I'm hungry."

"Me too." Micah sent a woeful gaze my direction.

Kelsey shoved him. "Stop copying me."

"Kids, get in the car." My whipcrack command headed off their whines.

As I leaned awkwardly to adjust Micah's buckle, compunction caught up to me. I'd been snapping at the kids far too often. We seemed to rush everywhere these days. Hurry through breakfast, fight traffic to drop kids at school and day care, scramble through the pile of work on my desk in the church office, race home with

Kelsey and Micah for a few hours before returning to pick up Dylan from fourth grade. I was supposed to be on staff part-time, but directing our church's women's ministry didn't fit into three-and-a-half hours a day and a few nights each week. As the program had grown, my stress level seemed to simmer on a constant low boil. I didn't want to take it out on my children.

"Tell you what. After we take care of the problem at church, we'll stop at Burger King, okay?"

Both faces beamed at me. I was hero mom again. So what if it was just cupboard love?

I pulled out of the parking lot and headed back to church. A quick stop to help the committee find what they needed—then we'd grab some burgers to bring home. I'd turn off my phone and spend some quality time with the kids—reading *I'll Love You Forever* and playing Candy Land—and make a nutritious supper to compensate for the junk-food lunch.

When I headed through the church doors, I was swept into a chaotic chase scene. Questions and needs darted around me. The church secretary chirped a reminder that she needed my article for the October newsletter and warned me that my voice mails were piling up. I steered the decorating committee in the right direction but then found a young mom sniffling in my office, crumpled tissues around her. "Oh, Becky, I'm so glad you're in this afternoon. I really need to talk to someone."

Kelsey and Micah studied me with knowing eyes, watching their hoped-for cheeseburgers disappear. One of the women on the retreat committee offered to take them downstairs and scrounge the church kitchen for a sandwich.

I gave my children approving smiles when they trotted away without complaining. They were so adaptable. When they disappeared down the hall, my thoughts steered rapidly into an alley of remorse. I tried to zig past the guilt kiosk but couldn't avoid it completely. I had crashed into my children's hopes, sending their trust tumbling. Again.

There wasn't time to stop and fix it. Problems pursued me—right on my tail. I kept trying to find an open road so I could aim us toward home, but by the time I'd counseled the weepy young mom, handed in my article for the newsletter, and returned the most urgent phone calls, it was almost three o'clock—time to pick up Dylan from his fourth-grade classroom in the education wing.

I loaded all three kids in the car. Pressure behind my eyes throbbed in rhythm with my pulse. As we pulled out into traffic, I dreamed of turning left instead of right, of driving away from town and out into the country. Off into the sunset. Away from the insistent responsibilities.

Some folks might crumble under the pressure. Not me. I was Becky Miller. I could build a women's ministry program, raise my children, keep an orderly house, get delicious suppers on the table, and be a caring wife to Kevin.

My cell phone rang. When I flipped it open, Kevin's hearty greeting buzzed in my ear, as if my thoughts had conjured him. "Hey, hon, I found it."

"I didn't know you lost it."

An impatient sigh answered me. "The house."

Now it was my turn to sigh. "Not another one. It's been a rough day."

"I'm telling you, this is the one. Come on. It'll only take a few minutes to look at it after supper."

Where did he get his energy? For months, he'd been dragging me around to explore "dream homes." We were outgrowing our tiny rambler, but I was weary of the hunt and skeptical we'd ever find anything we could afford.

"Can we make a deal? Wait—Dylan, stop poking your sister. Okay, I'm back. If this one doesn't work out, can we take a break from house hunting?"

"Oops, the signal's breaking up. See you soon. Bye."

My car lurched through a pothole, and I eased off the gas pedal. The light ahead turned red. I coasted to a stop and rubbed my temples. Worry blossomed along with the building headache. Kevin and I had often been at cross-purposes in recent months.

We'd taken the suggestion of various marriage books and started having a regular Saturday "date night." We couldn't afford a baby-sitter, so we usually rented a movie and snuggled on the couch after the kids went to bed. At least it gave us a few hours to escape each week. No matter how bad my life felt, the characters in the movies had worse problems, and I drew encouragement from how every woe could be resolved by the last scene.

Unfortunately, we had trouble agreeing on which movies to rent. Kevin loved any epic or spy film. I voted for chick flicks or old classics. Even our movie selections became a power struggle.

All marriages go through rough patches. We're just busy right now.

The light turned green, and I gunned the engine and hurried toward home, fighting to ignore the anxiety grinding like an over-heated engine.

"So, Mom," Dylan said from the backseat. "What's for supper?"

I took a deep breath. "Leftovers. And we'll need to eat fast. Dad wants us to see another house tonight." I wove through the streets, wondering why I felt something chasing me the whole way home.

Chapter Two

Yards of French silk billowed around my ankles
as I stepped into the jade dress. The skirt wasn't as full
as the wide hoopskirts in fashion before the war, but it still
set off my tiny waist. With so many men fighting the Yankees, and shortages
gripping Atlanta, most women had let themselves go and looked as dowdy
as maiden aunts. A true Southern girl knew the value of charm, a coy smile,
and fabric that set off her eyes. And I'd need all my ammunition to convince
Kevin to stay.

The front door crashed open. My heart pounded, and I raced for the
balcony overlooking the entryway. Kevin never entered a room quietly. He
strode across the marble foyer and tossed his hat toward a chair. Energy and
confidence radiated from his tall frame. I had expected marriage to tame him,
but Kevin was still a scoundrel. I could never predict how he'd react, and
suddenly I found it hard to breathe. Maybe my corset was laced too tightly
again.

I leaned forward over the railing and tilted my head. "Kevin dahlin',
I'm so glad you're home."

He paused at the base of the wide staircase and looked up. His gaze
raked over me. A slow smile raised the ends of his dark moustache. "Worried
about me?" His deep voice was rich with humor.

Why did I always feel as if he were laughing at me? I pursed my lips
in a pout. "Of course not." I sashayed down the stairs, slowing as I neared
to let him enjoy the view. "You're too smart to get into any trouble you can't
get yourself out of."

He threw back his head and laughed. When I reached the bottom step,
he grabbed me and kissed me hard. He lifted his head and one eyebrow

quirked. "So what do you want this time?"

With my pulse pounding, it took me a moment to remember my plan. Drat those corset stays. They made it impossible to think clearly. I lowered my voice to a wistful purr.

"Honey, let's stay home tonight. Please? Dylan needs help with his spelling, Kelsey and Micah had a long day, and you look tired, too." I tucked the last dish into the dishwasher and hit the button that made it wheeze into action.

He gave a low chuckle. "*I* look tired?" Kevin's arms wrapped my waist from behind, and his five-o'clock shadow tickled my neck as he nuzzled.

Annoyance flared and I pulled away. "Okay, *I'm* tired. We're busy enough, and I'm sick of spending every free moment driving out to see houses that never work out."

He waited until I turned to look at him. A muscle flexed along his jawline. His hickory brown eyes studied me with an expression I couldn't read. "I'm doing this for you. Think of all the time you'll save if we live closer to the church. This one has a huge yard for the kids. New appliances."

Seductive words. I peered out the kitchen window to our post-age stamp-sized yard. Tiny houses elbowed each other along the block. Rusty compacts and "old lady" cars hugged the curb. Real estate agents called ours a "starter neighborhood." Young couples or retired folk. No one for the kids to play with. And the crime rate had been rising. Sirens interrupted our sleep more and more often.

"I know we need more room, but can't we wait a few years?"

He rubbed his neck. "There've been rumbles at work about opening up a new branch of our office in Hastings. I found out today that they want me to head it up. That's a long drive from Richfield. My commute would be three times longer."

"And the last thing we need is less family time every day."

"Yep. I need to give them my answer soon, but if we don't find something closer to Hastings, I'll let it pass and keep working in the Minneapolis office." He sounded like a woebegone little boy giving up a chance to throw in the opening-day ball for the Twins.

I folded the dish towel and draped it over the oven door handle. "All right. I'm game. But if it's a wreck, or we can't afford it, we don't get attached, okay?"

Kevin grinned. "I'm telling you, this is the one. I drove out to see it at lunch today. It's perfect."

"It's perfect," I whispered later as we pulled up a long dirt drive. Faint streaks of sunset lit the dusky sky with enough light for me to appreciate the play of bronze oak leaves against weathered gray clapboard. The farmhouse sprawled across the hill like a stately plantation.

I shoved the van door open and scrambled out, leaning on my cane. A tall pine guarded one corner of the wide porch, its needles sighing as the wind tousled the limbs. Even though this was no longer a working farm, I was sure I smelled fresh-cut hay. Light poured out through a row of windows, promising a warm hearth, fresh-baked peach cobbler, and a slower, simpler life. Living in a house like this was guaranteed to reduce stress.

Kevin's arm wrapped around my shoulder. His breath warmed my cheek as he murmured against my ear. "Was I right, or what?"

"Oh, Kevin, it's amazing. I'm afraid to get my hopes up."

His chuckle rumbled low in his chest. "I knew you'd love it. And there's extra room. In case we ever need it." A worried undercurrent leaked through his words.

Before I could puzzle out what he meant, the real estate agent's car pulled up beside us. Brenda Finney was an enthusiastic, middle-aged woman in a square-cut blazer, who never tired of waxing eloquent about selling points. She climbed out and flashed a penlight at her listing. "The owner's family were some of the first to farm in this area. He's sold off most of the land to a developer, but the house still comes with two acres."

Beyond the wide yard and sprawling meadow, expensive brick houses congregated in precise cul-de-sacs. I hunched into my jacket.

"This can't possibly be in our price range."

"Right on target," Brenda insisted. "These older homes that need TLC are a bargain. Let's go on up. They're expecting us."

I had wanted to hate the house. Then I could convince Kevin we needed a break from the tedious search. And I could avoid the exhausting prospect of listing our house, getting it cleaned up to show, sorting, packing, moving—a mom's nightmare.

The kids scampered out of the van and raced ahead of us and up the porch steps. The wide front door opened, and three golden retriever puppies bounded out to greet them. Micah sat down and opened his arms. His laughter was soon muffled by fur. Kelsey and Dylan promptly forgot the house and began cuddling the pups, as well.

I shook my head. Every real estate agent should provide puppies as a welcoming committee. We hadn't set foot in the house and we were lost already.

I nodded a quick greeting as Brenda introduced the owner, a grizzled old man in stained denim and a baseball cap. The house drew me further in. The wood-floored living room was three times the size of ours. Sure, walking across it felt like being on a ship, as some parts sagged a bit. But some of my parts sagged, too, and I'd managed to ignore that fact.

The view out of the north window showcased a stand of pines. "It feels like we're way out in the country," I whispered to Kevin. "Look at the scenery."

"And it's only five minutes from the church and school. From here, my drive to the new office won't take any longer than it does now." He avoided saying "I told you so" but still couldn't hide all his smugness.

We explored the rest of the main floor and found the large kitchen. Sure enough, updated appliances gleamed over chipped linoleum. Kevin twisted the faucet at the sink. A deep moan vibrated from the pipes. Finally, water sputtered out with a gasp. Brenda appeared at my elbow. "The disclosure statement indicates the plumbing may need updating. But at this price, you'll be able to afford a few repairs."

I nodded, unconcerned. Rusty pipes couldn't dampen my adoration of this house. From the window over the sink, a wide meadow promised healthy outdoor playtime for the children. A harvest moon hung low in the sky. Kevin and I would sit on a porch swing each night and watch the stars come out. This piece of land would heal our marriage, strengthen our family, and provide a refuge for generations to come. I leaned forward to press my nose against the window. "Look, I think there's a garden."

"Oh yes." Brenda tapped a pen on her listing sheet. "The barn was taken down ten years ago, but there's a large shed that's used as a garage. The owner stopped farming the land but kept up his vegetable patch."

A garden. Think of the money we'd save. I could grow our own food. There was something so secure about owning a large plot of land. Like Scarlett O'Hara, I could grab a fistful of dirt and radishes and shake it at the sky, defying every enemy.

"Come on." Kevin pulled me back from the window. "Let's take a look at the upstairs."

As we maneuvered the narrow wooden stairs, I tightened the grip on my cane, pausing to catch my breath in the upstairs hallway while Kevin searched for the switch. A dim orange fixture on the wall flickered to life. The corridor needed overhead lighting, but that was probably an easy weekend project.

Kevin ran a hand over his dark buzz-cut hair and looked down the stairs toward where our agent was chatting with the owner. "Honey, I don't know about these steps."

His voice took on the gentle, worried tone he used whenever he skirted the mention of my limp. In the two years since my accident, I had refused to be an object of pity. Kevin had learned to be sparing with his sympathy. When he got too solicitous, I tended to bite his head off.

"Exercise is good for my leg. Besides, I'm up and down our

basement stairs a dozen times a day. This won't be a problem." To prove my point, I moved quickly toward the first door on the left, ready to explore the bedrooms.

"Yeah, but this house has a basement, too. And an attic. That's a lot of stairs."

I reached the second door and gasped. "Look at that claw-foot tub. What a beauty."

Kevin laughed at my enthusiasm. "If I'd known that was all it took to impress you, I could have found something a long time ago." He stepped up behind me and rested his chin on the top of my head. "Honey, I've been wanting to ask you about something—"

"So what do you think?" The eager voice of our real estate agent pulled us apart. "Should I put together a bid?"

I turned to face Kevin. One dark brow canted upward, and his teeth gleamed from the shadow of whiskers on his jaw. We'd been married over ten years, and the scoundrel could still charm my socks off.

This time he didn't need to. The house had already won me over. I gave him an answering smile. "Let's go for it."

"We'll want to hire a home inspector to come and take a look."

Fiddledeedee. An inspection wouldn't turn up any problems we couldn't solve. "Fine, but let's get moving on this. Wouldn't it be great if we could settle in before Thanksgiving?"

"Don't worry. I know a guy." Kevin bounded down the stairs to steer the kids back to the van.

I followed more slowly, teetering a bit on the steep stairs, but feeling a rush of anticipation strong enough to wash away my weariness. How fast could we figure out a bid? How many other people had seen the house? We would never find another home as perfect as this. We absolutely had to get it. Modern life had been tearing a swath through our family like Sherman's march through the South. But I was convinced that this house would change all that.

Chapter Three

"Pull over. I'll walk from here." I fumbled a few
dollars from my purse. My heart raced as the taxi drew
closer to the Empire State Building.

The bulbous yellow cab swerved to a stop against the curb, across the
street from my goal. *"What's the rush, lady?"* The gruff, genial voice of the
cabbie made me smile. 1950s New York had its own cadence. Voices blurted
out opinions with the same abrupt enthusiasm as the car horns and jack-
hammers on the busy streets.

I leaped from the taxi, feeling the pressure of time. It was five o'clock in
the evening, and I still needed to take the elevator to the top.

Even so, I paused long enough to offer my gloved hand to the driver and
give him a generous tip. *"I'm going to be married."* I wanted to tell the
world.

I stared up at the skyscraper and smoothed the folds of my skirt. I loved
the poetry of this tryst. The Empire State Building was the nearest thing to
heaven in New York. What better place to reunite?

I'd missed him so much. Every day during those long six months, I'd
been haunted by memories of our shipboard romance.

Now we could finally be together.

I darted across the street. Suddenly brakes shrieked—an almost human
cry of pain. The impact barely registered.

Why was I crumpled on the street? Why were so many faces staring
down at me? I needed to get to the elevator. What would Kevin think if I
didn't show up? Would he hear the approaching sirens from way up there?
It was the last thought I managed before a fog of darkness smothered me.

From outside, the garage door rattled open, and Kevin's brakes gave their customary soft squeal before the engine cut out.

I pushed myself up on the couch, bleary and confused. I'd fallen asleep with a movie playing. I rubbed my cheek and felt the impression of a pillow button imbedded in my skin. Kevin's occasional late-night appointments always seemed to fall on the nights when I didn't have a church meeting. We'd become tag-team parents, always missing each other.

Wincing as my bad leg took my weight, I eased to my feet. I should have gone to bed after tucking the kids in, but I needed to talk to Kevin. We had to make some decisions about the move. And I wanted to hear about his day.

But now my mouth felt woolly, and my brain cells had called it a night.

My cane squeaked against the linoleum as I made my way across the kitchen to meet Kevin. He sprang through the side door, slid his briefcase toward the corner, and tossed his keys into the basket on the counter. If he wore a fedora, he could have flipped it to a perfect landing on a hat rack.

His dark eyes sparked when he saw me. I knew I looked rumpled and sleep creased, but his slow grin showed appreciation and even a flare of carnal interest.

"Hi, hon. I'm glad you're still up." He closed the space between us for a hug and a deep kiss. He tasted like coffee. No wonder he was revved up. "We had a great meeting. And Harry says he can go out and look at the house on Saturday. How was your day?"

"Better now," I murmured, leaning into his chest. He smelled of fall leaves, smoky restaurant, and a hint of French fries. "Problems came up at church, and I ended up staying through the afternoon again."

"You work too hard. You need to delegate."

It was an old argument. I'd explained a dozen times that it took more time to supervise someone else than to do it myself. I eased away from him and sank onto a kitchen chair. "Things will slow down after the retreat."

His brows lifted, pressing a skeptical wrinkle into his forehead. "Mm-hmm. Until the women's Christmas tea. And the January parenting classes. And the mentoring training. And the spring fashion show."

I snorted. "We don't have a spring fashion show."

"Well, it's about the only event you don't have." He loosened his tie and pulled out a chair kitty-corner to mine. "But I've got just what you need."

His enthusiasm was contagious, and I felt my spirits lift in spite of my fatigue. "A week at a spa? A live-in maid?"

"Better." He reached into his jacket pocket and pulled out an envelope with a flourish. "Tickets to the Vikings' game. The rep we met with tonight gave them to me. Dylan and Kelsey haven't been to a game in years, and Micah hasn't ever seen them play in person." He made it sound as if social services would be hounding us for neglect.

I giggled. "Sounds like a great plan. When is it?"

"This Sunday."

My giggle transformed into a groan. "Teresa scheduled a staff meeting for this Sunday after church. I can't go."

Kevin's torso deflated. "When did this come up?"

"A few days ago. I forgot to tell you."

He left his chair and prowled the narrow kitchen like a caged Doberman. The sheen of his dark hair and hint of stubble on his face added to the likeness. "We agreed that Sunday afternoon would be family time."

"I know. I'm sorry. It's only this once. We've had some problems with relationships in the staff with all the rapid growth, and Teresa thought . . . But you and the kids can go. You'll still have fun."

Kevin pivoted at the far end of the stove and his gaze met mine. Distance stretched between us, wider than the kitchen floor. Wider than this scheduling conflict.

I pushed to my feet, wanting to erase some of the space between us. "Honey, it's for the church. I know I've been too busy, but it's just a phase. Aren't you happy that God's blessed our church so much? It's a good problem to have."

I hoped that some of the tension in Kevin's muscles was caused by too much caffeine and not his frustration with me. He gave a tight smile. "Yeah, I wouldn't want to stand in the way of God's work."

My knees buckled at his sarcasm, and I lowered back onto the chair. Things had been chaotic for a while now, but our mutual frustration had been leavened with humor. This new edge of bitterness in Kevin's words scared me.

"That's not what I meant." My voice sounded small.

He turned away, fists pressed against the counter. "I know. It's not your fault." After a long pause, he sighed and came back to the table. "Doesn't the church want to support marriages?" His rueful smile was only half teasing.

I perked up. "Actually, I wanted to talk to you about that."

He blinked at my sudden liveliness and lowered to the edge of his chair, wary.

"Teresa is planning a marriage workshop for our church in early November and asked me if you and I would team teach some of the sessions."

Kevin's hooded eyes were impossible to read, so I rushed on. "I know things have been crazy lately. We hardly see each other coming and going. This could be fun." I infused every ounce of appeal that I could into my voice. I did everything but bat my eyelashes at him. "Please?"

He rubbed his neck. "I don't know. Besides, if the farmer accepts our offer, we'll be busy selling our house and getting packed."

I leaned forward. "It would be a chance for us to do something together."

"You want us to teach other people about marriage?" Something sad flickered in his eyes, but I didn't have time to analyze it.

Teresa wanted my answer soon, and I had to convince Kevin this would be fun.

"Yeah. I have tons of ideas. We can talk about things that put a strain on a marriage—like when you were out of work. And we can share ideas for keeping the romance alive even when you have young kids—like our date night. Although I suppose they won't think renting a movie once a week is very exciting. Still, we can come up with some good ideas for them."

Kevin turned and rifled through the stack of mail and school papers on the table. "What did we decide about Dylan playing basketball this year?"

I let him divert me from my sales pitch and tried to ignore the hurt that pressed my sternum. If he wanted to change the subject, I'd go along. "He really wants to be on the team. All his friends are."

Kevin nodded and slid the form toward me. I studied the complex schedule of practices and tournaments and winced. We already squeezed too many events into each small calendar square. How were we going to juggle Dylan's basketball games? Kevin glanced through the conglomeration of spelling tests, finger-paint pictures, bills, and flyers.

He picked up a personal letter. A printed rosebud adorned the corner of the envelope. When he pulled out the letter, the paper held spidery, cursive letters that stayed inside careful margins. The letter from Kevin's mom was addressed to both of us, so I'd already skimmed it. Her arthritis was getting worse, and the doctor was urging her to sell her house. Other than that update, the brief note was innocuous. Warm, but nonintrusive—like her presence in our lives. Although I'd made an effort to involve Grandma Rose with the kids, she rarely left her home in Florida, and we didn't have the budget to visit her often. I knew Kevin worried about her. She'd had him late in life, after years of trying, and he was her only child. I'd met women in their seventies who still had a lot of zip, but Rose wasn't one of those. Her difficult life had taken a toll.

Kevin lingered over the letter, seeming to see something

between the lines. "Maybe now she'll think about moving up here."

"You've tried before. She's been in the same house since you were a baby. She'll never give it up." Was I wrong to be relieved that she had never listened to our suggestion that she relocate closer to us? "Besides, the Minnesota winters would be too hard on her."

"Maybe."

"So, about the marriage workshop—"

"Mommy." Kelsey tottered into the kitchen, squinting against the fluorescent light over the sink, knuckling tears off her cheek. "My tummy hurts."

I opened my arms, but she noticed Kevin and veered toward him. He hefted her onto his lap. "What did you eat today?"

"I don't know." She sniffled and rested her blond curls against his shoulder. Kevin looked at me.

What had she eaten? Something scrounged from the church kitchen for lunch. I couldn't remember supper. I scanned the kitchen table for clues in the crumbs. "We had leftover chicken, Cheez-Its, and grapes." She'd been having a lot of stomachaches lately, but the doctor hadn't found anything wrong.

"I think they were bad grapes," Kelsey moaned.

My worry eased back, and I hid a smile. "The grapes were fine. You just got mad when they touched your chicken."

Her lower lip pressed into a Mick Jagger pout. "I told you not to put them on my plate."

Kevin covered his chuckle by planting a kiss on the top of Kelsey's head. "Come on, princess. Your tummy'll feel better if you're back in your bed."

She wiggled her bare toes as he stood up, cradling her. "And it'll feel better if you tell me a story."

"Okay, but let's be quiet. We don't want to wake the boys." Kevin headed down the hall in an exaggerated tiptoe, and Kelsey clapped a hand over her mouth to smother her giggles.

Affection flooded me. Kevin was an amazing dad. He had so much more energy to give the children than I did. When he read bedtime books, he always did full character voices and never skipped a page. He wrestled the kids in the fall leaves. He suggested spontaneous walks to the park.

A familiar wave of discouragement lapped at my self-image. I wanted to be a better mom. More cheerful. More lively. A mixture of Mary Poppins creativity, Maria von Trapp enthusiasm, and Claire Huxtable unflappability. Of course, it wasn't fair that Kevin always played "good cop" to my "bad cop." He left discipline to me. He explained that, because of his past, he didn't trust his temper. A convenient excuse.

I scribbled my signature on the basketball form and signed a field-trip permission slip. After another glance at the school papers, I lowered my head into my hands. It had been a long day. That's what was causing the funny ache that felt perilously close to loneliness. Kevin and I couldn't seem to find a rendezvous high enough above the chaos of our busy days.

Grow up, Becky. Busy schedules, conflicting needs, juggled priorities. Such things were the realities of life.

Good thing tomorrow was Thursday. My Thursday night Bible study group was like a brief cruise in calm waters. I needed my girlfriends' support and prayers before the big fall retreat on Saturday. I couldn't wait to tell them all about the house we'd found. This was a divine opportunity, and I wanted them all praying that our inspector wouldn't find any problems and that the farmer would accept our offer.

It wasn't until I turned out the lights and limped down the hall toward the bedroom that I realized Kevin hadn't given me his answer about the workshop.

I peeked into Kelsey's room. She was asleep, with sweaty curls framing her face. The jaw that sometimes jutted forward in rebellion was slack and vulnerable. I almost woke her up so I could cuddle her and croon over her. Instead, I pulled the quilt up to her shoulder and backed out of the room on tiptoe.

The boys' room floor was scattered with wadded-up socks,

crumpled jeans, and sports equipment. We really did need more room. I picked my way around a Star Wars model and checked on Micah. He had wedged himself into the corner of his crib, one arm clutching a lime green Stegosaurus. He'd outgrown his crib, but to fit him in a big-boy bed we'd need to get bunks, and somehow we hadn't found the time to do that yet either. After straightening him out, I stroked the round curves of his chubby face. A dynamo of mischief all day, now he was an appealing bundle in his fuzzy, footed pajamas.

Dylan took a wuffling breath from his side of the room. I made my way toward him and removed the dog-eared copy of *Treasure Island* from his chest, then risked a gentle kiss on his forehead. He didn't wake up, but his sigh sounded happy.

My smile faded when I reached the master bedroom. After Kevin had tucked Kelsey back into bed, he'd slipped into his pajamas and crawled into our bed alone.

Light from the hall illuminated his shoulders and the hard line of his back. His even breathing continued as I slipped under the covers beside him. So much for our conversation. Another missed rendezvous. I was beginning to wonder when we would ever manage to connect.

Chapter Four

After the gnarled branches of the dark forest, the field of poppies reminded me of sunny afternoons in Kansas. "I think we're going to make it." I shifted my basket to my other arm and waded into the midst of the blossoms.

"Of course we are." The Scarecrow kicked up his heels in celebration. "I may not know a lot, but doesn't that look like an Emerald City in the distance?" He galloped forward, tripped over his own feet, and collapsed in a pile of limbs, laughing.

I caught his enthusiasm, and my ruby slippers seemed to sparkle with extra brightness. Our answer was almost in sight.

"Oh, oh, oh. I don't know about this. There could be thorns. There could be snakes in the grass." The Lion's shiver set his mane quaking.

"Let's keep moving. It's still a long way. Say, could you oil my knee?" The Tin Woodsman waited while I found the oil can and helped him loosen his joints again. Linking arms, we stepped into the meadow.

Where would I be without these dear companions? We each had different dreams, but traveling together had helped us past some frightening moments.

I yawned. The sunlight and soft fragrance made me feel the most relaxed I had been since the tornado. No, not merely relaxed. Sleepy. I wanted to curl up in a ray of sunshine and rest.

"Come on, Becky. Don't stop now." The Tin Man's voice sounded far away. My legs grew heavy. It was too hard to take another step.

"Mrs. Miller?" A voice pulled me back to the present. It took me a moment to absorb my surroundings. Orange mums lined the sidewalk toward Heather's front steps, and light spilled from the open door.

"Mrs. Miller, come on in." One of Heather's eleven-year-old twins greeted me from the top step of the porch, her eyes looking huge through her thick glasses. I moved slowly. I'd had to park halfway down the block. This late in the day, my bad leg protested against more steps.

"Mom's in the kitchen. She'll be right out." She ushered me through the hallway, took my coat, and disappeared.

I'd looked forward to being with my Thursday night Bible study girls all week long: Heather, with her free spirit and inner flowerchild who made horrible organic food; Doreen, the pulled-together power player who tackled the corporate world and still cared for her three kids; Sally, the plump, blond busybody who gave too much advice but always had practical help to offer; and Lori the tall, conservative African-American who had her pulse on every political cause and had memorized half the Bible. We were an odd stew, but somehow the flavors blended, and we were all better because of one another.

The living room wrapped me in warm textures and creative color combinations. The tweedy sofa and macramé plant hangers gave me flashbacks to the early seventies, and the heavy wood chest that served as a coffee table invited guests to prop up their Birkenstocks and mellow out. Heather's latest home business was candle making. Scented tapers and hand-rolled beeswax adorned every available surface. I took a deep breath and let my muscles relax into a willow rocking chair. Every time I visited Heather, I could feel my pulse slow.

Tonight I craved the fellowship of my friends more than ever. Kelsey had woken at three in the morning, throwing up. I'd had to work from home all day, making phone calls and falling further behind with each hour. A bunch of last-minute registrations had thrown my fall retreat plans into a panic.

At dinner, when I reminded Kevin about Teresa's marriage workshop, he changed the subject. And when I fussed about how hard my day had been, trying to work with a sick child in my care, he'd shaken his head and given me a look that reflected disappointment more than sympathy. I'd been tempted to skip Bible study and keep working on my talk for the retreat, but stress was hounding me like a pack of flying monkeys. I needed this break.

"Hello, Mrs. Miller." An identical match to the girl at the door padded into the room and offered me a mug. Spicy steam rose from the hot cider.

"Thanks, Charity." I cupped the mug in my hands, warming my palms. The threat of winter was already teasing the fall air, and my fingers felt like Popsicles. I should have worn gloves, but digging out the box of our family's boots, hats, and mittens hadn't made it to the top of my to-do list.

The girl gave a shy bob of her head. "You're welcome. But I'm not Charity."

"Argh! I'm sorry, Grace. I can't believe I still get you two mixed up."

She giggled. At age eleven, Heather's twins found humor in everything. I envied them. The doorbell rang, and Grace skipped along the wood floor to answer.

Heather homeschooled the girls, although she called it "unschooling." Visiting their household was like strolling through a bohemian art fair. Lilting music, handcrafted pottery, and incomprehensible paintings filled every corner. The girls were shy but incredibly creative, and they had unending patience for the younger children in our group. Two matching moms-in-training.

Grace pulled the door open and welcomed an anachronism into the flower-child living room. Sleek modernity invaded the house in the form of my friend Doreen.

"Hi, Grace." Doreen's voice was crisp and strong. Her heels clicked into the room with a purposeful pace. Doreen never got Heather's girls mixed up. In the high-powered corporate world, people didn't make those kinds of mistakes. She peeled off her black leather gloves and tucked them into the pocket of her suede jacket.

Grace reached for the coat. "Would you like some cider?"

Doreen tilted her head. Her perfect auburn hair swung out in one silky piece. "Did your mom make it?"

Grace giggled again. "We bought it at the orchard. But she did make some muffins."

"I'll just have some cider, thanks." Doreen marched to the couch and took possession of it. She rubbed her neck and grimaced in my direction. "What a day."

I wouldn't go so far as to say that Doreen needed a heart. But she could be a bit stiff sometimes. Still, she was a loyal friend. And I aspired to be an organized grown-up like her one day.

I gave her a smile of sympathy. "You too?"

"Always. Today the boss threw me an extra project. Since I'm not traveling like the other account managers, he said I could pick up the slack because my schedule is lighter."

"Yeah, right." I rolled my eyes. "Single mom with three kids, and your schedule is lighter."

The perfect curves of her eyebrows flattened. "I know. And when he hired me, he said it wouldn't be a problem that I couldn't travel. Now he's punishing me for it." She opened her leather purse and pulled out a slim Bible. "Never mind. I'm trying to stop complaining so much. How about you?" She gave me an assessing look. "Sick kid?"

"How can you tell?" I glanced down at my baggy jeans and rumpled sweat shirt. "No, don't answer that."

I was tempted to launch into my litany of woes, but I'd never win in a comparison of hardships with Doreen. We both had three children and the various challenges that accompanied that role. But her husband had cheated on her and waltzed out of her life two years ago. She won my sympathy vote, hands down.

"How's Judy?" Doreen asked. "Is she coming into town for Thanksgiving this year?"

"She's fine, I guess." I'd introduced my sister to my circle of friends one Christmas, and instant kinship sparked between Judy and Doreen. "She doesn't know if she'll be able to fly into town yet.

She'll probably let me know the night before, and then suggest we all go out for sushi instead of having a turkey dinner."

Doreen laughed. "Well, tell her hello from me, okay?"

"Yoo-hoo!" The front door nudged open, and Sally's mane of blond curls poked into the entry. Her face lit when she saw us, and she trotted into the room, not waiting for an invitation. "Brrr." Sally's high-pitched voice had a shrill edge. "It's getting nippy out there." She settled her ample hips onto the couch next to Doreen. "Thank heaven Heather got rid of those beanbag chairs. So, how is everyone?"

Doreen and I looked at each other and moaned. "Don't ask," I said.

Sally pursed her glossy lips. "Now, now. Remember, we're supposed to give thanks in everything."

Sometimes I just wanted to pinch Sally's chubby cheeks. Hard.

Doreen elbowed her. "Hey, how about a little compassion?"

Sally's face fell into lines of heavy concern as she looked at me. "Oh, Becky, is your leg bothering you this week?"

Every time I was able to put my disability into the background, she was quick to remind me. I sighed. "No more than usual. Kelsey's had the stomach flu, and the big retreat is this weekend."

Sally beamed. "That's right. We had ours last weekend. It was okay, but we sure miss having you in charge. I hope Faith Church appreciates what they got when they hired you."

Gratified, I decided Sally wasn't too irritating after all. "Thanks, but they may decide to fire me if I don't pull things together for Saturday."

Sally pulled out her thick day-planner and opened to a well-worn tab. "I'm adding it to my prayer list. You can do all things through Christ who strengthens you." Platitudes seemed to give her courage. She glanced at her watch. "Where is everyone?"

Heather drifted in as if on cue. Her mop of kinky chestnut hair was as unfettered as her spirit. She sank gracefully to the floor, smoothing her broomstick skirt around her legs. "Lori just called.

She's not going to make it tonight." A hint of worry colored her musical, breathy voice.

I'd counted on seeing Lori. I needed her moral support after the week I'd been having. "Is she okay?"

Heather hesitated. "She said she's under the weather. Have you talked to her this week?"

"No, I've been crazy busy."

Sally, Heather, and Doreen kept looking at me.

"I meant to call her." Why was I feeling guilty? "Did any of *you* check in with her? It's not like her to miss two weeks in a row."

Sally pointed her pen in my direction. "We've been praying for your life to get in better balance. How's that going?"

I stiffened and tilted the rocking chair forward. "Fine. I admit I haven't quite figured out balance. But that's the way things are. Work at church is going to be intense for a while. And Kevin and I think we found a new house."

I launched into an enthusiastic description that would have made my real estate agent proud. "Of course, it's all kind of stressful. And if . . . no, *when* we get it, there'll be a ton of work fixing it up."

Sally made a note in her planner. "I thought you were trying to slow down."

I bristled. I'd like to see Sally handle the huge women's ministry program I oversaw—while raising three children. Her one daughter—sweet, compliant, nine-year-old Chelsea—put Sally in the minor league of parenting. "Everything is fine. It takes juggling to make everything fit, but I manage. Unless something goes wrong . . . like one of the kids getting sick."

Heather stared into a candle flame on the coffee table. "But shouldn't there be room in our lives for children to get sick or for things to veer in a different direction?" She spoke slowly, almost to herself, and I wondered what idyllic world she was picturing. Honestly, sometimes I thought her head was full of straw and fluff.

Doreen defended me. "That's not realistic. How can you plan for the unexpected?"

"I just meant we should have margins . . . room to breathe . . . slow down a little." Heather's tone was wistful, not scolding. But it still triggered resentment. Her girls were older. She'd forgotten what it was like to chase little ones in circles.

Doreen barked a short laugh in Heather's direction. "If you Type B folks didn't have Type A's around, nothing would ever get done."

Sally squirmed. "Who else has prayer requests?"

I was glad she was moving on. Conflict made my bones itch. I hated it when we argued. I was also eager to get the focus off of me. "How about you, Heather? How are plans going for the mission trip?"

Heather glowed like a bayberry candle. "We're so excited. Ron got two of his colleagues to come along. We're bringing the girls and a whole bunch of medical supplies." She turned to Sally. "Thanks so much for the box of books. We shipped those ahead."

Sally shrugged. "Oh, it was easy. I put a note in the church bulletin, and people dropped off all kinds of things."

Sally's twittering annoyed me seventy percent of the time, but she had a good heart. She might boss, nag, and meddle, but she'd be the first to arrive with a casserole when there was a need. And I knew she'd faithfully pray about every request we discussed.

I was relieved when we finished our prayer time and started the Bible study. I hoped to avoid any more probing about how my life felt out of control. Of anyone in the world, these were the women I could be real with. But even here, it was more comfortable to maintain the illusion of being Becky Miller, Super Christian.

I wanted sympathy, encouragement, and—if I were honest with myself—admiration for the terrific job I was doing at the church and the new adventure Kevin and I were undertaking with the farmhouse. Instead, my friends were sometimes like an extra conscience. My own conscience battered me enough on its own, thank you very much.

As the Bible study finished, Heather smiled. "That was so awesome."

"But I miss Lori." Doreen snapped her slim Bible closed. "She always has great ideas for applying the verses."

"Do you think it's something serious?" Sally's eyes gleamed. She might love Lori like a sister, but she was always eager for juicy gossip.

Heather ignored her. "Let's close with a worship song."

The rest of us exchanged uncomfortable glances. Sally and Doreen were the "pipe organ and hymnal" types. And while I liked contemporary praise and worship songs, I didn't have the voice for singing in someone's living room. I preferred being drowned out in a crowd.

Heather was oblivious to our unease and launched into a praise chorus. We joined in unsteadily, and Heather just ignored any sour notes. Sitting on the floor, she lifted her hands and swayed with the music, like a scarecrow in a breeze, shooing away crows of doubt.

Our varied group had formed years ago, when we were all members of the same church. In spite of scattering in new directions, we had decided to continue our weekly Bible study. These women were my yellow-brick-road companions through life. I wouldn't be able to face the hazardous adventures of the journey without them.

As we gathered up our Bibles and notebooks to head out and face another week, I felt Lori's absence again. She was a Glinda in my life. Whenever my situation turned dire, she showed up with the perfect words for me. She reminded me how to find my way home.

I had never known her to miss our meetings. I decided to e-mail her as soon as I got home. If something was wrong, I wanted to know about it.

I climbed into my minivan and started the engine. Heather's home was only a mile from mine—a mercy tonight. I was exhausted. Before pulling away from the curb, I closed my eyes for a moment.

There's no place like home. There's no place like home. There's no place like home.

But a few minutes later, when I walked into our kitchen, I was tempted to turn around and flee. Kevin was on the phone, lines compressed around his eyes, shirt untucked, scribbling something on a scrap of paper. The room looked like a tornado had swirled through it.

He didn't acknowledge my arrival, although his knuckles whitened around the phone. "Are you sure that's the earliest flight?" His voice grated with tension. "Yes, yes. Book that for me."

Chapter Five

Fog swirled over the tarmac, creating ghosts of regret. The plane's propellers sputtered in the darkness. The sound of the blades cut into my heart. The man I loved—the only man I had ever loved—was about to fly out of my life. And I had to encourage him to go. The knowledge burned in my throat like cheap whiskey. I had to convince him to fly to safety.

The Nazis were closing in on him, and he couldn't stay in Morocco another hour. I had plenty of connections at Becky's Café Americain—my bar attracted expatriates, black marketeers, and some of the local constabulary—but even I couldn't keep him safe from the Nazis.

As he turned up the collar of his trench coat and prepared to leave, I decided that reading about noble sacrifices was more rewarding than living them.

Shadows softened his bone structure, and I could see the pain in his eyes beneath the brim of his fedora. If I didn't stay firm, he'd refuse to get on the plane.

I squared my shoulders. "If that plane leaves the ground and you're not with it, you'll regret it. Maybe not today. Maybe not tomorrow. But soon and for the rest of your life."

He gave me a last searching look and turned to board the plane.

As my heart taxied down the runway and lifted off, a German staff car roared into the airport. I was unimpressed. Mortal danger couldn't alarm me now. My decision had already tortured me more than the Nazis ever could. I lifted my chin and turned to face the car.

A horn beeped, and I pushed back the living room curtains. "The taxi's here."

Kevin rolled his suitcase down the hall. "Are you sure you'll be okay? I could wait until after the retreat."

A magnanimous offer since he knew good and well his trip was set in motion. I opened the front door and followed him along the sidewalk. Micah skipped behind us in stocking feet and Spiderman jammies. "Kev, you need to go. Tell her I'm praying for her."

He gave me a quick hug. "Thanks, hon."

The cab driver hefted the suitcase into the trunk, and Kevin slid into the backseat.

"Oh, don't forget to bring back the DVD we rented to the movie store," he said.

Bummer. Another Saturday date night that wouldn't happen. Maybe I'd watch our "movie of the week" by myself.

"I'll take care of it. Just hurry back. We've gotta move on the new house."

"I lined up the inspection. He'll call you with his report."

"Okay. I love you." I closed the door and let my fingertips linger on the window. When the driver shifted out of park, I stepped back and grabbed Micah to keep him from chasing the taxi down the street.

"Come on, bud. We've gotta line up some serious baby-sitting."

Irritation scraped my nerves like sandpaper on a blister, followed immediately by shame. How could I be annoyed? Kevin had received the call last night while I was at Bible study. His mom was in the hospital. A flu bug had gotten out of control, and she had pneumonia. Of course he had to catch the first flight to Florida. I'd insisted on it. It was the noble thing to do.

Sure, I had a million things to prepare for tomorrow's retreat. After all, the retreat was one of the biggest events I organized at the church each year. Of course, I had counted on Kevin to take care of the kids tomorrow while I ran things, but emergencies happen. I would cope.

I limped up the front steps, dragging Micah along behind with one hand. "How many times have I told you not to run outside in your stocking feet?" He solved the problem by plopping onto the step, peeling off his socks, and wiggling his toes.

I crouched beside him, nuzzled my face into his hair, and blew a raspberry against his cheek. Good thing my kids made me laugh so hard. Some days it was either laugh or cry. I shooed him inside and aimed for the phone to start my hunt for baby-sitters. First, I indulged in a deep, cleansing breath. If Lamaze breathing worked during labor, maybe it could help me through today's crises.

Micah pulled open one of the kitchen cupboards and rummaged for food. He upended a cereal box and shook it hard. Crumbs of Cheerios sifted to the floor. "All gone." He coupled the proclamation with an accusing glare in my direction.

"Don't worry, bud. Let's go see how Kelsey's feeling today. I'll make toast for all of you."

Kelsey had slept through the night and was feeling better, but she insisted she couldn't go to school yet. I was tempted to press the point and coax her to try, but my guilt meter couldn't handle the spike today. I smoothed her sweaty tangle of curls. "After we drive Dylan and Micah to school, you can make a nest in my office. I have to work this morning, but I'll try to keep it short."

She gave a listless assent as I helped her into a comfy sweat suit.

"Mom, I can't find my good socks," Dylan's panicked voice called from across the hall.

I nudged Kelsey toward the kitchen and ducked into the boys' room. "What do you mean? You have plenty of socks." I waved at the evidence scattered around his bed and floor.

"But, Mom, those aren't my good ones. I have basketball today. I need my good ones."

I rubbed the bridge of my nose. I really should have a cup of coffee before engaging anyone in a clothing debate. "Dylan, honey, these are all good." I picked up one of the white sport socks, found another with a matching blue stripe, turned it right side in, and handed it to Dylan.

He dropped the pair to the floor. "I need the ones with the red stripe. I can't play basketball with these."

I counted to ten while scooping up socks and stuffing them back into Dylan's dresser drawer. He crossed his arms and waited, bare foot tapping the rug.

I slammed the drawer shut and whirled around to face him. His eyes blinked up at me from under his thick lashes. He no longer had the Beatle-bangs he wore as a toddler, but even with the buzz cut that mimicked his dad's, he was too cuddly and endearing. I couldn't possibly stay irritated with him.

He clutched his hands to his heart. "Please, Mom? Help me find them."

What kind of parent would send their son to basketball practice without his favorite socks? "Okay, run downstairs and see if they're in the dryer. I'll look around in here."

I poked through some more drawers, then hobbled to the living room to check under the couch cushions. I found some squashed Skittles, enough change to provide a week's worth of milk money, and a decapitated Barbie . . . but no socks.

"Micah, don't touch!" Kelsey's screech echoed from the kitchen.

Now what? I abandoned the sock search. Wise plan. When I rounded the corner into the kitchen, Micah was fiddling with the dials on the front of the stove.

"Micah, no!" I wrenched him away, gripping his arm hard. As I dragged him to the table and scolded him into his chair, I had a visual flash of one of the pages of the retreat guide. *Setting the Tone of Love in Your Household.*

"Yeah, well, you know what they say," I told my conscience. "Those who can, do. And those who can't, teach."

I dropped bread into the toaster, grateful we had three slices left besides the end piece. None of the kids would eat the heel of the loaf. I poured apple juice into small cups and set one in front of Kelsey, where she slumped, elbows on the table, still looking pale.

Dylan charged up the basement stairs. "I found them!" He waved some dirt-streaked socks over his head.

"Were those in the dryer?"

His glee faded. "Not exactly." His eyes pleaded with me.

Would a good mother let her son wear dirty socks to school? I looked at the clock. Of course she would. Desperate times called for desperate socks. "Well, hurry and get ready. We're late."

He scrambled to obey and soon joined his siblings at the table. While their mouths were busy with toast, I grabbed the phone.

I punched in my favorite number. It rang several times before someone answered. "Hello?" Lori's voice sounded heavy, almost slurred.

I knew it was early, but she was the ultimate Proverbs 31 mom—up before the crack of dawn every day. "Did I wake you up?"

"Oh, hi, Becky. No, it's okay."

Her voice didn't brighten as much as I had expected. "Is something wrong?"

"Wrong?"

"I mean, you don't sound like yourself . . . and you weren't at Bible study last night."

"I'm fine." She seemed to make an effort to infuse life into her voice. "How are you?"

"Stressed to the max. Kevin's mom is in the hospital, and he just left for the airport, and the big retreat is tomorrow. I was wondering if you could watch the kids tomorrow. I know it's short notice, but we don't have enough child care lined up for the retreat as it is. A bunch of people signed up after the deadline, and we don't want to turn them away. Anyway, you'd be saving my life if you could watch them."

She hesitated too long. "I'm sorry, but I can't." Her tone was flat, dull.

I waited for an explanation, a reason, or a few helpful suggestions of other folks to ask. She didn't say anything more. Maybe I'd interrupted a homeschool session. Lori ran a tight ship with an organized, tightly honed schedule and an advanced curriculum for ten-year-old Abby and even six-year-old Jeffy.

"But I'm not only organizing the event, I'm leading one of the sessions. This is really important." My panic propelled me into begging mode. But I wasn't ashamed to beg. Lori was my best friend. She never made me feel small.

When I'd first met her, she reminded me of Whitney Houston. Tall, black, regal, with a syrup-smooth voice. But that's where the similarities ended. Lori was anything but a diva. Her poise and spiritual depth would have intimidated me if she weren't such a warm, genuine friend.

"Look, I need to go. Sorry. I hope you find someone." The abrupt dial tone stung my ears.

Lori hadn't explained, hadn't helped, hadn't even offered to pray for me to find someone else. I felt as if I'd stepped into a creepy movie where everyone was taken over by aliens. She'd become a pod-person—a distant, distracted, disconnected pod-person.

I hung up the phone, shaken. Then I glanced at the clock. No time to figure this out now.

A plane sailed over our neighborhood, making the loose kitchen window rattle. That might not be his plane, but somewhere out there, Kevin was about to take off into the sky and leave me to cope with a sick kid, an overbooked retreat, my best friend acting weird, no baby-sitter, and a talk that I was barely prepared to give.

I looked heavenward. A water stain spidered across the ceiling where the roof had leaked last spring. *Lord, I'm doing this retreat for you. Could I get a little help here?*

Kelsey knocked over her apple juice, and it splashed onto Micah's Spiderman pajamas, setting him into a wail that rivaled an air raid siren.

I mopped, kissed, comforted, cajoled, and somehow got everyone dressed and out to the van. A trace of morning fog swirled across the blacktop of the driveway. As I cranked the ignition, I thought about everything I needed to take care of in the next few hours. Stress fed my self-pity. Did God even care how much I was dealing with?

Pulling into traffic, I glanced at the sky and made another attempt to pray. *Sometimes I think the problems of one mom don't amount to a hill of beans in this crazy, mixed-up world.*

Chapter Six

"*Come on, folks!* Gather round." My voice carried over the crowd milling past tidy storefronts. In my snazzy suit and shined-up shoes, I mounted the steps of the band shell in the center of town. Wholesome, homegrown—pride of the Midwest. The good people of River City, Iowa, watched me with the mixture of expressions I'd learned to expect in my extensive travels.

The mayor's chest swelled, buttons straining at his vest. He wanted to put his town on the map. His wife waved a scarf and gave a coquettish "yoo-hoo." She saw herself as the patron of all arts and was eager to back my proposal. The local barber crossed his arms and leaned against his striped pole, his face set in a glower that said, "Don't try your flimflam pitch on me."

Young faces looked up at me, as well—buckteeth, freckles, and the earnest hope that I'd be able to separate their parents from some hard-earned cash to buy them band instruments.

"I'm Professor Becky Miller, delighted to offer my services to your fine city. You are clearly men and women with good hearts and sharp minds."

The barber snorted, and the librarian shifted a stack of books in his arm and shook his head. They didn't realize their dubious expressions fed my fire. I loved a challenge.

I lifted my voice. "And I know you care about the children of this fine town."

A murmur of agreement ignited my energy. I gathered it, spun it, and expanded it. "And you've seen the dangerous temptations facing young men and women today."

"The pool hall!" a querulous biddy testified from beneath her flower-covered straw hat.

"Exactly!" I paced the top step. "But I'm here to tell you, I can solve that problem."

Polite applause answered me. It was a start. Soon they'd be cheering. Soon I'd be leading a marching band down Main Street.

"Let's welcome Becky Miller as she speaks to us about problems facing twenty-first-century families."

I flicked on my cordless microphone, left the front pew, and marched up the steps to the podium with confidence, barely leaning on my cane. Our church was packed with women ready to be encouraged, edified, and inspired. And I was the one to do it.

Lord, speak through me. Touch hearts that are weary.

I smiled out at the full pews. "Thank you so much for coming to the Faith Community Church Women's Retreat on this fine October day. Have you been blessed so far?"

The audience shook off some of their after-lunch lethargy and applauded.

I beamed. "That's great. And I know the rest of the day will minister to you, as well." The vortex of stress and nerves that had swirled around my plans for this retreat now fed my adrenaline. I launched into my talk, acknowledging the discouragement and fatigue I read in so many slumped shoulders. I attacked the flaws in our society that threatened our children—the rushed pace, the luxuries that produced notions of entitlement, the corrupting influence of the media, the broken relationships. And I countered it all with the dream of a Christ-centered family life.

I paced the front of the church. "God can work through even the ordinary moments of your life." A few years ago I would have spoken about doing big things for God, but I'd learned that chasing heroic images of the Christian life only left me feeling I could never measure up. God worked in my ordinary life. And I loved doing all the little things. Helping people. Cheering them up. Solving their problems. Just call me Mrs. Becky Fix-it.

"God is at work through you, even when you don't see it. Now let me share my seven-point plan to take charge of your life, so you can be more available to God."

For a second the words had a hollow echo, as if the microphone was adjusted poorly. I stopped and took a breath, distracted by the frisson of unease that chose that moment to ripple through me. I recognized the sensation. The same feeling sometimes hit me when I was reading my Bible—as if God beamed a penlight onto a certain thought.

Okay, Lord. You want to tell me something. But let me finish this first.

Enthusiasm infused my voice as I explained my tips and charged into the conclusion. "So, don't be afraid to be intentional. When you see a problem, make a plan to fix it. Be open to the new opportunities God may bring your way." A wave of satisfaction buoyed my heart upward. I was doing exactly what I was preaching. I'd seen the problems in our family and was making a plan to fix it. Kevin and I would grow closer as we worked side by side sprucing up our new house. The kids could romp in the huge yard, and we'd all slow down and reconnect.

I pulled an index card from my pocket and glanced at it. "Before Pam comes up to lead us in some worship time, I want to let you know about some of the new programs here at Faith Church and invite you to get involved."

This brief commercial had been Teresa's idea. She had a true marketer's mind-set and had taught the staff to never miss an opportunity to promote all that we offered at the church. Her coaching had been a big part of the church's rapid growth. When I finished the announcements, I settled into a back pew, eager to open my heart and ears to God during the worship time.

One verse into the first song, I felt a tap on my shoulder. "Becky, I'm sorry, but Bonnie can't find the list of resources we're supposed to hand out at the door." Cheryl, one of the retreat committee members, bounced on her heels as if she were about to launch over the pew and grab me.

"The box is in my office."

"I looked there." She had no intention of leaving until I produced the missing handouts.

Sorry, Lord. I need to take a rain check.

I slipped out the back of the church and into work mode. The retreat flowed along like a river in a carefully constructed channel. I rushed from place to place, patching any leaks—keeping the activities in their boundaries. Handouts found. Overwhelmed nursery volunteer soothed. Worship leader signaled to move along when prayers ran long. I loved feeling in control. The women's faces glowed with gratitude as they left at the end of the day. I felt warm and full, knowing I had done my part to fix their problems.

Later, a worship song hummed through my head as I drove toward Sally's house. She'd been kind enough to take my kids all day when at least a dozen other possibilities had failed. I hated turning to her for help. Of all my friends, she was the most likely to make tsking sounds at the jams I found myself in as a working parent. She worked part-time as a church secretary but never seemed to struggle with balancing that role with her family life.

Sally answered the door with her blond curls in disarray. Her smile was automatic and a bit tight. "Becky! How was the retreat?" She made a valiant effort to hide the relief in her voice.

"It was awesome. How were the kids?" I stepped into the foyer, careful not to bump the porcelain statues clustered on her Victorian end table.

"Fine, fine. It was no trouble. Not a bit of trouble. Happy to help." If Sally talked any faster her dangling earrings would vibrate right off her lobes.

Three somber faces greeted me as my children trudged toward me from the French Provincial living room. Given the white carpet, glass tables, and fragile knickknacks, I suspected little actual living ever went on in the room.

"Tell Mrs. Fustering thank you," I coached my children.

Dylan and Kelsey muttered the words without looking at Sally, and Micah grabbed my leg. Sally's daughter, Chelsea, entered the hall from the kitchen.

"Hello, Mrs. Miller." She offered me a sheaf of papers. "Here's a list of what we did all day, and what each of the children ate."

Chelsea was only nine, but she had big plans for a baby-sitting agency when she was older. Although she was outwardly sweet, she had strong opinions on how other people should spend their time—a pint-size duplicate of her mother, bossiness coated with sugar. No wonder my kids looked glum.

"Any word from Kevin? How is his mother doing?" Sally took a few subtle steps toward the front door as she spoke.

"I'm calling him as soon as I get home. Last night he said she should recover all right, but he sounded worried."

Sally nodded. "I'll keep praying for her." She opened the door and gave me a quick hug. "Good-bye, children. Be good for your mother, now."

We headed to the van. I heard the sound of Sally turning her bolt-lock with a firm click.

As soon as the kids were buckled in, the clamor began. "Chelsea wanted to play tea parties all day," Dylan grumbled. "They don't even have a football."

"Mrs. Fussy hollered when I played with that thing from her bookcase." Though only a kindergartner, Kelsey gave the teenage eye roll she'd perfected.

Micah absorbed his siblings' unhappiness and squawked in his own minor key. "Don't touch." He captured Sally's tremolo perfectly. "No, no. Don't touch."

"No, no. Don't touch," Kelsey and Dylan joined in.

I lowered the baton before the anthem gained any more volume. "I'm sorry you had a rough day, but it was very nice of them to watch you. You should be grateful."

Sour faces glared into my rearview mirror. Time for a new tactic.

"Thanks for being good while I did the retreat. You deserve a reward, so we'll order a pizza tonight, okay?"

Cheers rang from the backseats like a trumpet fanfare. I still had it. Find the right angle, and you can turn anyone's attitude around.

Flushed with success from the retreat and bolstered by pizza, I sailed through the evening of parenting like a drum majorette waving her musicians into formation. We even had family devotions and a special prayer time for Grandma Rose.

Once the kids were all asleep, I hobbled to the couch with the cordless phone and called Kevin.

His cell kicked over to voice mail on the first ring. Must be in one of those voids where cell phones cut out. I tried his mom's house for good measure. He was staying there, taking care of things for her. I let it ring twenty times. No answer there either. Grandma Rose didn't believe in answering machines, so I couldn't even leave a message.

Is there anything more wistfully lonely than the sound of a ringing phone when no one answers?

Disgruntled, I stood to put the phone away, and my hip screamed in pain. I caught my breath and lowered myself onto the couch. I hugged my knee toward my chest, then flexed my leg a few times. I was supposed to do physical therapy exercises every day, but I didn't even have time to take my vitamins, condition my hair, floss—or do any of the other "good for you" things people were always telling me to do.

Lord, what's happening to me? Is serving you supposed to feel like this?

I said the rest of my bedtime prayers while limping down the hallway. *Lord, please heal Grandma Rose. Be with Kevin while he's in Florida. Help Dylan with his high energy, teach Kelsey to be less bossy, and help Micah stop whining. Help us get the new house, if it's your will. Oh, and Doreen's work problems. Please help her. And bless Heather's mission trip.*

There was something else I had planned to talk over with God, but I couldn't remember now. I nestled into bed and edged toward

Kevin's side. His pillow held a hint of his aftershave. Longing grabbed me with a sudden force.

I missed him. Not just because he was out of town. Lately I had been lonely for him even when he was home.

That was a scary thought.

And, Lord, help our marriage.

We had to hold on a little longer. Everything would change when we had the new house. Life would slow down. Relationships would mend. The quiet peace of the country would erase our stress and give us a movie-script happy ending. On that optimistic thought, I fell asleep.

The next morning, getting three munchkins ready for Sunday school without Kevin was a daunting task, but somehow we all made it to church on time. I tried to focus on worship, but I spotted the woman who had been crying in my office earlier in the week and made a mental note to follow up with her. Then I noticed a woman who had helped with the retreat decorations. I'd forgotten her name on my list of people to send thank-you notes to. I jotted notes to myself on the margin of the service bulletin.

During the sermon, Pastor Bob mentioned God preparing a home for us, and I wondered when Kevin's friend would call with his report on the house inspection. That sent my thoughts into a delicious frenzy of mental furniture arranging. Our couch would look wonderful facing the large front windows and would take advantage of the view, and we'd want to put a couple of chairs near the fireplace. Our tiny kitchen desk could have its own alcove—it could even have its own room. We could have an actual home office in one of the upstairs bedrooms. The possibilities were endless.

After church, I trudged into Pastor Bob's office for the staff meeting. Pastor Bob's wife had offered to entertain my kids in the church nursery while we talked. The church's staff had grown since I'd been hired. The music director, church secretary, school principal, preschool director, and youth pastor all squeezed into the room and settled in with cheerful greetings. I tucked myself into a corner, thinking wistfully of the Vikings tickets. Had Kevin given them to someone before he left for Florida? The kids would have loved some family time. Instead, they were with a sitter again.

Teresa charged in last, carrying a few bags of bagels. I perked up. The woman knew her stuff. If you're going to call an extra meeting, bagels do a lot to boost morale. She launched into an agenda while our mouths were full of cream cheese. Teresa was a whippet—wiry, tall, with a long nose. She didn't merely chase a rabbit of church growth around the track, she pulled us all along in her wake.

She started with a team-building exercise, then moved on to conflict resolution and addressed some emerging problems in our cohesion as a staff. Discussion swirled about budget problems, new forms to fill out when reserving space for church events, coordinating our various programs, and brainstorming about vision statements. It took a half hour for me to realize we had forgotten to start the meeting with prayer. When had church work begun to feel so corporate?

My mind continued to drift. I'd heard this pep talk before. Various staff members expounded on their vision for growth, complete with metaphors. Overflowing nets of fish. Huge harvests.

A strange sense of unease churned in my stomach. Or maybe it was the onion bagel. While energetic voices chimed in around me, a heretical question popped into my head. Would it be so terrible to be small?

I thought of my high-energy pitch to the women the day before. Suddenly the words seemed too practiced and polished. Was I selling snake oil so I could lead a marching band of followers through pearly gates one day?

As the staff continued to enthuse about scriptural examples of the big and dramatic, I wondered about the solitary lost lamb, the quiet conversation Jesus had with a woman at a Samaritan well, the washing of twelve pairs of dusty feet.

I was probably just tired from the stressful week. I didn't want to bring down the unified mood of the staff by raising these questions.

"Isn't that right, Becky?"

Teresa's question pulled my attention back to the meeting. "I'm sorry . . . what?"

"Your work." She poked the air with her PDA stylus. "It's expanded way beyond fifteen hours a week."

Relief seeped through my pores. I wanted to hug her—if she would ever hold still long enough. Someone was going to rescue me from the expanding pressure and the schedule that had been overwhelming me. "Yes. The women's programs are growing fast."

Teresa beamed. "That's why I propose we expand Becky's position to a full-time salaried role."

Throwing a bagel in the air and collapsing on the floor in tears didn't fit staff-meeting protocol. Instead, I swallowed hard.

"I'd need to pray about that." Always a good answer to give when in a panic.

"Fine, fine." Pastor Bob glanced at his watch. He was probably hoping to get home and catch the end of the Vikings game on TV. "Let us know next week."

When the meeting adjourned, I hurried to escape. I needed to reach Kevin to find out how his mom was doing. I hadn't talked to him since Friday. Telling him about the request that I go to full-time status could wait. I could imagine his reaction to that one. He didn't need the added stress right now.

Driving home, the same ripple of wrongness I'd sensed during my talk at the retreat invaded my thoughts again. I turned on the radio and leaned back. I wasn't selling snake oil. I was trying to inspire people—help them fulfill their potential and take control of their lives. There was nothing wrong with that. And the church's focus on "bigger and better"? Sure, it could get a little out of balance. But maybe that's why God had planted me here. Because of my past experiences, I could be an influence to remind everyone that numbers and media attention weren't the only ways to measure success.

With that settled, I began singing along to the *Tribute to Musicals* blaring through the car speakers. Something about seventy-six trombones.

Chapter Seven

Blaster cannons fired from hidden alcoves framing my course. "Red 2, what's your position?"

My ship rocked as a percussive wave slammed me from behind. I keyed in my comm link. "There's an enemy fighter on my tail."

"I'm on it, Becky."

I tilted my wings, skimming too close to the corridor walls. My screen registered the flare of an explosion behind me. Immediately my wing commander's voice crackled in my ear.

"You're clear, Becky. Go for it."

I had one chance. If I hit the target, I'd destroy the worst menace to threaten the free worlds in known history. I struggled to absorb the flashing readout on my navigation screen, my palms sweating inside my flight gloves.

If I missed . . .

No, don't go there. *I took a deep breath and shut off the computer guidance. Immediate chatter from base demanded an explanation. I tuned them out. I needed to shut out everything else. With another slow breath, I closed my eyes and pressed the fire button.*

Tones from the rapid dial chirped as I released the button and lifted the phone to my ear. I squeezed my eyes shut. *Please let him answer. Let him be there this time.*

"Hi, hon." Kevin's deep voice was distorted by the empty space of long distance, but it was still the best sound I'd heard all day.

"Where have you been?" My words burst out with more than a hint of desperation. After my busy Sunday, I'd been eager to tuck the kids in bed early, but now the house felt too quiet and dark.

"Sorry. I had a care conference yesterday with the doctor and the hospital social worker. How was the retreat?"

"Great. But I'm missing you. Is your mom doing better?"

"The antibiotics are helping. They think she'll be off oxygen tomorrow."

I leaned back against the couch and stared at the tiny lights on the stereo. I saw the dire death star of separation exploding in a satisfying conflagration. "So when are you flying home?"

"Oh, Harry called. He's mailing us his inspection report, but he sounded pretty concerned about things that weren't up to code."

"Are they things we can fix? Tell him you're good at do-it-yourself projects. We can't give up now."

"I don't know." He sounded tired, too defeated to tackle a new challenge.

Suddenly I felt angry as well as forsaken. He had introduced me to the house and now it filled my thoughts and even my dreams. How could he throw off our plans at the first little wrinkle?

"Look, we're not going to find anything this big, with so much land, in our price range. This place is a miracle."

When he didn't answer, I chewed my lip in frustration. "When are you coming home?"

Kevin's deliberate breaths into the phone sounded like Darth Vader. His sigh hissed and crackled, bouncing off some distant satellite. "It could be a while."

I didn't want to whine. But he had led me on—gotten me excited about a new house, then flew halfway across the country before we could lock into anything. "You said your mom is doing better."

"She's getting over the pneumonia. But there are other issues. Look, I'm beat. I'll call you tomorrow, when I know more."

"Sure." I struggled to hide the black emptiness swirling me away. Anxiety tapped my hull like tiny meteors. "What should I do about the bid on the house? Someone else could snatch it up if we don't move on this."

"I'll talk to Harry again. You still want to go ahead, even if he doesn't recommend it?" A little of Kevin's usual life surged back into his voice.

"Yeah. I just wish you were here instead of in a galaxy far, far away."

"What?"

"Never mind." My fingers tightened around the phone. What wasn't he telling me? *Why* wasn't he telling me? "I love you."

"Love you more." Kevin shot the automatic greeting my way and hung up before I could give him our standard "love you most" response. Not fair.

I could feel his worry and distraction even from a thousand miles away. Why wouldn't he tell me about everything? Why couldn't he be more open? Didn't he realize I wanted to help?

And what about your secrets, Becky?

That was different. I batted away my conscience. This was not a good time to bring up the staff meeting and the request that I move into full-time work at the church. And he didn't need to hear about all the mounting stress I was feeling. He had other things to think about.

Still, I needed to talk to someone about it all.

I hit my second rapid-dial button on the cordless phone. It was after nine at night, but Lori would still be up.

It wasn't until she answered that I remembered how strange she'd seemed the last few times we'd talked. And she still hadn't told me why she'd been missing our Bible study group.

"Becky? Oh, I'm so glad you called. How was the retreat? What's going on with Kevin's mom? How have you been? We haven't talked in ages." Lori's lethargy from our last conversation had been replaced with warp speed. Her familiar and caring tone made my eyes prickle with sudden emotion. I needed to feel understood, and Lori always understood and accepted me.

"Everything seems out of control," I confessed. "I mean, it's nothing terrible, but there's so much happening I feel like my brain is going to explode." I was ready to start my recitation of struggles but pulled out of my self-absorbed force field long enough to remember that she'd missed the last two weeks of Bible study. "What about you? I've missed you. Are you okay? You sounded really funny last time I called."

Her pause was so long, I thought she was going to offer a Kevin-like evasion. "Beck, I think I need to talk to you about something. Could I come over?"

"Now?" In my college days, I'd chat with friends half the night. That was before I'd become an old, tired mom. "I mean, yeah. That would be great. The kids are in bed, and I'd love to see you. But . . . what's wrong?"

"I'd rather talk in person. I'll be there soon."

For the second time that night, I listened to an abrupt dial tone, not sure how to react. I was glad she was coming over. We'd had little chance to spend time together lately. I wanted her to help me sort out all the parts of my life that were spinning into an out-of-control free fall.

But I was also worried. Lori had been acting so strangely. What did she need to tell me? Was something wrong with Abigail or Jeffy? I'd watched her children grow up and loved them like my own. Abby's dark eyes flashed from under her neat cornrows with the same political fervor as her mother's. She was only a year older than Dylan, but recently she had sent a letter to the editor of the local paper with an earnest plea for better care for the elderly. Six-year-old Jeffy always greeted me with a shy grin and galloped away—long limbs hinting that one day he'd have the willowy frame of his mother. *Please, God, don't let anything be wrong with them.*

It couldn't be trouble in her marriage. Kevin played basketball with her husband, Noah, most Friday nights. Kevin would have told me if Lori and Noah were having problems.

On the other hand, men didn't always pick up on things like that. When Jeffy was born six years ago, Kevin answered Noah's phone call. After a brief conversation, he hung up, turned around, and announced that Noah and Lori had a baby boy. When I drilled him about how the labor and delivery went, how Lori was feeling, and how much the baby weighed, he shrugged. Men sometimes missed things.

I pushed up off the couch and limped to the kitchen to start a pot of tea. Lori and I both loved jasmine green tea. We could savor the exotic flavor and feel healthy and virtuous at the same time. My hip was progressing from a dull throb into a more piercing pain. The crisp fall weather had retreated today, and balmy Indian summer had moved in for a last visit. The change in air pressure made my aches worse, but I loved the unexpected tropical feel to the air. I opened the kitchen window and smelled a hint of woodsmoke and the peppery tang of the marigolds in my backyard flower box.

Inspired, I opened the back door and dusted off two lawn chairs. We could sip our tea in the backyard and talk under the stars. Practice for when Kevin and I had the new house and would sit with friends on the veranda. *If* he clarified all the facts with Harry and we could get the bid in before someone else bought our dream home.

With some effort, I dragged my thoughts away from throngs of offers beating ours—all because Kevin was out of town. It was far too easy for me to slip into irritation toward Kevin these days. Resentment could become a habit as easily as biting my nails. Instead, I went back to worrying about Lori. I hoped there was nothing seriously wrong. Or even worse, that she was mad at me about something.

By the time I had the tea brewed, Lori arrived. We settled into chairs with a squeak of aluminum. A moth bumped against the kitchen window screen, and an occasional car swooshed along the street in front of our house. Canned laughter from a TV sitcom carried from my neighbor's open window. When we moved to the country, I'd have a more tranquil place to invite friends.

"So what's been going on? We've missed you at Bible study." I shifted to find a comfortable position against the plastic slats of the chair.

Lori blew across the top of her cup. "I'm sorry. And I'm sorry I was so . . . short with you the other day. How did the retreat go? Did you find someone to watch the kids?"

"We had tons more people than we expected, which was great. But things were pretty crazy setting up for it. Sally watched the kids." I giggled. "Dylan doesn't appreciate tea parties."

In the light spilling from the back door, I could see Lori's faint smile, but her eyes focused on the tea in her cup. "I bet you gave a great talk at the retreat. You have such a gift for motivating people."

Her comment was typical Lori. Kind, warm, supportive. So why did I have the feeling she had simply hit an automatic-play button to recite the words, while she was really someplace else?

Before I could probe, she tilted her head up. "Your maple tree still has some leaves. Ours are all down already. So how is Kevin's mom?"

"She's recovering, but something is weird with Kevin. I—" She had almost caught me. Steering me toward my issues. Not this time. "Never mind that. We can talk about it later. Lori, what's wrong? You've been acting strange."

She took a sip of tea, then set the cup down in the grass. Even though the air was muggy and in the seventies, she wrapped her arms around herself and shivered. "I'm sorry."

I reached out and gently touched her arm. "Lori, it's me. Don't keep apologizing. What's wrong?"

Her long neck bent, and she curled into herself like a snail pulling into a shell. "I've . . . I've been under the weather."

Vivid scenarios played through my mind like a commercial for a movie-of-the-week. I set my teacup aside, as well, somehow thinking I needed my hands free. "Lori, you don't . . . it's not cancer, is it?"

She laughed suddenly. A brittle, eerie sound. Not her easy, generous laugh—the one I'd heard so often over the years. She blinked a few times. "Don't be silly. You have such an imagination."

Annoyance almost diverted me, but I tried again. "Yeah, we've established that. But I'm not imagining that something is wrong with my best friend. You've always been here for me. Let me help. What's the matter?"

"Been here? Have I? Really?" She choked out another laugh that ended in a sob.

I scooted my chair closer and wrapped an arm around her. "Yes. You know that. You've helped me grow in my faith. You've supported me when I thought I would fall apart. Remember when Kevin and I had that big fight? And you found the support group for him when he lost his job? What would we have done without you?" A new worry grabbed me. "Is it Noah?"

She stood up suddenly and paced away. I worried she'd trip over the edge of the sandbox in the dark, but she stopped and looked up again. "Noah is fine. The kids are fine. Everything is fine." Her flat tone became more agitated and her voice rose in volume. She threw her arms wide. "Fine, fine, fine."

I huddled in my chair, watching her. "No, it's not. Just tell me. Are you upset at me about anything? Did I do something?"

She slumped, gaze dropping back to planet Earth. "I wish it were that simple." She looked directly at me for the first time, her eyes glistening against the shadows of the night. "This has nothing to do with you. I promise." For a second I saw the real Lori again, gentle eyes set off by her dark caramel skin.

I nodded slowly. "Okay. So what's wrong?"

"Look, this was a mistake. I've gotta go. Just pray for me, all right?" She ducked around the side of the house and left without another word.

The chirp of a few leftover summer crickets mocked me. A plane flew overhead. I picked up her deserted teacup and held it while its warmth faded. My worry for her melded with an aching loss.

First Kevin, now Lori. I'd lost my wingmen. I was flying solo, and I didn't like it. How was I supposed to fight all the death stars in my life without help?

Chapter Eight

The chill English damp burrowed through my coat and made me shiver. Aching loneliness weighted me like the glowering sky. Each day was the same on this joyless estate—dull, vast, and empty. I missed India. The burnished sun, the silks, the scent of curry. But when my parents died in an earthquake, I was sent to this dreary land to be a burden on my uncle.

A robin chirped at me, braving the distance between us and perching on a nearby fence. Then, with another throaty carol, he flew a short distance and waited. Curious, I followed—out of the formal gardens, past the mulched beds, and through a deep thicket.

For the first time since I'd come here, my heart beat with curiosity. I pushed aside a wall of ivy and found an ancient door. It resisted my gentle push, so I pressed harder. Brushing against the overgrown foliage, the door eased inward. I slipped through it and caught my breath in wonder.

A snarl of dead branches guarded a solitary and neglected place—a hidden garden. I broke off some of the twigs in my path with a satisfying snap. A weathered statue smiled down at a murky lily pond. I ran my finger along the marble nose and chin in wonder. How many years had it been since he had a visitor?

A flicker of green drew my eye, and I crouched down. Brushing aside dead leaves, I freed several green shoots. They pushed through the cold earth with the same lonely determination with which I pushed through each day. Resolve welled up in me. To feel anything besides emptiness was a gift I wanted to grab. I could transform this abandoned garden. I could pull out the weeds, help it heal and bloom again. It wouldn't be too much trouble.

"But I don't want to be any trouble." Grandma Rose's voice

sounded frail and uncertain over the phone line.

"Don't be silly. You're family. And the kids will love seeing you." My brain scrambled to figure out how to get Kelsey's room prepared for Grandma Rose's visit. I hadn't had my morning coffee, and Monday mornings were tough even without new wrinkles.

A few rasping coughs echoed in the phone, followed by a pause while she caught her breath. "I don't want to intrude."

"It's not any trouble. You flew all the way out here to help Kevin with the kids after my accident. The least we can do is help you get your strength back." A little tender care, and she'd bloom again. Kevin and I had neglected her for too long, but we could nurture her now.

"But Kevin told me you're getting ready to move. Such a head-ache to have an old lady come visit."

"It will be a treat for all of us."

"Kevin said it would be fine, but he doesn't understand how it is for a woman. And you with all those children. And work."

I shoved aside the image of my life as a perennial bed, already crowded and overgrown. *What's one more rose?* "It will be a pleasure. Besides, with you here to play with the kids, it will be easier for me to get my work done. You'll be doing us a favor." I projected warmth and reassurance. "And I miss you." I was a little surprised to realize that I meant it.

Rose Louise Miller had always been an enigma. Strong enough to survive an abusive marriage and then raise Kevin alone after her husband was killed in a car accident. Stubbornly remaining in her home in Florida, even as the neighborhood changed around her and friends moved away. Always accommodating—even frail—on the surface, but deeply opinionated and able to make things happen her way.

Kevin's voice boomed through the headset after the wispy tones of his mother. "Honey, thanks so much. I think it will do her a world of good to stay with us for a while."

"I'm glad you thought of it. Family comes first."

"Oh, and I talked to Harry about the Woodbury house. He was worried about the plumbing and a few other things. I'm sure it's all stuff we can fix. The problem is, we're maxed out with our down payment and the new mortgage. We can't afford the supplies we'll need to make the improvements."

"Even if we do the work ourselves?"

"Yeah. But I did have one idea. . . ." He didn't sound very confident.

I saw my dream home dissolving into a mist, along with our shared adventure that was supposed to strengthen our marriage. "What's your idea?" My words were breathless with desperation.

"We could take out a construction loan in addition to the mortgage. As soon as the work is done, we can apply for a new mortgage with low interest. Combine them. But we'd have to work fast . . . get our permits, schedule our inspections. We couldn't afford the high-interest building loan for more than a month or so."

I was no expert at high finance, but this sounded scary. I took a deep breath. We needed this change. It would give me the fresh ground I needed to fix our family life. "Let's do it."

I heard a sound from Kevin's end of the phone that sounded like a sigh. "Okay. Call the agent, and have her submit our bid, okay?"

"Are you sure this will work?" One last concession to my fears. I wanted the house the way a dieter wants hot fudge-drizzled cheesecake, but I needed Kevin to reassure me. This was a huge decision to make when we couldn't even look in each other's eyes to discuss it.

"The house is an investment in our future." He was trying to muster some confidence. "We'll have to scrimp a little, but it'll be worth it."

My breastbone ached with yearning. Our dream home in the country. Our own hidden world to create and restore. I shoved aside my anxiety about the financing and embraced excitement. "Will do. See you tomorrow."

After setting down the phone, I rallied the kids to help me fix up Kelsey's room for their grandma. We decided that Kelsey would camp out on her sleeping bag in our room—a treat that made the boys jealous. My spirits lifted as we worked. Kevin was on his way home. And doing something kind for his mother was bound to earn me extra points with him. Disapproval and frustration had haunted our marriage in recent months, like mournful ghosts in an old English manor. We needed something to ease the tension. Even our date night hadn't kindled new romance. We laughed at different spots in the movies we rented. We used to laugh at the same things.

Dylan helped me pull Winnie the Pooh sheets off the bed and replace them with clean, floral-print linens. "Family is important," I told him. "We want to make Grandma feel better."

He pummeled Kelsey's pillow like a boxer working the bag. "So can I stay home from school to help you get ready?"

"Guess again, squirt. Go get your backpack. We hit the road in five minutes."

Kelsey squashed her clothes to one side of her closet to make space for Grandma, then popped her head out. "Mom!" she squealed. "You can't move my Barbie house. I have it set up just right. You'll wreck it."

"Honey, Grandma will break her neck if she tries to get around in here. We'll move it down to the basement. Be a good helper. It's just for a little while. And she's family. Family comes first."

At least that's what I longed for. My sister, Judy, and I had negotiated an uneasy truce over the years. I didn't cram my faith down her throat, and she watched her language around the kids and stopped sending them inappropriate toys. And some of our conversations on her last visits bordered on the sisterly connection I'd always dreamed of.

As far as extended family went, my sister and Kevin's mom were all we had. My mom's addictions had hastened her death shortly after Kevin and I married. My dad's workaholism and rages spiraled further out of control after she was gone. Their marriage had been unhappy but symbiotic. Without Mom there, Dad seemed to implode—dying of a stroke a few years later.

Not the model I longed for in my family. Kevin and I strove to create the ideal family—close-knit, loving—but in many ways, we were starting from scratch. An Adam and Eve without human parents as role models, standing in our suburban Eden, bewildered.

Grandma Rose's visit would be exactly what we needed.

With all the extra time I'd put in at church over the weekend, I could have justified a morning off. But positive feedback was still pouring in on the women's retreat, and I wanted to indulge in a little basking. After getting the kids to school and day care, I aimed for my office.

I planned to tackle paper work, then slip into the sanctuary for some quiet prayer time. I needed to ask God about Teresa's suggestion that I switch to full-time staff. Maybe God would give me a loud no, and I wouldn't even have to mention the notion to Kevin.

Or maybe God wants you to be honest with Kevin and confront any conflict the topic might uncover.

I stopped in the outer office to pour a cup of coffee. As I turned to walk toward my office, my knee buckled for a second. I stumbled and splashed a few drops of coffee on the carpet.

"Are you okay?" The church secretary was quick with her concern.

I grabbed a napkin and crouched to blot the spill. "Caught my toe on the carpet."

Her eagle eyes followed me as I fought to walk steadily into my office. Why had my leg become extra wobbly lately? The unpredictable weakness upset me more than the recurring pain.

I sank into my chair. "Lord, is it okay for me to pray for healing when I haven't been doing my physical therapy?"

Instead of a voice from heaven, a quavering soprano called from the doorway.

"Yoo-hoo. Mrs. Miller, do you have a moment?" Ruth Angelicus's cheerful face dimpled with fine lines like a hand-stitched quilt, and her white hair tufted in fluffy chaos like cotton batting escaping from a seam.

"I wish you would call me Becky." I soaked in the peaceful warmth of Ruth's smile.

"Oh no, dear heart. It isn't respectful to call a church worker by their first name."

"Well, come in. It's always great to see you."

She hobbled into my office and lowered herself into my extra chair, propping her cane near mine against the desk. They created a poignant still life. My modern, sticker-endowed aluminum with rubber-tipped base beside her classic, polished wood hook-handle. I admired Ruth so much that any traits we shared made me happy— even our canes.

She clutched her purse on her lap and sat with the dignity of the Queen of England.

"How can I help you?"

Her sunny smile clouded. She opened the clasp on her purse and pulled out several forms on sage green paper, creased neatly in half. "It's these papers. I'm so confused."

I recognized the new volunteer application forms that our staff had designed to aid in getting more of the congregation involved. "I'm happy to help. What has you concerned?"

She took a deep breath and placed the forms on the edge of my desk. "I want to teach second-grade Sunday school. Like I always do. Where do I write that?"

The taste of coffee soured in my mouth. My cheer sank into my stomach as I began to understand the problem.

Mrs. Angelicus drew my gaze with her guileless eyes. "All I can find is *facilitator, craft designer, music leader, curriculum presenter.* Nowhere can I find *Sunday school teacher.*"

I was tempted to send her down the hall to our children's ministry director. She had redesigned the Sunday school program and should be explaining this. But Mrs. Angelicus was one of my favorites. I owed her this.

"The church is changing the format of Sunday school and mid-week classes. We've had a hard time finding committed teachers like you, so to get more people involved we've designed roles that aren't as demanding. The professional staff present the Bible lesson to the large group, and then the facilitators take each of their small groups to do crafts that have been prepared for them."

I was beginning to sound like I was making a sales pitch, so I stopped.

Mrs. Angelicus' creases deepened. "When do I tell them the story? When do we pray?" She brightened. "You know, I have my own flannelgraph board and pictures for all the Bible stories."

"Maybe we can find a way for you to use your flannel board sometimes." An inadequate answer. The church was moving into PowerPoint and DVDs and didn't seem to have a place for the old guard.

She reached across my desk and gave my hand a gentle pat. "I understand." She stood up and grasped her cane, listing to one side. "It's all right, dear heart. You're doing a good job here."

I hated myself for the resignation in her voice—for the way her shoulders forgot their prim discipline and drooped. After she hob-bled out of my office, I looked down and realized she had left the blank volunteer forms behind.

I hid my face in my hands.

Lord, what's the answer? All these changes have been tested at successful churches. They aren't evil ideas. We can't refuse to change if we want to draw in new members. How do we do it all? How do we reach out to postmoderns, use marketing savvy, promote our church . . . and not lose our soul?

Again, I hoped for an audible answer. Again, a human voice intruded instead.

"Becky? Are you okay?" Teresa blitzed into my office before I could lift my head.

"Yeah, I'm just worried—"

She rubbed her hands together. "Well, I'm sure you'll handle it. You always do. Say, I wanted to apologize."

I needed at least three more cups of coffee to keep up with Teresa. I blinked and waited, not even trying to figure out what she was talking about.

"I hope I didn't put you on the spot at our staff meeting. About the full-time position."

Relief rose in my chest. "Well, actually, I've been feeling a bit overwhelmed already."

She nodded as if we were on the same side. "Exactly. You're already putting in a zillion hours a week, so you should be paid for it. And the way that the church is growing, we can certainly afford it in the budget. Pastor Bob is in favor, too."

"That's not what I . . . I mean . . ."

"Great job on the retreat, by the way. I hear we had a record turnout. I think the *Woodbury Ledger* is going to have an article in their next issue emphasizing all the great programs we provide for women."

I rubbed my temples. I had to find a calm, professional way to tell her I felt like I was choking—overgrown with clinging vines and gnarled thorns. I didn't even want to imagine what would happen to my marriage if I started working full time. My husband needed me. My kids needed me. My friends needed me. Now my mother-in-law needed me. There wasn't enough of me. I was confused and exhausted, but I knew enough to remember that family has to come first. Concentrate on those few tender shoots of green.

"Teresa, I really don't know if I can handle more responsibility. At least not now, while the kids are young."

She winked, as if I were joking. "You just have to weed out the unnecessary things, like I do."

I closed my eyes and squeezed the bridge of my nose. By the time I opened my eyes, Teresa had disappeared—off chasing another rabbit.

Chapter Nine

The chimney sweep moved aside with a tip of his hat as I marched up the sidewalk toward my home. The smell of soot barely registered. My eccentric neighbor fired his cannon and shouted a greeting. I hurried past, through the wrought-iron gate, and up the steps into our house.

My meeting had been long, and our nanny would be furious. I had promised she could have the evening off. I only hoped the children had behaved.

Dylan and Kelsey waited in the foyer, subdued and staring at their feet—an attitude they presented only after major mischief.

Cook stood behind them, her ample arms crossed in anger, her mouth holding a sour pucker. "She's off and gone, she 'as."

"The new nanny?"

"Yes, ma'am."

I glared at my children. Why couldn't they understand that my efforts were important? And that their father's long hours at the bank were for their benefit?

Cook stomped back to the kitchen. The children hung their heads. Now what would I do?

"We have to find someone. Quickly. And this time, no toads in her bed or pepper in her tea—"

A firm rap on the front knocker interrupted my lecture to the children. Perhaps the nanny had reconsidered. I smoothed my collar and pulled the door open.

The most unusual woman stood on the stairs, her heels lowering from tiptoe as if . . . well, as if she had drifted down with the wind. An umbrella *furled above her head, and an enormous carpetbag rested at her feet.*

"Here I am." Grandma Rose smiled shyly under the porch light. Her beige pantsuit was unadorned, as if her goal were to be as bland as possible. Brown hair—the flat shade that comes from a drugstore box—framed her sallow skin. The seriousness of her illness suddenly hit home with me.

"I'm so glad you're here. Come in, come in. How was the flight? Did they give you some supper?" I escorted her to the couch, noticing the wobble in her steps and the sigh of relief as she sat down.

"Oh my, yes. We had a nice flight. I would never complain. Although, who could eat that cardboard they called food?"

Kevin slid an olive green, hard-sided suitcase the size of a small state into the hall, then ducked out. A moment later, he jostled his bag through the door. He stopped and rolled his shoulders. "Those airline seats are getting smaller all the time."

I jumped up and clambered around the luggage to hug him. "Or maybe you're getting bigger." I nuzzled my face into the familiar crook where his neck met his shoulder.

"Hey, was that a fat joke?" He pulled back to pat his flat stomach.

A laugh tickled my chest. "I'm just saying . . ."

He pulled me in close again and breathed against my ear. "I missed you." Love, longing, and the pain he'd had to confront in seeing his mother so weak . . . all vibrated in his throat.

"I'm so glad you're back. I should have gone with you."

"Grandma! Grandma!" Kelsey and Dylan thundered up from the basement and launched onto the couch, fighting for a prime location beside her. Micah galloped in from the bedroom and trumped his siblings by leaping straight for Grandma's lap.

"Why, who are these big children?" Grandma Rose peered over the top of her glasses. "I don't recognize them."

Dylan and Kelsey giggled, but Micah poked at her glasses.

"Broken." Then he cupped his hands near her ear. "I'm Micah," he bellowed.

Grandma Rose winced. Kevin sidestepped past me to grab Micah and rescue his mom from more vision or hearing tests. "Hey, buddy, did you take care of the house while I was gone?"

Dylan jumped to his feet on the couch cushions and beat his chest. "I was the man of the house." His bouncing drew another grimace from Grandma Rose.

Great. My mother-in-law was seeing my kids at their rambunctious worst only minutes after her arrival.

"Kelsey, why don't you show Grandma how you fixed up your room for her?" I frowned at Dylan, and he trampolined off the couch and ran ahead down the hall.

Kelsey grabbed her grandmother's arm and tugged. Grandma Rose eased to her feet. "Whoa. Slow down, Goldilocks."

"Grandma, my name is Kelsey. Did you forget?" Kelsey trotted in place like a racehorse at the gate, impatient with their slow progress. They disappeared down the hall.

Kevin was still holding Micah. I looked at my husband and shoved my bangs off my forehead. "I'm sorry. I coached them to be polite, but they're too excited."

Micah chose that moment to wriggle like a greased pig, and Kevin let him slide down to the ground. Our youngest toddled at full speed after the rest.

I limped closer to Kevin. "How is she? How are you? I missed you."

He drew me close, and we connected with a happy sigh like two sides of a zipper joining. "After the kids are in bed, let's go to Betty's." Betty's Tea Shop was an easy walk and one of our favorite places to hang out on the rare date nights when we had the energy to talk instead of watch a movie.

I rubbed my cheek against Kevin's velour sweat shirt. "Mmm. You're so cuddly in casual clothes."

His chuckle bounced my face off his chest. "Maybe I should

check into changing the dress code at work. Although I don't think insurance managers are supposed to be cuddly."

"If we're going out, should I call around for a sitter?"

"We don't need a sitter with Mom here. We'll just wait until the kids are settled down."

"Mo-om." Kelsey careened around the corner. "Dylan pushed Micah." Micah's shriek rose on cue.

Kevin and I unzipped our embrace so quickly, I almost heard the ripping sound.

Dylan charged in right behind Kelsey. "It's not my fault. He was touching Kelsey's horse. Tattletale." He gave Kelsey a shove for good measure. "And he didn't listen when I said no."

Kevin knelt down and began the litigious process of sorting out culprit from victim. The phone shrilled an added voice into the chaos, and I used the interruption to slip away from the conflicts. Besides, Kevin needed a chance to get back into the swing of parenting after a few days away, right? Let him have a chance to handle discipline issues.

Our perky real estate agent was on the line. "He accepted the offer. You can close on November first. Of course, with your contingency clause, you have to sell your house before then. We'll do a big showing this Sunday."

I shrieked the news to the household and managed to ignore the rest of her blathering about getting our little rambler ready for the open house. Time enough to worry about that later. We'd passed the first huge obstacle toward getting the house. We could handle the rest.

Another hour of laughter and commotion passed before tired children, and an equally tired grandmother, were all tucked securely in various beds. Kevin placed our cordless phone on Grandma Rose's nightstand and gave strict instructions to call his cell phone if the kids woke up or she needed anything.

Kevin and I grabbed jackets and headed out. Indian summer had blown away and the dry air held a chill. Now that we were alone with only the occasional purr of a passing car, we walked in silence for the two blocks to Betty's. A squirrel darted into the street, changed his mind, and zoomed back toward a tall elm on the boulevard. The streetlight caught a few candy wrappers tumbling across the sidewalk to snag on our neighbor's lawn. On the next block, the fluorescent lights of the corner gas station, the Laundromat, and Betty's Tea Shop drew us forward.

Kevin reached for my hand. "You're freezing."

"Cold hands, warm heart."

"What does that say about me?" His warm paw squeezed my fingers.

I giggled. "Don't know. Should I be worried that your warm exterior hides a chilly psyche?"

"You should be more worried that I won't buy you a Cocoa Supreme."

"No fair. That's extortion."

"What do you expect from a guy with a chilly psyche? At least Florida was warm." He pulled open the glass door of Betty's and spicy scents swirled around us like steam. I settled at one of the tiny tables near the window, tucking my cane behind my chair. Kevin headed for the counter.

A gangly teen pointed to a chalkboard listing specials. "Would you like to try our new Lemon Blend?"

"Nah. Lemon tastes like furniture polish. We'll have a Cocoa Supreme and a Jamaican coffee—"

I cleared my throat loudly.

Kevin sighed. "Decaf."

The teen grinned and turned to fill tall Styrofoam cups with our drinks. For as long as we'd lived in this neighborhood, there had never been a Betty at Betty's Tea Shop. The owner's name was Lloyd, and he tended to hire high-school boys too spindly to be on the local sports teams, because they were available more hours.

I surveyed the rose-patterned tablecloths with their lace ruffles and the doilies dripping from the display shelf, trying to picture

Lloyd arranging them. "I'm going to miss this neighborhood," I said as Kevin handed me my cocoa and pulled up a chair.

"Yeah. I hadn't really thought that far, but I guess I will, too."

I licked at the whipped cream melting on my drink and took a cautious sip. "Mm. Perfect. Doctors should prescribe chocolate. You know what they say about a spoonful of sugar."

Kevin stared into his coffee, his jaw clenching and unclenching as if he were chewing on his thoughts.

I reached across the table and teased the cup out of his hands and toward me. "Come on. Talk. If you ever want to see your precious coffee again."

He looked up. Affection in his eyes melted some of his underlying distance.

I leaned forward. "What happened in Florida? What's wrong?"

"It's bad."

I nodded. I had a strange ability to push a deep Inner Calm button when Kevin needed me. I leaned hard on that button now and reached for his hand. "Tell me."

"I can't believe how run-down her house has gotten since the last time we visited. And the neighborhood isn't safe at all. She can hardly go out. And a lot of her friends have died or moved." He coaxed the coffee away from me and took a sip. Now that he had started, the words tumbled out of him as if the Jamaican blend were a full-caffeine version. As he talked, I watched worry, guilt, and a healthy dose of anger chase across his face. Worry about his mom's living conditions and health, guilt that he hadn't been aware of how much had slipped, and anger at her stubborn desire to keep living in the house she'd maintained for thirty years.

I sipped my cocoa and listened. By the time he had given me gruesome details of the house Grandma Rose could no longer maintain, and listed all the possible solutions he'd proposed and she'd rejected, I was down to a last lukewarm swallow of chocolate.

Kevin scraped his chair back a few inches and rubbed a hand over his head. "So I told her she had to move up here. At least we'd be nearby. There are plenty of nice senior apartments."

"You *told* her?" I bet that went over well. Had he forgotten everything he'd learned in a dozen years of marriage? "What did she say?"

He crossed his arms. "She agreed to come for a visit, but about the rest . . . she said she'd think about it."

I raised my eyebrows. She'd given the standard mom answer for "never in a million years, but I don't want to waste energy arguing." Kevin glared at his coffee. The poor man. I should be as worried as he was, but it felt good to be on the same side of a problem for a change. I was almost enjoying this. We hadn't felt like a unified team for a long time.

"I'll talk to her. Don't worry."

His face lit with gratitude. Then he looked down and tore off a fragment from the rim of his cup. "There's something else."

While I waited for him to continue, a picture blended into focus, as if a sidewalk artist had connected chalk lines into a recognizable image. "You want her to live with us."

He looked up at me and held very still, shocked at my guess and gauging my response at the same time. "How did you—"

"You've been worried about her for months now. And when we looked at the new house, you kept talking about how great it would be to have the extra room. Not hard to put the pieces together."

He held my gaze. "What do you think?"

What did I think? Kevin needed me. All the tension of the past few months, the sighs of disappointment, the interrupted conversations, the withdrawal, the feelings of becoming adversaries competing to see who was the most exhausted—this challenge gave us a reason to be a team again. I'd been a harried, cranky wife recently. This would win back my status as a supportive partner. Fixing Rose's living situation would help fix our marriage.

I swallowed hard and smiled even harder. "It's a wonderful idea."

Thankfully, Kevin wasn't one to dig too deep. Otherwise, he would have noticed my qualms. He swigged down the last of his coffee and jumped up. "You're amazing. Have I told you that lately? I thought that in the new house she could have the room off the kitchen for her bedroom. It's close to the downstairs bathroom, and she wouldn't have to handle so many stairs. And she can keep an eye on Micah and Kelsey in the afternoon if you have to run back in to work once in a while."

It could work. Maybe. "It'll be like having a nanny in the house."

Kevin held the door for me as a gust of cold wind tried to rattle it from his hand. "We still have to convince her."

"Don't worry. A few days with her grandkids, and she'll never want to leave."

Kevin kissed the top of my head, then wrapped an arm around me. I appreciated the warmth as we meandered along the sidewalk. "She really can't keep living in that house. The hospital social worker said she was malnourished. Her arthritis is worse. She hasn't been taking care of herself."

"We'll help her realize she needs a little help. Give her time to adjust to the idea."

"Yeah. She's always been this way. Her first reaction to new people or situations is resistance. But sometimes she comes around." Kevin picked up his pace, and I tried to stretch the stride of my cane. He took a deep breath of night air, and I saw the weight of the past few days lift off of him and float away. Whatever the coming months would bring, the challenges would be worthwhile if I could make him happier—if I could bridge the colorless, unspoken distance that had spread between us.

He looked up. A gray wisp trolled past the moon and melted into the dark atmosphere. The Big Dipper emerged as a pattern amid the chaos of stars.

"There's still one problem," I mused.

"What?" He firmed his jaw, as if expecting an argument.

"We still have to sell our house."

Kevin grinned at the sky. "Piece of cake."

Easy for him to say. I'd be the one keeping the house clean. And had he noticed how much our neighborhood had deteriorated in the past years?

"Can you believe it?" he asked. "A new house, room for the kids to play, my mom coming to live with us. It's super."

Yep. Just super. Supercalifragilisticexpialidocious.

Chapter Ten

I pushed a mass of cobwebs aside and ducked under a rocky outcropping. The dank smell of the tunnel melded with the odor of rotting vegetation from the jungle outside and another scent—one I was quite familiar with after years of archeological digs. Death. The unique signature of dried bones and decay.

My pulse quickened. We were close to the treasure. My guide was excited, too, and lurched ahead of me.

"Stop!"

The fool turned to grin at me as his foot triggered an ancient trap. An arrow hissed from the wall and narrowly missed his head. His grin froze, and his knees began to shake.

"Stay behind me." I scanned the rocky path for more hidden traps. A few more paces, and a chasm cut across our path. I uncoiled my whip and flicked it toward a wide branch breaking through the rocky surface above. I swung easily across, then tossed the handle back for my guide. After a combination of coaxing and threats, he finally leaped awkwardly across the space. I caught him and pulled my whip out of his death grip.

My studies had warned me about the traps in the main chamber. I frowned at the guide. "Don't move. Don't touch anything. I'll be right back." Placing each foot with deliberation, I made my way up a series of carved steps to the pure gold statue bathed in a renegade stream of light. The university museum would throw me a party for this one.

I estimated the weight and pulled a bag of sand from my belt. If I managed the switch, I'd be on the plane for home within the hour.

I snatched up the statue and slid the substitute weight into place.

If I miscalculated . . .

A subsonic rumble shook my feet. The bedrock growled. Oops.

Forgetting subtlety, I flew down the stairs and across the chamber, duck-ing as a slew of arrows sang overhead. My guide had already disappeared down the tunnel. I spared a glance behind me. A mammoth stone was bear-ing down, rolling toward me with gathering speed.

"Honey, look out!" Kevin barely maintained control of the dolly as he wheeled our filing cabinet toward the front door.

I dove toward the couch and got out of his way without a sec-ond to spare.

Kevin disappeared out the door. A few seconds later Heather skipped in with a stack of flattened boxes. "I found some more. And Kelsey is at my house playing with Grace and Charity. What do you want to tackle next?"

I wiped my sleeve against my forehead and struggled out of my sprawl on the couch. "I don't know. It's not fair that we have to move all this out before we even sell the house. This isn't how I wanted to spend my Saturday."

Heather laughed. "Maybe your real estate agent is into feng shui."

"I'll shui her feng," I muttered. But it was token grumbling. I knew our house looked crowded and cluttered. Clearing out some of the things we wouldn't need for a few weeks would definitely help the showing tomorrow. "Are you sure you don't mind having our stuff in your garage?"

Before Heather could answer, a shriek rose from the basement. I grabbed my cane and rushed for the stairs. From the top step I could see Micah's little body sitting on the lower steps, but his screams seemed to be coming from the center of the basement. People can't yell if they've been decapitated, can they?

Dylan popped into view below, eyes wide. "Mom, hurry!" I could barely hear his shouts over Micah's screeches. Heather and I hurried down the stairs to discover the problem. Micah had pushed his head between two vertical balusters connected to the handrail on the bottom part of the staircase.

I hurried around and crouched down in front of Micah's face. "Shh. I'm here. It's okay."

His wail cut off with a few sniveling gasps. "Mommmmy. I stuck!"

Dylan pushed against one of the railings, grunting with effort as if he could bend solid oak. "I bet him he couldn't fit through." He stopped pushing and grinned with a sudden realization. "Hey, I was right."

That started Micah crying again. "I stuck forever."

I fought to give a stern glare at Dylan and a soothing reassurance to Micah, all while chewing the insides of my cheeks so I wouldn't laugh.

"Would it help if I pushed from this direction?" Heather asked cheerfully.

I tried twisting Micah's shoulders and pulling, pretending to be a midwife. "No, I think we need to go back the other way. Micah honey, stop screaming. It doesn't help, and Grandma is trying to nap."

"Look out, his ear is getting stuck." Dylan tried to be helpful.

I couldn't get enough leverage to push or pull, with my bum leg. "Dylan, go find Daddy."

Heather came down the rest of the steps and joined me in front of Micah. "Let's pretend you're a jungle animal in the zoo, and you're getting ready to escape."

That got Micah's attention enough to stop his ear-shattering wails. I pulled out a Kleenex and blotted at the sweat, mucus, and tears coating his chubby face. No wonder he couldn't get out. His face was puffy from bawling. "That's my big boy. Don't cry."

Kevin charged down the stairs, took in the sight, and burst into laughter. Dylan followed him and grinned.

I shot a warning frown at Dylan. "It's not funny. And someone is in big trouble for talking him into this."

Kevin pulled off his work gloves. "If his head fit through, it'll fit back the other way." He studied the angle for a moment. "Hon, get me some Crisco."

A noisy, messy fifteen minutes later, Micah was free. Dylan was grounded to his room, Kevin and Heather left to drive a load of furniture the mile to her house, and I steered Micah toward the shower. It never ceased to amaze me how many booby-traps were hidden in the average home. And my kids were the kind of adventurers who always discovered them.

Grandma Rose opened Kelsey's bedroom door and peered out into the hall. "Is everything all right?" She spotted her lard-coated grandson and gave me a puzzled look.

"I'm sorry for all the noise. Everything's fine. Please go back to your nap. You're supposed to be resting."

"I'd much rather help. I feel so useless." She shuffled into the hallway. "Besides, no offense, but it does get a bit too noisy for napping around here."

Before I could apologize again, the doorbell rang. "Here." I pushed Micah her direction. "Could you help him get cleaned up? I'll be right back."

I hurried to the living room and pulled open the door.

A burly black man jogged in place on our steps. "Is this the packing party place?"

"Noah! Am I glad to see you!" I looked over his shoulder. "Where's Lori?"

He stomped into the living room and blew on his hands. "Fall is definitely on the way."

"I thought she was coming."

Noah scanned the room. "Where's that feeble husband of yours who can't move a few boxes by himself?"

"She e-mailed me."

When our real estate agent presented us with a long list of suggestions to prepare our house for selling, I sent out an e-mail SOS to my Thursday night gals. Sally and her family were out of town for the weekend, and Doreen had promised to take her kids to the zoo. But Lori and Heather both sent e-mails saying they were glad to help.

Noah scuffed his foot very much like Dylan did when caught at one of his schemes. "She asked me to answer her e-mails. Where's Kevin?"

I maneuvered in front of Noah and waited until he looked at me. "Every hard time I've gone through, she's been here for me. When I had the accident, she listened to me day after day until I could cope again. If something's wrong, I want to know. I want to help. What's going on?" My eyes pooled and I blinked hard.

"I really can't say." Noah spoke softly.

"She's my friend. I don't understand."

He rubbed the back of his neck, and furrows dug into his forehead. "I'm glad she has a friend like you. I've told her to talk to you, but she . . . she's not ready."

Micah galloped out in his best Sunday clothes. Grandma Rose followed close behind, wiping her hands on a plush bath towel. My best one. She handed it to me. "You'll want to wash that right away to get the grease out." She gave me an affable smile.

I wondered what would happen if I started yelling like Micah had when his head was stuck. I wanted Lori to talk to me. I wanted Kevin's mother to leave my good towel alone. I wanted Teresa to stop calling to ask about whether Kevin and I would teach at the marriage retreat, and what I'd decided about working full-time. I wanted my hip and knee to stop throbbing and my leg to stop buckling at odd moments.

Instead, I introduced Noah to Grandma Rose. She pushed a strand of damp hair back from her face and pressed her lips in a prim line. "It's nice to meet a friend of Kevin's. I came for a little visit until I get over this bad cold. You know how doctors like to fuss."

I escaped down the stairs to start a load of wash.

The past few days had challenged me more than I'd expected. Kevin kept asking if I'd talked to his mom about a permanent move. I was trying to establish a relationship with her first, but it was a slow process. Grandma Rose was polite but withdrawn. If a conversation made her uncomfortable she shut down. So far, I couldn't get her to acknowledge that she might not be able to live alone anymore. She wouldn't even admit that she had been seriously ill.

I knew her history. When Kevin was a boy, his dad had lost his job, and their family life crumbled. Kevin's dad began to drink and then to batter them. No wonder Grandma Rose seemed so desperate to fade into the woodwork and avoid conflict.

But Rose had also held down a job and raised her son after Kevin's dad died. She had firm opinions on how things should be done. I was feeling the strain of her unspoken disapproval. The smallest misstep could trigger a sniff or a cluck from the woman I was trying to win over. I'd spent the last few days dodging arrows and tiptoeing around hidden snares.

Since I was afraid my frustration was about to force its way out in some biting words, I retreated to the basement. When Kevin got back from Heather's garage, he found me doing laundry therapy. I'd developed this system out of desperation to find moments to pray during the busy day. As I pulled clean clothes from the dryer, I prayed for the owner of that item as I folded it.

He watched me for a moment as I finger-pressed the collar of Kelsey's blouse while muttering. I admit it might have looked weird, but he didn't have to stand there staring at me as if my sanity were about to fracture.

"Beck, can't this wait? We've got a houseful of people wanting to know how to help."

I pasted on a smile. "Sure. My list is upstairs."

I clumped up the steps, and we rallied the troops in the living room. "The bathroom needs a good scrubbing. We have to vacuum everything, especially the spots where we moved furniture. We have a can of paint for touch-ups. Oh, and the real estate agent wanted us to clean all the windows."

Soon the house was humming with a combination of laughter, the vacuum cleaner, and Steven Curtis Chapman on the stereo. I attacked cobwebs and dug out more dusty artifacts to store until the move. Kevin and Noah repaired the leaking faucet in the kitchen. The house began to sparkle.

As Kevin nailed down a loose threshold that we'd meant to fix for months, I scrubbed the kitchen floor nearby. "You know, it's not fair," I mused. "We're making our house perfect for someone else to enjoy."

"Yeah," Kevin said around the nails in his mouth. "I thought the same thing." He gave a final thump to the setter and stuffed the spare nails into his pocket. "And the new place needs so much work. We're getting the short end in both directions."

"But it'll be worth it, right?"

"You bet. The kids can run and build forts. They can go on treasure hunts. We can fix everything the way we want it. You'll have a shorter drive."

"But yours will be longer."

"Not to the Hastings office. I told them I'd take the transfer." He chuckled. "We better get this house sold. There's no going back now."

I squeezed my rag into the soapy water and released another whiff of lemony ammonia. We'd rarely been alone in a room together in the past few days. I better take advantage of this moment. "Teresa had an interesting idea."

Kevin pulled a screwdriver from his back pocket and tightened a loose knob on a kitchen cabinet. "I think we should pass on that marriage retreat. Tell her we're adjusting to a lot of changes right now."

I'd already told Teresa that, but I may as well let Kevin enjoy himself. "Okay. I think you're right. We'd never have time to get a class outline ready with everything going on."

He beamed at my cheerful acquiescence. Now that he'd turned down one request, it was the perfect time to bring up the more difficult topic. Besides, Kevin had been extra sweet to me the last few days—grateful that I had suggested having his mom move in with us and thrilled that I'd volunteered to talk her into the move.

"No, this is a different idea. Teresa noticed that I've been putting in way over my fifteen hours a week." I wrung out my rag and scrubbed a stain in front of the fridge.

Kevin squatted down beside me. "I'm glad you brought it up. I've been thinking it's too much for you, but I didn't know how to say anything."

"Too much for me?"

"Yeah. You haven't been taking care of yourself. The kids spend half their lives at church or in the van. And you've gotta admit you've been a little stressed lately."

My rag dropped into the bucket. Soapy water splashed over the sides.

I grabbed the refrigerator door handle to pull myself to my feet. "Too much for me?"

Kevin scrambled to stand up, skidding a bit on the wet linoleum. "Isn't that what you and Teresa talked about? That you're working too much?"

Steam built inside my skull. He thought I'd been failing as a mom?

No, don't explode. That will only prove his point.

"Actually, Teresa wants me to work full-time."

Kevin snorted. "That's ridiculous." He pulled out the silverware drawer that always stuck and began poking inside. "I think the slider thing is bent."

"I think it might be a great plan." I tossed the idea in his direction with casual confidence and turned to clamber up onto the counter so I could wipe down the top of the cabinets. Okay, I didn't really believe it, but I was hurt and wanted to shake him up a bit. "Hey, there's a Frisbee up here."

He pulled back from the cavern of the drawer and looked up at me. "Forty hours a week? Are you nuts? How in the world could you think that's a good idea?"

I wasn't about to admit that I had been every bit as appalled when Teresa mentioned it. Now that my pride was wounded, I saw plenty of reasons why it could work.

"With the new house, we could use the extra income. And I'd hate to lose my job if I refuse to take on more hours. They might have to get someone new. I'm good at my job. The church needs me. Plenty of moms work full-time. Besides, like Teresa says, I've practically been working that much anyway. I may as well get paid for it."

I reached over the sink to lift off the curtain rod. "Whew, these valances are filthy."

Kevin still hadn't said anything, so I twisted to look at him. His arms were crossed, and there was no movement in his face. His jaw was solid granite. How dare he give me the cold and stony? He was the one refusing to have a fair discussion.

The curtain rod was stuck in its bracket. I braced myself and gave it a tug. My bad leg buckled and I lost my balance. My arms flailed, but this jungle full of booby-traps had no handy vines to grab.

I shrieked as I fell backward. The ceiling seemed to pull away from me.

Kevin leaped forward to catch me. His foot hit a wet patch on the floor, and his legs slid out from under both of us. He hit with a crash.

I landed beside him. I had a second to gasp for breath before searing pain cut through my leg. An unheroic wail rose from my throat. My vision grayed. I felt as if I'd crashed into a deep crevice and would never be able to claw my way out of the pain.

Chapter Eleven

Alpine skies shone clear blue against distant snow-capped peaks. On this mountain, spring bluebells and wild roses already dotted the sloped meadows. From our tiny loft window, the new day beckoned. Goats bleated and rattled their bells. The cheerful whistle of the goatherd on his way up the slope reminded me it was past time for breakfast.

"Heidi, wake up," I said. "Today is an important day."

Heidi pushed her head out from under her burrow in the feather bed. "Your papa will be so surprised," she said. "You must wear your best apron."

I giggled. The simple clothes of the mountain were so different from the frilly dresses I had worn in the city. Would Papa even recognize me?

Grandpapa lifted me down from the loft and helped me to the table. I ate my porridge and drank fresh goat's milk without complaint. After the simple meal, Grandpapa helped us settle on a blanket outside. Heidi and I braided daisy chains, but I made no progress because I kept staring down the footpath, searching for my first glimpse of Papa.

Then he appeared, breathing hard from the climb. I flung away my flowers in excitement. Heidi helped me to my feet.

"Becky, my child. Is it you? Your cheeks are like roses." Papa's welcome voice was full of surprise and delight.

My heartbeat quickened. I released Heidi's arm. It was time to show him the best surprise of all. Arms reaching toward him, I stepped forward. The wheelchair that had broken my spirit for so long was in pieces at the bottom of the mountain. And the love of Grandpapa and Heidi had worked a miracle.

Unsteady without my cane, I took another step.

Dr. Lorton scribbled a note on his chart. "All right. Have a seat. Now tell me if this hurts." He set aside his clipboard and prodded my knee.

The sudden pain took my breath away. And Kevin had wondered why I'd opposed this visit. It was a miracle Dr. Lorton could see me first thing Monday morning, so I didn't dare back out of the appointment. But I wanted to hurry through it and get on with my day. The weekend had been bad enough.

After my tumble from the kitchen counter, I'd had to lie down and ice my leg while everyone else finished getting the house ready.

We spent Sunday afternoon at the zoo while our real estate agent hosted an open house. The kids had a ball, but Grandma Rose and I spent the whole time limping from bench to bench. At least the painful afternoon had given us a chance to talk. She changed the subject whenever I mentioned how difficult it must be for her to keep up a whole house by herself, but after much wheedling, she agreed to visit my doctor along with me—to keep me company.

Dr. Lorton pushed his wheeled stool back a few feet and shook his head. "How often do you do your physical therapy exercises?"

Why did white coats make me feel about five years old? "Um, I've kind of let it slide. I mean, with three kids, I barely have time to brush my teeth."

He gave a carefully neutral nod, but the wrinkles at the inner edges of his brows pinched together. "If you want to be able to take care of your children, you're going to need to make time to take care of yourself. I'm seeing an extreme regression in your range of motion and an unusual amount of inflammation. If we can't reverse this, you may be looking at another surgery." He grabbed his prescription pad. "We should try a new anti-inflammatory, and I want to see you for a follow-up appointment in two weeks."

He continued his lecture as I made contrite nods. I left the examining room as if I were leaving a confessional with a huge penance assigned. Grandma Rose had already been ushered into a different exam room, so I chose a chair in the waiting room, grabbed a three-year-old *Good Housekeeping,* and stared at the pages blindly.

Time for a little honest introspection. Deep down, I had figured if I ignored my handicap, it wouldn't really exist. Besides, heroes discounted their pain and kept moving. I wanted to be heroic. I swallowed back a surge of anger. There were few enough minutes in a day. I didn't want to waste them on making concessions to my injuries. Doctor's appointments, therapy, monitoring my nutrition and daily activity—not how I wanted to spend my time.

And who owns your time?

The quiet thought startled me, and I lifted the magazine so no one could see the tears that welled in my eyes.

Yes, Lord. I've given my life to you. So, my time is yours. But we could do so much more if you'd heal this.

Amid the sounds of coughs, sniffles, trilling phone, and the murmur of the receptionist's voice I heard a deep silence. A gentle rebuke.

For some reason, God had given me this body. A body that needed sleep, needed to be fed, and—in my case—needed extra care. Lately, I'd started to think that my valuable work at the church, and in my home, would somehow negate those needs.

Okay, this was the perfect time to make a fresh start. The new house would provide a life of simplicity and a slower pace. Like Heidi on the mountain, our family would thrive with sunshine, fresh air, and wholesome food. And I'd celebrate all the simple graces of life instead of fighting against them. I'd embrace it all: a good night's sleep, a day of rest, gentle exercise for my leg, taking my vitamins, breathing deeply.

I looked at my watch. I had hoped to get to church to catch up on some paper work before it was time to pick up Kelsey and Micah. Grandma Rose's exam was taking a long time.

I forced my clenched shoulders to relax. This was the new go-with-the-flow Becky. If I didn't have time or strength to accomplish everything today, God would figure out another way to get it all done. The happy endings were in His hands, not mine. The thought should have comforted me, but instead, I felt vaguely depressed.

When Grandma Rose hobbled out to the waiting room, she looked as glum as I felt. She sank into a nearby chair.

I tossed aside my magazine. "What did he say?"

She thrust her jaw out. "He threatened me with a walker."

"What?"

Her chin retreated as she slumped. "He says my balance isn't so good. Something about my inner ear. *Pfft.*" She dusted some lint from her skirt. "And you?"

"He threatened me with surgery if I don't do my exercises."

"*Humph.* Doctors."

I nodded. We sat side by side for a moment, contemplating our various mountains to climb. A nurse came out and called for a bleary-eyed four-year-old boy. His mother's haggard face looked familiar—I had seen the same expression in my bathroom mirror this morning.

Grandma Rose opened and closed the clasp on her purse a few times. "Did he scold you, too? Doctors do like to scold."

"Tell me about it."

She held up several prescriptions. "For my heart. And arthritis. And something else for my cough. And a lecture for not taking them for the past months. Who can keep track of it all?"

I showed her my scrip. "New pills for me, too. Plus a speech about taking care of myself."

We sighed in unison.

I planted my cane and stood up. "I have an idea. It's sunny. Let's drive to the park near church until it's time to pick up the kids." Besides, there would never be a better time to break through her denial and talk to her about moving. Maybe after this shared suffering, she'd even open up and reveal some feelings to me.

"I don't know. It's cold. And you have better things to do."

I was getting used to the pattern. What did antiwar protestors call it? Passive resistance. Rose was an expert.

"We both have coats, and we could use some fresh air."

"If you insist." She slipped her purse handle over her arm and came to her feet with a slight wobble.

"Want to share my cane?"

"No, thank you." She pulled her shoulders back primly, but the corner of her lips twitched.

We drove up to the small park a few minutes later. Canadian geese paddled across a pond, ignoring kin who honked from their precise V formation overhead. The sun spotlighted the remaining colored leaves, but a chill in the air reminded me that this brief encore performance was coming to a close. Soon the branches would be left with the stark gray shades of winter. I empathized with them. Sometimes I felt like my colorful, sparkling days were past. And if I felt that way, how must Grandma Rose feel?

I led Grandma Rose to a wooden bench near the water. "Are you warm enough?"

"Of course." She tied a gauzy scarf over her hair and tightened the belt of her brown felt coat. Then she scanned my navy hooded sweat shirt hanging unzipped over my sweater and corduroys. "You should have something on your head. You'll get an earache."

"I'm fine."

"What did the real estate lady say last night?"

"That's right. You slipped off to bed so fast, I didn't get to tell you."

She leaned back slightly, almost letting her spine touch the back of the bench, but not quite. "I didn't want to intrude."

I was tempted to reassure her that she wasn't an intrusion, but if she hadn't heard me the first fifty times, she probably wouldn't now. "No one came in with an offer yet." My shoulders curved forward with discouragement. I was exhausted from cleaning and from obsessing about our new house and terrified we wouldn't get an offer on our house in time. "We have to sell it soon. The contingency on the contract for the new house only gives us thirty days." I ran my fingers through the breeze-tossed layers of my hair. "I have to keep the house spotless, because buyers might want to look at it anytime. That's going to be a nightmare."

She opened her mouth but then snapped it shut. She didn't need to say anything. I could almost hear her thoughts by now. *A place for everything, and everything in its place. It always worked for me.* Or *If you didn't spend so much time over at that church, you'd be able to keep things orderly, not that I would ever criticize. I'm sure you know what you're doing.*

I didn't have the strength to smile and nod at her comments today, so I was glad she refrained. Now, how to approach the delicate topic? I decided to dive right in. "You know, with the new house, we'll have plenty of space. We'd love to have you come live with us."

Not as subtle as I'd planned, but we had to pick the kids up in twenty minutes. I shifted to face her and gauge her reaction.

Her eyebrows lifted, and her mouth formed a perfect circle. It was the face Kelsey made when the weatherman said a tornado was heading our way. Or the face Dylan made when we told him he'd have to wear a suit to our friend's wedding. Something close to horror.

"That's what you've been wanting to ask me?" she squeaked.

"You knew I was trying to—"

"Of course." She sniffed. "You and Kevin have been whispering in corners and giving each other looks, and you've started conversations with me a dozen times and then never gotten to the point."

So, she wasn't as clueless as I'd thought. Or as delicate as I'd feared. "So will you do it?"

She gave a negative shake of her head. "I thought you were going to ask me to move to an apartment up here—not come live with you."

"You mean you've thought about it? Moving to an apartment?" I could have yodeled with happiness. If she had already been considering a move, it should be easy to convince her to come live with us.

Her lips pressed into a hard line for a moment before she

answered. "I've lived in my house most of my adult life. And I've done fine on my own."

I took her hand. "You've done great. You raised an amazing son. You've worked hard. But it's all right to accept a little help."

She sat carefully still and watched the pond, not answering.

Was she touched by our offer? Offended? I couldn't read her, so I tried to forestall some of her arguments. "Would it be hard to leave your friends?"

She frowned. "Most everyone I knew back home has moved away. Or died."

Compassion warmed my veins. What would it be like to be old and alone? Seeing your friends die one by one? No wonder she seemed so closed off. "So why not move up here and be close to family?"

Her head bowed, and she seemed to be considering the invitation, so I pressed forward. "I know change is hard. It's hard for me to think about moving into a new home. I brought my babies home to the old house. But sometimes change is a good thing. Look at us. We're giving up our house, but the new one will have more room— room for you. That's a good thing."

She slid her hand away from mine and gripped her purse. "No. Maybe I need a little help. Maybe it's time to give up my house. But I refuse to be a burden. You have enough to manage. Always running here and there." She shook her head again. "It's never a good thing. Two women in the house. Different ways."

The words were resolute, but I heard the tired breathiness of her tone. She was weakening. I'd let Kevin have the next try. I understood her fears. No one liked change.

But it wasn't like I was asking her to move to a hermit's cottage in the Alps to raise goats. Our family was moving to a great new home and would find all sorts of blessings there. We just had to convince Grandma Rose. Oh, and sell our old house, too.

The geese on the pond took to the air in a noisy flapping of wings. "They're heading south," I said. "Moving on. Sometimes a new home is a good idea."

Grandma Rose looked at her watch and stood up. "Don't we have to pick up the children?"

So much for my clever analogy. I followed Grandma Rose to the van.

She looked out the window as we pulled out onto the road. "You know, I never much cared for geese."

Chapter Twelve

The noise of the crowd in the arena was a growling beast. I strode up the ramp and into the beast's jaws, leaving behind the stench of animals, human sweat, and fear that permeated the halls beneath the coliseum. Overhead the sky glared a sharp blue. Today was a good day to die. I felt no fear. A person who has already lost everything has no need for fear.

As a gladiator, my life was no longer my own. Not that I had ever really owned it. Even in my glory days as a general, I'd been a servant to Rome. The chains had simply been of a different kind.

The crowd cheered, and I brandished my sword. They knew my emblem, even though my helmet hid my true identity.

I turned to take in the wide scope of the stadium until I located the silk-draped balcony of the emperor. Now a true emotion surged hot in my blood.

If I defeated every opponent, the emperor might step out into the arena to acknowledge my victory. Then I could finally repay him for what he had done to my family and die with honor. The hunger for revenge fed strength into my muscles.

A new roar rose from the crowd, and I turned to gauge my first opponent. A giant with mace and spear lumbered toward me, eager to strike the first blow. His spear flew wide and burrowed upright into the ground. I grabbed the shaft to add leverage to a flying kick that sent him stumbling back. I dodged his flailing mace, and my sword found the gap at the side of his breastplate.

One after another, new adversaries confronted me. I conquered them all. The frenzied cries of the tiers of Romans faded into a hum, as meaningless as distant bees. Sweat stung my eyes. The sound of my rapid breaths echoed

loud in my ears. My vision narrowed to the sword of my next rival. My
arms shook with fatigue as I blocked his first blow.

Then he spun past and smashed his shield into my back. I fell forward.
I tasted hot dust and the copper tang of blood. A quick roll brought me back
to my feet. I couldn't hold him off much longer. My movements felt slow,
tangled, shrouded. I had to break through my own exhaustion, or my next
breath would be my last.

"'Finally, be strong in the Lord and in his mighty power.'" Pastor
Bob's voice held the deep tremolo that signaled intense emotion. He
took a breath and turned the page of his Bible. "'Put on the full
armor of God so that you can take your stand against the devil's
schemes. For our struggle is not against flesh and blood . . .' Do you
hear that?"

All of the staff who had gathered in his office nodded.

"I think one of the devil's schemes is to cramp our vision. Make
us afraid to use all the means we can to share the gospel. Cripple us
with thinking we can't."

Teresa bounced her head in counterpoint to her tapping foot.
"And Galatians chapter six tells us, 'Let us not become weary in
doing good, for at the proper time we will reap a harvest if we do
not give up.' We are at a crucial point of growth in our congregation. We're all tired and overwhelmed. But that's exactly when we
need to work harder."

I squirmed. Why did everyone seem to have more zeal than me?
I used to love the imagery of battle to describe the Christian life. It
was easy to relate to feeling attacked on every side. I had a keen
awareness of our battle with the unseen enemy. But today I had
really hoped the theme of Tuesday morning staff devotions would
focus on verses like Jesus' words "Come to me all you who are
weary and burdened, and I will give you rest."

I cleared my throat and all heads turned toward me. "I was
thinking about all our ideas for helping our church grow, and I
found this verse in second Corinthians, 'The weapons we fight with
are not the weapons of the world.' I think it's great that we send out

press releases, and run a Web site, and are exploring media ministry. But I also think we have to be careful not to rely too heavily on 'weapons of the world.'"

Awkward silence filled the room. Someone coughed, several people shifted in their chairs.

"What do you mean? Can you expand on that?" Teresa said in a pseudo-supportive voice—the one she had probably learned in her small-group-communication classes.

I pressed my arms against the knot in my stomach. I hated being a voice of dissent—especially when I agreed with much of what they were saying. But I had to raise this issue.

"Don't we still need to focus on prayer, and seeking God's direction, and digging into Scripture? I think sometimes these other tools—the proposals and marketing and surveys—get us focused on numbers. God doesn't measure success the same way we do."

Teresa tilted her chair back. "How could there be anything wrong with bringing more people to hear the gospel?"

"There's not." I looked around at the faces of the staff. How could I explain the unease I'd been feeling? "But it's easy to get off track when we start running church like a corporation." I saw a few nods and took heart. I told them about Mrs. Angelicus and her sadness at no longer having a place in the new structure of Sunday school.

Pastor Bob's thick brows waggled between surprise and concern as I spoke. "Becky, I'm glad you brought this up. In our rush to embrace twenty-first-century models, we have to remember that God cares for each individual."

Teresa cleared her throat, looking put out. "Of course. We all realize that. Now, let's move on to staff reports. Becky, have you made a decision about going full-time?"

Oh boy. Out of the frying pan and into a self-cleaning oven set on Clean. My face felt hot and my heart raced.

Get a grip, Becky. You're too young for hot flashes.

"I'm so honored that you asked, but my family needs me. I

couldn't handle committing to a full-time schedule. In fact, I need to find a way to stick more closely to my contracted hours. My work here has put a lot of stress on my family lately."

I was tempted to tell them about sick kids and a grumpy husband. About racing in circles with no time to spend with friends. About not being able to worship on Sunday mornings because work was always on my mind. About becoming cranky, losing my temper more and more, and not taking care of my health. About the building tension as we wondered if our house would sell in time.

But I didn't want to start crying. Tears didn't fit Teresa's professional model for church workers. Instead, I swallowed hard. "I realize that you might feel we need a full-time Women's Ministry Director and will want to replace me, but I hope you won't. I love working here."

Pastor Bob smiled. "Very sensible. I'm sure we all understand. And of course we want you to stay. In fact, I think we've all been in danger of spreading ourselves too thin. Let's all do some praying about refocusing our priorities. Okay, how about the music department? What's new this week?"

As easily as that, the meeting moved along. Tension released its grip on me, and I sagged into my chair. Gratitude and surprise at Pastor Bob's reaction mingled in my chest.

There had been one stubborn part of me that wanted to take on the extra hours just to prove to Kevin that he was wrong and I could handle it, but I didn't need to assert my I-am-woman-hear-me-roar identity. It had taken more courage for me to stand against the church work encroaching into more and more of my time. I had prepared myself for losing my dream job.

And from the frowns that Teresa was casting my direction, that still might happen. But for now, I'd done the right thing—taken a step to slow down . . . or at least stop the acceleration.

After the meeting, I attacked the work on my desk with new vigor. Each phone call, each e-mail, each form fell like foes beneath a sword. I no longer felt like a slave to my work. I was even humming when I picked up Micah and Kelsey at lunchtime.

"Hey, kids, I've got a great idea. Let's drive by the new house and say hi to it."

"The one with the dogs?" Kelsey bounced in her car seat.

Micah beamed. "Doggie. Arf, arf."

"No, silly. It's ruff, ruff." Kelsey demonstrated. The kids began howling and barking every canine impression they could invent.

At least they weren't growling and snapping.

I turned left out of the church driveway instead of right. In five minutes, we had left the suburbs behind and drove along pastures and clusters of new developments. Dry corn stubble filled one field, and the kids cheered when they spotted a pheasant lift off from its cover.

In just a few more minutes, we pulled up the long dirt driveway. The house rose beneath sharp autumn sunshine. Did one side lean a bit? I hadn't noticed that when we visited the house last week. And the grey clapboard looked chipped and disreputable instead of quaint. The old oaks near the house had surrendered their leaves, and gnarled branches thrust out in all directions. When I turned off the engine, I could hear a haunting squeal as one limb rubbed against the side of the house.

"Let's see if the dogs are home." Kelsey threw off her seat belt and reached for the door.

"No, kids. Stay buckled. We can only look today. The house isn't ours yet."

"When will it be?"

"After we sell ours. That's why we all have to pitch in and keep the house neat and clean all the time." Which could be one of the most challenging battles of all time.

I soaked in the peaceful setting and let myself fall more deeply in love. This homestead was my ally in the battle to fix our family's problems. I could see myself bringing a colander of fresh strawberries in from the garden while Grandma Rose tended the jars heating in boiling water and explained the intricacies of canning homemade jam. Gingham curtains would flutter in the open window, and the children's happy whoops would carry into the house as they galloped around the wide meadow behind the house.

My leg would improve because of all my gentle morning walks down country paths. And my prayer life would flourish as I chatted with God on those same walks.

Micah's feet thumped against the back of my seat. "Weetoh."

"What, sweetie?"

"He's saying he wants a burrito," Kelsey translated. "Me too. I'm hungry."

I laughed. "You're right. It's lunchtime." I started the car and carefully backed down the rutted driveway, then pulled out onto the road. "I think we still have a few in the freezer."

With the promise of food, and a Slug-Bug contest, the drive home passed amiably. When we pulled up to our house, I groaned. Two strange cars were parked at the curb, and our front door stood open. We'd been invaded.

Our real estate agent, Brenda, had warned me. In addition to open houses, there would also be visits by individuals wanting to take a closer look. She had promised to give me as much warning as possible.

"Okay, kids, here's the plan. We'll sit here for a little while, and you can tell me all about your day at school."

"But I'm hungry," Kelsey whined.

Micah sneezed. "Me too."

I passed him a tissue. "I know, kiddos. But remember what I said about selling our house? If we stay out of the way, it will help."

Kelsey frowned. "But Grandma's in there. Why does she get to be there, and we don't?"

And why didn't the agent call me, like she promised she would before bringing anyone through? I hoisted my shoulder bag onto the seat and rummaged for my cell phone. "Phooey." I'd shut off my phone for staff devotions and had forgotten to turn it back on.

"Mommy said a bad word. I'm telling."

I ignored Kelsey and thumbed through messages. Sure enough, she had left several messages asking me to call her back because she had some hot prospects eager to see the house.

"Phooey, pooey. Need to poo-poo," Micah announced to the world at large.

Brenda had given me strict instructions. She could do her job much better if we stayed out of the house during showings. Too bad for her. I wasn't going to risk an accident with my barely potty-trained youngest.

"Okay, kids. Into the house." I had never realized how much of my life would revolve around bodily functions once I became a parent. As we hurried up the sidewalk, I punched the key on my phone to listen to the last message on the queue.

"Hey, sis. It's Judy." She gave a short laugh. "Like you wouldn't figure that out from me calling you 'sis.'" My eyebrows climbed. My self-assured sister never dithered.

I steered Micah toward the bathroom, grateful that the potential buyers were apparently in the basement. I hit a button to start Judy's message over.

Yes, she definitely sounded odd. I hovered outside the bathroom while Kelsey skipped to the kitchen and pulled the freezer door open. My sister's message continued. "Beck, something's happened. Look, I don't want to explain it in a message." She made a strangled sound. If it hadn't been Judy, I'd have guessed she was crying. But Judy didn't cry. "Just call me, okay?"

Grandma Rose tottered out from Kelsey's room. "There you are," she stage-whispered. "I was going to fix lunch for you all, but those people came. I don't know how you can live like this."

I stared at my phone, then at Grandma Rose. "I'm sorry—"

"Oh, what a cute little girl." A woman's voice shrilled from the kitchen. "Does she come with the house?" I heard our agent give a polite laugh, while heavy footsteps pounded up the stairs behind her.

"Don't know about that water heater. Looks mighty old to me. Could need replacing." The gruff man's voice irritated me, and I left

Micah to himself and hurried out to the kitchen, where Kelsey continued to rummage through the freezer searching for burritos.

I planted my cane in the kitchen doorway. "The water heater is fine. With three kids, we go through a lot of hot water."

The older couple in the kitchen blinked at my appearance. Brenda gave me a look that said *I* was in hot water for interrupting her tour. "Well, I think you've seen everything inside. Let's take a look at the backyard."

"I love how you've decorated," said the woman, trying to appease me.

I set my cell phone on the counter. "Thank you. We've really enjoyed living here. We've just outgrown—"

"Yes, it sure is a nice house." Grandma Rose joined us in the kitchen. "But I do wish there weren't so many city buses going past. It's hard to take a nap with all the noise."

Brenda quickly opened our back door. "Let's go out—"

"Mommy," Micah hollered from the bathroom. "Wipe me."

The older couple tried to hide their grins, Brenda glared, and as Kelsey pulled a tub of ice cream out of the freezer, it slipped and fell onto her foot. She screamed and started hopping around. I stood, paralyzed, unable to decide which direction to move first.

Pain trumps mess. I reached for Kelsey and awkwardly comforted her, wishing it were easier to bend my knee to get myself to her level. "It's okay, sweetie. Put something cold on it."

"That's how it got hurt," she wailed. But my hug seemed to help, and she lowered the decibel of her crying.

Brenda popped her head in the door, with the couple hovering right behind her. "They have a few questions about the roof."

"Mom! Wipe poo-poo!" Micah sounded frantic.

Micah trumps selling the house.

"Coming!" I hobbled toward the bathroom as quickly as I could. Behind me, I could hear Grandma Rose cheerfully answering the potential buyers.

"They've lived here a long time, and they've never replaced the roof. So, it must be pretty old. Don't cry, sweet pea. Here, have some ice cream."

As I helped Micah, I heard my cell phone trill from the kitchen. "Kelsey, don't answer—"

"Hello, Miller residence." Kelsey managed to be polite between her snuffles. "Oh, hi, Aunt Juju. Yeah, she's here."

"Tell her I'll call her back." I was helping Micah lather up his hands.

"She says it's a 'mergency."

Sister trumps my sanity. I left Micah to splash, toweled off my hands, and hurried to the phone.

Chapter Thirteen

"*At last, they realize who I am.*" The grande dame of silent films swirled down the marble stairs with scarves and flowing gown trailing in her wake. "*I knew one day they would want me back. Beg for me.*" She paused on the landing and looked at the throng of people in her foyer.

"Yes, madame," I answered. Why hurt her with the truth? I'd shielded her for years.

Cameras flashed and she posed. Triumph shone in her deranged eyes. Her makeup was thick and garish. Her smiles tight and too extreme. But she lifted her arms in a confident gesture, causing her bracelets to sparkle. Sparkle the way she had years ago.

As she continued down the stairs toward me, I could smell the cloying heaviness of her perfume. Age wasn't wearing well on her or on this mansion. The red flash of police lights outside highlighted each tatter in the draperies, each scratch in the pipe organ, each faded spot on the oil painting that hid her film screen. How many nights had we sat on the scuffed upholstery of the couch together and watched the movies of her glory days?

"All right, Mr. DeMille, I'm ready for my close-up," she said imperiously.

"Of course." I offered her my white-gloved hand and led her toward the waiting police car with a semblance of dignity. She deserved that much.

More flashbulbs flared, and she preened. Let her believe the newsmen were here to capture her return to stardom, instead of to report on a sordid murder. Her whole life had focused on nothing but her work. She hadn't cared whom she used along the way. That's why she had been one of the greats.

The headlights of my minivan caught Judy's figure standing beside her luggage right outside the airport's baggage claim area. The evening flight from Chicago had landed on time. Of course. I chuckled to myself. It wouldn't dare do otherwise with Judy on board.

Her tailored pinstripe suit fit her figure flawlessly. Her blond hair gleamed, even in the flat light of overhead fluorescents. Her makeup was a bit harsh—dark brows, dark lips—but that was the look she preferred. Maybe it helped intimidate her business competition. Although she didn't need the help. She'd always been a star—my parents' golden child, and now the VP of marketing for a major toy company.

I pulled up to the curb, got out, and lifted the hatch. She slid her stylish carryon into the back, leaving me to wrestle a large matching suitcase. Braced on my cane, I managed to heft it in with some one-armed contortions. Then I turned to her.

Close up, she seemed brittle and unapproachable. Too bad. She needed a hug, and I could handle a few prickles.

I wrapped my arms around her and squeezed. "I love you, sis. Everything's going to be okay." Warm concern swelled in my heart, surprising me with its strength. "Now will you tell me what this is about?"

Judy had been evasive in her phone call. But even with our real estate agent asking me about the furnace, Grandma Rose wanting to know what to make for lunch, and Kelsey trying to show me the bruise on her foot, I had heard the desperation in Judy's voice. When she said she needed to see me, I didn't hesitate.

"Of course you can come visit. But I did tell you about Kevin's mom staying with us, didn't I?"

"Are you saying you don't have room for me?" Judy's plaintive tone ignited my worry and nurturing instincts.

"No, no. There's room. If you don't mind the basement couch. No one's staying there." Yet. If you didn't count the strangers traipsing through. The way things were going, I could hang up a sign. *Becky's Home for the Troubled.*

Now that Judy had arrived, I needed to find out what had sent her into such a tailspin. I limped to the driver's side, maneuvered in, and slid my cane into its place between the seats.

Judy opened the passenger-side door and picked a granola bar wrapper from the front seat, holding it as if it were radioactive waste. I ignored her obvious dusting of the seat and pulled out into a lane. This late in the evening, there weren't too many cars trying to nose into a spot near the doors.

Judy stared at my cane. "How's the leg been?"

"Oh, no, you don't. You are not diverting me. What's wrong?"

Instead of answering, she reached forward and cranked up the heater. "I always forget how cold it is here."

"The weather? That's the best you can do?" I cleared the airport and merged onto the freeway. "Besides, Chicago is just as bad."

"Maybe, but I spend more time in L.A. and Houston."

"Poor you."

She laughed as if she'd forgotten how. "Can we go somewhere?"

"You don't want to go home?"

"I want to be able to talk."

She had a point. Kevin was probably giving Micah a noisy bath. Grandma Rose was most likely rearranging all my spices in alphabetical order. Kelsey and Dylan were supposed to be having quiet time on the couch, reading. But they were probably whacking each other with books.

I took the next exit ramp and headed toward a small overlook of the Mississippi that Kevin and I had discovered when we were dating. Judy stared out the window as we drove, hands clenched in her lap.

I gave up trying to coax any information out of her and waited until we'd pulled into the deserted parking area. The van had warmed up, so I turned off the ignition. Moon-tempered darkness surrounded us, and a wide band of water stretched beneath us.

"Talk."

Judy tried another weak laugh. "When did you get so bossy?"

"I learned everything from my big sis."

She looked at me. "Thanks for letting me come." Quiet. Almost tender.

Now I was getting scared. "Cancer? Do you have cancer?"

"No. Would you shut up and let me tell you?" She squared her jaw and stared out the windshield. "They fired me. My career. It's gone." Her despair swelled and filled the van, squeezing out the air.

I sucked in a short breath. "But you helped make them. You were so big."

"I am big. It's the company that's too small. We were bought up by a global conglomerate. They brought in their own people, and just like that—I was out."

My heart ached for her. "Oh, Judifer." The childhood pet name slipped out. "I'm so sorry." A few years ago when Kevin had lost his job, it had devastated him. But he had family, friends, and his faith to lean on. Judy had thrown every ounce of her life into career success. She'd had a series of casual flings and no real trusted friends. And faith? In her mind, that was for sissies.

"Becky, what am I going to do? I don't have anything else."

"You have me." I touched her shoulder. "You can stay with us as long as you want, until you figure out what you want to do next."

She nodded but then quickly turned her head away.

I heard her sniffle and handed her a tissue, but otherwise I pretended I didn't notice her tears. Judy hated to cry. Even worse, she hated for anyone to see her cry.

The windshield was fogging up, and I rubbed a patch clear. "Besides, we could use your help decorating our new house. Did I tell you we decided to move?"

"You're moving? And you didn't ask me for advice?"

Ah. My true sister had returned. "We found a big old farmhouse with a couple acres of land. And it's only a few minutes from my work."

"Has it been inspected? Did you check on zoning? How about the property taxes?"

I shrugged. "A friend of Kevin's checked it out. We bid for it 'as is' so we could get it for a bargain. Sure, it'll need some work. But that's part of the fun."

"Let's go. I need to talk to Kevin. I can see I got here just in time."

I started up the van, relieved that she'd forgotten her despair now that she could orchestrate my life. "Fine. Now let me explain Grandma Rose. She wants to help out, but she has a lot of health problems. And she's critical of everything I do." I seemed to attract that in my life. "But she won't always tell you directly. She'll shake her head and mutter under her breath about how things used to be done properly when she was a young mom."

"Oh, really?" The ferocious gleam returned to Judy's eyes.

"You be nice to her. Kevin and I are trying to convince her to live with us."

"What? Why on earth would you do that?"

"I told you. She has lots of health problems and shouldn't live alone anymore."

Judy tucked a strand of hair behind her ear, revealing a perfect pearl earring. She settled back against the seat. "That's what nursing homes are for, sis."

I decided to turn on the radio instead of risking any more conversation.

Several hours later, I was beside Kevin under our fluffy comforter. Kelsey snored softly from her sleeping bag in the corner by the closet. An unusually large space stretched between Kevin and me, and I wasn't sure what to do about it. "Do you think your mom will be happy with us?"

"Sure." He spoke softly in the direction of the ceiling. "She didn't like the idea of selling her house, but she's started to accept that. It'll take a little more time for her to get used to us all."

"I hope so. She hasn't seemed very . . . comfortable yet." I wriggled deeper under the covers. Kevin always turned the thermostat too low at night.

He made no move to scoot closer to warm me.

"Kev?"

"Hmm?"

"Aren't you glad I told the church I can't work full-time?"

He sighed. "Of course I am."

"Then why are you over there, and I'm over here?" After the words blurted out, tears sprang into my eyes.

He reached for me and wrapped his arms around me. "Oh, honey, I'm sorry."

My throat felt thick, and more silent tears ran down my face. "I don't mean only now. There's been a space between us all the time lately."

The muscles of his back tightened under my hands. "Well, you've been busy."

"Are you blaming me?"

"I didn't say that. Come on. Don't cry."

I rolled away to reach for a tissue. "I can't help it. We never talk anymore."

He groaned. "Beck, my mom is here. And your sister. Even at night, Kelsey's in our room. We can't relax on the weekend because of open houses. It's a weird time. It'll get better."

I blew my nose and then snuggled back into Kevin. "Promise?"

"Yes. It's just a rough patch." As easily as that, he put aside the topic and settled in to sleep.

"Kev?"

"Hmm?"

"Judy's not going to want to sleep in the basement for more than a few nights. She's used to star treatment. I'd ask Lori, but she's still not returning my calls. And I hate to suggest a hotel when Judy's just lost her job."

"How about Heather? Do they have room?"

I plunged toward him and planted a big kiss on his lips. "You're a genius! Their whole family is going on that short-term mission trip. I bet she'd love to have Judy house-sit. And that's only a mile away, so Judy can hang out here all she likes. Brilliant."

He grunted.

I moved my elbow off his stomach. "You're right. Everything is going to get better. I'll figure out how to manage my time better. I know I can cheer up your mom and get her to enjoy living with us. Especially once we move into the new place. We just have to get this house sold. I heard that you should simmer cinnamon on the stove and have a bouquet of flowers on the table when people come. Do you think that would help?"

No answer.

"Kev?"

His even breathing told me I'd been talking to myself. I smiled and tugged a little more of the comforter onto my side of the bed. Now if I could find out what was wrong with Lori, I'd be well on my way to fixing everyone's problems.

Chapter Fourteen

Smoke rose as the train prepared to pull out of the Istanbul station, adding coal fumes to the smells of spices and unwashed bodies. The shriek of the whistle almost covered my companion's gasp.

"What is it now?" I asked.

He pointed down the platform where a mustached Bulgarian quickly pulled back into the shadows. "We have been followed." His Russian accent sounded strained with tension.

This mission had been an obvious trap. But the chance for MI-6 to get their hands on the electro-decoder was too good to pass up. So, I took the bait and arrived in Turkey, introducing myself to the local consul. "The name's Miller. Becky Miller."

From that moment, I'd been pulled into a web of agents and counter-agents, assassination attempts and betrayals. All in a day's work for me. But the Turkish consul had become a friend. And now he was dead. I had no more patience for cat and mouse.

"Let's go," I yelled. We leaped onto a car as the train began to roll, hurried into a sleeper car, and locked the door. I whirled around and confronted my companion—the Russian who claimed he was planning to defect. "No more games. Who do you really work for? I want answers now."

The train rocked as it picked up speed, and the whistle pierced the air again.

I shivered on the steps and rang the doorbell again. Lori's daughter, Abby, pulled it open. As always, she wore a neat dress—the old-fashioned kind that seemed to be the uniform of sorts among my homeschooling friends. Abby's plaits ended in red, white, and blue beads. Her glasses were the same golden brown tones as her complexion. She looked much older than her ten years, partly because her demeanor was so mature.

"Hello, Mrs. Miller." She blocked my way, uncertain.

It had taken a week for me to find time to escape my chaotic household and come check on Lori. Judy and Rose squabbled with each other, and they both argued with me. The kids were wound up, and keeping the house presentable for real estate agents bringing clients through left me exhausted. I wasn't going to be turned away today. I reached forward with my cane and hobbled inside. "It's all right. I know she doesn't want to see anyone, but I've got to talk to her."

Abby sighed, more a sound of relief than failure. "She's in bed."

"Where's Jeffy?" I looked around the neat country living room and dining room. Maps and cursive writing charts covered the walls. A shelf displayed carefully labeled collections of rocks and shells. In spite of being a daily classroom, Lori's home was comfortable and welcoming. Checkered upholstery and restored Shaker-style antiques kindled my decorating urges. Our new house could look like this.

"Dad took him in to work today."

A six-year-old at Noah's computer programming office? That would be interesting. On the other hand, Jeffy was probably apprenticing for a software designer. Lori's kids were truly exceptional.

I shrugged out of my jacket. "So, is she all right?"

Abby studied the planks of the floor. "You can go on upstairs."

I needed the help of the railing, as well as my cane, to coax my aching hip and knee to cooperate. So much for a sneak attack. A charging rhino with tap shoes would be subtler.

Trying to regain my secret-agent nerve, I peered around the frame of the open door.

Lori was propped against the headboard of the bed, staring at the wall across from her. My noisy approach hadn't caused her to turn. She had always looked like an Alvin Ailey dancer—tall, supple, elegant. Today she seemed smaller, almost frail. And she wasn't in her usual denim dress. The loose cotton sweat suit looked like it belonged on someone else.

I stepped into the room. "Lori?"

Her head moved slowly, and her eyes registered my presence as if she were drawing herself back into the room from a far distance. Her mouth opened and closed, and tears filled her eyes. "Oh, Becky."

I hurried forward and we hugged. Lori began to cry onto my shoulder, deep shuddering sobs.

I cried, too. From my worry, and also from the relief of seeing her. I'd missed her so much and feared she no longer wanted my friendship.

"You're really sick, aren't you? Why didn't you—"

"I've missed you, but I—"

"—tell me. I want to—"

"—didn't want anyone to see me like—"

"—help. What can I—"

"—this. There's nothing you can do."

"—do?"

I sat on the edge of the bed, and we stopped hugging so we could look at each other. We were both a wet, sloppy mess. We stared at each other, and suddenly we were both giggling.

Then I sobered. "Okay, talk. No more hiding. Whatever is wrong, I'm your friend. I'm here for you."

"All right. But first tell me how everyone is."

"Sally is collecting blankets for a local women's shelter and keeps telling me how to fix up my house. Without you around to keep her in line, she's bossier than ever. Doreen is crazy busy but still shows up for Bible study in perfect makeup and shoes that match her suit. Heather is helping Ron get ready for the mission trip."

"And how's it going with Kevin's mom? Noah said she agreed to move?"

"Sort of. She decided she wanted to sell her old house. Kevin is down there now boxing and shipping some of the things she wanted and putting her house on the market. But she still hasn't agreed to live with us. She put herself on a waiting list for an apartment building she likes." I twisted my wedding ring. "I'm hoping once we're settled in the new house, she'll decide to stay with us."

She studied me. "Why? I mean, why is that so important to you?"

"It's for Kevin. I want to do it for him."

"Are you trying to prove something?" Lori's voice was gentle, but her words prodded motivations I didn't want to examine.

I lifted my gaze from my ring. "Enough about me. No more stalling. Please. Tell me what's wrong."

Lori sighed. "You have to promise not to tell anyone. I'm not ready."

I was already nodding. "Of course. But we're best friends. You aren't allowed to keep secrets from me."

She smiled, but her lips twisted as if the effort caused her pain. I felt guilt for browbeating her, but I was sure I'd be able to help if she'd open up.

Her eyes filled with weary sorrow again. "I feel so . . . ashamed."

Frustration made my temples throb and my stomach ache. "Lori, talk."

She leaned back and stared at the wall again. I held her hand in both of mine.

"I've battled depression"—she said it as if she were confessing a deep horror—"off and on for most of my adult life."

I was tempted to say, "Is that all?" Everyone I knew fought the blues once in a while. Even my driven and competitive sister was down in the dumps these days. But I held my tongue and waited.

"The last few years I've done pretty well. I kept to a careful schedule, exercised, and got plenty of sleep. I'd have some low times, but I was able to fake it and get through the day."

Depression didn't fit my picture of Lori. "But you've always been so organized and efficient. Everyone in our Bible study aspires to be like you."

The pained smile returned. "I need to be organized. I need to stock my freezer ahead with meals for the bad days, figure out options and backup plans for our schedule."

"Why didn't you tell us? We would have helped."

She sighed. "Because you'd all try to fix it."

I shook my head in denial but then realized she was right. I squeezed her hand.

Lori rubbed her forehead. "Before we moved here, I had a bad spell. And I told my friends at our church there what was going on. Remember when you had the car accident? Remember everyone at church pounding you with advice? 'God's trying to teach you something,' or 'You should claim your healing,' or 'Here, buy these vitamins I sell.'"

"Yeah. It drove me nuts."

"Well, multiply that. Add comments like 'Depression is a sin. You're supposed to rejoice always,' or 'You must have some unconfessed bitterness. Or maybe it's a demon.' When we moved here, I decided I didn't need to deal with all that . . . and people looking at me funny—like I was nuts."

"Okay, so people can be idiots. But you didn't have to hide this from me."

She turned toward me, and this time her half smile didn't seem to hurt her as much. "I should have told you. But you've had so much going on. And this gets so ugly sometimes. I didn't want you to see me."

"Ugly how? Like head-spinning-and-spitting-up-pea-soup ugly?"

She choked out a laugh. "No. But . . ." The energy bled from her face, and the deep sadness returned. She shrugged, giving up the effort to explain anymore.

"Okay, would it be too meddling and annoying of me to ask . . .

have you thought of taking medication for it? There are lots of anti-depressants around."

"No, you aren't meddlesome. Don't ever worry about asking me about this stuff, okay? It helps to talk to someone besides Noah and my counselor."

Warmth spun through my veins. "I care about you."

She nodded, let that sink in. "Okay. Medication. Yes, I'm on it. But it's tricky for me." She stared at me for a long moment, battling some last inner reservation. "It's not just depression. I'm bipolar."

Images of the Antarctic popped into my head.

She saw my confusion. "Used to be called manic-depressive. Some folks have it really bad. They get psychotic when they're manic. Go on shopping sprees, take risks, make grandiose plans, go for days without sleeping."

I tried to hide the shock I was feeling. None of this sounded like the carefully controlled, gentle woman I knew.

"Don't worry. I don't get that bad. But the problem is that treating the depression the wrong way can cause mania. It's a tough balance."

I shook my head. "How on earth did you hide this from all of us for all these years? That's impossible."

She shrugged one shoulder. "The meds were working. I've had good doctors. When the depression sneaks in, I withdraw for a while until it's better. When I'm up, I just talk a bit more, and faster. Or if it's really bad and I'm not sleeping, I stay home until we get it under control."

"And now?"

"The meds stopped working. It happens sometimes. Something that has worked for years doesn't do it anymore." Tears started rolling down her face again. "And I hate what this is doing to Noah and the kids. They'd be so much better off without me."

My stomach knotted. "Whoa. That's the depression talking. You know that's not true."

She nodded, mopping at her tears with her sleeve. "Part of me knows that, but I can't stop the feelings. They're so strong. And I don't want to be a nuisance to my friends."

I wanted to shake her, but instead I gave her another hug. "You'll never be a nuisance. And I think you should tell them. Wouldn't it help to have your friends supporting you right now?"

"I don't want everyone treating me differently. Tiptoeing around this."

"Hey, we're all a bunch of nuts. So what if you're certifiable?"

Her laugh sounded deeper and less subdued this time. "You're right."

"Come on, Lori. We've helped Doreen through her divorce. And Heather through all her failed home businesses. And you all didn't start treating me weird because of my limp. We're here for one another."

She gave a tired nod. "Maybe. I'll think about it."

"Now." I stood up and grasped the handle of my cane. "What can I do to help?"

She frowned as if the effort to think was too difficult for her. "Ask Abby if she finished her math worksheet. The head of our homeschool group is picking her up for a field trip soon."

"You got it. And how about if I pick you up for Bible study tomorrow night? If you're up to it? Then you don't have to waste energy driving."

"That might be nice. I've been so groggy from these new meds, I haven't wanted to do anything. But it's a little better this week. Maybe I could handle it."

"I'll call tomorrow and see if you feel like going. It's at Heather's . . . and the last time we meet before they leave for their mission trip."

A flicker of determination brightened Lori's eyes, and she nodded. Then she patted my knee. "Thank you."

When I left Lori's house, it was time to pick Dylan up from school. I felt drained from my visit with Lori. Relieved to finally know why she'd been withdrawing from our friendship. Devastated by the struggle she faced and that she hadn't confided in me sooner. Desperate to find ways to reassure her that I respected and loved her as much as ever.

And it wasn't only Lori. There were so many people I cared about. Why couldn't I do more?

I wanted to be a support to Kevin, but someone had to stay with the kids. So now he was alone in Florida handling all the difficult decisions without help.

Grandma Rose was subdued and a bit cranky now that she'd admitted she couldn't keep up a house on her own. She seemed to focus her resentment on me, and nothing I tried cheered her up.

Judy wasn't having the spiritual breakthrough I had hoped to encourage. She grumbled about sleeping in the basement—though that problem would end in a few days when she started house-sitting for Ron and Heather. She'd stayed out late several nights, and I feared she was following our mom's example and finding comfort in a bottle.

Teresa was still stressing out about wanting to do more with our church programs, and I could tell she was angry with me for not putting in the same crazy hours she did. Even while I wondered if her husband, Ben, ever saw her, I wished I had her energy. I hated knowing I was disappointing her.

Lord, show me how to fix these problems. I'm exhausted. I thought your burden was light.

A soft thought brushed through my mind. *Are these your burdens?*

Of course they are. These are my family and my friends and my work. They are all my responsibility. If I don't care for these people, who will?

I pulled up to the school and watched Dylan elbow one of his classmates before noticing my van. He grabbed his backpack and jacket from the sidewalk and charged toward the curb, shouting some taunt over his shoulder.

I shook my head. He was getting more unruly every day. I really needed to start addressing some of his attitudes.

With so much on my mind, I drove home hearing his chatter

but not really listening. Dylan raced into the house ahead of me. I limped along behind and closed the door, shutting out the sharp October wind. Grandma Rose was sitting on the couch with Kelsey and Micah, reading them *The Velveteen Rabbit.*

The warmth of the house wrapped around me and coaxed a happy feeling to the surface of my heart. The kids were finally experiencing the blessings of an extended family. This had been a good plan. "Hi, kids. I'm home."

They jumped up and ran to hug me, careful to be gentle so they wouldn't knock me off balance. Then they barreled back to the couch, where Dylan joined them.

Grandma Rose tousled his hair, then smiled at me like a queen acknowledging her subject. "I started supper. I wasn't sure when you'd be home." She made it sound like I was running wild every night.

"You didn't need to do that." I headed toward the kitchen and nearly tripped over Dylan's backpack. "Dylan, you forgot something."

He growled but trudged over to his backpack and carried it to his room. I opened the fridge. "Where are all the vegetables I chopped for the stir-fry?"

"Oh, is that what they were for?" Grandma Rose's voice carried from the living room. "You can't put meat on your bones with just that. I used them in a casserole. And I added some beef I found in the freezer."

I yanked open the freezer door.

Oh no. Two sirloin steaks—the big splurge for a special date with Kevin—gone.

I opened the oven door. Yep. There it was. Chopped up into a casserole and smothered with cream of mushroom soup. I groaned.

She meant well. She was only trying to help. I should have labeled everything with fluorescent Post-its saying *Don't Touch.*

I hung up my jacket and then joined everyone in the living room. I eased into my rocking chair. The pain in my hip reminded me I hadn't done my physical therapy exercises again.

"Thank you for watching Micah and Kelsey. I had a good visit with my friend."

Grandma Rose smiled. "A pleasure. My grandchildren are delightful." She leaned forward. "Although, when Kevin was Kelsey's age, I had already taught him to read."

I fought the urge to roll my eyes. "Kelsey's learning plenty in kindergarten. We don't want to rush her."

She sat back and tugged a short curl of hair forward over her cheek. "Well, I didn't mean to offend you. I don't want to meddle."

Now I didn't know what to say. Every day I seemed to get stuck in more and more of these conversations that I couldn't win. She was a double agent in my own home. Playing the ally, but undermining all my efforts. I massaged my knee and didn't say anything.

"Oh, that sister of yours called. She said she wouldn't be coming home for supper. She's going to some club." Rose sniffed her disapproval.

This time I was smart enough not to comment. "Mmm. Thanks for taking the message."

"Your phone never stops ringing, does it?"

"I told you, you can let the machine get it, and I'll listen to the messages when I get home."

She frowned. "That doesn't seem polite. Oh, and a woman called. I can't remember her name. But she said it was about the house."

"Brenda Finney—our real estate agent? Did she schedule another showing?"

"No, no. I would have remembered that. But you're supposed to call her. She said something about an offer."

"What?" I launched from the chair, grabbed my cane, and made it to the kitchen desk in record time.

As I reached for the phone, it rang, almost under my hand.

I jerked my hand away, then reached forward again to grab the receiver and give a breathless "Hello."

"Hi, hon. The real estate agent called my cell. She said she tried to reach you."

"Yeah, I was—"

"Guess what? We have an offer on our house."

I whooped and did a one-legged jig. Kevin rattled off details, but I barely heard him. It was really happening. We were moving to our dream home.

Chapter Fifteen

The hot wind attacked from the west and drew deep ruts in the dirt, killing off fields of wheat, drying farmers' skin into the tight lines of poverty. Dust exploded from the roads. Dust wafted through screen doors. All of Oklahoma sifted like ashes in a bowl.

The whole country felt the drought, the Depression, but none more than my family. Dust coated my clothes as I trudged down the path toward home. Prison had hardened me, but it also started a low burn deep in my gut. A hunger for something I'd never had.

I'd tried to find them at our house, but the home I knew stood stripped and empty. So, I continued trudging to my uncle's farm. Sure 'nuff. My family was here. "Becky's home!" My kid brother shouted the news as I drew closer.

My granddaddy stepped out onto the porch and spit into the dry dirt. " 'Bout time. We is leavin' tomorrow."

Crazy old man. "What do you mean, leavin'?"

"Kicked off the land. But don't you worry none. We is headin' to California. There's work for any with a strong back. Reckon you'll be runnin' the place in no time."

Freedom tasted new after being in prison. And now I had an appetite for more. I smiled. "Reckon I will."

The next morning we loaded what we could onto the old jalopy. Precious little, but with the whole family crowded in, we had to heap the pieces up high. A strange parade we made . . . joining the others heading west for a better life.

I looked out the window, bemused. A trace of dry snow dusted across the sidewalks in shifting patterns. The last few weeks had been less than tranquil. Sorting, packing, pressures at work, and Rose's constant sideways criticisms had me convinced I'd be in a straitjacket before moving day. Our real estate agent managed to move up our closing date a few days, so we could move in on this last Saturday of October. Our front yard was full of activity as friends carried boxes out to the waiting caravan. The odd assortment of vehicles consisted of one U-Haul that Kevin planned to drive if he could figure out the clutch, my van with two tall houseplants sticking out the window and Grandma Rose patiently waiting in the front passenger seat, Kevin's car that Sally had promised to drive holding the boxes marked *Fragile*, Noah's pickup truck with Doreen riding shotgun, and Sally's compact loaded with cleaning supplies.

I could hardly believe the day had arrived. With our friends helping, we'd be settled into the new house by sunset.

Noah huffed past me with an end table that he wedged into the bed of the pickup. I almost expected to see a rocking chair lashed to the top of the cab. The hodgepodge of our possessions was taking longer to load than I'd expected. The couple buying our house would soon arrive for the final walk-through.

I hurried to the kitchen. Sally was wearing pink rubber gloves and wiping out the fridge. She shook her head, and her blond curls bounced. "Honestly, Becky, I don't know how you didn't all get food poisoning. You had some really old stuff in here."

I was so grateful for her hard work, I ignored the dig and gave her a quick hug. "Thanks for helping." Sally might have her faults, but she never failed to roll up her frilly sleeves and offer practical help. Judy had begged off the day's adventure, saying she planned to work on her résumé. Lori wasn't up for this commotion, but Noah said she was improving. She'd been back to our weekly Bible study twice now, though she still hadn't talked about her bipolar disorder with any of the other women. Heather and her family were in the Dominican Republic on their mission trip, and Judy was house-sitting for them. She was relieved to be out of our basement and got a kick out of Heather's flower-child décor. The past weeks had been stressful, but the excitement of the new dream home had eased some of the distance between Kevin and me.

He bounded past me and down to the basement.

"Kev, don't put too much in the van," I called. "I still have to pick up the boxes we stored in Heather's garage."

He popped back up the stairs. "You and my mom won't be able to lift those all yourselves. We can take the whole caravan past Ron and Heather's house. It's on the way." Then he flashed his teeth. "And we can get Judy to help."

I giggled. "Good plan."

"I'll do a last check of the basement. You make sure we didn't forget anything on the main floor."

"Okay. We're almost done."

Sally nodded. "The kitchen is cleared out. I checked the drawers and cabinets."

"Thanks. I guess we're ready."

Sally gathered up her mops and rags. "I'll wait outside. I know you'll want to say your good-byes."

Suddenly, the house we'd lived in for ten years was empty— hollow as a dry husk. A poignant ache pressed against my rib cage. Kevin jogged up the stairs two at a time. He skidded to a stop when he saw me standing alone in the middle of the living room.

I reached for him with one arm, my other hand braced on my cane. My knees felt wobbly, and I didn't dare let go. Today, the weakness wasn't from my old injuries.

"Kev, what are we doing?"

He wrapped me in a warm hug. His grungy flannel shirt smelled like crisp winter air, with a hint of dust and sweat. "We're going to fix up the new place and have a ball." He leaned back. "Are you crying?"

I sniffed. "No. I'm happy. It's just . . ."

Suddenly I didn't want to explain my mix of emotions to him. He was in such a great mood, and he wouldn't understand anyway.

I gave a small shrug and looked away.

He kissed the top of my head. "Great. Well, we better get moving."

He hurried out of the house, and I looked around one more time, feeling lost and lonely. Then I walked out the front door, locked the door behind me, and limped to the van, where Rose and the kids were waiting.

I climbed in and gave a wan smile to Grandma Rose.

She pursed her lips and the lines around her mouth deepened. "Hard, isn't it?" That edge of resentment still colored her conversations with me. She still grieved letting go of her old home.

I patted her hand. "Yeah. Lots of good memories. It must be even harder for you. You were in the same house for decades."

She slid her hand away and looked out the window. "It's where Kevin grew up. I could see him in every room."

I struggled to think of a way to comfort her. "But now you can see the real live Kevin every day instead." I looked at the kids in the backseat. "All set?"

Kelsey and Dylan checked their seat belts and nodded.

"Wait. Where's Micah? I thought he was in here with you."

"Nah," Dylan said. "He had to go potty."

Panic gripped me. I'd just walked through the house, and he hadn't been there. I threw open the van door and yelled for Kevin. He couldn't hear me over the roar of the U-Haul engine, but he saw me waving one arm and stopped cranking the wheel to pull out.

Without waiting to explain, I hurried back to the house. He caught up while I was fumbling with the key.

"Sweetie, you already said good-bye. It's time to go."

I spun and glared at him. "Micah's missing." How dare he treat me like a sentimental wimp when our baby had disappeared?

"I thought you put him in the van?" His words sounded suspiciously like blame.

My panic fueled a flame of anger. "I did. He got out. I can't be everywhere . . . contrary to what everyone expects of me."

He looked at me as if I were a stranger. "I'll check around back . . . and the neighbors' yards, too."

I didn't bother answering. Instead, I hobbled into the house and slammed the door behind me. My leg shrieked a protest as I raced in a lopsided sprint from room to room. "Micah! Micah, where are you?"

Why hadn't I stayed in the van and watched the kids? Why had I insisted on helping with the last cleanup of the house? I stopped shouting for Micah so I could catch my breath. What kind of careless mom was I, anyway?

The front door creaked open, and I hurried back to the living room.

Kevin stood in the doorway. Micah squirmed in his arms, his knit cap still protecting his ears, his patched jeans and winter jacket coated with dirt. "He was in the sandbox." Again, Kevin sounded as if he were accusing me. My relief at seeing Micah was threaded with anger, and I shot a glare at Kevin.

But he had already turned. "I'll buckle him back into his car seat. Let's go."

I counted to ten and then followed him. This time no sentiment welled up as I locked the front door.

Micah was already in his car seat, and Kevin was back in the U-Haul when I reached the van. Kevin gave a couple quick taps of his horn. I suppose it's possible he meant it as a cheerful signal that we were setting out. But I ground my teeth, convinced he was being impatient with me.

I turned the key and revved the van engine. Grandma Rose shook her head. "Good thing Kevin found him. Micah could have frozen. Poor Kevin. He works so hard and then he still has to help with the housework and kids. In my day we took care of our husbands."

This time I mentally counted to twenty. Not daring to speak, I quickly turned on the radio and pulled away from the curb toward

Heather's house. In the few minutes it took to reach her block, my frustration had cooled a bit.

"Kids, do not move. Stay buckled. You can sing the new song you learned to Grandma." Two hundred verses of "Throw it Out the Window" was a sweet revenge.

Kevin pulled up behind in the truck. He jumped out and jogged up the sidewalk to the front door. I saw Judy open the door and chat with him as I made my way to the garage. In spite of my crankiness, a bit of excitement stirred in my stomach. After we gathered up this last load of boxes and furniture, we'd be on our way. Moving into our dream house.

Judy sauntered toward me in silk lounging pajamas and greeted me with a yawn. "Good morning, sis. How did the packing go?"

"All right, I guess. Can you help us load up our last boxes?"

She tightened the belt of her matching robe. "In this? Don't be silly. But I've got the key to the garage. Come on."

She scuffed along in her slippers and unlocked the garage's side door, reaching inside to push the button for the automatic opener.

The wide door rattled upward, and Kevin stepped forward, then stopped.

"Where is everything?" His voice echoed against the concrete floor. I shoved past Judy to join Kevin.

The garage was empty.

So deserted, I could practically see tumbleweeds rolling past.

"Judy, tell me you moved our stuff. Tell me this is a practical joke."

She came up behind me. "Where'd everything go?"

"You're supposed to know. You're staying here." My voice rose.

Kevin put an arm around my shoulders. "Judy, we had all our extra stuff stored along the right wall. Have you seen anyone in here?"

Judy fluffed her hair and wrinkled her forehead in concentration. "Sure. Heather told me the folks from their mission board were going to pick up some boxes to be shipped down to Haiti or Belize, or whatever little poverty-stricken country they were going to."

"The Dominican Republic," I said.

"Whatever. They came over yesterday while I was washing my hair. I gave them the key and told them everything was in the garage."

Kevin and I looked at each other and back at the empty garage.

"Judy," Kevin said slowly, "did you explain that a friend of Ron and Heather's also had some things stored in the garage?"

"Um . . . I don't remember." She began to look genuinely worried. "I figured Heather had told them what to ship."

I wanted to cry. Instead, I gave a quiet moan.

Kevin squeezed me closer. "What was stored here?"

I struggled to remember. It had been several weeks since we decluttered the house to put it on the market. "Things we figured we wouldn't need. Some books. Winter stuff. Ice skates. Christmas decorations. A couple end tables. My box of maternity clothes."

"Well, you weren't going to need that again."

I managed a short laugh. "No. And I guess if we haven't missed the rest of the stuff in the past few months, it's not a huge disaster."

Kevin kissed the top of my head. "Guess we made a donation to the medical mission in the Dominican."

Judy watched both of us, her arms crossed defensively. "I'm . . . sorry."

"Judy, it's okay." I gave her a quick hug, which she returned stiffly. "It's not your fault." Well, technically it was her fault. But making a federal case out of it wouldn't help our fragile relationship.

"Really?"

"Really. It's not important." And strangely, I meant it. Like most Americans, we had too much stuff anyway. We had stowed away the stuff we rarely used, not our most precious belongings. I wasn't about to let this latest wrinkle ruin our dream move.

"Good." Judy gave me a genuine smile. "*Brr*. It's freezing out here. I better get back inside."

"Wait a minute, O favorite sister-in-law." Kevin used his mock-stern voice. "The least you can do is get dressed and ride with us to the new place. You can help us figure out where to put things. We need all the help we can get."

"Oh, come on. I'm not into the *Better Homes and Garden* stuff. I had a decorator do my condo."

I jabbed in her direction with my cane. "Well, I don't have a decorator. So get yourself pulled together."

She yawned again. "Okay, okay. Besides, I do want to see this place. And can we stop at Target? I need to buy a copy of *Fortune* magazine. All Heather has around here are *Organic Gardener* and *Mother Earth News*. And some religious stuff."

A nervous burn moved through my stomach. The farmhouse was a far cry from the kind of places Judy had lived. I'd kept her away for a reason. I didn't want to deal with her mocking and criticism until we'd closed on the house and everything was final. Now it was too late to back out, so hopefully she'd forgo her derision.

Kevin and I waited for Judy to dress and returned with her to our vehicles. The caravan pulled out once again. So far, nothing about the move was going right. But our situation had to improve. I pulled onto the freeway and headed toward the land of opportunity.

Chapter Sixteen

How had an afternoon visit turned into such a disaster? When we were invited to tour this remote island park, I hated to lose time away from my paleontology dig. On the other hand, we couldn't turn down the offer of funding. Seemed like a great deal at the time.

When I caught my first glimpse of a living, breathing dinosaur, my awe overcame any common sense or fear. Not many people get to see genuine T. rexes and Triceratops.

I didn't even worry when a storm rolled in and our automated car was stranded far from the visitor's center. They wouldn't let people in the park if it wasn't safe, right?

But now the power was out. That meant the electrical fences weren't working. That meant . . . trouble.

I'd volunteered to search a hidden bunker for the circuits that had been shut down. My flashlight cast a weak beam on the dusty walls. Somewhere in this shed, I was supposed to find the switches to restore power. But I turned a corner and confronted a bare wall. I lifted my walkie-talkie, trying not to sound as scared as I felt. "There's a wall in front of me. Which way do I go?"

"It's okay. Just follow the pipes."

I aimed my light up and found the conduits. Who could blame me if the beam of light quivered as I crept along? Anyone's hand would be shaking. Even without prehistoric monsters lurking outside, this place was creepy. I felt my way down another corridor. The narrow beam finally hit on a box.

"I found it. What do I do?"

The guy on the other end of the walkie-talkie guided me through the start-up, switch by switch. Fluorescent lights flickered to life.

I leaned against the far wall in relief and turned off my flashlight. I'd done it. Saved the day.

Giddy with relief, I hurried back up the hall. I raced around a corner . . . and screamed.

My worst nightmare faced me.

The raptor saw me the same instant I saw him. Slavering jaws gaped open and beady eyes zeroed in on me. A screech rose from the creature as he leaned his weight back on his tail and waved his claws in anticipation.

My knees turned to water. The flashlight dropped from my numb hand.

"Would you hand me the flashlight?" Kevin's head pulled out from behind the washing machine. Dust smudged his nose and a cobweb wafted from his hair.

I passed him the flashlight and leaned on the shiny deluxe-model dryer. "I can't understand why it's having problems. All the appliances are new."

Kevin grunted and thumped something with his wrench. "But the pipes aren't. It's been leaking by this hookup."

"Can you fix—"

Something huge and slimy wriggled past my toes.

"AKKK!" I jumped onto the dryer, clutching my cane toward my heart.

Kevin jerked upright, banging his head on a shutoff valve. "Yow! What happened?"

"A centipede! Huge! Ran under the washer. Get it. Get it!"

Kevin rubbed his head and sent me a glare that should have been reserved for the centipede. "It's just a bug. Old houses have lots of them."

"This was not just a bug. This was a genetically engineered mega-monster." I was still hyperventilating. I could handle an occasional attack of city ants each summer, or a few spiders in the corners. But I wasn't prepared for insectoids the size of small farm animals.

Kevin tried scooting the washer out a few more inches. "I can't see any—"

A sudden spray of water exploded from the pipe beside him. He sputtered, yelped, and fumbled to find the valve.

I laughed. I confess. Who wouldn't?

Kevin got the water shut off, blotted his face with the hem of his shirt, and lasered surly eyes in my direction.

Honestly. He had no sense of humor. I pressed my lips together, trying to stifle my giggles. "I think I'll put another coat of spackle on the living room walls."

"You do that."

I scanned the basement floor for further signs of multi-legged creatures, but the concrete looked clear. I raced for the steps in a lopsided hobble and clattered up to the kitchen in record time. How was I going to do laundry if I was afraid of our own basement?

Grandma Rose puttered around the kitchen, making sucking sounds through her dentures. She set a soup can on one of the cabinet shelves. "I'm almost finished reorganizing this for you."

Not again. She'd already refolded my towels her way and arranged the kids' dresser drawers by some sort of logic known only to her. "You really don't need to do that. You should be resting."

"Oh, it's no trouble. It's the least I can do."

I'd never find anything in the kitchen again. I tamped down my frustration. She meant well. In fact, she seemed driven to justify her existence. Did she really think I'd kick her out if she didn't pitch in around the house? If I could find a way to reassure her, would she stop rearranging everything?

We were trapped in mutual guilt. She felt guilty for living with us. Kevin and I felt guilty for the grief she experienced in giving up her Florida home.

Judy strolled in, hooked a chair with her foot, slid it out, and slouched into it. "Is there any coffee?" She turned to grin at Grandma Rose. "I love spending Saturday like normal people. I used to work most Saturdays, or use it as a travel day."

I crossed my arms. "It's two in the afternoon. The *normal* people were up hours ago working on the house." On one hand, I had Grandma Rose working herself to the bone. On the other, I had Judy enjoying every lazy moment of her new unemployed status. As soon as we'd gotten the furniture set up, Judy had moved into the guest bedroom upstairs. My huge new house was feeling too small already.

"Now, now." Grandma Rose had already pulled out the box of coffee filters. "Don't pressure poor Judy. She needs time to get her bearings."

I stomped out of the kitchen and into the living room. How was Judy getting her bearings by going downtown to clubs every night and sleeping most of the day? Cheerful chatter carried from the kitchen and fueled my irritation. And why had Grandma Rose made such a quick turnaround in her feelings toward my sister? Suddenly she was defending Judy. Just like during our childhood—Judy was always the favorite. When was Grandma Rose going to warm up to *me*?

I slapped spackling compound over a crack in the wall and slid the putty knife over it with a satisfying scrape again and again. My temper cooled. I was getting good at this. Hiding all the blemishes felt good. We'd be ready to paint tomorrow afternoon.

Suddenly the front door burst open. Kelsey and Dylan barreled in as if pterodactyls were chasing them.

"Mommy! Something bit me." Kelsey wailed and jumped up and down flapping her hands in panic.

My brain zipped through a catalog of possible predators from bugs, to snakes, to rabid pheasants. Who knew what lurked in the meadows around the house? I grabbed Kelsey for a hug and felt something bite my palms.

"Yipes!" I turned Kelsey around and found the culprit. The back of her winter coat was covered with burrs. When she stopped jumping, I saw more on her cuffs, biting into her wrists.

"Mommy! What are they? Get them off!" Kelsey's nose was

running and tears smeared her cheeks.

"Hold still, honey. They're just burrs."

"Birds?" she shrieked. "Where? Why did they bite me?"

"No, honey. It's just little prickles from weeds. See, they come right off." I pried one from her sleeve and showed her the little round thistle. One down, about six thousand to go.

She began to calm down—enough to point at Dylan in rage. "He dared me to look in the jungle."

"Jungle?"

Dylan tried to sidle toward the door.

"Hold it, buster. You were both supposed to stay on the porch."

He tried a cherubic smile that didn't have the same effect now that he was a lanky fourth grader. "We were pretending."

"Dylan Jacob Miller." My voice rose. "Did you tell your sister to go play in the weeds?"

"No, Mom. She just went." He grinned.

Kelsey wailed a denial and gave a furious shake of her curls.

I saw more burrs tangled in them. What had she been doing? Rolling in thistles?

Grandma Rose tottered in from the kitchen. "Oh, don't yell at the poor boy. It's my fault. I promised you I'd check on them."

"Dylan, go to your room." I turned to face Grandma Rose. "It's not your fault. Kelsey knew she wasn't supposed to leave the porch. And Dylan shouldn't have talked her into it."

"Grandma, the birds bit me." Kelsey turned on the waterworks again.

"Come to the kitchen." Grandma swooped in to do some comforting. "You need a cookie. Oh dear, your face is like ice. Your mother shouldn't let you play outside on such a cold day."

I followed Dylan up the stairs, planting my cane with a loud thump on each step. "This isn't Florida," I muttered. "It's Minnesota. If I kept the kids in on cold days they'd only play outside about one month out of the year."

Thankfully, Dylan didn't pay attention to my grumbles. He was too busy preparing his defense. He spun to face me the second we entered his room. "But Dad promised to take us for a hike around the house. We waited and waited." Dylan's lower lip tried its best to convey the depth of his misery.

"Watch out, or your face will freeze that way."

Dylan's eyebrows rose and his lip popped back into place.

I took a deep breath and settled on the edge of his bed, pulling him close so we could meet eye-to-eye. "Dylan, I trusted you to obey the rules. You and Kelsey could have gotten hurt. It's important that you obey."

He flung himself across his bed. "We were bored. You never have time for us anymore."

Claws dug into my heart. The wound stung with the poison of my own self-doubt. "Things are crazy right now. Once we get the main repairs done, Dad and I will have more time to play. But this isn't about me. You know it was wrong to convince Kelsey to disobey."

A flicker of genuine remorse moved across his eyes. "Will they hurt her? The burrs?"

"She'll be fine. But it will take a long time to pick all the thistles off her clothes."

"I'm sorry." Half tremulous, half sullen.

"I forgive you. Now go tell Kelsey you're sorry, and then you can start picking burrs off her coat. That's a fair consequence."

His eyes lit up. "Can I put one under my microscope? I want to keep one for my collection."

Micah chose that moment to toddle in from his room, dragging a teddy bear by one foot. "Nap all done."

I pulled him up onto my lap and nuzzled him. He smelled of little-boy sweat and . . . What was that smell? Sandalwood?

"Micah, were you in my cologne?"

His snuggly body stiffened. "Me in bed."

"The whole nap time?"

He reached up and patted my cheek. "Mommy pretty."

That did it. He'd been up to something. I wedged him against my hip as I stood, leaning on my cane to counterbalance. Then I hurried to my room. He wrapped his arms around my neck and pressed his face into my hair. He was still at the developmental stage of believing that if he couldn't see the problem, it didn't exist. Sometimes I wished for that skill.

The strong smell of perfume assaulted me at the doorway of the master bedroom. The laundry basket was upended and shoved against the dresser to provide a step stool, leaving a trail of clothes across the floor. My top dresser drawer sagged open at a crooked angle. Lipstick, face powder, and hand lotion spattered the surface and the attached mirror, looking like an abstract work by Pollock.

Eight hours later, when Kevin and I sank into bed exhausted, the room still reeked. The entire day had been loaded with mishaps, whining, and crankiness—not only from the kids.

"At the old house I could keep track of what they were up to. It was so much smaller." I tucked a spare pillow under my knee, trying to get comfortable.

"Is your leg hurting again?" Kevin rolled to his side and twiddled a strand of my hair.

I batted his hand away. "No more than usual, why?"

He flopped onto his back and stared at the ceiling. "I thought maybe that's why you've been so . . ."

I bristled. "What?"

"You know. Crabby. You haven't been yourself lately."

I ground my molars together and scrambled to think of a Bible verse about controlling my tongue. I couldn't.

"Crabby? You try chasing three kids in circles 24-7. Half the time I have to work with them underfoot. If they're sick, they have to come to the office with me. And if I'm at home making calls for work in the afternoon, they're screaming in the background. And I know the staff is ticked off that I'm trying to limit my hours. Everyone is overworked right now. And then we're trying to settle in to this dinosaur of a house, and there's so much to take care of.

And your mom is always criticizing everything I do. And you don't ever stand up for me—"

"I was wondering when you'd get to the part where you blame me." Kevin's voice was tight and angry.

I propped onto one elbow and stared at the man I'd loved for more than a dozen years, and for a horrifying moment couldn't remember why I loved him. "I'm not blaming you. I'm asking for a little compassion. Instead of accusing me of being crabby."

"Well, what would you call it?" He used his ultra-reasonable voice that drove me mad.

"Of course I'm crabby." My voice rose. "Who wouldn't be? I was hoping that if I could care for your mom, you'd . . ." Too close to the truth. I swallowed my words. "Never mind." I tugged on the comforter, trying to snag a little more warmth in the chilly room.

Kevin tugged back. "That reminds me. Mom said she put her name on another apartment waiting list."

"What? I know she said she didn't want to live with us permanently, but I thought she was just worried about being a burden. I thought once we settled in here . . ."

"Well, she's not happy here." He rolled away from me, taking an unfair chunk of blanket with him. He muttered something that sounded like "Who can blame her?"

"What did you say?"

In the long silence, I heard the plunking of the leaking faucet across the hall. Even the claw-foot tub was crying.

Kevin sighed. "Never mind. Let's get some sleep. This isn't getting us anywhere." Another several plops echoed. He groaned. "I've gotta get that faucet fixed tomorrow. It's driving me crazy."

I curled away from him, stared at the faded wallpaper, and seethed. In only a few minutes, his deep breaths began to rumble softly.

Lord, I'm so frustrated. We really believed you were leading us to this house. Did we make a mistake? And why do I feel so stressed all the time? And why can't I get Kevin to smile at me the way he used to? There are so many things that need to be fixed. Not just with the house—everywhere. And there isn't enough of me to go around. Tell me. What am I supposed to do?

I squeezed my eyes tight shut and listened as hard as I could.

The wind growled outside. Kevin moaned in his sleep. Water continued dripping an erratic rhythm into the bathtub. Images played across my mind from the film we'd watched on our last date night. Noble characters confronted problems and everything fell quickly into place. One-hundred-and-three-minute solutions.

I wanted that kind of clarity.

I fell asleep mid-wish.

Chapter Seventeen

The distant howl of a wolf rose from the dark forests like a moan of pain. Lightning crackled across the sky and lifted the hair on the back of my neck. The horses that had pulled my carriage up the mountainous roads shied and quivered.

No wonder this remote province of Eastern Europe spawned so many myths and tales of horror. The jutting Carpathian Mountains and menacing weather exaggerated the foreboding atmosphere. Never had a real estate agent had to travel so far to sell a London property.

The angular edifice seemed to lean toward me, conjuring all the warnings I'd heard from peasants as I journeyed.

Well, nothing to be done now but to meet the eccentric owner and secure his signature. I climbed from the carriage and studied the crooked gables and gloomy face of the castle.

The count would have been wiser to spend some of his resources on repairing this monolith.

I rapped on the door, hearing the low, hollow sound echo like the thud of my heart pounding a warning in my ears. Rain poured from the eaves, splashing against the hard ground and seeping through my saturated mackintosh.

At last, the door opened with a shuddering creak. I stepped into the entry and studied the gloomy interior. Cobwebs wafted down from crooked candelabrum. The flutter of wings sounded high in the rafters along with the eerie squeak of bats.

As the servant closed the door behind me, I shivered.

"Sorry it's so chilly." I closed my front door behind Sally as she arrived for Bible study, stamping snow from her boots. "The furnace works, but there's no vent into this room. Apparently they sealed off this part of the house and didn't use it in the winter."

After moving in, we learned that the front room and wide porch had been added to the structure long after the original farmhouse was built. Our chilly living room was only one of the many quirks we continued to discover. And we'd blown our budget buying the house, so we had to weigh the cost of each repair. If we didn't get the house up to code fast, we couldn't get a new mortgage that would absorb the separate construction loan. We had planned on one month to pass the inspections. If we weren't ready, we'd have to sell the house. We couldn't risk going further into the hole, or missing payments and having the bank foreclose. Pain gnawed in my stomach every time I thought about how far over our heads we were. I felt sick at the thought of losing our house.

"N-n-no problem." Sally shuddered so that her blond curls bounced, and closed her pink down jacket. "A space heater might be a good idea, though."

Doreen was already perched on our rocking chair, her cashmere sweater visible in the opening of her long wool coat. She had been checking her schedule in her PDA, and tapping in notes, but now she pulled her attention away from her ever-present technology. "We could move the Bible study to your kitchen."

I sighed. "We can't. Grandma Rose is in there." We'd only been here about a week, and already she'd staked out the kitchen, the main floor bedroom, and the half bath as her territory.

"How's Judy? I'd love to see her," Doreen said.

I shook my head. "When Judy heard the words *Bible study* she hightailed it out of here."

A loud thump sounded overhead, followed by a shriek and running footsteps.

Doreen looked up at the ceiling, where the light fixture quivered. "Kevin's watching the kids?"

"Yep. We haven't finished the basement yet, so it's the only other place for the kids to play right now."

Sally raised a brow.

"Don't give me that look. This place will be awesome with a little elbow grease." I took in the freshly painted walls and new curtains. A few cracks had reappeared in one wall, even after my careful spackling and painting. And Dylan had discovered that if he set a marble on the floor, it would roll toward one side of the room. But other than those problems, I loved the living room. One room done. A dozen more to go.

The doorbell rang—a flat, fractured sound. I pulled open the door and Heather swept in, along with more cold air. "Happy almost-Thanksgiving," she sang out. She had a lopsided handwoven basket hanging from one arm. "I brought some treats."

I stifled a groan. Her all-natural concoctions usually tasted like cardboard.

She kicked off her oversized boots and promptly settled on the floor. "Stop making faces. These are health candies. You mix honey and peanut butter with wheat germ and soy nuts and roll it into balls. You'll love it."

She passed the basket to Doreen, who picked one out between a finger and thumb and stared at it. "How's Grace feeling?"

"Almost back to normal." Heather's bubbly energy deflated a bit. Grace had developed a stomach bug that wouldn't go away, so Heather and Grace had cut their trip short and flown home. Ron and Charity were still finishing up their time at the medical mission in Santo Domingo.

"I'm glad she's feeling better." I settled onto the couch and passed the basket along to Sally. "I've been having some stomachaches lately, too. Maybe I have the same thing."

Heather laughed. "I doubt it. Unless you've been visiting the Caribbean. Kind of hard to pick up those bugs here."

"I don't know. The plumbing in this house is so old, who knows what's breeding in the pipes?"

Heather pulled off her hat, and her chestnut mop of hair tumbled around her shoulders. "Becky, I'm so, *so* sorry about your boxes of stuff."

We'd been through this already. "It's not your fault. Besides, it's nice to think of our extra things doing some good."

"Yeah," Doreen said around a mouthful of health candy. "But somewhere in the Dominican Republic, an orphanage director is going to be confused when he opens a box of donations and finds ice skates and snow pants."

The doorbell squawked again, and Heather sprang up, waving me back to the couch. She pulled open the door, and Lori walked in amid a chorus of greetings.

"Sorry I'm late." She balanced on one foot while pulling off a boot, then switched sides with the grace of dancer. "My tummy was bugging me, and I wasn't sure I should come."

Doreen nodded. "Lots of stomach things going around. Becky thinks she caught a Caribbean parasite."

Sally nibbled the edge of a second candy. "Naw. Becky's probably getting an ulcer from stress. Maybe that's Lori's problem, too."

I shot Sally a quelling look. "It's just Lori's medicine."

The room froze in silence, and all eyes turned slowly toward Lori. Stricken, I realized my mistake.

Lori met the questioning gazes, then looked down as she pulled knit slippers from her pocket and slid them over her socks.

Sally broke the silence first. "I knew it. I knew something was going on. What medicine?"

"Is this why you missed our meetings last month?" Doreen leaned forward with her corporate-aggressive intensity in full force.

I covered my face and tried to sink into the couch. The cushions bounced as Lori sat down beside me. "I'm sorry," I whispered into my palms.

What kind of friend was I proving to be? It had taken Lori forever to finally trust me with her secret. Now I'd slipped and set her up for poking and prying.

"It's all right." Lori's voice was quiet but composed. "I've never loved a group of friends more. And part of love is trust."

When I pried my hands away from my face, I saw Doreen, Sally, and Heather all staring at Lori like a bunch of slack-jawed zombies. Poor Lori.

She found my hand and squeezed it. "I shared this with Becky a while back but asked her to keep it private." She gave a sad smile. "Please keep this in our group, okay?"

They all nodded slowly, in thrall to the promise of a revelation. She explained the side effects of the new medicines she was on—nausea, fatigue, dizziness. Murmurs of sympathy bolstered her as she moved on to explain what she needed the medication for.

As Lori had predicted, once she had explained bipolar disorder, the responses were varied and questions flew. She answered them patiently, doing her best to dispel myths and reassure everyone that she was still the same Lori she always had been.

"I read an article the other day," Doreen piped in, "about pharmaceutical companies pushing for diagnoses of all kinds of things. Depression, anxiety, attention deficit. They get people with normal ranges of emotion to think they need medication . . . just so they can make money."

My irritation built. I wanted to jump in and protect Lori.

But my best friend wasn't fuming like I was. She nodded, the expression on her dark-caramel face placid and composed. "I'm sure that some people don't really need medication," she said gently. "I do."

Sally squirmed in her chair. "Something smells good in the kitchen. Becky, what is your mother-in-law baking?"

Heather swatted Sally's shin. "Don't ignore this. Lori needs our support." She stood up. "Can we pray for healing for you?"

Tears welled in Lori's eyes. "Of course. I'd appreciate that."

Heather came around the couch and rested her hand on Lori's head. Doreen and Sally left their chairs and gathered around us, as well.

Prayer was a wonderful suggestion. But I hoped this didn't pressure Lori . . . or make her feel that if she wasn't miraculously delivered from this tonight, she had failed somehow.

Doreen, in typical strong fashion, pounded the gates of heaven for a swift and complete answer. Sally mumbled prayers about showing Lori if there were things she needed to change in her life or lessons she needed to learn. Heather reminded God of how special Lori was, and asked for His help with a childlike confidence. Tears clogged my throat as I prayed that God would show us all ways we could support Lori in this struggle and help her feel loved.

I was about to say amen, but Lori interrupted.

"Lord, you know how much I hate this battle, especially bouts like last month when things got so bad. I hate feeling like I can't be a good wife or mom or friend. I ask you to heal me and remove this from me permanently. But I also thank you. Thank you for friends I can be real with. Thank you for doctors who care. Thank you for a family that is patient and supportive. Thank you for tools to help me. If this is a thorn that you intend for me to carry the rest of my life, thank you for using it to remind me to rely on you moment by moment."

We were all sniffling by the time she finished, and I grabbed a box of tissues from the end table and passed it around. I was grateful Heather had steered us into prayer before everyone badgered Lori with more questions.

Lori's smile gleamed against her dark skin. She took a deep breath. "Okay, now that that's off my chest, how about everyone else's praise reports and prayer requests?"

We spent most of the next half hour hearing about the mission work in the Dominican Republic and the desperate needs that Heather had observed. After that, I was too embarrassed to share how tenuous our future in the new house was and how frightened I was that we'd made a mistake. And I kept my fears about my marriage hidden even deeper. Still, it felt good just to be with these friends.

After another general prayer time, Lori kept us on task. "Time to dig into our chapter." She unzipped her Bible cover and flipped to the book of Romans, and we all did the same.

"Okay. The study guide focused on disappointment. We were supposed to write times we've felt disappointed by God. What did you come up with?"

Sally tapped the page of her study guide with a pen. "I thought the question was wrong. God can never disappoint us. I'm more worried about disappointing God."

I could relate to that feeling. Lately I was falling short in every role in my life.

Heather stretched her legs out in front of her and leaned back on her elbows. "Let's get real here. If we really believe that God is all-powerful . . . when things go wrong, it's easy to feel confused by Him."

Those words from happy-go-lucky, trusting Heather shocked me.

She looked around the room at our faces and shrugged. "Like last week. Having to leave our mission trip early was frustrating. We really believed God called our whole family to spend two months there, and everything fell into place. When Grace got sick, we prayed and prayed. But eventually we felt I needed to bring her home. Grace was disappointed, I was disappointed, the mission staff in the Dominican was disappointed. It made us question whether we had made the right choice in even making the trip."

"Of course you did," Doreen insisted. "We all felt confirmation in our prayer time. And even if you came home early, I know God is doing important work through your family."

"But isn't it normal to ask why? Grace and I talked about it on the plane home because she was feeling worried about ruining the trip. We decided that maybe God allowed it so Charity would have a chance to blossom apart from her sister." She sat up. "You know Charity is much more shy than Grace."

I nodded even though I'd never noticed. I'd never been able to tell the girls apart.

Doreen was tracing a circle over and over on her study guide. "It helps when you can guess a reason. The hard thing for me is when I can't make sense of it. Like Jim leaving the kids and me. Did I make a mistake in marrying him? I thought I was following God's will. Was I wrong?"

Heather scooted closer to Doreen and patted her knee. "You made the best choice you knew how. Jim had free will to make stupid choices. That doesn't mean it was all a mistake. The point is what you do with the reality in front of you now."

Her words resonated inside me. We had our house. Yes, the renovations were a heavier burden than we'd expected. Kevin and I were snippy with each other. But God could still use this experience to strengthen our family. I just wasn't sure how.

"But aren't we supposed to fight when things don't go the way they're supposed to?" Sally twisted a charm bracelet on her wrist. "I was listening to a guy on the radio yesterday who said the Christian's life is supposed to be full of victory."

Lori looked at her Bible. "That's why I loved these verses in Romans 5 about rejoicing in sufferings. It doesn't say we won't have sufferings. And it doesn't say God will remove all sufferings as soon as we pray. It says suffering produces perseverance. To me that says that some things will have to be endured a long time."

I rubbed my knee. The cold air had tightened it, and the ache was growing bad enough to distract me. "The chain of qualities that Paul lists finishes with hope . . . that does not disappoint us. So why did the study guide ask us about being disappointed with God?"

"Probably so we'd stop trying to be brave," Heather said. "And so we'd admit there are things we're confused about."

While the Bible study continued, my pencil traced the words I'd written in my study guide. Question marks danced around them all. My job at Faith Church—it's what I'd always dreamed of doing, but the pressure to excel was stirring up some bad habits in me. Our new house—instead of giving us extra family time, we were busy fixing things every spare second and feeling new stress about how we'd afford repairs. Grandma Rose—having her stay with us was wearing down my spirit a little each day . . . especially when Kevin seemed to take her side. Inviting my sister, Judy, to visit—instead of being a spiritual influence on her, I simply had a front-row seat while she self-destructed. My attempts to fix everyone were failing.

I doodled more question marks. The decisions themselves didn't seem wrong. I'd prayed before making them, and continued to pray for God's direction. But something wasn't going right. I was exhausted. I woke up each morning feeling like a vampire had drained my blood during the night.

"So, Becky, when are you having the house blessing?" Heather's voice pulled me from my musings.

"The what?"

"Whenever Ron and I move to a new place, we have friends come to pray over each room and consecrate the house to God."

I squinted at her. "This doesn't involve incantations in Latin to chase away ghosts or something, does it?"

Heather laughed. Lori leaned toward me. "I think it's a great idea. Let us know the date."

I shook my head. "Maybe after we get everything fixed up."

"Yoo-hoo. Dessert is ready." Grandma Rose's tremulous voice carried from the kitchen doorway. My friends all jumped up, salivating from the scents of baking that had wafted to the living room during the past hour. Rose smiled in delight as they each thanked her on their way into the kitchen. "Oh, that's all right. I know Becky doesn't have time to bake. Young women have different priorities these days."

My traitorous friends laughed and nodded. They didn't seem to feel the wooden stake of accusation. Grandma Rose's words reduced my ministry efforts to self-indulgent dust. And my friends didn't notice. All they cared about was heaping their plates with apple cobbler and fresh whipped cream.

On cue, Kevin jogged down the creaky stairs and aimed for his mom and the dessert. He didn't even look my direction.

Lori noticed my distress and pulled me aside. "Don't take her comments personally. God's called you to different things," she said in a low voice. "If you spent your days baking, you wouldn't be able to manage the women's ministry at Faith. You're a blessing to a lot of people."

"Maybe," I whispered. "But she makes me feel like I'm not measuring up as a wife and mom."

"By whose standard? Beck, ask God to show you how to order your priorities. You can't do it all, and that's okay."

I gave Lori a grateful hug. "I know. And I could kick myself for making that comment about your medications."

She shrugged. "I was going to tell them anyway. You gave me the nudge I needed." Concern washed across her face. "Do you think they won't respect me anymore?"

I laughed. "Lori, we all respect you. Sane, nuts, or anywhere in between. And if anyone gives you a hard time, you just let me know, and I'll pack them off to . . . to Transylvania."

She giggled. "Okay. Pass me some of that cobbler. How are the house repairs going?"

"Every time we start to fix something, we find three other things that need to be repaired. It's going to take forever to take care of the major things so life can get back to normal."

"Or maybe you have to get used to a new normal." She looked around the rustic kitchen full of people.

Grandma Rose's barbed comments, Kevin's preoccupation with do-it-yourself projects, a gimpy leg that wasn't improving, kids testing every limit in their new environment, my control slipping more each day . . . My life looked like a scene in someone else's movie, not mine.

A new normal? I didn't like that idea at all.

Chapter Eighteen

The ship's deck shuddered beneath my feet.

"What was that?" I shivered in the night air. The low shoulders of my formal gown did little to protect me from the glacial salt-tinged breeze.

The ship shook again, groaning against an unseen impact. Suddenly, the hull scraped against some hidden mountain. Chunks of ice crashed to the deck.

Kevin pulled me back. "We hit something." He grabbed my hand. "Come on. Let's find out what's going on."

Thirty minutes later, I'd been separated from Kevin in the chaos. People milled around the grand staircase, asking questions, speculating. I overheard a snatch of conversation between a few officers who hurried past us.

The ship was going down.

I raced below decks to find Kevin. Behind me, faint strains of the orchestra reached my ears. The halls were crowded and noisy as stewards handed out life belts. Beyond the portholes, I heard the creak of ropes and pulleys as lifeboats were lowered.

I pressed through, racing in the opposite direction of the terrified guests, deeper into the ship. Soon I was sloshing through knife-cold water, struggling to keep my footing. The water rose from my ankles to waist deep. The ship listed, and waves rolled toward me in the narrow corridor. Lights flickered off, then back on. Another swoop of water tugged at me, threatening to cover me, to sink me, to drown me.

A stack of folders slipped from the filing cabinet beside my desk and showered down on my head. Now I knew where the phrase "drowning in paper work" came from.

Teresa chose that moment to pop into my doorway. "Becky, what are you doing?"

I swam up from the papers, sputtering. "Reorganizing a few things."

"Can you give me your notes on the women's mentoring program?"

"Sure, why?"

"I found a young single woman who volunteered to chair the program. I want to show her what you've done so far."

"But that's one of my projects."

Teresa looked around my office, probably searching for a lifeboat. "You can't have it both ways. You need to limit your hours. I get that. But that means someone else has to take on some of the women's ministry programs."

I clutched a folder protectively. "I've been excited about this one. I've been collecting survey sheets and matching up pairs." Was that a whine in my voice? I was sounding like Kelsey when she wanted one more bedtime story.

Teresa picked her way over manila folders and settled into the spare chair in my small office. "I'm sorry." When she slowed down enough to breathe, Teresa could be sympathetic. "I know it's hard to let go of something you've worked on. But there's no way for everything to get done if you're limited to fifteen hours a week."

I dug my fingers through my hair. "I know."

"Want to reconsider coming on full-time?"

"The way our remodeling bills are piling up, I probably should." I forced a lopsided grin. "Why didn't I know that place would be a money pit?"

Teresa leaned forward and patted my shoulder. "It'll be worth it when you get it fixed up. So, what do you say? Would you consider switching to full-time?"

I glanced at the picture of the kids on my bulletin board. Smirks, freckles, and mischief beamed at me. "My family has to be my top priority. Fifteen hours is all I can handle." *And I'm not even handling that very well.*

Teresa sprang to her feet. "I understand. I can't imagine how I'd do my job if I had kids to worry about, too." She followed my gaze to the photo on the bulletin board, and her shoulders sagged for a second. Then she brightened. "Pastor Bob needs to see everyone this morning. Ten o'clock, okay?"

I nodded and booted up my computer. "I'll e-mail you my files on the mentor program."

But she had already disappeared down the hall, back to her usual pace of full speed ahead.

Lord, multiply my time. Help me prioritize. Help me get this all under control.

Multitasking served me well. I skimmed through e-mails while making phone calls. With one hand, I sorted mail and tossed much of it into the circular file. When one of the women I called wanted to chat about her daughter's problems at college, I recommended a good book from our church library and wrapped up the conversation efficiently. By ten o'clock, my office was less of a disaster, and I even found a notebook and pen to bring with me to Pastor Bob's office.

"Tom Richland has been kind enough to meet with us today to give us a preview of the evangelism board's report for the next congregational meeting," Pastor Bob said as we cozied into his office. Tom had a blaze of fervor in his eyes. If he couldn't convince someone of the need for salvation, he'd drag them kicking and screaming into the kingdom. His intense focus sometimes inspired me and sometimes frightened me.

"Let's pray," he said in a tent-revival voice.

The staff obediently bowed heads while Tom demanded that God stir up lukewarm souls and help our church reach out to more people. He insisted that God multiply our efforts.

The bossy tone troubled me. I flinched as I recognized echoes of my own "multiply my time" prayer. When had I started telling God to support my agenda?

Tom paused, then uttered a crisp "Amen" that startled me. Other staff members jerked their heads up.

"I've got the statistics our committee has developed. After our Easter musical was televised, we had two hundred inquiries—phone, visits, or e-mails. We've determined that we drew in twenty new members from that follow-up. The expenses were roughly one thousand dollars, with another two thousand to pay for the special to be aired."

He stopped and waited for our reaction. Pastor Bob reached for his cup of coffee.

Tom slapped his hand on the desk. "Get it?"

We all jumped, and Pastor Bob pulled his hand back from his mug.

"It's simple math." Tom's eyes glowed like a signal flare. "Three thousand dollars equals twenty new souls saved. So, the committee has proposed that we televise two musicals this year, to double that result. Each year we can build on our media outreach. There are hundreds of people in our community who don't know Christ."

I doodled on my notepad as he continued expanding on his long-term plan that would involve televising all our worship services and Bible classes. When I glanced up, I noticed Pastor Bob's face had turned a pale gray. He gave a weak smile. "This is certainly exciting news. Let's focus on one thing at a time. Staff, what do you think about televising our Christmas program this year, in addition to our Easter drama?"

"Will the construction in the sanctuary be finished by then?" With all the power tools and ladders everywhere, there wouldn't be room for a television camera.

Pastor Bob rubbed his chin. "The contractor said they'd be done by December fifteenth, but—"

"There you go. Plenty of time to prepare for a broadcast," Tom said quickly.

Teresa lost no time in assigning tasks. "I've got the adult interest inventories, so I can begin contacting those with skills in costumes, set design, and lighting. We'll need to do something classier than our normal production."

Brad, the music director, pushed his glasses higher on his beak nose and squinted. "If we begin with this week's choir practice, we can add a small orchestration to the pieces we're preparing."

"Great." Teresa looked at Doris, the Sunday school and children's ministry coordinator. "Can we get the Sunday school involved? Have the kids do a processional and sing 'Away in a Manger'? Audiences love that kind of thing." Teresa was turning into Cecile B. DeMille. She'd probably stage a parting of the Red Sea, except that wasn't a Christmas scene.

The level of enthusiasm from the staff surprised me. I kept my gaze down, hoping no one would think of a way for the women's ministry to help with this burgeoning extravaganza.

"Wait." Pastor Bob cleared his throat.

Most sensible word I'd heard yet in this meeting.

"Tom, as you mentioned, the cost was three thousand dollars for televising our Easter musical. We don't have the budget to do another production so soon. And can we even get a broadcast time on a month's notice?"

Tom threw his shoulders back, dislodging his wide paisley tie. "I took the liberty of calling my contact, and we can have a six in the morning Saturday slot the week after Christmas. And as far as money . . . we must convince people to give a love offering. When we explain the simple statistics, who will dare refuse to give? What's more important, money or the salvation of souls?" Tom's tent-meeting voice was hitting a tremolo.

Pastor Bob stood up. "Well, thank you, Tom. You've given us a lot to discuss. Thanks for coming in."

The meeting broke up, and I hurried back to my office, unsettled. Was it really a simple formula? Throw enough money into a television production and more people are saved?

I pushed aside my unease. At least no one had fingered me to dive into this extra project.

As I drove Micah and Kelsey home at lunchtime, a Christian radio host was sharing about the incredible success they'd had the past year. They had reached sixty-five countries and wanted to go into eighty by next year. The host promised that if I would only send him half my annual income, his ministry organization would no longer be limited. They'd be able to save the world.

"That's what doesn't fit." I pulled into our driveway, and the minivan lurched along the packed dirt.

"What?" Kelsey tried to lean forward against the straps of her booster seat.

"It's true that God wants His gospel to reach the whole world. But that radio minister isn't the only one working toward that goal. Maybe God plans to reach those other fifteen countries with a different program. Or, if God wants him to reach eighty countries, He'll supply what they need . . . without heavy-handed pleas. Right?"

I shoved the gearshift into park and turned to my kids.

Micah and Kelsey looked at each other. Kelsey wrinkled her nose. "Mom needs lunch."

Micah nodded somberly.

I laughed, feeling suddenly free. Free of the guilt and pressure I'd been carrying—for not working enough hours at church, not being excited about a televised Christmas musical, not wanting to impoverish our family in order to help the radio ministry.

Gray November skies spread a comforting blanket over our two acres. The farmhouse slouched as if enjoying an afternoon nap. Our new home looked like it intended to remain casual and relaxed in spite of the frenetic demands of the modern world.

The kids clambered out of the car, jumping and clapping at their suddenly uncranky mom. We burst into the back door, jabbering about lunch ideas. Then we all froze. My good cheer drained away.

A plume of water sprayed from the kitchen sink. Buckets and

kettles tried to catch the torrent, but more water was rolling from the lower cabinet. Our kitchen floor had become an ocean.

"Kids, wait outside. Stay right by the door." I didn't need them paddling around in the mess.

"There you are." Grandma Rose tromped in from the living room with an armful of towels. "I couldn't find the shut-off, and I lost the slip of paper where I wrote your phone number." She scattered towels around the room, where they were as effective as blotting up the Atlantic with a kitchen sponge.

"Where's Judy?"

"She left to talk to a headhunter. At least that's what she told me." Rose had to raise her voice over the hiss of spraying water.

Judy had picked a fine time to abandon ship. Okay, this was up to me to solve.

Fortunately some of my evolving home-improvement instincts kicked in, and I clumped down the basement stairs and found the water meter and shut-off valve. Of course, I couldn't get the round gear to turn. I fumbled through Kevin's pile of tools for a wrench and tried again.

"How's that?" I shouted up the stairs.

"It's still running." Grandma Rose sounded exhausted. "No, wait. That was the water that had collected under the sink. Yes. That did it."

The stairs felt steep and long. Probably because I had no desire to face the disaster.

"You did it!" Grandma Rose shrieked and hugged me as I sloshed across the linoleum.

The hero's welcome bolstered my courage as I faced the mess. "Could you holler outside and ask the kids to go around to the front door? I'll let them in that way."

My cane kicked up splashes as I navigated toward the living room. By the time I opened the front door, the kids were jumping up and down on the porch.

"Wow, Mom. Something broke." Kelsey stated the obvious.

My youngest looked worried. "Micah not do it."

Poor kid was used to getting blamed for everything. "No, sweetie, it's not your fault. We're having trouble with the pipes."

They accepted that cheerfully enough, until they learned the mishap would delay lunch.

I snagged them some granola bars and juice boxes and told them to have a picnic on the living room floor. That was sufficient adventure to keep them happy.

Kevin deserved fair warning, so I left a message on his voice mail at work, telling him the plumbing problems had escalated to a new level. Then Grandma Rose and I began the mop-up work.

A new camaraderie blossomed between us as we worked. She was so impressed by my ability to find the shut-off valve that she didn't criticize the kids' impromptu picnic or remind me again how I dragged the poor children back and forth too much. Instead, we commiserated on the unending chores involved in running a household.

"You know, when I was Kelsey's age, we still didn't have indoor plumbing." Grandma Rose surveyed the kitchen and gave a wry smile. "I've come to enjoy it." She coughed a few times, and I heard the rattle that had been so common in the first days she was with us.

"Rose, please go and rest awhile. I'll finish up here. You don't want to have to visit our doctor again, do you?"

She didn't argue.

That was worrisome. She always argued. I followed her into her bedroom and helped her settle onto the bed. She refused to pull back the bedspread, because she claimed only sick people got under the covers during the day. But she didn't protest when I pulled a hand-knit afghan in Joseph-coat hues over her polyester housedress.

I turned to leave, then paused.

Her room was crowded with boxes that Kevin had shipped up from her Florida house. Knickknacks could look like junk to a stranger's eye, but each of them probably held stories and memories.

Her knitting bag rested beside a small armchair—also from her former home. Doilies protected the arms, and a needlepoint cushion rested against the back. The closet door was neatly closed, but I knew what it held: rows of lightweight dresses and dull pantsuits.

I sank into the chair, feeling sad. Would my life one day fit into a single, crowded room? "You know, I have to take you shopping soon. You need a good winter coat and some warmer clothes."

She closed her eyes. "I'm knitting a sweater."

"That's great. But it won't be enough." Sitting felt good. The chair was just cushy enough. "Whew, I'm tired. I don't know how you managed working full-time and raising Kevin on your own after . . . well, after."

She rolled over, closing me out with her back. "You do what you have to."

I recognized the signals. We weren't going to have a heart-to-heart conversation. At least not today. "I'll try to keep the kids quiet."

When Kevin came home after work, he brought in a large pizza and was the instant hero of the whole Miller clan, including me. We waded through all our usual evening activities while Kevin tried to diagnose the plumbing problem, and I bit my tongue to keep from suggesting he call someone who knew what he was doing.

It was after eleven before we settled into bed. I kicked off the comforter and did some leg stretches. I'd tried to be more diligent with my exercises, but today had gotten away from me—again.

Kevin turned out the lamp on his side of the bed. "Hon, I'm thinking of calling Harry."

"Harry who inspected the house for us?"

"Yeah. He's retired, but he used to be a contractor. If I take some vacation days and get Harry to help, we'll get the major things fixed up."

"But what about our summer vacation? You can't use up your vacation days." I tried to hug my knees to my chest and curled my chin up. My bad leg jutted above me, stiff as an oar—a splintered, battered, crooked oar.

Kevin rolled to face me. "With the extra expenses, we can't afford a trip this year."

I felt his eyes on me, waiting for my response.

No vacation? Not that we ever took grand cruises across the Atlantic on a luxury liner. But I'd miss our annual drive to the north shore of Lake Superior.

My leg dropped to the mattress with a thump. "Teresa asked again about having me go full-time."

He sat up and gently kneaded the muscles of my bad leg. "Do you really want to do that?"

"No, but maybe we should think about it. . . . And besides, I don't know if I trust Harry. He inspected this house for us."

"He gave me a list of problems. It's all fixable. I'm just not an expert. And Harry won't charge me too much." Kevin slipped into his sales manager voice. "We've put too much into this house. I've spent most of the construction loan on supplies. If we can't finish the repairs quickly and apply for the new mortgage, we could lose everything."

"What if we're just throwing good money after bad?" I gnawed my bottom lip.

Kevin didn't notice. "The trick will be to get the work done faster. With Harry's help, it'll be a snap." He used the brisk, efficient voice he used when he was putting a gloss on a problem he wanted to hide from me. He was scared. And he wouldn't admit it.

"Aren't we sinking too much into this place?"

He pulled up to punch his pillow and settled back down. "Naw. I've got it figured out. Our finances will float. No problem."

Yeah, that's what they said about the Titanic.

I turned out my bedside light and sank down with a weary sigh. Kevin reached for me and I scooted closer. His lips found my mouth. In spite of my fatigue, my body came to life. One good thing about the new house—no more kids camping out in our room. But even while I savored our closeness, I felt another flare of loneliness. Why could Kevin communicate so well physically but still seem so distant when we talked? When had that sort of intimacy disappeared? Or was I expecting too much?

Then I surrendered to his touch and stopped thinking.

Chapter Nineteen

Two thoroughbreds blocked my path, their jockeys crouching low, silks splattered with mud from the wet track. I took my weight higher in the stirrups. "Come on, baby. Let's show them what you're made of."

We took the inside position around the final curve and wedged our way past one of our opponents. "Eat my dust!" I screamed. The powerful horse beneath me gathered his muscles for the final charge, egged on more by my yell than my crop.

I willed my bad leg to support me in my forward crouch. After a riding injury where a horse fell on me, doctors said I'd never ride again. Crushed and mangled bone backed them up. Of course, the naysayers said this horse would never be a champion. Not enough heart. Too small.

Wrong on both counts. We showed them.

I breathed every bit of my will into the horse's ears, letting the mane lash my face. I gave him his head, and held on.

My damaged knee screamed from the strain and threatened to give out.

Only a few more seconds.

We pulled alongside the lead horse. Neck and neck into the homestretch.

My poorly mended hip throbbed with the pulse of each stride of the gallop.

A swift glance to the side showed me that we were pulling ahead.

If we won this race, every bit of the pain would be worth it.

Come on! Just a few more seconds.

My joints sent spears of pain through every cell of my leg.

"You can do it, Mommy." Kelsey cheered from the stands—in this case the living room couch.

Sprawled on my side on an old blanket, I held the leg lift for another second, then tried to maintain some control as I lowered my limb. I had finally decided that the only way to fit in my physical therapy was to include the kids.

"Why does your face get all funny when you do that, Mom?"

Micah looked up from his Duplos and frowned when he realized he'd missed the grimace.

"Because it hurts." I switched to my other side. The exercises hadn't hurt this badly months ago. I'd really let things slide. "Don't worry, Micah, you can watch on this side."

Classy pumps clattered down the stairs. "Sis, the hot water ran out again. I was only in the shower a few minutes."

I sighed and sat up. Judy looked professional and polished. Blond bob, navy power-suit, a few elegant pieces of jewelry. I instantly felt shabby in my old stretch pants and sweaty hair.

"Sorry. We're getting the new water heater on Saturday." I stretched forward, coaxing my hamstrings to relax and letting my back curl. We'd experienced Murphy's Law of buying and selling a home. While the buyers of our home insisted that we replace our water heater before the closing, we bought the new house and immediately learned we had to replace the same appliance here. At least the freezing front room was an easy fix. Two space heaters— one on each side of the room—made it bearable. But hot water had been in short supply.

"Oh, good. I won't be back until Tuesday."

"You're going somewhere? Do you need me to drive you to the airport?" Did that sound too eager?

"Yeah. I'm going to meet with a few people in New York. Check out my options. Can't hang out in suburbia with you forever."

I uncurled and sat up tall. "Technically we may be in a suburb, but I like to think of it as a hobby farm."

"Whatever. Wish me luck."

"I'll do you one better. I'll pray for you."

Judy rolled her eyes and headed for the kitchen in her aggressive Miss America stride. She paused at the doorway and did a model's half turn, flicking her hair back with a knowing toss of her head. "The way things have been going for you, you better save those prayers for yourself." She disappeared in search of Grandma Rose's coffee.

Kelsey galloped after her. "Aunt Juju, can I go with you to New York?"

Duplos crashed to the floor as Micah looked up again. "Me too!" He maneuvered to his feet and toddled after her.

I eased back to rest on my elbows. The slightly canted floor stretched out around me, golden in the afternoon sunlight.

Sure, we'd had a few hitches, but this house was going to work out for us all. By the time there was an opening in the apartment building Rose liked best—they estimated two months—she would turn it down with a grateful smile. She'd hug Kevin and say, "You have such a wonderful wife. I hope you appreciate her. She loves you so much, she made a home for your mother."

Kevin would swoop me into his arms and spin me around this wide-open living room. What was that verse in Proverbs 31? "Many women do noble things, but you surpass them all." Kevin would tell me that over and over while I sat in my rocker and hand-quilted a new wall hanging for our country-motif bedroom.

"Becky, aren't you going to start supper soon? Poor Kevin never gets a square meal." Grandma Rose stood in the doorway with fists on her hips, wearing a full apron no less. "Or if you're too busy"—her eyes scorned my sprawl on the floor—"I could start a pot of soup."

"No, no. I'll figure something out." Maybe after I drove Judy to the airport and picked up Dylan from basketball practice, I could swing by Taco Bell. Our budget could handle that . . . barely.

Or could it? We'd put every penny of savings into our down payment. And penny was the operative word. With three kids, our savings account was more of an emergency fund, and somehow there were always emergencies. Since moving to the "country," our expenses had mushroomed. Cloud-from-an-atomic-test sort of mushroom. Not only did everything need repair, we had two extra mouths to feed with Judy and Grandma Rose.

Grandma Rose had offered us her social security checks while she lived with us, and Kevin had refused. After several tight-lipped conversations and stubborn silences, they compromised and applied her checks to the unpaid portion of her hospital bills.

I'd never been more grateful that Kevin worked in the insurance industry. Grandma Rose's paper work made my eyes cross. Each doctor's appointment and each prescription created a new puzzle of forms. I was happy to consign that mail to him.

And Judy? She had lived on an expense account for so long, she had forgotten that food cost money. She didn't exactly flaunt her severance package, but she never gave a thought to household finances. It wouldn't occur to her to chip in for groceries or utilities, and it felt petty for me to ask.

Maybe I better forget Taco Bell.

I blotted my face with my sleeve and lurched to my feet. The kids were cantering around the kitchen table, playing horses. Judy hurried out to finish packing.

Grandma Rose rubbed her temples. "I think I'll take a little nap." She coughed a few times as she shuffled to her room.

I really needed to get another appointment for her. Ever since her pneumonia, her lungs kept acting up.

"Okay, kids. If you help me fix supper, you'll get a surprise."

Kelsey skidded to a stop. "What's the surprise?"

"If I told you, it wouldn't be a surprise." I watched wheels turn in Kelsey's head. Was it a worthwhile gamble? Stop playing and help Mom for some unknown goodie?

She shrugged. "Okay."

We surveyed the cupboards and the fridge. Why hadn't I followed Lori's advice and developed a monthly menu plan? I hated figuring out what to make each day.

I pulled out the slow cooker, poured in a can of stock, and organized my troops. Micah scrubbed a few limp carrots while Kelsey peeled potatoes with a special safety peeler. I chopped an onion and dumped a box of frozen peas into the slow cooker for good measure.

Good thing Grandma Rose was in her room, where she couldn't watch my improvisations. She wouldn't approve. Any meal not built around a pot roast or a whole chicken didn't count in her mind.

"Okay, kids. You earned your surprise. You don't have to have quiet time this afternoon. Instead, you get to come with me to drive Aunt Judy to her airplane. Won't that be fun? Go get your shoes on."

Micah and Kelsey's bare feet padded out of the kitchen and up the stairs.

"Wait! That means socks, too," I hollered.

Even in November they'd go outside barefoot if I let them.

Judy strode into the kitchen. "Sis, I can get on the earlier flight if we leave right now."

And suddenly I was in a race. No time to change out of my grubby workout wear. Jackets, shoes, kids. Where had I dropped my purse last? Keys. Were the keys in my purse? I didn't see them on the counter. Had Grandma Rose moved them again? No, they were in the purse. Good.

We hurried to beat the afternoon traffic on I-494. I wove from lane to lane while Judy tapped her foot and checked her Rolex. As we approached the airport, the kids whooped and shrieked as a low-flying jet came over the freeway on its way to landing. Instead of joining their glee, I kept an eye on the van's clock. My pulse zoomed over the speed limit, and my stomach started the queasy ache that was becoming a familiar companion.

These days I was always hurrying to catch up, convinced that if I crossed the next signpost all the pressure would lift. But there was always another post calling me forward. And the finish line never got any closer.

Judy sprang from the car, slid her compact black suitcase to the sidewalk, and gave a quick wave. "Don't worry. I'll be back in time for Thanksgiving."

Thanksgiving?

I'd forgotten it was only a week and a half away. The last two years I'd gotten the scrawny birds left at the bottom of Cub Foods' freezer. I had promised myself not to leave it too late this year.

"Guess what, kids?" I navigated the lanes on the way out of the airport. "We're going to the store before we pick up Dylan. Won't that be fun?"

My rearview mirror reflected Kelsey and Micah exchanging dubious looks.

"And I'll buy you a box of animal crackers if you're good helpers."

They perked up.

"Can we ride on the merry-go-round?" Kelsey knew to negotiate for more perks.

What demented soul ever came up with the idea of positioning miniature merry-go-rounds at the entrance of a store? Didn't he realize all the pleading and tears it would cause hurried moms?

"No rides. We won't have time." The grocery store near our new house wasn't laid out the same as our old one, so shopping had been taking me longer.

I got trapped behind an old lady pushing a cart with a crooked wheel, but I passed her on the inside and hurried to the next lane. We were out of potatoes. What else? Celery, onions, stuffing mix, yams. A can of jellied cranberries that no one liked but was a tradition. Maybe Grandma Rose would eat some this year. She'd never been with us at Thanksgiving before.

The kids were terrific helpers. Micah rode in the cart, throwing his body forward to urge on his mount. Kelsey kept up a running commentary as she spotted various things she was convinced we needed.

"No, sweetie. Super-deluxe Sugar Popping O's are not on the list."

"You don't have a list."

I tapped my temple. "It's in here."

We checked out in record time, and I turned my trusty steed toward the church-school. Dylan's basketball coach had sent home a letter reminding parents to pick their children up on time from practice. I'd blushed when I'd read the note, sure it was personally directed at me.

This afternoon we made it with time to spare. Dylan meandered out sans jacket and wearing his practice shorts. How many times had I told him to change back into his school clothes after practice? Snow was in the forecast. Did all kids have a defective inner thermostat? Mine sure seemed to. I tooted the horn lightly so Dylan would spot my van in the long line of parents, but he didn't notice. He was preoccupied, nudging a friend and laughing.

Another boy called something, and suddenly Dylan dropped his knapsack and raced toward him. Before I could absorb his intent, Dylan shoved the boy, sending him reeling back several steps. Both boys began shouting, their faces red—two stallions pawing the ground.

"Don't move," I commanded my two youngest. I jumped from the van, dragging my cane behind, and then hobbled quickly to the fight.

Doris, the children's ministry director, stepped outside and placed a calming hand on each boy's shoulder.

When I reached them, she was addressing Dylan. "Tell Matthew you're sorry. Shoving is not acceptable."

Dylan's stony jaw suddenly reminded me of Kevin's. "I won't. It's his fault."

I grabbed Dylan with too much force. "It doesn't matter whose fault it is. You apologize this instant."

He registered surprise and a flicker of embarrassment that I'd observed the scene. He kicked a tennis shoe against the concrete and muttered a sullen "Sorry."

Doris smiled at me. "Dylan's a good kid. I'm sure this was a misunderstanding. You might want to talk to him about it when you get home. I'll talk to Matthew's mom when she gets here."

As we pulled out of the car-pool lane and toward home, the queasiness in my stomach grew into full-fledged nausea. I'd skipped lunch, and my anti-inflammatory pills were bugging my stomach. I tried to concentrate on that instead of my anger, but I couldn't rein in my thoughts. Dylan knew better. I couldn't believe my son was violent. And unrepentant. What kind of mom was I?

"Matthew's a creep." His muttered defense didn't win him any points.

I pressed my lips together and leaned toward the steering wheel, wanting to be home. "We'll talk about it later. Right now I need to drive."

Even Micah and Kelsey sat in wide-eyed silence until we pulled up into the driveway.

"Dylan, help me carry in the groceries. Then you can go straight to your room. I'll talk to you after I put everything away."

Kelsey grabbed a bag with eggs balanced on top and almost tipped it over. I caught it just in time. "Honey, take this instead." I passed her a lighter one with toilet paper and bread.

Dylan thumped his bag on the kitchen table and stomped up the stairs. Kelsey and Micah disappeared.

I counted to ten as I emptied each bag. It wasn't until I folded the last bag that a sick realization hit me.

I'd forgotten the turkey.

My frustration climbed, and I sank into a chair, letting my forehead drop to the table. I didn't dare climb the stairs to confront Dylan until I'd calmed down.

I needed to let my adrenaline fade after the race to the airport, and the race through the grocery store, and catching my son causing trouble. Maybe some herbal tea. Heather kept giving me canisters of the stuff, trying to convert me away from coffee. The mint and rose hips actually smelled pretty good.

I popped a mug of water into the microwave and hit the Beverage button. Then I lifted the lid of the slow cooker to see how the soup was coming along. No warm steam rose to my nose.

I tapped the side of the appliance with my fingertip. No heat.

The socket above the counter was empty.

A moan escaped me. I'd never plugged it in. So much for supper.

Grandma Rose popped her head out of her room. "Oh, there you are. Is there any cough syrup in this house?"

I immediately felt guilt for not stocking a complete pharmacy. "I don't think so. Wait." I pulled our childproof box from the top shelf of the pantry and rummaged through our first aid kit and various bottles. "Here's something we keep on hand for the kids." I passed her a bottle of red cough medicine. It wasn't very strong. The strong stuff tasted so horrible none of us would use it. This was probably only a step above a teaspoon of honey and lemon.

Rose squinted at the label. "Hmm. This is all you have?" She sniffed, coughed, and retreated to her room.

I grabbed the note pad on the card table in the corner that served as an office area. Cough syrup. Turkey. One mega bottle of Valium.

I scratched that out. Make that a case of Jolt. Something to help me keep up.

Out of reflex, I phoned Kevin at work. Even though we'd been cranky with each other lately, he was still the first person I turned to when I was slogging through muddy turf.

Kevin's voice sounded weary when he answered, so I spared him the details.

"Hon, can we afford Taco Bell for supper?"

"You've got a hankering for Mexican?"

"Something like that. And I forgot to turn the slow cooker on."

"Oh, sweetie." Laughter and empathy blended in his words.

"Yes, I'll pick it up on my way home. I was just leaving. Hey, and I'll stop by Mr. Movies and pick up a rental. We can have a movie night with our tacos."

In that moment, I forgave him for every time he'd extolled his mom's way of doing things. "Thanks. I might survive today after all."

He laughed, and some of the fatigue left his voice. "Honey, I'd always put my money on you to win."

Sure, he said that now. But wait until he heard about Dylan's shoving match at school. I forced a smile into my words. "See you soon."

I dropped the receiver into its cradle. The answering machine light was blinking so I checked messages. One was from Lori, asking for prayer. I'd told her to call me anytime she was struggling, so I could support her. She had finally taken me up on it, but today I felt like a spiritual misfit with nothing to give. I breathed a quick prayer for her anyway and jotted myself a note to call her later.

The next message was from Harry. "Uh, yeah. Kevin, I checked my schedule, and I can start on the plumbing work tomorrow morning. We better go ahead and replace all the pipes, so I'll need to cut through some walls and tear out part of the ceiling. Not to worry. It shouldn't take long. Couple of weeks."

Would anyone think less of me if I admitted that I burst into tears?

Chapter Twenty

The light from Lori's staff threw the caverns into a contrast of shadowed edges. Sunlight seemed a lifetime ago, even though we'd only been trekking through these mines for a few days.

"The dwarves knew what they were doing when they built this." Grandma Rose's voice echoed in the chamber—sturdy, opinionated. "This is how people are meant to live."

"The sooner we get out of this maze, the better." Judy hefted her shield and repositioned the horn that hung from her shoulder. "It's a fool's task anyway. Why throw away our chance at power?" She glared in my direction.

The ring burned cold against the skin over my heart. How could I know whom to trust? Dread pervaded all my thoughts—even my dreams.

Kevin strode forward brandishing his torch as he checked our path. "Orcs are near. We need to get moving."

My three small companions sprawled on the rocks, catching their breath. Kelsey, Dylan, and Micah didn't understand the full import of our journey, but they were loyal and cheerful allies.

As I adjusted my small scabbard, a soft blue glow appeared from the blade. "Orcs!"

"Hurry! This way!" Kevin led us back to a more protected room and bolted the wide doors. His broad sword promised that he would protect us with his life's blood.

The whole ground seemed to shake as something battered the door, splintering it.

We braced ourselves, weapons at the ready.

A monster knocked aside timbers as if they were matchsticks. He lumbered forward, weapons in hand.

A cave troll! We were doomed.

Harry lurched through the door, wrench in hand. His bib over-alls did nothing for his portly figure. An untidy fringe of gray hair surrounded a dull bald spot, and his face bristled with gray whiskers. He shrugged out of his down jacket, sending a few stray feathers flying from a ripped seam. His metal toolbox hit the floor with a thud.

"G'mornin'. Let me get the rest of my stuff."

He disappeared back to his truck before I had a chance to greet him. Not that I could muster much enthusiasm.

At least I'd planned to work from home today. Micah had a nose as leaky as our upstairs faucet, and the day care had strict rules about contagious kids. I'd organized some volunteer lists during our movie date last night, so I almost felt like I was staying on top of things. This morning I'd dropped Kelsey and Dylan at school and hurried home. Micah and I would protect our walls as much as possible while Harry began his work. Well, at least I would. Micah was planted in front of the TV in the corner of the room, watching a big red dog solve everyone's problems.

Dirty work boots tromped back into my line of vision. A mammoth sledgehammer hung from one of his fists.

"Harry, I know Kevin's explained. His mom is in poor health . . . and this place means a lot to us . . . and we've already painted—"

He wiped the sleeve of his flannel shirt across his bulbous nose. "Now, don't you worry, missy. I'll take care of everything."

Missy? I gritted my teeth and forced myself to step back and let him invade my home. "Where do you want to start?"

"I need to check out the basement."

"The cellar stairs are through the kitchen." I'd taken to saying *cellar* to sound more country. Besides, the dark, rough space was more of a cave than a basement.

Harry followed me into the kitchen, where Grandma Rose was picking at a piece of toast, sturdy arms resting on the table, the sleeves of her polyester blouse rolled up. Her whole wardrobe seemed to center around browns or grays. Gray roots had begun to grow into her lifeless brown hair. I should schedule an appointment for her at Great Clips, but she'd probably refuse to go, thinking a haircut was an indulgence.

"Mm-mm." Harry patted his belly. "That coffee sure smells good. How about a cup to wet my whistle?"

Grandma Rose gave him a scalding glare.

"Rose, this is Harry. He's the man helping Kevin with the plumbing."

She sniffed and looked over her glasses at Harry. "Where I come from, we work first and have refreshments later."

Harry seemed to take no offense at Rose's comment. He pulled up a chair and squared off with her. "Where would that be?"

"Florida."

He barked a laugh. "Folks in the South don't know a plug nickel about work." He gave me a conspiratorial wink. "Too much heat. Makes folks lazy."

I winced. He couldn't have accused her of anything worse.

Grandma Rose's chair scraped back with force and she jabbed a finger in Harry's face. "And apparently the cold weather up here has frozen your brain cells."

She stormed out, and I heard her slam the door of her bedroom.

Harry shrugged like a good-natured giant. "Is she always like that?"

I wasn't sure how to answer that, but Harry didn't seem to expect a response. He was throwing a longing gaze at the coffee-maker.

"Harry, the basement is that way. Go ahead and check things out, but don't start smashing things until you talk to me."

He waved a dismissive hand and lumbered down the cellar steps.

I started a fresh pot of coffee. Lori was coming over this morning. When I'd returned her phone call late last night, we'd agreed we both needed some friendship therapy.

Harry hollered up the stairs. "Okay. I'm shuttin' the water off now. No flushing."

Great. Not the words you want to hear with a not-quite-three-year-old in the house.

I limped to Rose's door and tapped. "Did you hear that? We can't use the bathrooms for a while."

"You could hear him bellowing all the way to Wisconsin. Keep an eye on that man. I don't trust him."

Since she couldn't see me, I rolled my eyes. I highly doubted that Harry was going to steal the family silver. Especially since we didn't have any.

I hobbled back to the living room. Micah sat on the floor in one of the impossible contortions that only toddlers can manage—as if he'd been sitting on his heels, but then let his feet shift out to either side. *Clifford* was wrapping up, so I turned off the television. "Abby and Jeffy are coming over to play. Don't forget to share."

Micah rolled to his feet and did a little jig, hopping from one foot to the other, his pudgy face alight under his mop of hair. When the doorbell rang, he charged across the living room to answer, pumping his little arms, chin tucked in. Pure little-boy determination and vigor.

Since Lori homeschooled, Abby and Jeffy could bring their work anywhere . . . or even postpone lessons until later in the day. She didn't have to configure car pools, plan events around a school calendar, or sign a zillion permission slips and homework forms every day. Maybe I should consider homeschooling my brood. The idea held a lot of appeal.

On the other hand, we loved the Christian school at Faith Church, and since I was on staff at the church, we got a generous break on tuition. The opportunity was too good to pass up.

Micah flung our front door open and squealed. Lori came in and smiled as her kids carefully lined up their shoes on the rug and draped their coats over the bench I had positioned near the door.

"My people," Micah crowed. "Come on, come on." He

gestured his friends up the stairs. His life was divided into "his peo-ple"—the ones he knew—and everyone else.

Abby smiled at me, her glasses giving her a mature look that contrasted with her playful cornrows. "Hello, Mrs. Miller. Your new house is lovely."

Charmed, I gave her a hug. "Thanks, Abbs. Make yourself at home."

"Horsie!" Micah threw himself against Abby. She crouched so he could squeeze his legs around her waist and grab her neck. Jeffy picked up Abby's book bag and followed behind.

They trekked up the stairs, already beginning a game of Let's Pretend. I heard snatches of negotiations about who would be a warrior and whether Abby should be an elf princess or a monster.

I took Lori's coat. "Your kids are the most polite I've ever known. You're an amazing mom."

Lori lifted one shoulder. "They're just good-natured."

Now that I knew about Lori's battle with the depressive side of her bipolar disorder, I recognized the self-diminishing way Lori brushed aside compliments. I gave her a hug, and before pulling away, I met her eyes.

"You're an amazing, beautiful, special person. Don't shake your head. You've got to hear me and let this sink in, okay?"

"Yes, Mom."

"That's better. Now, make yourself useful and pour us some cof-fee. I just made a pot." I settled into the rocking chair near the space heater. If I closed my eyes, I could imagine we were cozying up to a fireplace.

Lori returned with mugs and set them on the coffee table, pull-ing it closer to the space heater. "We could sit in the kitchen."

"No, I need privacy so I can vent."

She breathed in steam from her cup. "I see our Bible study on taming the tongue went right over your head."

I made a face. "I promise not to get too specific about anyone. But seriously, I don't know what I'm going to do. Grandma Rose still isn't happy here. I've tried so hard to win her over . . . for Kevin's sake. But it's not working. And instead of appreciating me, Kevin just takes it for granted. And Dylan got in a fight at school. It's so embarrassing when I'm on the staff. And speaking of staff, the chairman of the evangelism committee has hatched a plan for televising our Christmas program. And Judy will be back next week. I thought after getting laid off she'd want to look for more meaning in her life, but all she's been looking for are fun nights out and cute guys. Now I've got a troll in my basement threatening to rip apart my house . . . and it's almost Thanksgiving. My leg's been getting worse, I've been having stomach aches, I feel like I'm going insane—"

I clapped a hand over my mouth, distressed at my insensitivity. "I didn't mean . . . that is . . . no offense."

Lori had been listening with her coffee mug hiding her lips. Now she set the mug down and laughed—hard.

As I thought of how ridiculous my life must sound, I started to laugh, too. Soon we both had tears running down our cheeks.

"Well, at least now I'll have company in the asylum," Lori gasped. That sent us both into another round of giggles.

I'd worried about how to treat Lori after finding out she was bipolar. Lori begged me not to treat her differently. Still, I admired her ability to joke.

"Whew." I blotted my eyes with the cuff of my shirt. "That felt good. Okay. Now tell me how I'm supposed to fix everything. I'm seeing a theme here. I've got a leg that needs fixing, a house that needs fixing, kids and relatives who need fixing."

Lori sipped her coffee. "Are you sure you're supposed to fix everything?"

That question stalled out my righteous indignation about the struggles I'd been facing. "Aren't I?"

A sharp ring interrupted from my belt. The cordless phone. I'd taken to tucking it in my pocket or waistband during the day. I couldn't run for it, and it annoyed Grandma Rose if I let the

189

machine pick up. But I didn't want any distractions. Lori and I needed this visit.

Lori waved her hand. "Go ahead and answer."

Throwing her an apologetic glance, I punched a button. "Hello?"

"Oh, Becky, I'm glad I caught you." Teresa's conversations were as warp-speed as the rest of her. "I know you aren't coming in today, but I wanted to give you as much notice as possible. Could you get the Mom's Time Out group to work on publicity for the Christmas program? Press releases, posters up around town—you know. And will you rustle up some volunteers to baby-sit for the singers and actors who have children? And we're planning an additional rehearsal for the Saturday after Thanksgiving. I'll need your help to contact everyone."

My ears started ringing, and my throat felt thick . . . as if I'd tried to swallow and it had gotten trapped halfway. "Um. Look, I can't talk right now. I'll call you back."

Surprised by my own terseness, I said a quick good-bye and turned off the phone. Then I started to shake. "I can't," I whispered. "I can't do one more thing. I can't. I can't." The lump in my throat turned into a low sob. "What am I going to do?"

Lori jumped from her chair to hug me, then knelt by my chair. "What is it?"

Through tears, I told her about the latest new time-consuming, stress-creating event that demanded my involvement. "And the thing is, my Mom's Time Out group is already busy the next few weeks organizing our annual Christmas Tea. This would put everyone over the edge. It's a busy time of year anyway. What am I going to do?"

She listened calmly and waited until I'd caught my breath. Then she handed me my mug. "Drink."

She sat back down in her chair. "I think the answer here is easy, isn't it?"

I glared at her. "Maybe getting all that work done would be easy for you . . . you are the queen of organizing."

"No." She knocked the heel of her hand against her forehead. "Don't you get it? It's simple. You have to say no."

I froze. My mind instantly clamored with all the reasons that notion was impossible. Still I trusted Lori enough to try on the idea for size. Could I? What would happen?

"Beck, if it's going to cause you and all the women you work with ridiculous stress, I think saying no is the only option."

"But it's to lead people to Christ. . . ."

"So they can be as harried and exhausted as you are?"

"That's not fair. It's only this one event. After that I could start being firmer about my hours."

"And then there'll be another event. And another. No one else is going to set limits for you. They'll take all you're willing to give."

The poignant thread in Lori's voice hooked my swirling thoughts. "Is that . . . I mean, did you . . . ?"

She nodded. "Part of what my counselor has worked with me on is catching on when burnout is approaching so I don't spiral as far."

"But what if you can't make the stress go away? I mean, I have a husband and kids, and a mother-in-law, and a job. That isn't going to change. No matter how careful I am, that's a lot of responsibility on my shoulders."

"Is it?"

Defensiveness flickered to life. "You don't think that's a lot?"

"Of course it's a lot. But is it on your shoulders?"

I opened my mouth to explain that of course it was all up to me. That's what being a woman was all about. And being the sandwich generation. And being a working mom.

I closed my mouth and rocked my chair back. "Okay, I get it."

She grinned. "You're not as slow as everyone says you are. How about if we pray and put a few of your problems on bigger shoulders, okay?"

"Hey, I was supposed to be cheering you up. Doesn't it bother you that I've been burdening you with my problems?"

"It makes me feel great." Lori snickered. "Wait. That sounded wrong. I don't mean I'm glad you're having so many issues. But it makes me feel useful." Heaviness seemed to press her shoulders forward, and she took a deep breath. "Which I don't feel a lot lately."

Feeling strangely shy, I wondered how much to ask. "What is your doctor saying?"

Her thin brows drew together, creating creases in her chocolate-caramel skin. "My psychiatrist says to give this new medication a few more weeks. I'm still sad most of the time and have to use every ounce of willpower to do the simplest thing. But it's not as bad as it was."

I shuddered. Sounded bad enough as it was now.

"My counselor is a Christian. She's been great. She's coaching me to rest in God and not beat up on myself. I've always tended to take the manic energy and develop tendencies that are . . ."

"Compulsive? Driven?"

She stuck out her tongue at me. "I was going to say workaholic. Anyway, she keeps reminding me this illness is cyclical and I'll get better."

"What can I do?"

She shook her head. "There you go. Wanting to fix it. You don't need to do anything. Just be here."

"I am. Okay, let's pray." We reached for each other's hands.

A thundering crash sounded below our feet. Then heavy feet pounded up the stairs. "Missy?" Harry yelled.

Not now. Please, Lord. I needed this prayer time with Lori.

"Missy?"

I sighed. "In here."

The moment for prayer fizzled as he marched into the living room. "I'll need to run to the hardware store. I don't have enough of the right connections. And I should talk to Kevin about how he wants to route some of the new pipes."

"Okay . . ."

Grandma Rose shuffled out in her backless slippers. "Is that man gone yet?"

Harry popped a stick of gum in his mouth and grinned. "I have to buy some supplies. But don't you worry. I'll be back before you can miss me."

"Oh, good," she said dryly.

Harry snapped his gum and sauntered out, neglecting to pull the door closed behind him. Lori jumped up to close it before all the cold air could blow in from the porch.

Grandma Rose cleared her throat but then slipped into a series of wrenching coughs. "Becky, about that cough syrup . . ."

Lori cast me a look of sympathy, then walked to the foot of the stairs. "Abby, Jefferson, time to go."

I wanted to tell her to stay. In fact, I was desperate to savor some prayer time. But I needed to get Rose some different medicine. Lori must have seen the regret on my face. She gave me a hug as the kids scampered down the steps. "I'll be praying for you."

Suddenly, she was gone, along with the brief moment of camaraderie. Reality swept back in, and I struggled to hang on to my good intentions. I had to call Teresa back and tell her no. I felt responsibilities pulling me down like a heavy weight strung around my neck. But I determined to put the burden on stronger shoulders.

Lord, I feel like I'm in a dark cavern and don't know the way out. There are scary monsters every direction I turn. And they keep coming. There's too many of them. Be my guide. Fight for me.

"I tried that red stuff you gave me, and it didn't help at all." Rose coughed again.

I turned away from the door and looked at her with concern. "I'll get you some cough medicine when I pick up Kelsey at kindergarten, okay? What would you like for lunch?"

She retreated toward the kitchen. "Don't go to any trouble on my account."

Chapter Twenty-one

Cloying heat rose from the jungles and shimmered over the river. My blouse clung to me, and I wished my missionary modesty would allow me to unbutton a few more buttons. Instead, I settled my broadbrimmed hat more firmly on my head and turned to smile at the cantankerous pilot of this small steamship. He was convinced we'd never manage the journey. I believed in the power of determination.

After all, my determination had convinced him to take me down the river even after he had refused in no uncertain terms.

"A lovely day," I shouted. The grinding chug of the engine made conversation difficult.

Kevin squinted at the water ahead, his grizzled features strong. He played the role of a curmudgeon, but I knew human nature. His gruffness hid a tender heart and a boatload of courage.

Suddenly, a higher-pitched wheeze rose from the boat, then a sharp clank. The engine died. We coasted toward the riverbank. Kevin waited until we were securely anchored before flinging his hat to the deck.

"I told you this was a mistake." He pulled out a bottle from a hidden cubby and took a long swig, then wiped his filthy shirtsleeve across his mouth. "Engine's broken. We're stuck."

I stuck my jaw in his direction. "Then we'll fix it."

"Lady, you don't understand. It'll need dry-dock. I can't even reach the problem."

"Why?" I had no choice. I had to reach our destination.

He passed the bottle to me. "It's underwater."

"Can't you swim?" All he needed was a little coaxing. "Come on. I'll help."

194

Kevin grimaced from the stepladder as he worked his wrench against rusted pipes. I focused the flashlight on his work. The pale bulb in the cellar didn't shed much illumination, so I'd offered to help.

"You can do it," I cheered.

Kevin grunted and threw all his weight into the torque. The coupling finally loosened with a groan. The sudden movement threw Kevin off balance. He fell from the ladder, his pipe wrench hitting the concrete with a heavy clatter.

Instead of springing back up, he rolled to a sitting position and rubbed his knee. "Why did we buy this house?"

I summoned a positive attitude and reached out to stroke his buzz-cut hair. "We're closer to church and school. There's more space for the kids to play. There's room for your mom, so we can take care of her. And we wanted to enjoy family time fixing up a home together."

He growled.

I decided this wasn't a good time to remind him that the house hunt had been his idea in the first place. "When is Harry getting back?"

Kevin swiped the back of his hand across his sweaty forehead, smearing a mix of dust, rust, and cobwebs. "Should be here by now. He said he had a lead on a good deal for some copper pipes. I don't know why it's taking him so long."

"Kev, are you sure Harry . . . well . . ."

"Knows what he's doing?"

"Yeah."

Kevin stood up and rubbed the small of his back. "Well, he knows more than I do. And he's hardly charging me anything."

"Okay, then. Let's get the rest of this old iron piping pulled out for him."

Kevin stepped in for a hug. "You know, you're a good sport."

Warm pleasure lapped over me, counteracting the chill of the concrete floor. "I know. Okay, what tool do you need next?"

He climbed back up and rattled the next pipe. "Hand me the reciprocating saw."

"Check." I passed him the power tool, proud that I could assist. I plugged it into the extension cord.

As Kevin began cutting, the saw screeched, then lowered its pitch to a heavy grind. The blade moved farther in, and the pipe began to rattle. I backed out of the way.

Kevin wobbled as the saw cleared the pipe, but he caught his balance. He stepped down, shifted to the next location, and checked to be sure I was out of range. He made the next cut. "This puppy's coming down!" he whooped.

A few seconds later, he leaned out of the way as a large segment of pipe crashed to the floor.

I grinned at him. "I knew you could do it."

Flushed with exertion, Kevin set down the saw. "Time for lunch."

"Good plan." Finally, it felt like Kevin and I were actually sharing the journey instead of always sniping at each other. I limped toward the stairs and began making my way up.

"Becky, are you all right?"

"Sure, why?"

"Your limp seems a lot worse. Are you doing everything the doctor told you?"

"Yes. Sort of. I don't always have time for my physical therapy exercises. And he said I should avoid stairs . . . at least until the inflammation calms down some more."

Kevin followed me into the kitchen. "And this house has a ton of stairs."

I shrugged and sank into a chair, massaging the ache out of my thigh and knee. "I'll deal with it. It's fun having you around the house. I wish you didn't have to use your vacation days, but this is kind of nice."

Grandma Rose peered into the kitchen from the hall. When she saw no sign of Harry, she padded in with Micah on her heels.

"Kevin, you look exhausted. What was all that crashing? Are you all right? Becky, why don't you pour him some ice water?"

"Mom, Becky needs to rest her leg. I can get my own water."

I looked up at Kevin, surprised by his support.

Grandma Rose pursed her lips in disapproval while Kevin got out two glasses, poured water out of a pitcher, and handed me my drink. She adjusted her apron. "Well, I suppose I better make some lunch if no one else is going to do it." She managed to spread peanut butter in a way that broadcasted how offended she felt.

Kevin ignored her and pulled up a chair, letting Micah crawl onto his lap. "So what did Teresa say?"

"She was at a district adult educators meeting this morning. I plan to call her this afternoon."

"Good for you."

I shook my head. "I don't know. Maybe Lori's wrong. It feels selfish to put limits on my service."

Kevin reached across the table and held my hand. "We all have limits. Even you."

"Back in my day," Grandma Rose seemed to be talking to the jar of peanut butter, "we didn't think and talk and fuss about everything. We did what needed doing. Before all that psychology and nonsense. Nowadays people have to follow their bliss and be fulfilled, and have boundaries. I've seen it on *Oprah*." She sniffed and shook her head, stabbing the knife back into the jar.

"You're right." Harry lumbered in from the living room and joined the conversation. "My grandson cheated on a test, and his parents are all worried about his self-esteem instead of grounding him for a month like they oughta."

Grandma Rose gave Harry her first approving nod. "Exactly."

Harry scratched the tuft behind his bald spot. "Kevin, I got the new piping out in the truck. Wanna help me carry it in?"

"Lunch first," Grandma Rose stated. She cut off the crusts of a sandwich and set the plate in front of Kevin. Micah reached for a segment but his grandma shook her head. "No, no. That one is for

your daddy. I'll make yours in a minute." Then she handed a sandwich to Harry.

Kevin raised his eyebrows at me. I didn't know whether to giggle at Rose's coddling of Kevin or at the fact that she had conde-
scended to feed Harry.

"So, Harry." I nodded my thanks to Rose as she slid a plate
toward me. "Do you think we'll have running water by Thanksgiving? My sister will be here, and I'm making a big dinner. It's hard
to cook without water." I smiled so he would know I wasn't whining.

He shrugged and took another large bite of sandwich. "Thas
good," he said with his mouth full. "It's nithe to be wiff family on
Thankthgivin." Even through the peanut butter, he conveyed a hint
of wistfulness as he accepted a glass from Rose and took a swig of
milk.

"What are your plans for the holiday?" I asked, hoping he'd
answer before taking another bite.

"Oh, I'll just have lunch in the dining room at Eldercare Estates.
My daughter and her kids live in Nebraska, and they aren't going to
make it up until Christmas. They don't get here so much since Ellen
passed away." This time there was no hiding his sadness as he leaned
against the kitchen counter.

Grandma Rose stepped behind me and nudged me. I twisted
my neck to look at her, but she was staring at the ceiling, so I
thought I'd imagined the poke. I turned back to the table and felt
another nudge.

"Oh, for pete's sake," she muttered. "Since Becky is busy eating," she said more loudly, "I guess it's up to me to invite you. You
should have Thanksgiving dinner with us."

I choked on my crust.

Kevin quickly jumped up and circled the table to pat me on the
back. "Keep chewing," he whispered in my ear.

"Really?" Harry's grizzled face turned in my direction, eyebrows
raised in question.

I finished coughing and swallowed hard. "Of course, Harry. We'd love to have you."

I needed to make another run to the grocery store for the turkey anyway. I could buy an extra pie and some more stuffing mix.

Everyone focused on sandwiches and carrot sticks for the next few minutes while I did a mental count of chairs. Where would I put everyone? How had I become the hostess for this odd conglomeration of people?

Harry got up to put his plate in the sink and dusted his hands together. "That was tasty, I don't mind saying. Let's get those pipes in, why don't we?"

I lurched to my feet. "Come on, Micah. We need to pick up Kelsey from kindergarten."

He looked at his half-eaten sandwich and sighed.

"I'll watch him," Rose volunteered. "He shouldn't go out today. It's so cold. You'll give him earaches again."

I'd explained a dozen times that Micah's infant ear infections and need for tubes had nothing to do with going out in the cold. How was it that she found a way to blame me for every problem? *This is Kevin's mom. It's my job to make her happy.*

"Thanks so much," I said too brightly. "I'll be stopping by the store to get your cough medicine, so let Kevin know if you get tired. He can watch Micah." I'd bought her some strong stuff that hadn't helped either; so we finally called the clinic to ask the doctor to recommend something.

"I don't want you to go to any trouble." Rose suddenly looked lonely at the counter, surrounded by lunch fixings. We'd all blazed through in a hurry—not the pace of life she'd been used to in her little house in Florida.

I carried my plate to the sink and stopped near her. "You're family. You aren't trouble." And I gave her a gentle hug.

She stood stiffly and coughed. When I stepped away, her cheeks were pink, and I thought I saw a hint of a dimple appearing at one side of her mouth. Kevin had that same dimple. His was easier to see because he didn't have wrinkles hiding it, and because his smiles were usually wider and more frequent.

"It was sweet of you to invite Harry to Thanksgiving," I said. "I know he annoys you."

She sniffed. "It's a woman's duty to care for the less fortunate, even when it's unpleasant."

Leave it to Rose to turn a kind gesture into a put-down.

On the way to get Kelsey, I stopped to buy every brand of cough medicine I could find at the drugstore, including the expensive elixir the doctor had suggested. When I reached the church, I avoided the car-pool line. Instead, I parked and walked in to get Kelsey.

She skipped when she saw me and tugged my hand toward the bulletin board in her room so I could see some of her projects. Then we walked down the hall to the church offices so I could pick up a folder I needed.

Teresa swung in through the main entrance, dodged around construction tape, and met me at the office doors. "Oh, good. I was hoping I'd catch you."

All my well-rehearsed words flew from my mind like a flock of African cranes rising from the sand flats. "I was planning to call you this afternoon. Sorry I couldn't get back to you last night."

"So how many of the women in Mom's Time Out will be able to help? And can they all come to the meeting the Saturday after Thanksgiving?"

The shaky feeling started to return—the roaring in my ears and fear that I might cry. I blinked, letting myself picture Lori's hug, and Kevin holding my hand across the table. Then I looked at a point on Teresa's long nose—not quite able to meet her eyes. "I won't be able to coordinate it. And to tell you the truth, my young moms are all maxed out already. A lot of them are traveling or hosting company on Thanksgiving weekend, so that Saturday would be a big hassle for them."

In my peripheral vision, I saw Teresa's mouth drop open.

I took a step back, hoping to retreat.

"You can't do that. All of the staff are taking on extra work for this. We're all maxed out. That doesn't matter. Everyone is making sacrifices. We're suffering together for the faith."

Uncertainty tugged at me like a deep river current. But I breathed a prayer and met her eyes. "I'm sorry I can't help."

"What if we can't televise our program because of your decision? Have you thought about the people we won't reach?"

Now a full waterfall of condemnation beat on my head. I sucked in air and held firm. "Maybe if this project means ruining our health and hurting our families, it's not meant to be. Maybe God will reach those people some other way. We're a piece of the body, not the whole body by ourselves. We've been doing the part He's called us to. I'm not saying it's not a fine idea. Next year, if we have more preparation time, perhaps we can get the moms' group involved instead of doing our Christmas Tea. But we can't keep adding more things on to people, without subtracting something else."

Whew. Where had that speech come from?

Teresa stared at me as if she were asking the same question. Then she looked down at Kelsey, who was squatting by my cane and pulling the Velcro tabs of her shoes open and shut. I thought for a moment that Teresa's expression softened. But when she looked back at me, her glare was in full force. "This will hurt the morale of the staff." She bit out the words. "We need to be united."

"I'll be happy to discuss this with Pastor Bob . . . and with Tom, too." That was a scary proposition. "My job description involves ministering to the needs of our women . . . and they don't need a new project thrown at them. Most of them feel overwhelmed already."

Teresa didn't even answer. She yanked open the door to the offices and let it slam behind her. I decided not to bother fetching my folder.

I escaped to the van with Kelsey.

She sang to herself, swinging her legs in her car seat as I drove.

Was I wrong? Tom and Teresa were right in stating that many people in our community needed to hear about Christ. Shouldn't I "pour myself out" like the apostle Paul wrote? I felt hopelessly confused.

Lord, show me what to do. I'm in murky water full of crocodiles and hippos. There are tigers on one shore and hyenas on the other. I feel like I'm sinking.

Like light playing on the surface and drawing me up from the bottom of the river, a verse flickered into my mind from the gospel of Matthew. *"Love the Lord your God with all your heart and with all your soul and with all your mind. This is the first and greatest commandment."*

Oxygen filled my lungs as I sighed.

But what does it look like to love you, Lord? More time caring for my family, or more time reaching out to the community? There's not enough of me.

Another verse surfaced in my memory from our Thursday night group. We'd been studying 2 Corinthians 8. *"For if the willingness is there, the gift is acceptable according to what one has, not according to what he does not have."*

But some people can work full-time and manage a family and . . .

A scripture flowed through my mind, complete with melody. *"One thing have I desired of the Lord, that will I seek after, that I may dwell in the house of the Lord all the days of my life."*

Then the Mary and Martha story played out in my thoughts.

No, Lord. Not that old chestnut.

But the words were insistent. *"Mary has chosen what is better."*

Warmth permeated my tense muscles in a mixture of shame and relief. Working at Faith Church had been so all-consuming, I'd stopped focusing on *what is better*—on adoring Christ and drawing close to Him. How can someone so involved in the work of God forget to know Him, love Him, revel in Him?

As I pulled the van into the driveway, I stayed in my seat while Kelsey scrambled out of the car and raced to the house.

Lord, teach me to love you again. When I'm not sure of my decisions, at least let me live them out with love instead of duty or guilt. Guide me. I'm trying to listen. I want to hear you.

Tears began to journey down my face. Love and forgiveness wrapped around me in warm colors. One by one, I held each worry out to His waiting hands.

Chastened and refreshed from the prayer time, I opened the door and slid from the front seat. The November air had a bite, and I could see my breath as I planted my cane in the uneven gravel of our driveway. But my heart was warm.

Before I could reach the back door, it flew open. Kevin raced out and aimed for his Corolla.

"Where are you—?"

He skidded to a stop and saw me. "Mom's having trouble breathing. I'm taking her to urgent care."

Panic gripped me. Why hadn't I made a trip for the cough medicine sooner? Why hadn't I noticed how tight her breathing had been getting? "Do you want me to come?"

"No, someone needs to stay with the kids and get Dylan from basketball. Go help her down the steps. I'll pull up the car. Hurry."

Chapter Twenty-two

Whistling, I marched along with my pickaxe over my shoulder. It had been a rewarding day in the mines. I'd unearthed some large gems. Good thing, because we had more expenses ever since she moved in.

Not that I would complain. She fixed up our small cottage and found a hundred ways to give little comforts to the seven of us.

Of course, she was rather fanatical about cleaning, and Grumpy didn't approve a bit. But even he would have to admit our lives had grown brighter since she arrived.

In the lead, Doc entered the glen surrounding our home. "Shh. Let's go in quietly in case she's taking a nap."

Dopey opened the door, began an exaggerated tiptoe, and immediately tripped over his feet.

"Quiet!" we all shouted at him.

No sweet-natured woman skipped out to greet us, even after all our racket. We often heard her singing her way through her chores when we approached the cottage. Today we heard only silence.

"Do you think she went somewhere?" asked Sneezy. His hand brushed a vase of flowers, and pollen floated down. He began a fit of sniffles and snorts.

"She knows the woods can be dangerous. She wouldn't have wandered off alone, would she?" I asked.

We all looked at one another, fearing the same thing. Had we been too difficult to live with, after all? Had she decided she didn't want to stay with us?

Then Bashful poked his head into the main room. It took him some *time to get our attention, but finally he pointed urgently. We all raced forward.*

There she was. Napping in a very peculiar position on the floor. No, not napping. Doc tried to rouse her and couldn't. A shiny apple with a bite missing rested in her slack palm. She was pale as snow.

"She looks so white," I whispered to Kevin. Grandma Rose snored softly, propped up by hospital pillows. When we tiptoed farther into the room, she opened her eyes.

"What are you staring at?" She fumbled for the remote and found the button to raise the head of her bed. She tugged the sheet up to her chin.

"How are you feeling?" I eased down to sit on the side of her bed.

"I'm fine. I was fine all along. All I needed was some cough medicine, and I would have been fine."

I squeezed the bridge of my nose. I wanted to give all the arguments for why she was wrong, but she looked too frail to confront.

Kevin pulled up a metal chair and settled into it. "That's not true. The doctor said you were having a lot of trouble with your lungs again. Did he explain to you about using oxygen at home?"

She flapped a veined hand toward the tube below her nose. "I don't need it. I'd take this off, except then they all run in and cause a fuss. Did you bring my scarf? It's the cold Minnesota air that's been giving me trouble." She turned and stared at the curtain near her bed. "I should have stayed in Florida."

Kevin's skin turned pale around his mouth. The wounds of a little boy who failed to please his mother settled over his adult face.

My stomach knotted at his expression. "I'll get us some coffee. There's a vending machine down the hall." I patted his shoulder on my way out. Maybe Rose would mellow if I left the room.

I'd been terrified when Kevin called me from urgent care, telling me they wanted to admit Rose to the hospital. I was positive that our house's uncertain heating system, water problems, and construction dust had made her worse. Guilt poisoned my emotions as I remembered all the complaints I'd harbored in my mind about her. If I could magically free her from her illness, I'd do it. But I didn't know how.

As I squeaked along the hallway, coffee sloshed onto my hand. My other hand gripped the handle of my cane. I'd decided on only one coffee. Carrying two while negotiating my cane was too tricky.

I paused outside the room. Kevin's deep voice carried, even though it was twisted with pain. "But I always wished I could have stopped him. I should have done something."

I held my breath. A word of absolution from Rose would do a lot to heal Kevin's scars.

The bed creaked. "I'm tired," she said, her embarrassment clear in her tone. "Go find that wife of yours."

Kevin emerged from the room. "Thanks." He grabbed the Styrofoam cup.

We crossed the hall to sit in a small waiting area.

"Kev, are you okay?" I rubbed his arms, feeling the tension holding him together.

He tilted his head back and closed his eyes. "I'm fine."

He'd just been incredibly brave. He'd raised a painful subject with his mom. And she'd cut him off.

"It's good to talk about your feelings." I put some gentle teasing in my voice. Pastor's last Bible class had been about communicating, and the different needs and approaches of men and women.

Kevin was more talkative than most of my friends' husbands, but he often diverted conversations from anything touchy-feely. I tried to acknowledge that as his style, but it continued to frustrate me. Now I could see that his mom had him beat in the ability to hold firmly to denial.

He gave me a half-grin and pulled his head up so he could sip his coffee. "I *feel* . . . worried. I'm sad that Mom isn't feeling good. It bugs me that she still wishes she was in Florida."

I waited, but he took another drink and set down his cup. Then he picked up a newspaper and checked out the sports page.

"That's it?" I tugged the paper away. "You *are* allowed more than a dozen words."

He draped an arm around my shoulders. "Okay. I feel grateful that I have a wife like you."

I rested my head on his shoulder, content for the moment. If he needed to delve deeper into his psyche, it could wait.

Dr. Lorton exited Rose's room and spotted us. He pulled up a chair across from us and tucked a pen into his white coat pocket as he sat down.

My heart fluttered. He wouldn't need to sit down for good news, would he?

"Rose is ready to be discharged, but I wanted to talk to you about her follow-up. I advised that she go into a nursing home temporarily for rehabilitative care, but she is"—he fiddled with his stethoscope—"opposed."

"And I'm guessing that's an understatement," Kevin said dryly.

The doctor sighed. "Exactly. She has multiple health problems, and they exacerbate each other. The issues with her heart, blood pressure, arthritis—they all add to her susceptibility to infections and this recurring bronchitis. She needs to be monitored." Both Kevin and the doctor looked discouraged.

"But she's living with us now." I sat up taller, trying to look capable and efficient. "We can take care of her."

Dr. Lorton brightened. "Are you home all day?"

"Well, no. I work part-time, but . . ."

He rubbed his forehead. "She shouldn't be on her own. The social worker will be coming up this morning. She can talk to you about arranging some home health care support. But you may want to prepare Rose for the nursing home option."

Dr. Lorton checked his pager, gave us a chagrined smile, and hurried away.

Kevin rubbed the back of his neck and groaned. "She despises nursing homes. She's not healthy enough to be living on her own. And she hates living with us." He turned to me, eyes heavy with fatigue and worry. "Where does that leave us?"

I took his hand, sharing his helplessness. "I could quit my job." They were empty words. We needed the income—and the tuition for the kids' school that my job provided.

Kevin squeezed my hand. "It wouldn't be right. You're finally doing work you've always dreamed of. And you're good at it."

Something in his tone snagged my attention. Like a magic mirror on the wall, I quickly offered him reassurance. "So are you. You're the best."

He drained his coffee and crushed the cup. "Right." He tossed the Styrofoam toward a nearby trash can. He missed. Without looking at me, he shoved to his feet, scooped up the cup, dropped it in the can, and crossed the hall to his mom's room.

From this distance, the changes in him were easy to see. His bouncing confidence had flattened into a weary heaviness. For months now, he'd been laughing less, tussling with the kids less, frowning more. I'd noticed a few changes, but the shift had been subtle and gradual. Until this moment, I hadn't realized how different he'd become.

Lord, something is wrong with Kevin. It's not only worry about his mom. It's not only because I've been so busy lately. Something else is wrong. Please show me what it is, and how to help him.

A scared little voice deep inside me added a plea I hadn't wanted to allow . . . even in my thoughts.

And please save our marriage.

Had it come to that? Was our marriage in danger? Some instinct in me warned that whatever else was demanding my attention, I needed to focus on Kevin. He needed me right now.

I gave them a few more minutes and then approached Rose's room.

"Of course I'll stay through Thanksgiving. Becky needs my help," Rose was saying. "But the apartment building I like has a one-bedroom unit opening up on January first." She patted Kevin's arm. "I don't want to be any trouble, but could you help me find a company to move my things that day? Then I'll be out of your hair."

I moved into the room and stood behind Kevin. "You aren't in our hair. We want you to stay with us." Even I could hear the weariness in my voice that contradicted my words.

She made a face. "No offense, but I'm not used to all the . . . chaos. I'm getting too old to have children running everywhere—and for all the rushing around."

My head drooped forward. She wasn't making a token excuse because she felt like a burden. She honestly wasn't comfortable living with us.

I'd failed her. And because of that, I'd failed Kevin.

"I better go pick up the kids." I leaned toward Kevin. "Let me know what ideas the social worker has," I said quietly.

He gave an absent nod. "See you later."

I moved closer and dropped a light kiss on Rose's forehead. "I hope you feel better."

My kiss was hardly a magic touch to rekindle life . . . but Rose did give me a weak smile. "I'll be fine once I'm out of this place."

Later that night, Rose was settled in her room with a nebulizer, oxygen, and a bell to ring if she needed us. The weekend in the hospital had exhausted her. Our children had responded to the aura of serious illness and been subdued for a change. They didn't argue at bedtime. Dylan even offered to read a story to his younger siblings while we gave Rose her medicine.

The bed creaked as Kevin and I climbed in for the night. I tugged down the hem of my extra-long nightshirt, covering the scars at my knee.

Kevin didn't seem to notice. "Wow. It's only ten, and the whole house is quiet." He kicked off the quilt. We'd fiddled with all the vents to keep the kids' rooms warm, but now our bedroom had become a sauna.

"So what did the social worker say?"

"She said an assisted-living facility would be a good compromise. But I've already checked into those. With her social security and the money from selling her house, she could barely afford a normal apartment on her own. The assisted-living apartments are a lot more expensive, depending on how much care the person needs."

I rubbed my leg, which had begun to throb with each surge of my pulse. "Maybe I should find an assisted-living place for your mom and me to share. I'm going to need medical supervision soon." My joke fell flat.

Kevin propped up on one elbow. Our night-light cast a warm glow on his cheeks, but his eyes were shadowed. "This has been hard on you." His voice was rough with emotion.

Sudden tears stung my eyes, and I turned my head, not wanting him to see them.

He ran a finger down from my temple to my chin and turned my face toward him. "You've been amazing. You've tried everything."

I blinked, wishing I could see his eyes more clearly in the dark. "But?" My throat felt so thick, I had a hard time asking the question.

He shrugged. "It's not your fault."

"What?" I searched his face. "Please, talk to me." *Stop shutting me out.*

He sighed. "It's late. It's been a crazy day. Let's get some sleep. It can wait."

Right. Because tomorrow would be so much more tranquil. Judy was coming, Harry would return to rattle our pipes, and a health care worker would stop by to check my skills on the medical equipment. I was sure there'd be plenty of opportunities for Kevin to tell me what was bothering him.

I lay awake and listened. In a few minutes, his breaths were deep and even. Another tear trickled down my face and hit the pillow. I heard a loud plop and for a moment thought my tears had become as weighty as they felt. Then I realized it was the faucet in the bathroom. The water continued an irregular metronome while the emotions of the day trod circles around my brain. I was feeling so many things I couldn't keep them straight. Worried, lonely, scared. Grumpy, dopey . . . and finally, sleepy.

Chapter Twenty-three

The curved walls of the drainage tunnel seemed to shrink around me. My feet splashed through inches of runoff and sewage. I ignored the smell and pushed myself to run harder. Every sound echoed against concrete, reminding me of the clang of prison doors sliding shut—reminding me of how the justice system had failed me.

My mouth tasted bitter.

A scrape sounded far behind me, loud enough to be heard over my gasps for breath.

I reached an intersection. Faint light appeared down one corridor. The water ran toward it. Maybe I'd found my way out.

"Give it up, Mrs. Miller." An annoyed voice rang from somewhere in the darkness behind me. "There's nowhere to go."

No. They weren't bringing me back now. I had to find out who had really committed the murder, or my life was over anyway. The chance to escape was worth any risk.

Still, my anger exploded past my panic. "It wasn't me. I didn't do it," I yelled with all the grief, fury, and helplessness of the past few months.

A moment of surprised silence answered me. Then the same voice. "I don't care."

Fine. They were the ones who had turned me into a fugitive. Any doubt about my choice to flee dissolved. I raced toward the light, hobbled by the pain from the prison bus crash that had freed me.

The opening appeared in front of me, blinding me after my journey through the tunnels. I reached the circular rim and pulled up short.

Below me, water flowed out to join a massive surge. Hundreds of feet *below, the water broke into a violent cauldron of rocks. I heard footsteps sloshing closer behind me. There was nowhere to go. I wouldn't let them take me.*

Taking a deep breath, I launched myself into the pounding spray.

"Where is she?" The voice came from a distance.

A doorknob rattled, but I ignored it, letting water drown out my tension. I reached for the shampoo. The new water heater had been installed, and I planned to enjoy every minute of my escape.

"Mom?" Little fists pounded the door.

I thrust my head out of the shower curtain to make sure the ancient hook-and-eye lock was holding. "I'm in the shower."

"But Dylan hid my Barbie car."

"That's nice."

"Honey," Kevin's voice joined the bloodhounds baying in the hall. "Do you know where the tablecloth is? Mom said she wants to iron it."

I winced as soap stung my eyes. Iron a tablecloth? At eight o'clock in the morning? Rose was supposed to be resting. Tablecloths, cloth napkins, candle holders and other holiday decorations—they all would have qualified as rarely used items when we decluttered our old house in October. "Probably in the Dominican Republic."

Finally, blessed silence took over outside the bathroom door. Not that they had me fooled. I knew that the minute I stepped outside, they'd be after me again.

Mothers were pursued with more passion than criminals on the lam.

"Does this milk smell sour?"

"Where are my favorite jeans?"

"I can't find the Cheerios. Are we out?"

"He hit me—touched me, looked at me, breathed the same air as me."

"She's bugging me. Do something."

"Someone's on the phone."

Usually when I was desperate to escape, I could find a few minutes of peace in the bathroom, but today they'd discovered my hiding place.

After a quick rinse, I shut off the water.

The pipes shrieked and shuddered. Harry was making progress, but he hadn't tackled the upstairs bathroom yet. Yesterday I'd overheard Kevin and Harry debating about how much tile would have to be broken out. I had quickly stuck my fingers in my ears and started singing, "La-la-la. I don't want to hear this."

They had ignored me.

Now I wrapped a robe around my damp skin and limped across the hall to confront my closet. Yesterday I'd missed my Monday work hours because of spending the morning at the hospital. That meant I really needed to stay and work after I dropped off the kids. That meant choosing nice slacks and a sweater.

But Micah's cold was worse. And I needed to be around in case the health care worker showed up early.

I reached for a comfortable sweat shirt.

Wait. Teresa was already mad at me. I'd refused to take on extra projects, but I at least needed to carry out my normal responsibilities.

I pulled my tan Dockers from a hanger.

This was crazy. Rose needed to be coaxed into resting, and Kevin and Harry wouldn't be able to watch Micah while they worked on the plumbing.

I put the pants back on the hanger and grabbed my most comfortable, frayed jeans. It was the Tuesday before Thanksgiving. I had a million things to do here at home. Church would have to survive without me.

I stared at my jeans and suddenly wanted to burst into tears. How could it possibly be this hard to decide what to wear? I sank onto the edge of the bed.

God help me. I'm really losing it. Where do you want me today?

A wave of calm stilled my panic. My family needed me. These

were extreme circumstances, not a pattern of missing work. Just because I took an emergency morning off didn't mean I was sliding down the slippery slope of laziness. Besides, I could work on my newsletter article and return some phone calls from home.

I pulled on the jeans and slipped the sweat shirt over my head.

Heavy feet clumped up the steps. "Hey. I'm shuttin' the water off."

When had Harry arrived? He was getting to our house earlier each day. "Okay," I called.

The footsteps retreated, and I fell back onto the bed.

I should really do my stretches. I tried hugging my knee toward my chest, but pain stopped me. In spite of taking the anti-inflammatory pills off and on, the old injuries were getting worse. Kevin had been right. All the stairs in the new house had been rough on me. I hadn't realized how much easier our rambler had been. I'd been so excited to buy this house. Had I been wrong?

I squeezed my eyes shut. Too late to think about that now. We had our dream home, and we needed to make it work.

Lord, our new house would be a bigger answer to prayer if you would heal my leg so I can chase my kids up and down the stairs.

"Mom, come on." Dylan jogged in place in my doorway, playing with the zipper of his coat. "It's my turn to do devotions at school. I can't be late."

I propped up on my elbows and smiled. He looked more like Kevin every day. Same restless energy and enthusiasm. In spite of Dylan's recent behavior problems, Faith Christian School had been a good fit for him.

"Do you have your basketball stuff?"

He rolled his eyes. "I told you. I keep it in my locker."

Bet that smelled good. Sweaty practice clothes and gym shoes in a confined space for weeks at a time. At least he hadn't had to miss practice because he forgot his gear.

"Where's Kelsey?"

"Feeding Mr. Harry."

I groaned. Kelsey had a good heart, but she could destroy a kitchen in five minutes flat. "Tell her to get her backpack and coat. I'll be right down."

I stood up and reached for my cane. I wiggled my leg as an experiment. Nope. Not healed yet.

One step at a time. *Lord, get me through this day.*

And I was off and running. Well, limping. Chased by the panic that I'd forget something important or let someone down. The odds of that seemed to grow each day.

I settled Micah on the couch with a *Veggie Tales* movie. Kevin said he'd keep an eye on him if I hurried back. I dropped off Dylan and Kelsey at school and popped into my office to pick up a few files. I was about to flee when a form loomed in my doorway.

Teresa.

"Hi, Becky. How's your mother-in-law?"

I swallowed, wondering if I could dodge to one side and get past her. "She came home yesterday afternoon. I'm meeting with a health aide later, because she'll need some extra care for a while." I tried to edge around her, but Teresa wasn't moving.

"I'm glad I caught you." Teresa stepped closer.

I backed up. "Well, I—"

"I need to apologize." She sat on the edge of my desk and played with her watchband.

Surprised, I stopped trying to plan a quick route to the parking lot. "Why?"

"You probably noticed I was kind of . . . upset with you. It bugged me that you weren't putting the church first."

I chewed my lip. "I'm sorry that—"

"But when I quit being mad about it, I realized . . . Well, nobody knows about this, but Ben and I have been talking about starting a family." She looked up suddenly. "Don't tell anyone."

"Okay . . ."

"And I didn't see how kids could fit in. You know how church work takes over your life."

Especially with someone as ambitious as Teresa calling the shots. And I only had to work with her a few days a week. She had to live with the Teresa-drive in her head 24-7. Sympathy mingled with my confusion.

"So . . ." She stared at her watchband, tugging and releasing the gold segments. "Thanks."

I blinked, not sure what she was talking about.

She beamed at me, gave me a quick hug, and raced out the door.

Must be something in the water today. I stuffed the files into my bag and limped out into the hall. I had to make it to my car before any other people stopped me for bizarre conversations.

The parking lot of the strip mall near church was crowded, but I found a space near Discount Party Place. A couple of bright paper tablecloths would disguise our kitchen table and the card table I'd need to use for Thanksgiving. For good measure, I grabbed a wicker cornucopia. The kids could fill it with little toys to symbolize things they were thankful for.

The day was turning out pretty great after all.

When I got home and carried in my bags, I was in such a good mood, I didn't even groan when I spotted Judy's suitcase at the bottom of the stairs.

"Don't take your coat off."

I jumped at the sharp command. "Judy, don't scare me like that."

"I need a mocha Frappuccino. You're taking me."

"While you're job hunting, you should really consider law enforcement. You're great with the giving orders thing."

She ignored my sniping and grabbed my arm, guiding me back out the door. "We'll be back later," she called to the household in general.

"Wait. Where's Micah?"

"He crawled in bed with Rose, and they're reading *Winnie the Pooh*." She tugged. "Come on, everyone is fine. Believe it or not, the house can survive without you for a few minutes."

A loud, splintering crash sounded from upstairs. Apparently, work on the bathroom was under way. I stopped resisting and followed Judy out of the house as fast as I could.

As I turned the van around and headed down our long driveway, I longed for the familiar warmth of Betty's Tea Shop. But that was my old neighborhood—my old life. Instead, I drove back to the strip mall and the closest Starbucks.

People scurried in and out. Animated discussions rose and fell from small tables scattered in front of large windows. After we settled at a table, I studied Judy.

She was coifed and stylish as usual, with a crimson pashmina draped around her neck. But her eyes were red-rimmed, and a small muscle on one side of her mouth kept twitching.

I placed a hand over her coffee. "I don't think caffeine is a good idea. You look like you need a long nap instead."

She batted me away. "Har, har. Look who's talking."

"Okay, I'd love to trade insults all day, but I have to get ready for Thanksgiving. So, what's up? How was New York? How many corporations are fighting to snatch you up?"

She blew across her cup and took a careful sip. Then she leaned forward from her hips and drilled me with her out-of-my-way-world stare. "Right. Let's do this." She drew a deep breath. "I'm ready."

"Ready?" What was she talking about? Was everyone batty today?

She sat back and crossed her arms. "Yeah. You've been waiting for this for years. I'm ready. Lay it on me."

"What?"

"The God stuff."

I choked on my coffee. When I recovered, I took a careful peek at her face to see if she was serious. *Lord, help me here. She means it. She wants to hear about you.*

"So New York didn't go so well?" I asked slowly.

One side of her mouth pulled up. "Good guess. Got it in one."

I waited for more explanation.

Judy sighed. "Okay. All those friends in high places . . . They aren't so friendly now that I'm not a VP of Marketing. And I'm not like you. I don't have life outside of work. Work was my life. After a bunch of useless interviews, I was feeling like . . ." She pinched her lips together. "I mean, feeling crummy. I thought maybe . . ."

"It's time to try God?"

She wrinkled her nose. "It sounds weird when you say it like that. Don't give me a hard time. Just give me the facts. How do I do this?" She gripped her chair arms as if I were about to reveal torturous initiation rites.

Lord, help me.

My skin felt flushed, and I could count each heartbeat doing double time against my ribs. I'd prayed for this opportunity for a decade. In recent years, she'd become less sarcastic when I'd mentioned God—especially since my car accident. She figured suffering gave me more credibility. She'd even come along with us to church occasionally when she was in town visiting. But she had always yawned through the service. I knew what it was costing her to expose her desperation, and I didn't want to mess this up.

"Okay. Well, God loves you and—"

"Come on, sis. Give it to me straight."

"What?"

"The hoops to jump through." She pulled out her PDA and tapped the stylus on a few keys. "I know how it works. You go to church, stop swearing, donate some money. What else?"

I wanted to bang my forehead against the table. "Judy, knowing God isn't about jumping through hoops. That's the whole point."

She frowned at me.

Foam floated on the top of my drink, and I poked at it with a plastic spoon. "We can never do enough to earn a relationship with God."

"Sounds like a losing proposition, then. What's my incentive to try? The perks? The take-away?"

I shook my head. "You don't have to try anything. He loves us."

"And He sent Jesus to die on the cross, and somehow that fixes everything." She rattled off the words.

My mouth sagged open.

"Don't look so surprised. I saw the revival of *Jesus Christ Superstar* on Broadway. I'm not totally ignorant."

I struggled to remember what the musical conveyed about Jesus. Probably not the most accurate theology.

"So you know what happened. Jesus died in our place, so that our relationship with God could be restored."

"Yeah, I get that. But why do I want a relationship with God? What is the cost-to-benefits ratio?"

Didn't everyone want to know God? Didn't everyone feel that empty place? Maybe not. The world was busy and noisy enough so that we could ignore our misery, believing that God would invade and disrupt our lives too much if we let Him in. I'd known Him for many years, and I still slipped into that way of thinking.

I cleared my throat. "Cost to benefits? It's a gift. A free gift."

Judy's eyes narrowed.

Holy Spirit, help her understand. Help me explain. "We stop pushing Him away and give Him our broken, messed-up lives. He gives us—everything. Forgiveness, hope, eternal life, purpose, constant love."

"Why? What's in it for Him?" Her voice was raspy.

I struggled to hear her amid the hiss of coffee machines and laughter at nearby tables. I leaned forward. "You. You are unique and special and loved by Him. He wants a relationship with you."

Her eyes widened. Surprise and longing flickered across her face. *Lord, she's so close. She's so hungry for you.* Was the fugitive going to stop running? My throat felt thick with emotion.

A cash register drawer clanged open. Coffee beans whirred in a grinder.

The vulnerable expression on Judy's face shuttered, and she scraped her chair back a few inches. "I don't buy it. There's got to be a catch." She stood up decisively. Conversation over.

Once again, I'd faced an opportunity to save someone . . . to fix her deepest problem. And once again, I'd failed. The growing burden of defeat made my limbs feel like lead as I followed Judy out to the car.

Chapter Twenty-four

Rain drummed *against the dark pane of glass above my head. I squeezed my eyes tight and tried to imagine away the cobwebs and dreary bits of furniture.* With hard work, I could believe I was resting on a beautiful couch with down pillows. I could picture a bookshelf where bare rafters now stood. But no matter how hard I tried, I couldn't imagine away the cold.

I pulled my tattered black shawl around my shoulders and fought back tears. "Oh, Daddy, I've tried to be a good soldier."

It wasn't the silk party dresses that I missed. Or the beautiful rooms that had once been mine. Or even my pony. I didn't need those things.

But I couldn't live without my father. And no matter what they told me, I wouldn't believe—

"Becky Miller, stop your dawdling. Cook needs you to scrub the pots and pans." The head mistress glared at me from the doorway. "And Miss Judy wants more coal."

I scurried to obey. I needed to finish my work so I could slip away. I had to find my father.

As soon as Cook was busy elsewhere, I ducked out the door and raced down wet London streets to the army hospital. A new ship had arrived with more wounded. I hurried up broad stairs and past the soldiers at the door. It had taken earnest pleading, but now everyone was accustomed to my visits and let me pass.

I hurried into the first ward. Iron cots filled every space. Bandaged soldiers filled every cot. Longing filled my heart. He had to be here. He had to. I'd never believe he was dead. And when I found him, he'd hold me and call me his little princess.

Tears of yearning sprang from deep in my soul and washed down my cheeks. I buried my face into the comforter. Kneeling was painful, but this morning the weight of my loneliness had pushed me to the floor as I prayed.

"Lord, I miss you. This world wants to convince me you're dead, but I know that's a lie. I know you love me. I know I'm your dearly loved daughter. But life has been feeling like a cold, dark hovel. I feel so alone. Help me see you again."

Knuckles tapped lightly against the bedroom door. "Becky? It's time to go if we don't want to be late for church."

"Coming." I'd begged Kevin to give me some time. My devotional life had been squeezed out like so many other things. But I knew I'd never get through this Thanksgiving Day if I didn't grab a few minutes of time to pray. He'd gotten the kids ready and steered them away from my door.

Tuesday at Starbucks, Judy had continued to balk when I tried to explain the notion of grace. When we got back to the house, I felt drained . . . and inadequate. No wonder I had trouble telling her that God alone could forgive, heal, renew, and give meaning to life. Judy had seen me slaving to heal, renew, and renovate everyone who crossed my path—to the point of anxiety and exhaustion.

"So what do I do?" I stared out the window and struggled to my feet. "Quit? Quit my job? Quit trying to help Rose or Lori or Judy? Quit reaching out to Kevin? Quit parenting the kids?"

The door creaked open. "Honey, are you okay?"

I dashed the tears from my cheeks and turned.

Kevin looked delicious in his suit. He tugged at his tie. "We're going to look silly dressed up like this."

I smoothed the creases from my long skirt. "Come on. It's a small concession."

Kevin's mom had announced she wanted to come with us to the Thanksgiving Day service. Our parishioners tended to dress casually, but in honor of Grandma Rose, I made sure we were all wearing our holiday best.

Kevin ran a finger under his collar. "She's not going to like it if the praise band is playing today."

I limped toward him and adjusted his tie. "Stop worrying. I think it's great she feels up to coming. And that she wants to. Has she said much to you about her faith?"

Kevin rubbed his forehead. "Not a word. It's not something we ever talked about. I tried once after I became a Christian in college. It's like I'd broken the golden rule. Never discuss religion, money, or politics. How was your prayer time?"

I sighed. "Okay, I guess. Thanks for running interference for me."

He shrugged. "No prob. But why didn't you wait? You could pray at church—" A grimace crossed his face. "Never mind. Forget I said that."

He knew better. These days I did very little praying at church. Faith Church was my workplace. Everywhere I turned people needed to ask me questions. Every announcement in the bulletin reminded me of projects I was working on.

I followed Kevin down the stairs. The scent of roasting turkey reached the living room. The card tables were decorated and ready for our afternoon feast. We crossed to the kitchen on our way to the back door.

Judy stood by the kitchen sink, studying a glass of water. "The water still tastes funny."

"At least Harry got it turned back on for the day. What are you doing up so early?"

Dressed in a slim skirt and blouse in dappled autumn colors, my sister gave me a tentative smile. "Figured I'd start jumping through those hoops."

I opened my mouth to argue, but she lifted her hand. "Don't start. I know you claim there aren't any, but I have to do this my way."

I wanted to tell her that following Jesus had little in common with the Sinatra song, but I didn't want to squelch her interest. "Okay. Let's go."

On the drive to church, the melody crept into my brain. I couldn't shake the phrase. *Lord, is that my problem? Am I doing it my way? I don't mean to.*

Kevin pulled the van up to the church's main entrance. We emerged like clowns from a circus car. When I slid open the side door, Dylan, Kelsey, and Micah exploded out first. I reached in to help Grandma Rose. She wobbled and leaned on my arm. I braced us both with my cane. "Are you sure you don't want to use one of the wheelchairs? The church keeps several near the entry."

Her chin squared off. "Don't be ridiculous."

I didn't push the issue.

Judy climbed out and stared up at the church, throwing back her shoulders as if she were about to enter a boardroom for a tough business negotiation.

We waited for Kevin in the entryway while I struggled to explain the scaffolding and building supplies to Rose, keep Micah from toddling away, and introduce Judy and Rose to various friends.

Teresa spotted us and sailed straight through a cluster of chatting families toward us. "Becky! Happy Thanksgiving. This must be your mother-in-law." She grabbed Rose's hand. "It's so nice to meet you. I'm glad you're feeling better. We were all praying for you."

Instead of jerking her hand away, Rose pinked up and murmured a greeting.

"Teresa, this is my sister, Judy."

"Becky's told me all about you. And this is my husband, Ben." Ben wove through the crowd and stopped at Teresa's side to catch his breath.

Judy threw me a grin and turned back to Teresa. "Well, I hope you keep my sister in line."

Teresa gave an exaggerated sigh. "I try." Then she turned to me, vibrating with energy. "Did you hear? Pastor Bob got Tom to calm down and start planning for next year's Christmas program instead of this year's—thanks to you."

I felt creases deepen in my forehead. "Tom couldn't have been happy about that."

"Pastor told Tom we'd be doing a special vacation Bible school outreach this summer. That cheered him up."

Kevin stomped through the front doors and blew on his hands. "Whew. It's getting cold out there."

"And here's Mr. Becky Miller," Teresa crowed. She edged closer to Judy. "Becky has been an amazing blessing to our church." She led Judy away, still raving about me.

Ben slapped Kevin on the back. "I guess we're just the trophy husbands around here." He laughed and then hurried to follow Teresa.

I glanced at Kevin. His polite smile was frozen, and there was no humor in his eyes. I reached for his hand. It felt cold.

He pulled away and picked up Micah in one arm. He offered the other arm to his mother, and we made our way toward the sanctuary.

We were waylaid several times. When a young mom hurried over to tell me how much the Mom's Time Out group meant to her, I wanted to scream.

Don't fuss over me. Can't you see my husband's face?

But she couldn't see his stormy expression because he kept walking and followed the kids into a pew without me.

Somehow I nodded and smiled when I needed to and eventually was able to enter the sanctuary. Kevin didn't look at me once through the whole service.

Is he jealous of all the people who demand my time? That's not fair. I give the bulk of my time to him, his mother, his kids.

Does he feel like a "Mr. Becky" at church? That's ridiculous. He has his own career. His own skills.

God, there's a battleground between us, but I can't even figure out what it is. Give us a chance to talk. Help us.

A crazy prayer when I was about to host a houseful of people. Suddenly the thought of getting through the day made me want to cry.

Deliberately, I began to count my blessings. Rose and Judy were both here in church. Kevin had a job. My kids were healthy and happy—even if they were too squirmy. And we had a plump bird in the oven and several pies on the counter waiting for us at home.

I'm not sure if it was my efforts at soldiering on, or if everyone had absorbed some goodwill from the church service, but our Thanksgiving dinner actually went better than I expected.

Harry arrived in slacks with a collared shirt under a sweater. Without his stained bib overalls, he looked almost distinguished.

I served the food buffet style in the large kitchen. Everyone dished up food and carried plates out to the tables in the living room. The kitchen table plus a card table, end-to-end, created a grand dining room.

Kevin led us in a time of prayer. Rose and Harry remained silent, but Dylan attempted to thank God for everything on the planet.

Judy was seated next to me and squeezed my hand. "And thank you for my sister."

I blinked back surprised tears and cleared my throat. "Amen."

Kevin's chilly mood began to thaw after his first helping of turkey and mashed potatoes. He laughed as Harry told a story about the last time he'd been up north deer hunting. But when conversation moved on to home renovations, Kevin stopped eating.

"Yup, it's tough fixing it piecemeal this way." Harry burped and reached for another roll. "Too bad you can't move out for a month, bring in a crew, and get it finished."

"Well, we can't." Kevin shifted, bumping the card table and making the water glasses shiver. "So can we finish plumbing out the upstairs bathroom this weekend?"

I froze with a fork of stuffing halfway to my mouth, eager to hear his answer. Seven of us sharing Rose's half bath was no picnic.

Harry scratched his neck. "I got nothin' better to do."

"Well, at least you've made yourself useful." Rose folded her napkin. "Too many people retire and sit around being a burden."

Harry guffawed. "You should visit Eldercare Estates. Folks there do lots of stuff."

"Is there a swimming pool? The doctor said it would be good for my arthritis. And I'm looking for an apartment. I've got one in mind, but I'd look at some others."

"You needin' an apartment?"

"No, she's not." Kevin stood up. "The doctor doesn't want her living alone. Becky, can I help you get the pies now?"

I pushed out my chair, making the table lurch again. "Good idea. Who wants pumpkin, and who wants cherry?"

Harry ignored us and turned to Rose. "At Eldercare, they have what they call these 'assisted living' options. You can have someone check up on you or help you with things. But you still have your own place."

Kevin let his breath out in a huff. "Mom, we've talked about this. Medicare doesn't cover that." He glared at Harry. "Since the ladies did all the cooking, why don't we go dish up the pie?"

Amiably, Harry shuffled from the room with Kevin.

I slid my chair close to the table again. "So, kids, why don't you explain the things you put in the cornucopia?" I spoke loudly to cover the sounds of Kevin's gruff voice in the kitchen.

Micah lurched forward from his booster chair. I grabbed him before he could crawl onto the table. He pointed to a small stuffed turtle. "Animals. I like animals—can we get a dog?"

"Good, Micah. We should thank God for animals." I ignored the plea-for-a-dog clause that he'd been putting into all his conversations lately.

"I put my hair in it," Kelsey said.

"What?" I turned the cornucopia. Sure enough, a blond curl rested near the turtle.

"What does it mean? What are you thankful for?"

"I'm thankful I have pretty hair like Aunt JuJu." Kelsey gave a coy smile in Judy's direction.

I pushed my brown locks behind my ears and let the two blondes have their moment.

"Okay, Dylan, it's your turn."

"I put in my dead beetle, because I like science. And some of my baby teeth 'cause I'm thankful for food."

Judy stared at the centerpiece with alarm and edged her chair back from the table a few inches.

"Wanna see? On one of them, you can still see the blood. Remember, Mom? That one that bled a lot? There's still some on the tooth."

"Okay, I think it's time for pie." I shouted the line as if it were a stage cue.

Harry entered, looking chastened from his conversation with Kevin in the kitchen. He carried a platter with several small plates of pie. "Who wanted pumpkin?"

Rose and Judy lifted a hand. As soon as Kelsey saw Judy's choice, she raised her hand, too.

"I want one of each," Dylan shouted.

Kevin came in next with a platter of cherry pie. The tendon in his jaw was pulsing, but he tried to hide his tension.

Everyone dug in, and conversation moved on to safer topics. Judy's gaze shifted between Kevin and me, and she tapped a long fingernail against the table in a worried Morse code.

I picked at my slice of cherry pie. *Lord, Kevin and I need to talk. Please. Make a way.*

"I have a great idea." Judy turned in her chair, resting an arm on the back in a languid pose.

Everyone shifted focus to her. She might be out of work, but she still knew how to command a room.

"Since Kevin and Becky have welcomed us into their home and provided this great meal, I think we should all do the clean-up while they go for a little walk." She sent me a dazzling smile.

229

Wow. How was that for a quick answer to prayer? And from my sister, who was never sensitive or selfless. My spirits lifted.

Until I turned to share my smile with Kevin.

The side of his fork drove through the crust of his pie, sending fragments exploding. The hard lines of his jaw spoke as loudly as his frown. Going for a walk with me was the last thing he wanted to do.

Hurt grabbed my stomach and twisted. When had I become the enemy?

Chapter Twenty-five

"I can't do this." His voice was as sharp as the creases of his suit.

I gave the man before me a tender smile. "Of course you can. You'll love Paris."

He turned away, framed by the huge desk and glamorous artwork of his Manhattan office. He was a man used to being in control. Commanding corporate empires.

It was endearing to see him uncertain.

The past week had been a whirlwind. When I'd returned from a year in Paris with a new haircut and newfound confidence, his younger brother had first swept me off my feet.

But somehow this man edged his way between us, captured my heart, and invited me to fly to Paris with him.

Love surprised me and triggered delicious hopes. When I was a child, watching him from my perch over the mansion's garage, this man had awed me—even frightened me. Who could have guessed that I would be the one to draw him out of his cold world of work and success?

Now he spun to face me. The lines of his face tightened. "No. I can't do this."

His sneer stunned me. I stumbled back a step. "What do you mean?" My words came out breathless.

"It was a lie. All of it."

An uneasy laugh escaped my lips. He was joking. Playing some strange game. I shook my head. He should know I wasn't sophisticated enough to keep up.

His expression softened for a second, then closed off. "I was sent to deal *with you." His voice was cruelly bland. "To keep you away from my brother. You were . . . unsuitable. Don't you understand? There is nothing between us. Nothing."*

Black despair edged my vision. I felt dizzy, as if all the wind had been knocked out of me. A lie? I'd given my heart to this man. How could I have been so wrong?

"I told you, it's nothing." Kevin tugged his ski cap farther over his ears.

He was lying to me, and Thanksgiving dinner suddenly felt like a stone in my stomach.

The sun was low in the sky, with tatters of gray clouds diffusing the light. Behind us, the pines shimmied in the growing wind while the driveway stretched before us, rocky and uneven. Kevin offered his arm.

I closed the snaps of my collar against the cold and tucked my mittened hand into his elbow.

Lord, I don't want to say the wrong thing. I don't know what's going on. I don't know how to fix this. Help me.

We reached the end of the driveway. "Doing okay?" Kevin glanced over.

I tested my bad leg with a little shake. "I'm fine. It feels good to walk after that big dinner."

"The turkey was great this year."

"Thanks."

We picked our way along the shoulder of the county road. I sniffed and wiped a mitten across my nose. "Smells like snow's coming."

"Yeah. Remember that one Halloween when we got a couple of feet in one day?"

"Yep."

Kevin kicked a small stone and sent it skittering ahead of us. "Once we get snow, the kids can sled on the slope behind the house. That'll be great."

But as he said the words I could feel his mood sag downward like fog on the Seine. A clue.

"It's the house, isn't it?"

He stopped short. "What do you mean?"

"Well, something's been bothering you." A pickup drove past, stirring the gravel. Then silence settled around us.

His eyes finally met mine. Bleak, lost. "You aren't going to let it go, are you?"

"I'm your wife. Your best friend. Mother of your kids." I nudged him. "You're supposed to tell me stuff." I smiled, desperate to coax him out of the inner place to which he'd exiled himself.

His lips twitched. "I am? Was that in the marriage vows?"

"Yep. Love, honor, and talk."

His smile widened. Then he offered his arm again and we continued walking.

I braced myself for whatever he would say next.

We walked for a full minute while he gathered his nerve. "I'm tired of being a failure," he said at last.

I stumbled. "A what?"

"The house is a disaster. And it's taking too long to make the repairs."

"What did you expect? You work full-time. Of course it's going to take a while to fix it up."

"And my mom is—"

"You're awesome with her. I'm so sorry I—"

"Sorry? I'm the one who's sorry. I know it's not easy for you having her in the house. And if I made a better salary, we could find a good assisted-living place for her."

I stopped and planted my cane in front of Kevin. "You're doing the best you can. You're a great provider. You're making amazing progress with the house. You're a wonderful husband and father. And a great son to your mom. And we *will* get the house fixed up. The apartment your mom wants doesn't open up until the first of January. We have almost six weeks to make her more comfortable and convince her to stay. We can do this. Board by board. Paint bucket by paint bucket."

"Becky, you don't get it."

"Sure I do. You feel like a failure, and I'm telling you you're not."

"I'm a third-level manager in a third-rate territory of a third-place insurance company. Nothing to write home about."

How many ways could I reassure him? Aggravation pressed against my temples, making my head throb. *Easy, Becky. Don't blow it. He's finally talking.*

"Wanna know a secret?" I scuffed the toe of my boot into the gravel. "I thought you were disappointed in our marriage. In me."

"Why would you think that?"

"Because our life is so chaotic, and I haven't been able to make your mom happy—"

He snorted. "No one could make her happy right now. She's lost her independence, and she's furious."

"And because church was taking up too much of my time, and because of what Teresa called you this morning."

"Mr. Becky Miller?" He tugged the ends of my scarf and tilted his head downward for a quick kiss. "I'm proud of you. You've done a great job at our church. You have a lot on your plate. You have a lot of different roles to balance. I understand."

Sounded like he was reading a script from the *Supportive Husband Handbook.* He was going through the motions, but his eyes kept avoiding mine. I wrapped my arms around his puffy winter jacket. His answering hug felt as insubstantial as our relationship lately.

We turned and looked back at our house. The porch stretched wide with welcoming arms. In the dusk, the edges of clapboard blurred like a Monet painting. Light glowed from the many front windows—our own city of light.

There was every reason to feel content and hopeful. Instead, I felt uneasy. We began to stroll back up the road. "Kev?"

He gave an unencouraging grunt. We'd reached his limit of

heartfelt revelations, but I wasn't ready to end the conversation.

"Are you sure that's all that's been bothering you? Your job, the house, your mom?"

"Isn't that enough?"

I chewed my lower lip. "If you're not mad at me, then what . . . I mean . . . things haven't been good between us."

"Hey, we're on overload lately. With Mom and Judy around all the time. Harry. Not to mention the kids. We never have time alone. That's all."

"No, that's not all." A lump began to rise in my throat, but I wasn't going to stop now. "People make time for what matters to them. But you've been . . . We've been . . ." A tearful hiccup escaped.

Kevin picked up his pace. "We're fine."

"No. No, we're not." I struggled to keep up with him. "You've been pulling away."

"You're imagining things." He hunched his shoulders against another biting wind gust.

"Then why? Why have you avoided me?" My tears felt hot against the cold skin of my face.

He stopped. "I didn't mean to. But . . ."

"But what? What did I do?"

"Nothing." He cast a longing look toward the house, but I wouldn't move.

"I didn't want to see the disappointment in your eyes," he blurted out.

"What?"

"I dragged you to this messed-up house. I've seen how much pain you're in." His gaze darted to my leg and cane. "I couldn't protect you then, and I can't fix things now."

I thumped my hand against my gimpy leg. "This wasn't your fault. And the only way you've hurt me is by shutting me out." My voice rose, tight with months of confusion and worry. "I've been so lonely. It's like we've been on different sides. Like you thought I was the enemy."

"Don't be silly. I just don't like feeling helpless."

"Why didn't you tell me what you were feeling?"

He bristled. "You've had enough going on. I didn't want to be another burden."

I stuffed my fists into my coat pockets so I wouldn't swing one his direction. "So you thought you'd make me feel better by—what? Easing out of my life? Avoiding me? Yeah, that made me feel terrific."

"Sorry." His affronted tone was anything but.

"You should be. You've been insulting me."

He stepped back and thrust his fists into his pockets, as well. We squared off like two straitjacketed boxers ready to butt heads. "What are you talking about? I've never insulted you."

"Yes, you did." My eyes lasered his. "You decided what I could or couldn't handle. You didn't trust me. You didn't talk to me. Do you think my life is easier when you play Mr. Strong-and-Silent? I had no idea what was going on. I didn't know if . . ." My words choked off as serious tears ran down my cheeks. Fury and hurt poured out with them. I dropped my chin and watched gravel and sand swirl through my tears like an Impressionist's watercolor. "Don't do this to me," I whispered.

His arms gathered me close. Sobs wrenched from me, and I burrowed into his chest. All the fears, all the guesswork, all the worst-case scenarios that had been tormenting me broke loose.

"It's okay." His hoarse words resonated through his chest. "We're fine."

"I felt so lonely." I tossed back my head and studied his face. Were we really fine? What other things were eating at him . . . threatening our marriage? "We've been through this before. Don't hide things. Even if you're trying to make it easier on me."

He gave me another squeeze and released me. "You worry too much. I love you. That isn't going to change." Rote words.

Designed to soothe me like a pat on the head.

Something cold hit my eyelash. I looked up. Fat flakes of snow had begun salting the air. I stuck my tongue out trying to catch one.

Kevin managed a half smile. "We should head back. You're getting wet." He offered his arm again.

I leaned into him, feeling drained and still uneasy.

We paused in the driveway to look up. Snowflakes shimmered as they tumbled toward us.

"Beck, if you want me to tell you everything, there's something else you need to know."

"What?"

Kevin pressed his foot into a light coating of snow and pulled it back to study the imprint. His bleak look had returned. The hero who hadn't slain the dragon. "I don't know how to say this." He looked at our house. The red-shingled roof was dappled white with a first layer of snow. "The repairs are taking too long. We're in debt up to our eyeballs. It's not working. We need to get out while we can. Sell the house and put this mess behind us."

"Mess? It's our home."

He didn't answer.

"If we sold the house, where would we live?"

"I don't know, all right?" Impatience flared in his eyes. "Get an apartment until we find a house we can afford."

The suggestion felt like a fist to my stomach. "After all the work we've done?" *And all it represents.* "We can't give up. We'll be worse off than where we started. And what about your mom?"

Kevin turned away from me and faced the house. His chin dipped. "We can't do this anymore."

"Why on earth would you stop trying?"

He turned up his collar, effectively disconnecting his arm from mine with the gesture. "Let's not get into this now. We have company." He mounted the porch steps, knocked the snow from his shoes, and marched inside without looking back.

Kevin's words pierced me with fear. Did he think our marriage was a failure, too? If he wasn't willing to fight to save our dream home, maybe he wasn't willing to fight for our marriage either. Isn't that what I'd been feeling in the past months? The growing apathy? As if our love wasn't worth the effort anymore? Indifference inflicted a crueler wound than anger.

I swallowed my pain and trudged into the house. Kevin might be resigned to the emotional distance between us, but I wasn't. I still had some fight left in me.

Chapter Twenty-six

Several scrawny chickens scuttled across the yard as I shook out a freshly washed apron to hang on the line. I hoped the laundry would dry before Sabbath. *Where was that husband of mine? Probably stopped to chat with the rabbi, or dawdled to give away milk to some beggar who couldn't pay. These days, half the peasants in Russia fit that description.*

The jangle of the horse's harness drew my gaze. My husband was pulling his wagon up the lane, while his horse limped along behind. I rolled my eyes. More problems? A lame horse would make it hard for him to make his deliveries, and we needed every penny. Bad enough we had a house full of daughters and no dowries for them. We didn't need to go hungry, too.

I followed my husband into the barn.

"*If this is how you treat your friends, no wonder you have so many enemies,*" *he was muttering toward a point on the roof.* "*Would it spoil some eternal plan to send some riches this way?*" *He hefted a bale of hay into the stable.*

"*The matchmaker came today.*" *I crossed my arms and faced him.* "*You have to speak to our daughter. She could have a good husband. A butcher. But she says she's in love with the tailor.*" *The result of giving too much education to our girls. He spoiled them, and now they had no regard for tradition.*

"*Becky,*" *he said in a thoughtful, puzzled voice.* "*Do you love me?*"

"*Do I love you? What kind of question is that? Haven't I cleaned your house all these years? Cooked your meals? Raised your children? Milked the cow?*"

"Of course I love you," I insisted. "I want our marriage to work."

"Are you sure?" Quiet, resolute, Kevin confronted me with a question that I didn't want to look at too closely.

We'd endured the tense hours of entertaining our guests. As soon as everyone was tucked in bed, Kevin and I retreated to our room. My husband was ready to kiss and make up—his favorite way to solve any conflict. But I had perched on the blanket chest near the window, arms crossed, and insisted we talk about our problems. That was when he blindsided me with his question.

I felt affronted, insulted. "How can you ask me if I love you? Don't I take care of the kids, do the laundry, make suppers, give you emotional support, warm your bed? Didn't I offer to take in your mom?"

"That's just it." Kevin sank onto the edge of the bed and stared at the wall. "It's a duty. You do it because you think you're supposed to. Like all the other things you're so busy with."

"Don't be ridiculous," I snapped.

He took a slow breath, his shoulders caving in like Dylan when he couldn't solve a math problem.

Understanding pushed its way past my irritation. He meant it. Pain twisted around my heart and squeezed my lungs. "Kev, I do it because I love you."

"When you can fit me in." The eyes he lifted toward me were flat and empty.

I gasped and hugged a pillow to my chest as if it could stop the flow of blood from his lethal words. "That's not fair."

"You wanted to have this conversation. You begged me to tell you what was wrong. Now you don't want to hear it."

I swallowed. "I'm listening." Inside my skull, arguments and explanations gibbered, but I forced myself to silence them.

The mattress groaned as Kevin shifted to face me. "You're so busy fixing everyone, it's like you aren't even here."

Answers feel incredibly empty when they're spoken with the tired conviction that nothing will change, that knowing the reason for the problem won't solve a thing. Kevin had finally stopped brushing off my worries about our marriage. He was telling me what was wrong—but in a bleak voice that tempted me to join him in a mire of hopelessness. Fear twisted my stomach.

"You need more attention from me?" I asked carefully.

He gave me a level stare. "I don't want to be one more chore on your to-do list."

A tap sounded on our door, and the hinges creaked. Dylan trudged in, scowl first. "I don't feel good." He shuffled toward Kevin.

I intercepted him. "What doesn't feel good?"

"My stomach. I think I'm going to throw up."

I guided Dylan toward the bathroom. Behind me, Kevin sighed. Well, let him wait. Did he expect me to ignore our kids? After a few sips of ginger ale and some cuddling, Dylan decided it was a false alarm and I coaxed him back to his bedroom.

"How many pieces of pie did you eat, kiddo?"

"One," he said, wide-eyed and sincere.

I'd seen him eat two, and he probably grabbed more while Kevin and I were on our walk. Stuffing himself silly wasn't a big deal. After all, it was Thanksgiving. But telling lies *was* a big deal. So I launched into Mommy Lecture #601—complete with *The Boy Who Cried Wolf* and several appropriate Scripture verses. Not surprisingly, Dylan was soon sound asleep, innocent lashes dark against his cheeks; light, whuffling snores rising and falling with his chest.

I gave myself a moment to savor the sweetness of his face, free from snarling looks, rebellion, or guile. Kevin might complain that I was trying too hard to fix everyone, but I didn't see him doing anything about Dylan's behavior problems.

Are you letting him?

One of the hazards of a house after everyone else was asleep— God's quiet heart-whispers carried over the silence. I shuffled back to my room and found Kevin fully surrendered to turkey coma . . . and sprawled across our entire mattress. I shook my head and padded downstairs. My rocking chair was a good place to stew and direct a few thoughts toward God.

Lord, you're taking Kevin's side? Look at everything I do for this family. And he has the nerve to say he doesn't feel loved?

Why do you serve me?

Same reason. I love you.

Or?

It needs to be done. Someone needs to do it.

Ah.

As simply as that, my self-important busyness appeared in a stark floodlight—no longer dressed up in spiritual-sounding excuses. Kevin was right. I'd gotten lost somewhere, playing God. Thinking it was my job to fix everyone.

I shivered and pulled a polar fleece blanket from the couch to wrap around my shoulders. The tables had been stripped of their paper tablecloths and holiday decorations. The dark room felt bleak and empty.

But, Lord, it's a woman's job to take care of people. I can't help it. It's tradition. You made me like this.

Do you think you need to do my job?

Well, if you aren't doing it.

The faithless answer coming from my own mind shocked me to the marrow. Was that my core belief? Did I feel that God couldn't handle running the universe without my meddling?

Tears wove warm paths down my face.

Change my heart, Lord. Forgive me. Help me trust your timing, and your varied ways of bringing about your will. I trust you to heal our marriage, save our home, lead Judy toward you, guide our church, care for the women's ministry, strengthen my leg, watch over Rose, comfort Lori, work in our children's lives.

Whew. No wonder I'd been feeling lost and exhausted.

Help me stop trying to do it all in my own strength. A wry smile pulled my lips. *I admit it. I'm not you.*

Did I hear God's answering chuckle? I tugged the blanket around me more tightly.

I'm tired of thinking the universe can't run without me. I'm tired of feeling self-righteous about how much more I'm doing than anyone else. I'm not the only one who can do things the right way. Help me stop serving you for the wrong reasons. Let whatever I do be done in love.

I watched branches outside the dark windowpanes fidget in the wind like restless children, then calm so that snow could cling and coat each twig. I let my heart calm, as well, and felt peace coat my thoughts. Strange. None of my problems was solved. Yet standing against the strength and wisdom of God, each need shrank in its ability to badger me, drive me, terrify me. I suddenly understood the line from Browning's poem, "God's in His heaven, all's right with the world."

I prayed for a while, watching the snow flicker in the moonglow outside; then I pushed my stiff body out of the chair. I could sleep on the couch, but I hated the thought of explaining to Rose if she got up for something and spotted me. I limped up the stairs, pausing with each step as my knee screamed in pain. When I reached the bed, I nudged Kevin's back and managed to slip in to curl near him. "I'm sorry, honey," I whispered. "Don't give up on us."

The next morning before the rest of the house stirred, I locked our door and woke Kevin by twining myself around him. He was kissing me before he was fully awake.

I leaned back at one point. "I know we still have things to work out. But I love you. Okay? I love you."

He growled happily and pulled me close.

Later, we nestled under our quilt. I tried to tell him about my prayer time. The things God had shown me were hard to put into words.

"I thought this house would make our family a better team." I nuzzled my nose against the warmth of his neck. "But I've been acting like a team of one. Doing everything my way."

He stroked my hair. "So, should I call the real estate agent and get the house up on the market?"

"We could," I said quietly. "But I have an idea. Could we hold out a couple more weeks?"

He propped onto an elbow and stared down at me. "Do you really *want* to hold out a little longer? Things have been pretty insane around here. And we'll fall further into debt."

I pictured us packing up and moving far from the home we loved, like villagers loading their wagons and leaving Anatevka. "I think it's worth the risk." I grinned. "Let's give ourselves a few more sunrises and sunsets before we decide."

Chapter Twenty-seven

The ground hummed beneath our feet—a strange, heavy vibration. The pounding of collective hearts tortured by fear? The motley assortment of men certainly looked afraid enough to cause the earth to shiver. This loose alliance of clansmen had little love for the Scottish nobles about to lead them into battle. Some men were already turning to leave.

The rumble grew.

We saw the spears first, sprouting from the horizon. Then the horses. English soldiers in full armor added to the massive stallions' weight. They shook the ground—shook the last remnants of courage in the men.

The lords were pitiful in their eagerness to surrender. To lick the boots of the tyrants who had destroyed our country.

I rode forward, breaking through ranks until I could face the men. Several gaped in confusion or awe. With the blue woad of ancient Picts on my face, I hoped to summon forth the fierce heritage that had won these lands.

"You've come to fight for freedom. Will you run or will you fight?"

Rank upon rank of the English army filled the hillside across from us. The men's gazes held the fearsome sight and seemed to forget their purpose.

"Leave, then. Die in your beds. And spend each miserable day of your lives knowing you chose to surrender." I guided my horse along the rows of men in tattered plaids.

"Or fight."

Hope kindled. Men gripped their swords with more resolve.

My voice rose with the rage of years of injustice. "Yes, you may die. But you'll die as free men."

The men roared, pounding their shields.

"We won't surrender. We won't let a few problems defeat us. Right?"

The army of volunteers in our living room shouted their response. "Right!"

I nodded, satisfied. "The building inspector is coming on Monday to sign off on our new plumbing and the new wiring. We're going to be ready."

Kevin nudged me. "You're having way too much fun with this."

Noah's teeth gleamed from his teddy bear face. "Let's do it!"

Lori and Doreen grinned at each other and rolled up their sleeves. Our house seemed ready to burst with helpers—my Bible study girls and some of their husbands, a few friends from Kevin's work, and several from our church. I wasn't sure how they'd all be able to work at once. But Harry had drawn on his old contracting skills and had coordinated an agenda—our own mini-version of a home makeover show.

During my Thanksgiving night prayer time, the idea had formed like an inspired battle plan. The solution was simple. Finish the major improvements, get the new mortgage with low interest, happy ending.

At first Kevin had been less than thrilled by my insight. His exact words were, "What do you think Harry and I have been working our tails off doing?"

Lacking in the asking-for-help gene, Kevin failed to see the obvious.

We needed to rally the troops.

I might have a lot of inadequacies, but I was good at rallying troops. A few dozen phone calls, a few bribes, a few threats, and in the week and a half since Thanksgiving, I'd raised an army.

Today my heart warmed to see so many friends eager to help us. This wasn't a tragedy on the level of tornados, fires, or floods. We'd just gotten in over our heads. Yet they were willing to help because they cared about us.

Judy was conspicuously absent. She had invited herself over to

Heather's house. She needed to do some "networking" and couldn't get good cell phone reception at our homestead. I'd noticed the same wireless problems after we moved in. We seemed to be in a communications black hole. However, it didn't bother me, since I could always make calls on our landline. Being unreachable by cell phone enhanced our out-in-the-country ambience.

Rose was settled in her room with a stack of DVDs to watch on her little television. She had wedged a rolled towel along the door to block out Sheetrock dust and paint fumes, and had her nebulizer close at hand. We were installing a handicap-accessible shower in her bathroom, and I'd tried to interest her in the decision making. But when I showed her pictures of fixtures, she would only shrug. "Makes no difference to me. Don't go to this trouble on my account. I won't be here much longer." I assumed she was referring to her stubborn plans to move out and nothing more dire, but with Rose it was hard to tell.

Sally's daughter, Chelsea, had been recruited to play with the assorted children, including mine. Sally tugged on her pink rubber gloves and faced her daughter. "Remember. Don't let any of them escape. All people under twenty have to remain in the living room. It'll be the only safe room."

"And no tea parties," Dylan growled.

Chelsea looked down her nose at Dylan, a prim imitation of her mother. "We'll see what everyone else wants to do. I thought we'd start with paper dolls."

A cheer rose up from the little girls of various ages, and from Micah, who loved any chance to play with scissors.

"Mo-om." Dylan turned to me. "I could help Dad with the pipes."

I rubbed his buzz-cut hair back and forth. "Sorry, bud. I need you to help keep all the kids in the living room. But you can set up your Hot Wheels, okay?"

He jerked away from my hand and muttered a word under his breath. I decided to believe I'd misheard, because this wasn't the time to confront him. But as he stomped to the basement to get his box of Hot Wheels, I sighed. His temper was on a short fuse all the time, and I didn't know what to do about it.

Lori, too observant by half, walked over and threw an arm around me. "He's had a lot to adjust to. Grandma Rose, the new house, new rules. Kids have trouble with change."

"I know. And Kevin's been so busy repairing things, he hardly ever tussles with Dylan like he used to."

"It'll get better. Now, where do you want me?" Lori's eyes were bright with energy.

Too bright? Was her laughter strained? Were the muscles in her face unusually tight? Was she barely holding herself together? I found myself second-guessing when I was around Lori these days. When she was happy, I wondered if she was putting on an act, or escalating into an emotional intensity that would bleed the sanity from her. When she was quiet, I worried that she was trapped in the dark clouds again.

"Are you sure you're up for all this chaos?"

"Puh-lease. You want to see chaos? You should see our house when we host the homeschool association art class each month."

"Yeah? Well, I bet everyone is a budding Picasso," I said sourly. Sometimes I couldn't hide my annoyance at the brilliance of the homeschooled kids I knew. My irritation was just a cover for my own insecurities, but knowing that didn't always help. Would Dylan behave better if I homeschooled him?

Right. I should stop working and homeschool my kids. I should work full-time because that would help our budget situation. I should quit work so I could care for Rose. I should put in more hours at church because the needs are huge and immediate. Oh, and I should also do mission trips like Heather.

There was no way to win this mental tug-of-war. *I'm learning, Lord. I can't do it all. So reassure me that you've got it covered.*

I brandished my cane like a sword. "Let's get our orders from Harry."

And we plunged into the battle.

It was amazing what a ragtag bunch of untrained home improvement warriors could accomplish in a Saturday. Lori and I kept up a steady stream of sandwiches and coffee, and slipped away to paint one of the upstairs bedrooms when we had the time.

Harry had scrounged some bargain insulation and had a couple of men in the attic rolling it out. He promised the extra padding would improve our heating issues.

The upstairs bath had suffered from a lack of attention in the past two weeks. Remnants of smashed tiles, bare studs, and rusty pipes surrounded my once majestic claw-foot tub. I had wanted to cry every time I walked past and saw the destruction. I was thrilled that the bathroom was at the top of the day's priority list.

Sometime after the lunch break, Lori and I were painting trim in the bedroom across the hall while a great deal of clanging went on in the bathroom.

"Noah, help me carry up the backer board," Kevin called from the stairs. "As soon as Harry finishes the pipes, we'll get that in. I can do the first coat of mud tonight."

"Mud?" I looked at Lori. "Are they giving it a facial?"

Lori giggled. "Don't ask. Have you got any more masking tape?"

"I think there's some downstairs."

She glided from the room, and I put down my paintbrush and stretched, rubbing the small of my back. Beyond the newly installed windowpane, an inch of snow coated the slope around the house, the porch roof beneath me, and the pine trees along the north side of the house. The beauty flooded me with so much awe that it swept away the ache in my back, persistent throb in my hip, and weakness in my knee.

The day buzzed along with determination and good-natured chatter. Spending time with Lori was an added blessing. When she returned with more tape, we talked about everything and nothing, erasing the distance that had stretched between us over the past few months. Optimism swelled in me with each stroke of my paintbrush.

Until the phone rang.

I pulled the cordless from my overalls and held the receiver an inch from my paint-splattered face. "Hello?"

"Mrs. Miller? This is Mrs. McLain."

Dylan's teacher. My stomach dropped. "What can I do for you?" Maybe she just needed cupcakes for the class Christmas party.

"I hate to bother you on the weekend, but I wanted to update you on some issues with Dylan."

I moaned. "What's going on?"

Lori glanced at my face and tiptoed from the room, closing me in with paint fumes and impending mother-failure. I settled onto a stepladder, wishing Dylan was as easy to fix as chipped paint.

Mrs. McLain remained perky and encouraging as she filled me in on the latest problems. But even her positive attitude couldn't hide the fact that Dylan had been losing his temper, lashing out at classmates, and blowing off classroom assignments.

"It's not that he's doing badly. His grades continue strong. It's his attitude toward others. He's . . . impatient. Now, I'm sure you're familiar with our school policy on behavior problems."

Sure. Because I'd had loads of spare hours to read the two-hundred-page manual distributed on parent night each year.

"Um, could you remind me?"

"He's been given a warning, and some extra assignments. This is the phone-call-to-parents stage. But if we have another incident, you'll need to come and get him and schedule a meeting with the principal."

Lovely. Nothing would instill the congregation's confidence in the Director of Women's Ministries more than the news that her fourth grader was a delinquent. "I understand. I'll talk to him. We've had some disruptions in our normal routine, and maybe that's why he's acting out."

Pleasantly thanking each other for a conversation neither of us enjoyed, we finished the call, and I grabbed a paint rag to blot the sweat on my forehead.

This was progressing beyond a simple surly stage. What was I going to do to help Dylan? And when had my joyous little boy disappeared?

The door swung open and Harry pounded into the room. "Oh, sorry, missy. I was looking for Kevin."

I waved my rag toward the door, not trusting my voice at the moment.

Instead of ducking back out, Harry took another careful step into the room. "What's wrong, if you don't mind me asking?"

"Nothing. Dylan's just acting up at school." I tried to convince myself, as well as Harry, that it was no big deal.

He gave a sage nod. "Boy needs time with his dad. That's what he needs." And he lumbered out of the room.

I gave a strangled laugh. Great solution. Too bad Kevin wouldn't see it that way. Our house had become a battleground as we worked to settle in. We had fickle allies in our ranks—Rose, Judy, and Harry sometimes made me feel like we were losing ground as a family, not gaining.

Lori came back into the room and handed me a lemonade. "You looked like you needed reinforcements."

"Thanks." I took a long drink and then looked closely at Lori. She didn't seem too tired. She just seemed like Lori. But I hesitated to share my little problems. She'd battled some terrifying foes in recent months.

"You want to talk?" Lori pulled over a large spackle bucket and sat on the lid.

She had always been able to read my mind. "Are you sure you want to hear my silly problems? I mean . . ."

She gave me her fiercest don't-mess-with-me Zulu-warrior glare. "We've been over this before. It helps me to be a reciprocal friend—to feel useful. I promise I'll let you know if I'm ever not able to handle hearing your stuff. Okay?"

Gratitude soothed the sore places in my mother-ego. "Thanks. It's about—"

Suddenly the phone rang again.

Lori grabbed my glass. "Go ahead. I'll get us refills." And she disappeared.

Fearful, I punched the Answer button. "Hello?"

"Becky, what are we going to do?" Jill's voice was panicked. My Mom's Time Out nursery coordinator was a bit high-strung but rarely hysterical.

"What's the problem?"

"Didn't you hear? We lost two of our volunteers. I've tried everyone on our substitute list and can't find anyone for this Wednesday. And with the Christmas Tea coming up, none of the moms can miss the session on Wednesday. And—"

"Whoa. Jill, take a breath."

She gave a shaky laugh. "Okay. Breathing. But seriously, what are we going to do?"

Becky Miller, clan leader, mounted her steed. "Leave it to me. I'll figure something out."

A gasp of relief rewarded me. "Thanks so much. I'm out of ideas. Let me know who you find and how long they can volunteer. We could really use at least one full-time teacher for the older group. We have a lot of moms with kids in afternoon kindergarten, so they bring the five-year-olds to the morning Bible study."

"Don't worry. God knows what we need."

A few minutes later, Lori was back with more lemonade and a brown bag. She reached in and pulled out two extra-large Milky Way Dark bars. "When the going gets tough, the tough get chocolate."

We giggled and then tried to stifle our laughter so no one else would come to check on us and find us with our mouths full of chocolate . . . especially since Lori hadn't brought enough to share with everyone else.

"You are the best friend ever," I mumbled through a big bite of gooey calories.

"I know."

By the time our volunteer army had devoured pizzas for supper, I was feeling a lot less stressed about the condition of the house. Walls had been scraped and painted. Floors had been sanded and polished. The upstairs bathroom was on the way to being reassembled with plumbing that actually worked. Insulation promised us better temperature control.

As I carried a bucket of paint out into the upstairs hall, the lights dimmed, then flickered back up. Harry stood watching the fixture and scratching his head. "Don't like the looks of that. Oh well, there's always tomorrow."

"Don't worry, you'll get it fixed." I gave Harry a big hug, surprising myself as much as him. "I don't know what we'd have done without your help."

He turned red from his neck all the way up to his bald spot. "Oh, that husband of yours knows his stuff. He just doesn't have time to get it all done." He hurried down the stairs before I could embarrass him further.

Kevin bounded up the steps and spotted me. He grabbed me and spun me in a tight circle. "Honey, you're brilliant. It's amazing how much progress we made today."

I let myself bask in my success as a wife and renovator for a few minutes before drawing my thoughts back to my two current problems.

I'd need to tell Kevin about Dylan's school problems so we could sit down with our eldest for one of the serious talks that all kids hated. And I had to find some new nursery volunteers for the Mom's Time Out group—fast.

But first, I needed to get the blue paint off my face.

Chapter Twenty-eight

The clink of glasses and murmur of convivial conversation told me that the audience was in a good mood. I hovered behind the curtain, trying to tamp down the butterflies that threatened to fly right up my throat. A quick peek proved that the tables were full with guests dressed in their best finery.

We'd been booked to sing for the ski season, but without snow, audiences had been sparse. The hotel was in danger of closing.

"Come on," my sister hissed from the wings. "It's almost curtain."

We'd pulled together the best show we knew how. Great music, big dance numbers, amazing costumes and sets. The boys had called in favors to all their old army buddies. They'd bribed and cajoled to get a big crowd.

Would it be enough to save the general's inn? The guys wanted to help him, but the general would skewer them if he felt like an object of charity.

The orchestra lifted the overture above the sounds of chatter. Lights dimmed. The audience grew quiet. I tugged the sleeve of my costume and winked at my sister.

As the curtains slid open, the blinding spotlight found us. Polite applause welcomed us as we began our act.

In the past, our goal had been to get noticed, get bookings into better clubs, and maybe find a little romance. But tonight I was singing my heart out for a bigger purpose.

Stage snow sprinkled us from overhead. Regardless of the weather outside, in here we could celebrate a white Christmas.

"It's Christmas!" Kelsey proclaimed while jumping up and down on our bed.

"Huh?" Kevin rubbed sleep from his eyes and tried to sit up, but he was tangled in the sheets and comforter that were pinned in place by one of my legs. "Not for three weeks. G'back to bed."

I reached for my cane and slipped out of bed, then limped to the window. "Wow."

Several more inches of snow had fallen during the night, covering everything in sight. Even the county road was a distant blur of white. The wind scooted drifts into meringue peaks. We were inside a snow globe, and I could feel the sparkle of glitter in my heart.

Kevin joined me by the window and sneezed. "I hope they get the roads cleared so we can make it to church."

So he didn't have a poetic nature. He had plenty of other good qualities. I tickled his ribs. "Let's make cocoa for breakfast. I think we have marshmallows."

Kelsey cheered and scampered off to tell her siblings.

We savored our breakfast while we watched birds leaving tracks as they hopped under the oak. By the time we'd cleared the table and gotten the kids dressed, we heard the plows out on the road.

I tapped on Rose's door, then peeked inside. "Do you want to come to church this morning?"

She wheezed a greeting but waved me away. "Too cold out there."

"Okay, we'll see you later. Do you need anything?"

"Stop fussing. I'm fine."

I pulled her door shut gently and went to help the kids find their mittens and boots. Kevin grabbed the keys and went out to start the van. He came back inside a few minutes later, looking dejected.

"What's wrong?"

He slumped into a kitchen chair. "I don't know why I was so dumb."

"Hey, don't call my husband dumb. What's up?"

"They plowed the roads."

"And that makes you sad because . . . ?"

He raked a hand across his head. "Because our driveway isn't a road. It doesn't get plowed. The whole quarter mile of it is buried. We're stuck."

I gaped at him. How had we both overlooked this potential problem?

"Um, if the kids and I help you shovel?"

He grated his chair back. "Be my guest."

The magical mood of the morning turned brittle. I searched for some words of consolation but came up empty.

Knowing we'd never make enough progress to matter, I still told the kids to bundle up. It took several minutes to locate all the boots and mittens. Eventually they stood in a row like three well-insulated astronauts, barely able to bend their limbs. I zipped up Micah's snow pants and tied his scarf.

"Mommy. Need potty."

Of course he did. Dylan and Kelsey shifted impatiently as I began the tedious undressing process on Micah. By the time I got him to the bathroom and bundled back into all his gear, Kelsey and Dylan had shed a few layers.

"All right, kids. Back in your mittens and boots."

Suddenly, a horn tooted from the direction of the road. A roaring sound approached the house. Kevin and I hurried out onto the front porch.

Harry's disreputable truck pushed its way toward our house with a battered plow fastened to the front. It shoved aside the snow as we watched the progress. When he finally reached the shed that served as our garage, he turned off the truck, opened the door, and thudded down to the ground. "Thought ya might need to get plowed out. Folks who haven't lived in the country don't always think of it."

He pulled a paint-tarp bundle from the truck, marched up the porch steps, and nodded to Kevin. "Might wanna get yourself a plowing service. I don't think a big shovel would fit on your little car."

Harry stomped the snow from his boots and headed into the house. Kevin scooped snow from the porch rail and packed it together, then threw a vicious curve ball at the nearest tree. Dylan wasn't my only man with a short fuse.

I slipped my arm around his waist. "Maybe there won't be much snow this year."

He groaned. "We can't afford to pay for plowing. And I can't even afford a snowblower . . . not that one of those would do much good."

"Let's worry about that later. It's too late to head to church now, anyway. We can let the kids build some snowmen, and you and Harry can get a jump on today's projects."

"Folks, ya comin' in, or what?" Harry bellowed from the living room.

Kevin planted a quick kiss on my cold forehead. "You're right. One thing at a time."

We went into the house and found Harry surrounded by our children as if he were a backwoods Santa. "So this friend of mine at the lumberyard was gettin' rid of his old things, and I figured . . . it's about time Dylan . . . when I was his age . . ." He seemed to run out of words. Instead of saying more, he set his bundle on the floor and peeled back the tarp.

The sharp edges of the box he revealed had enough rust to guarantee a fatal case of tetanus. The metal clasp was crooked but somehow held the lid closed. Dylan fell to his knees and wrenched the top up. "For me?" His squeal was a welcome change from his recent surly tones. We all stared at the serious tools inside: a hammer, screwdriver, wrench, level, and miscellaneous hardware I couldn't identify. And was that a power drill?

"But . . ." Giving my hot-tempered boy heavy tools that could smash walls or siblings was a big mistake. I had enough stress.

Kelsey and Micah collapsed to the floor with Dylan as he lifted each item and examined it with reverence.

"What's that for?" Kelsey pointed at a chisel and looked at Harry.

Harry scratched the side of his face. "That's for Dylan to figure out. His dad will teach him."

"What's it for, Dad?"

Kevin shrugged. "You can use it for lots of stuff. I'll show you sometime."

Some of Dylan's excitement faded. "When?"

Harry tugged on his overall strap. "When you're helping your dad with the remodeling."

Kevin threw a startled look at Harry. "We'll see," Kevin hedged.

"Can we go out and play. Please?" Micah and Kelsey lost interest in their brother's new treasure and grabbed their mittens.

"Yes. But stay close to the house. Don't get in any trouble." Yeah, like that warning was going to do any good.

"Let's build a tree house," Kelsey screeched.

Dylan hefted his toolbox. "Sure. I can do that."

Micah nodded and galloped in place. "Me too!"

Harry cleared his throat. "Sorry, kids. Dylan, these tools have to stay inside. Don't want them gettin' rusty."

Dylan's face darkened for a moment; then he patted the dented metal and made a nod of decision. "Okay." Kelsey and Micah raced outside, but Dylan took the time to carry the box up to his room before putting on his boots and joining them.

Once all three kids were squealing in the snow, I glared at Harry. "What were you thinking? He's not old enough to handle all those tools. Some of them are sharp."

For someone of his bulk, Harry was able to slink quickly toward the safety of the kitchen.

"Kevin?" I redirected my stern look toward him. Someone had to stop this nonsense.

Kevin had the gall to laugh—a deep belly laugh. "Did you see Dylan's expression? How proud he was? Maybe Harry's right. Maybe it'll help him."

I'd told Kevin about the call from Dylan's teacher, but we had been so tired last night, we hadn't gotten far in discussing what to do. "But it's like rewarding him for getting into trouble. And who's going to make sure he's safe with them? Sure, he'll promise, but you know good and well that it'll be one more job on my plate." I tried to rev up my indignation.

Kevin gave me the weary shrug he'd been using too often lately, all humor drained from his face. "I'll teach him how to be careful with them."

When? During all that time you spend with him?

I managed to bite back the words—barely. But he might have seen me roll my eyes as I turned away. I stomped to the kitchen, put on a pot of coffee, and gave Harry the silent treatment.

Sadly, that didn't seem to bother him.

A few minutes later, Dylan came inside. "I'm ready to start working on the house. What do we do first?"

Harry turned his chair and faced the eager eyes and rebellious cowlicks beneath Dylan's ski cap. "You know, having your own tools is a big responsibility. You can only use them when you're helping your dad. Keep 'em locked up safe the rest of the time. Can ya do that?"

Dylan nodded, eyes somber.

Harry sniffed and wiped his sleeve across his face. "And ya gotta take good care of them. A man's tools say lots about him."

Something loosened around my heart, and I took a deep breath as I watched my son's earnest face.

"I'll take good care of them." No knight ever took a more sacred vow.

I gave up. "Fine. You can keep the tools. Go ask Dad what he needs help with first."

Dylan's smile split his face. "Sure, Mom."

I slumped into a chair. "Harry, you should have talked to us first."

"Sorry." His face turned a shade ruddier. "I'll be sure and do that next time. Is that coffee ready?"

Hopeless. It was all hopeless. No one listened to me. I had no control. Life was a crazy stage production.

So why did I feel happiness tickle through me? If all the world's a stage, could it be that I had the best role? Too many lines, to be sure. Too much slapstick. A good dose of melodrama. But over all, light cast a warm glow on the boards, the greasepaint smelled sweet, and somewhere in the distance I heard the sound of applause. Best of all, I was learning that I didn't have to be the director.

Rose shuffled out to join us, cinching up her quilted bathrobe. "What was all that commotion? I thought you were leaving for church."

"We couldn't get out because of the snow. But Harry came and plowed our driveway. And he brought Dylan his own toolbox."

Rose nodded as if it all made perfect sense. She tapped Harry's shoulder. "Do you have something for me?"

Harry sent me a worried glance. "Yep." He reached into his pocket and pulled out a mangled envelope that he handed to Rose. Then he cleared his throat and made a rapid exit stage right.

Suspicion bloomed. I tried a light approach. "Getting love letters?"

She gathered her dignity around her like her robe. "From that north-woods oaf? Please."

"Then what . . . ?"

"Nothing you need to worry about." She grabbed a mug of coffee and retreated to her room.

I needed to talk to Kevin. She was up to something. But first, I needed to find volunteers for the Mom's Time Out child care. I hoisted my shoulder bag to the table and rummaged. I pulled out a church directory and my cell phone. Maybe some other parishioners were snowed in. If not, I could at least start leaving messages. As usual, I couldn't get a signal, so I tossed the cell phone back in the bag and grabbed the cordless, getting comfortable at the table.

Judy sashayed into the kitchen, squinting against the snow-refracted sunlight coming in the kitchen windows. "They've started their clanging noises. Why'd they have to start so early? And where are the rug rats?"

"Kelsey and Micah are playing in the snow. Dylan's helping with the clanging."

My sister helped herself to coffee and collapsed into a chair, pulling up another to prop her feet. "Is it just me or did someone turn on a spotlight?" She rubbed her temples and groaned.

"How goes the job hunt?" Okay, it was cruel to pounce on her with that before her eyes were open all the way. But her cavalier flitting in and out of our home was getting on my nerves. Not to mention that I was honestly worried about her.

"I tried the indirect approach. Put out feelers about which places are having some problems—the weak links that'll need replacing soon." She trilled her nails against the table. "The trick is swooping in at the right moment."

Okay, maybe I didn't need to worry about her. The predatory gleam was alive and well in her eyes. "What time did you get in last night? I didn't hear a thing."

She breathed in her coffee. "Don't know. Late. It was just starting to snow."

"Heather drove you back?"

"Naw. When I was done making calls, I asked her to drop me off downtown. I checked out a few clubs, and I met a guy." A sly smile pulled at her lips. "He drove me home."

I knew my old script. Disapproval, warning, judgment. I also knew that those led to angry scenes. *Lord, help me find a new way to be with Judy.*

"Nice guy?" I kept my tone at a casual pitch.

"Yes." She peered at me, seeming disappointed in my lack of reaction. "I was at a jazz club, and it was so crowded, I ended up sharing a table with him. We like some of the same music. And get this. He's from Chicago, too. Not that it matters, with all the traveling I do. Or did." Her confidence slumped a fraction. "If something doesn't click soon, I may need to unload my condo there."

I reached across the table and rested my hand on hers. "You're always welcome here." And I almost meant it. "You're the best marketing guru around. This is a great time to pick and choose what you want to do next."

Her hand twitched in surprise. "Thanks." The voice sounded smoky and rough.

"Now, tell me about the guy." She'd had strings of miserable relationships. Usually short-term. Each adding another layer to her cynicism. With her new interest in spiritual truth, I had hoped the pattern wouldn't keep repeating. "What's he like?"

Lord, help the mister who comes between me and my sister.

Chapter Twenty-nine

In the dusky light of evening, I caught the eye of a college guy and sent him a teasing smile through the haze of bonfire smoke. A guitar thrummed, and someone picked out a scant melody on a harmonica. Laughter and beer were flowing, but I was bored with the pace of this small New England island.

I sprang to my feet and was gratified to see that the guy stood up, as well. Giggling, I ran up the dunes and along the erosion fence. Pickets were wired together in crooked clusters that looked like my braces used to.

The boy shouted something, but I laughed and ran down toward the water. We peeled off layers of clothes as we ran. I never paused when I hit the water's edge. The tang of salt met me as I splashed deeper. Even in July, the water was deliciously cool. In the darkness, the surface was slick as oil.

I stroked smoothly toward a buoy that lured me farther from the beach. I'd never been swimming in the thrilling danger of night before.

Suddenly, something grabbed my leg.

Too surprised to understand, I gasped for breath. Water pummeled me as I was jerked under. I struggled toward the surface and spat out water so I could shout for help. Something yanked me again. Pulled me through the waves. I forgot how to frame words, screaming again and again.

I struck out for shore, but my arms flailed. I couldn't make any progress. And somewhere beneath me, the monster was still lurking. Horror bit into my soul.

Twopenny nails snagged my skin through my wool slacks. Harry had decided one of the kitchen cabinets needed replacement after our little flood, but so far he and Kevin had only managed to rip out the old one. Washing out my coffee mug was now a hazardous adventure. Why had I ever thought fixing up an old house would make life peaceful?

I reached down to pry my pants leg away from a bare two-by-four. Monday morning felt like a relief today. I was eager to get back into the office, where I had a well-defined role and positive feedback for my efforts. The Sunday work crew had accomplished a lot, even with Dylan shadowing Kevin on every job, but we weren't sure if it would be too little, too late. The upstairs bathroom had been retiled and needed only grout. Harry claimed the new pipes would pass inspection. Kevin was taking a few more vacation days and planned to meet with the inspector in the afternoon. If he didn't sign off on our improvements this time, we might not be able to dig out of our financial hole. After all the work we'd done, and all the hopes we'd poured into our dream home, I felt like I was drowning. We couldn't go on like this much longer.

"Come on, kids!"

They pounded into the kitchen clutching backpacks.

Dylan saw me rubbing my leg and noticed the nails. "Oh, someone needs to fix that. Maybe I should stay home today and help Dad some more."

I hid a smile. Becoming Kevin's junior apprentice yesterday brought out my son's responsibility and confidence. "Don't worry. Dad can manage until you get home from school. Let's go."

Salt was doing its work on the county road, coaxing the snow to give ground on the blacktop. I shuttled the kids to their classrooms, then walked down the hall from the school wing to the church. I dodged around an electrician on a ladder as I made my way to my office.

Was I doomed to be surrounded by remodeling everywhere I turned? We were only in the first stage of the church's building program. There could be years of this chaos ahead.

I sank onto my desk chair and massaged my knee. Time for another anti-inflammatory pill. The new ones seemed to be helping, but they still bothered my stomach. It was a tough trade-off. Pain or nausea. The doc had suggested Vicodin if I couldn't manage the pain, but I hated the thought of anything fogging my brain even more than its normal weary-mom state.

First things first. The Bible that I kept in my office rested on top of file folders and several scrawled memos to myself. I pulled the book closer, breathed a quick prayer, and began to read where I'd left off last week—Ephesians.

A minute later, I burst into laughter. The words seemed to wink at me from the page *". . . built on the foundation of the apostles and prophets, with Christ Jesus himself as the chief cornerstone. In him the whole building is joined together and rises to become a holy temple in the Lord. And in him you too are being built together to become a dwelling in which God lives by his Spirit."*

Okay, Lord, you're in the remodeling business, too. Help me build on the right foundation today.

I bowed my head and prayed quietly for several wonderful minutes.

Then I heard a timid tap on my doorframe.

"Excuse me. Are you napping?" Ruth Angelicus waited across the threshold, one hand leaning on her cane, the other holding her purse.

"No, no. Come in."

She entered and perched on the chair near my desk. "I know what it's like to nod off. Happens to me all the time."

I smiled. "Actually, a nap does sound pretty good."

She nodded. "Well, I came to see if you've found a place for me."

I had to struggle to open my mental file. She'd been frustrated by the new designations in the Sunday school and wanted a place to serve. An idea fell into place. "Are you free Wednesday morning?"

"Well, my water aerobics class meets then, but I was thinking of switching to an evening class."

"We need a teacher for the kindergarten class of the Mom's Time Out program. It's not quite the same as second graders, but the volunteers always teach a Bible story and build relationships with the kids. And I know they'd love to see your flannelgraphs."

Ruth's face lit up. "I'd enjoy that."

"I know it's not perfect—"

Her laugh interrupted me. "Dear heart, nothing this side of heaven is perfect. We can never fix it all. That's so we'll keep longing for our true home." She pushed to her feet and reached over to pat my hand. "When do you need me?"

"This Wednesday?"

"Lovely." With a happy nod, Ruth went on her way.

By rights, she should have been bitter that the Sunday school program had been changed and she'd been phased out of the place she loved to volunteer. Instead, she was grateful and ready to share her gifts in an imperfect situation.

I couldn't have remained that cheerful. Not-quite-there-yet situations made me itch. And they created perfect opportunities for me to take control and fix things.

Some of my recent battlegrounds floated into mind, along with my excuses for compulsive efforts. If I fixed some of the attitudes in the church staff, we'd be able to do a better job. If I nagged Kevin to finish the remodeling, I'd be able to care for Grandma Rose more easily. If I called Lori more often, I'd be able to cheer her up. If I read more books on evangelism, I'd know the right things to say to fix Judy's spiritual life. If I taught Kevin to open up and reach out to me, my marriage would be stellar.

But the imperfect realities were the waters I swam through each day. Ruth's happy acceptance reminded me that wasn't going to change. I wanted to create happy endings for everyone I knew. *That's not how it works on planet Earth. Maybe in the movies, but not in real life with all its raw complexities.*

Teresa darted into the office. She looked at the projects spread on my desk. "Wanted to touch base. Fill me in. Current projects?"

Her rapid-fire delivery bumped against my contemplative mood. She was a lean, hungry shark, and I was chum. My heart pounded more rapidly every time she swam near me.

I envied her energy and drive, but I feared what it did to me. It was so easy to get sucked in. To be eaten up by nonstop intensity.

"Why don't you stop hovering and sit down?" I smiled to soften my words. "I'll fill you in on everything I've been working on."

Surprisingly, she pulled up a chair and settled down. When she stopped moving, I saw hints of fatigue around her eyes. We reviewed the status of some of my ongoing programs, as well as an update on Christmas Tea plans.

I pulled out a well-worn folder. "The committee has everything in place. But I'm still hoping we can draw in more women from the local community. Today I'm designing some invitations that women in our church can use to invite friends."

Teresa nodded. "Always more to do, isn't there? When does it end?"

A rhetorical question. A typical workplace moan. But because it had been my theme for the past several months, the words bit.

"It doesn't. Not this side of heaven. So, we go to bed each night knowing there are things unfinished. Things undone. And that's okay." I met Teresa's eyes. Two exhausted women who tried to fix everything.

Instead of jumping up to dart to the next item on her agenda, Teresa closed her eyes as if my words had wearied her more. "But it's our job. It's our calling."

Warmth and compassion flooded me—for Teresa and for myself. "Our calling is to show up each morning and say, 'Here I am, Lord. What little part would you have me do today?' And leave the rest to Him." My voice slowed as I spoke. Peace welled up in my spirit, a lingering memory of my prayer time Thanksgiving night.

Teresa's eyes popped open, and she gave an uneasy laugh. "Yeah, well. See ya later." She zoomed out the door, afraid to stop moving. I read somewhere that sharks have to keep swimming even when they're asleep. Poor things.

I began work on the Christmas Tea invitation. When I had a

mock-up, it occurred to me that Tom would be thrilled at how the women's ministry was reaching out to folks outside the church. I e-mailed a copy to him, no longer feeling guilt that I hadn't jumped onboard with his last-minute television project.

On the drive home with Kelsey and Micah, I refused to think about the work still on my desk. When worries about Rose or Judy or Kevin demanded attention, I pushed them aside. It was hard work, but I fully listened to Kelsey's chatter about her day. When Micah said he learned a new song, I asked him to sing it and joined in.

Contentment blanketed me like the layers of snow on the fields around our house.

We stamped the slush from our boots and went in the back door. Judy and Rose were at the kitchen table drinking coffee and laughing. I caught the tail end of a story Rose was telling about her dating life.

I felt a prick of frustration that Rose was so chatty with Judy, when she'd never been that way with me despite all my efforts. But I coached myself. *God's using someone else. That's okay. It's not all on you.*

"Guess what?" A bit of her old arrogance appeared as Judy flashed her teeth.

"You've won the lottery?"

She barked a laugh. "Almost as good. One of those companies I met with in New York has decided to expand in Chicago. Guess who they think should head the new division?"

I shrieked and lurched forward to hug her, nearly knocking her from her chair. "When did you find out?"

Kelsey and Micah joined the excitement with a couple whoops and a few jumps.

"They tried calling but couldn't get through on my cell. But when I checked messages I called them back on your landline." She grinned. "I owe you for a long-distance call."

"Don't be silly. When do you start? Are you excited? Tell me everything."

Judy cast a quick glance at Rose.

Rose nodded and patted Judy's arm. "Why don't you two go chat in the living room. I'll fix lunch for the kids."

"Look out!" Kevin's muffled voice carried through the wall. A crash sounded from Rose's bathroom. I lifted my eyebrows. Rose's lips tightened. "Yes, Harry and Kevin are busy in there today. I keep telling them not to bother."

And why were they ripping out something else, when the inspector was due this afternoon?

"Come on, sis." Judy was already halfway out of the kitchen.

I limped after her. "What's the rush?"

When we plopped down on opposite ends of the couch and faced each other, Judy couldn't meet my eyes. "Well, the thing is, they want me right away."

She tried to look apologetic about blowing back out of our lives, but she had too much sparkle in her eyes to pull it off.

"I'm happy for you. Tell me all about it."

She began rattling off company statistics and enthusiastic strategies she planned to implement. "And get this. Greg called. I gave him your number since my cell never seems to work here. I hope you don't mind."

"Greg?" I was having trouble keeping up.

"You know. The guy I met at the jazz club. From Chicago."

Oh, Lord, why did you have to let Judy zoom back into her normal life so soon? I was really hoping this crisis would make her want to get to know you.

Carefully neutral, I nodded. "Oh yeah. You didn't mention his name."

"So anyway, I wanted to thank you. For . . . you know."

"It's been great having you around." My feelings were deeper d more genuine than I would have expected.

"I probably won't get back here for Christmas." She turned

apologetic again. "I'll be on everyone's firing line, so I'll have to be on my toes and put in a lot of extra hours. But I'm glad we had Thanksgiving together. Please tell Heather thanks again for letting me house-sit. Oh, and say hello to Doreen for me, okay? I wanted to get together with her, and I never got around to it."

"Sure. But . . . exactly how soon do you have to leave?"

She nibbled her lower lip. "There's a plane at three o'clock. Can you take me to the airport?"

"Today?"

She gave an embarrassed shrug. "No time like the present."

But there was so much I hadn't said. I wanted to follow up on the conversation we'd had at Starbucks. I wanted to find out what she thought of our church. I wanted to explain again that she couldn't earn God's approval as if He were some CEO in the sky.

Lord, I needed more time. What kind of sister am I, anyway?

I recognized the old tape but couldn't stop it from playing through my mind.

"So, Beck, you take care of yourself, all right?" She glanced toward the kitchen. "And you're doing a good thing here. With Rose. She's quite a woman. I'm glad you guys could give her a home."

The phone rang, and I heard Rose answer it and call for Kevin.

"Thanks, Judifer." I felt a sudden pressure behind my eyes as tears threatened.

"Oh, and get this." She tossed her hair and looked away, hiding a sly smile. "I found out Greg plays guitar with a band . . . at his church."

My mouth did a gaping goldfish impression.

Deliberately casual, she picked a piece of lint off her slacks. "Yeah. He invited me to come hear him. I guess it's a real up-to-date kind of church right in downtown Chicago. Sounds more interesting than your church. I might check it out."

In spite of her insult to my congregation, giggly hope bubbled against my ribs.

Judy sprang to her feet. "Well, not to rush you, but we should think about leaving. Check-in takes forever these days."

I eased to my feet and reached to hug her.

Lord, you didn't need me to tie up the loose ends, did you? You're still working, aren't you?

"Call me anytime. And you know I'm happy to talk about God stuff whenever you want."

She gave me a squeeze and released me. "Don't I know it." But there was no sarcasm in her tone.

She went upstairs to get her suitcases.

I stretched out on the couch and did a few leg lifts, then a flutter kick that was supposed to strengthen my abs.

My corporate-shark sister was back in the feeding frenzy. But I had the feeling she'd be finding a new direction to swim in the coming days.

Kevin came into the living room. Instead of laughing at my backstroke impression, he looked grave. "That was Noah on the phone. Lori's in the hospital."

A chill gripped my bones and I stood up. "What happened?"

Judy bounced her suitcase down the stairs and stopped short as she felt the tension in the room.

Kevin drew me into his arms. "Depression. I guess it got really bad, so she checked herself in."

I pushed back. "I've got to go see her."

He stroked my back, still holding me. "Noah said she can't have visitors yet. Maybe next week."

Kevin's face looked as drawn and shocked as mine probably did.

"She seemed fine." I burrowed into Kevin's chest. "I shouldn't have let her help on Saturday."

"Noah said Lori loved being here. It had nothing to do with that. Holidays are always harder for her, and there were some conflicts with Noah's family at Thanksgiving, and . . . Oh, who knows what triggered it."

Judy stepped closer and patted my back. She knew Lori was my best friend. I'd told Judy how much I envied Lori's spiritual life.

I turned to thank my sister for her compassion.

But she tapped her watch. "It's those holy types that you need to watch out for. They all eventually snap."

Chapter Thirty

The penguin fell forward onto her belly, sliding along the snow for several yards. Stubby feet pushed against the ice, propelling her farther. Then she lurched to her feet and resumed the waddling gait that would carry her to her breeding ground. The month of March had arrived, and the South Pole winter had begun to freeze huge sections of the sea. More and more penguins leaped from the water and joined her on the trek inland. They traveled for dozens of miles across unforgiving terrain.

Weeks later, wind whipped the snow into such poor visibility that I despaired of getting a good shot. Then sunlight pressed through, the white haze cleared, and I could see through the camera lens again. The row of penguins stretched to the horizon line. One after another, they marched toward me. I waited and watched them come day after day. As the windchill dropped even lower, they huddled into a vast community, drawing warmth from one another—an island of life in the bleak Antarctic.

The noise at the rookery is deafening as potential mates sing to one another and pair up. Their marriage commitment has to be strong to face the months of struggle ahead. Finally, the moment I'd come to record took place. The female penguins began to lay their eggs. A careful ballet shifted the fragile orb to the father's feet so the mother could leave to feed. In spite of the harsh conditions, the penguin couple had formed a partnership that would ensure survival.

More frigid temperatures rolled in, and blizzards forced me to abandon my filming for several days. But even over the howling wind, I could hear the squealing reassurances as the penguins encouraged one another. The ice creaked under their weight, and I wondered what they dreamed about through the long nights.

The creaking noises pulled me awake Saturday morning. The heavy sound of a house settling and tiny pops of fatigued joists sounded ominous.

With a cautious eye on the ceiling, I made my way to the window. Our acres had been a winter wonderland yesterday. Now they were an arctic wasteland. Our house was a tiny island surrounded by a vast sea of snow. Waves of white buried the bushes and small maples, and obscured tall oaks. Snow fell heavily—too moist to swirl. The sun fought to cast pink streaks of dawn into the sky, but I expected to see the feeble ball buried by more snow.

"Kevin, wake up. It's a blizzard."

"Thas nice."

"Kevin, I'm serious. You've got to see this." Another rafter groaned from overhead. "And I think the house is going to cave in."

He sprang up in one adrenaline-charged movement. "What?"

"Listen."

We held our breaths, and of course, the house chose to remain silent. Kevin raised a skeptical brow, but then the nightlight and clock radio blinked out. Now our only light was the weak sunlight filtered through an eternity of snow.

"Power's out." He finally untangled from the covers and stood up. Attic rafters above us groaned, and he cast a startled look at the ceiling. "You might be right. I better check on the roof."

Our initial upgrades had passed inspection last Monday, but we'd been given a list of other things we had to fix before the finance company would write up a new mortgage. Still, the recent progress had bolstered Kevin's optimism. We clung to our hope that we'd get okayed for the new loan soon.

But that wouldn't happen if the roof fell in. "I'll get the kids and move them downstairs. Do you know where the transistor radio is?"

He was already pulling on his jeans, jumping to slide them up quickly. "The basement. I'll run down and get it. Can you check on my mom?"

"Sure."

Room by room, I kissed my children awake and watched them press noses to cold glass to see the snow. When I reached Dylan's room, I found him in his usual sprawl, with one hand dangling over the edge of his bed to rest protectively on his toolbox.

"Sweetie, wake up. We're having a blizzard."

He rubbed his eyes. "What a bummer."

"What do you mean?"

"It's Saturday. We won't have to miss school today. Why couldn't it blizzard during school?"

"Come on, bud. We need to go downstairs. And the way it's coming down, we might still be stuck here on Monday."

That cheered him up. He padded downstairs in his jammies, carrying his tools with him.

I picked my way down the steep stairs, out of range of an imminent roof collapse. Then I took time to feel the thrill of a genuine snow-to-the-windowsills blizzard. I did a little of my own nose-pressed-to-glass oohing and ahhing.

Finally, I pulled myself away from the view and tiptoed into Grandma Rose's room.

She stirred and looked in confusion at her blank-faced digital clock. "What's going on?"

"We lost power. We had a lot of snow. I wanted to check on you."

She coughed several times and drew in a rattling breath. I grabbed the cup of water on her bedside table and supported her shoulders with one arm as I guided the water to her lips.

"It sounds like you should use your nebulizer again."

She made a sound that was a combination of laughing and clearing her throat. "And how can I do that if we don't have electricity?"

Dread bloomed in the fear centers of my brain. What would we do if she got worse? We couldn't even get her to the doctor. The driveway was buried, and the snow was still falling.

"Maybe you should sleep some more. I need to fix breakfast for the kids, but I'll check in on you later."

"Oh, stop fussing over me. You have more important things to take care of."

I was weary of that theme. Over and over like a glacier grinding across the landscape, she eroded my good intentions, leaving me exposed as inadequate. I could never do enough to convince her that I cared about her and genuinely wanted her here. She never offered me affection or gratitude.

And why did that trigger such a deep feeling of rejection?

I slipped from her room and stood still in the hall.

Because her withdrawal reminded me of Kevin's. I sucked in my breath, shocked at the power of that connection. A raw wound lay exposed in my soul. For months I'd been trying to regain ground in our marriage while I felt Kevin roll toward me and then farther away like the tides. I'd submerged my own needs in order to make heroic efforts to win his appreciation. Be a good sport about the run-down house. Work hard at my career, but play down my successes so they wouldn't annoy or threaten him. Exhaust myself caring for his mom and smile through her critical comments.

No wonder Rose's indifference toward me burned. It touched the exposed abrasions of my loneliness. Trying harder hadn't worked—with Rose or with Kevin.

Kevin had made it clear that my sacrificial striving did nothing to make him feel loved. In fact, it had rubbed on his self-respect like sand between the toes. Could that be part of my problem with Rose? Did she sense the less-than-loving motives beneath my insistence that she stay with us? How could I strive less and love more?

Important questions. I filed them away for later. I had no time to work out the answers now.

My cane squeaked against the floor as I headed toward the kitchen.

Kevin was in a chair, pulling oversized jogging pants over his jeans.

"Is that going to keep you warm enough?"

"I've got long underwear on. I'll be fine." He tugged a ski cap over his ears.

"I hope they get the power back on. Your mom can't use her nebulizer."

Worry drew deep lines in Kevin's face. "And the furnace won't work either. While I'm outside checking on the roof, could you call the electric company? Probably tons of houses out, but we should let them know about ours since we're out here by ourselves."

"Sure. And I'll tell the kids to bundle up." The room already seemed colder, but maybe that was my imagination. "Don't worry. Harry will probably come plow us out, and we can always go hang out at church if our house gets too cold."

Kevin tugged thick gloves on. "Harry's visiting a friend in Duluth this weekend. He won't be coming."

Now I definitely felt a chill.

Dylan galloped into the kitchen. "Hey, Dad. D'ya need my help?"

Kevin beckoned Dylan over and perched him on his knee. "Yes," Kevin said gravely. "I need someone to take care of Mom and Grandma and Kelsey and Micah while I'm outside. Can you do that?"

My heart filled as I watched them. I needed to step back more often and let Kevin parent. He was exactly what Dylan needed right now. One more thing I'd been trying to handle on my own—playing the weary martyred mom and not accepting the help that was right in front of me.

"I'll handle it," Dylan promised. He hopped off of Kevin's lap and strutted out of the room.

I picked up a scarf and draped it around Kevin's neck. "Be careful out there."

"Don't worry. I can set the ladder up on the porch roof. From there I should be able to reach the house roof. I'll rake some of the snow off to relieve the weight."

"Wait." One of his Sorels was untied. I knelt awkwardly and slid the lace through the top eyelets and tied it securely. "You don't want to trip."

"Yes, Mother." His grin flashed above the scarf.

In spite of the very real dangers, he was enjoying this adventure. *Men.*

I opened the back door for him. The air felt warmer than I expected. Probably only a little below freezing. No wonder the snow was so wet and heavy.

Kevin launched into the deep snow and worked his way toward the shed. Each step seemed to take great effort.

The sun was fully up now but hidden by the overcast sky. The world had turned black and white like an old movie. Black tree limbs, white snow, gray shadows.

I shivered and closed the door, my eyes finding comfort in my red-checkered tea towel and blue ceramic cookie jar. What kind of storm had the power to bleed all the color from the world? Another icicle of fear slid down my spine.

I hurried to the living room where three kids had their noses pressed against the large window looking out across the porch. I would have giggled at the sight, but the house gave another ominous groan. I glanced at the stairs. How was I going to get them all dressed? I didn't want them going back upstairs.

"Kids, listen. I need your help."

They turned toward me, and I gathered them around me on the couch. Eyes wide, subdued by the sheer magnitude of the storm, they snuggled close.

"We all need to get dressed. And in lots of layers. The furnace can't work right now."

Dylan sprang to his feet and jogged toward the stairs.

"No!" I took a deep breath. "I don't think we should go upstairs. But I have an idea. Let's see what we have in the basement, okay?"

We grabbed a few flashlights and made our way carefully down to the cellar. Two large baskets of clean laundry waited to be folded and put away. If necessary, we could always grab a few layers from the dirty laundry.

The kids began to giggle as they found strange combinations of clothes to pull on—layer by layer until they swelled like marshmallows.

I sat on the bottom step and pulled on my exercise leggings, then flannel pajama pants, then wool dress pants, then a pair of Kevin's sweat pants over the top for good measure.

Maybe Kevin and the kids did have the right attitude. Adventures were kind of fun.

When we were all wearing as much as we could, we clomped up to the kitchen. "Hey, let's wear our boots in the house. Just this once." I could get into the spirit of fun as well as anyone. "We want to keep our tootsies warm, right?"

We donned boots, and then I settled my brood around the table. "Okay, kiddos. I need you to be good helpers. Dylan, you can get out the cereal. Kelsey, you get the bowls. Everyone help Micah. I have to make some phone calls."

They gave somber nods and began to get their own breakfast.

I grabbed my cell phone, but as usual, I couldn't get a signal. I picked up the landline phone and didn't hear a dial tone. I shook it, jiggled it, and stared at it in disbelief. Nothing. We were completely cut off from the outside world.

Forcing a smile, I looked at the kids. "Well, I'm sure the electric company knows we lost power. They'll send someone soon. Kelsey, don't hold the fridge door open. It'll lose all the cold air." Not that cold air was hard to come by. Soon the milk and eggs would stay chilled sitting on our kitchen table.

Muffled clomping sounded from the porch end of the house. The scraping sound must be Kevin dragging the ladder up behind him onto the porch roof.

I limped out to the living room in time to see the ladder floating in space in front of the porch windows. Then it disappeared. Snow began to fall in heavy cascades as Kevin cleared the porch roof. This part of the project didn't worry me. The roof was gently sloped and only ten feet above the ground. But the image of him on the steep attic roofs, starting small avalanches on purpose, made my stomach clench like a hard-packed snowball.

Becky, don't be silly. He has two working legs. Climbing a ladder and shoveling snow is not a big deal to him. He has to do something or the roof could collapse, and that would be a real danger.

My pep talk didn't work. I couldn't pull myself from the front windows. I watched signs of Kevin's progress as if my vigilance could keep him safe.

In a few minutes, the ladder creaked under Kevin's weight. I bit my lip. He was heading up to the next level. I prayed that the ladder was firmly wedged in place.

Scrapes and splats gave me a clue as to where he was working—first over the far end of the living room, then moving toward the stairs. With all the snow being raked down onto the porch roof, he'd have to shovel that all over again. But he had to do this in stages.

I began to relax. His plan was working. He was easing the weight on this whole side of the house.

Then the globs of snow stopped crashing down. As the silence stretched, my last nerve twisted in pain. What was he doing up there?

Suddenly, the kids squealed from the kitchen.

I attempted a lopsided gallop and made it across the living room in record time. "What's the matter?" I gasped.

Kelsey giggled. "Daddy's burying us. Look!"

"It's an avalanche." Dylan pointed out the kitchen windows with glee.

My chest tightened. Huge piles of snow poured down past the windows. That meant that Kevin was on the far side of the roof . . . or at least straddling the peak. I didn't know he planned to work on the steep side. What was he thinking? It had to be slippery up there. This wasn't worth risking his neck. If the roof started to buckle, we could always huddle in the shed to wait for help.

I reached for the doorknob.

A sudden loud scrape sounded overhead. A metal rake somersaulted past the windows and wedged into the snow. A second later a dark form plummeted down and hit the backyard.

Kelsey screamed. "Daddy! Daddy fell!"

Her voice sounded far away, projecting from a place where time still continued. In my world everything had frozen.

I gasped in a breath. My arms flung to the sides, blocking the kids from moving toward the door. "Dylan, watch the kids. Kelsey, it's okay. I'll go help him." I didn't wait to see if they'd understood me. I slammed out of the door and stumbled, half crawling, toward Kevin.

He lay face down in the cavern created by his fall. His left arm was hidden—twisted beneath him. His other limbs splayed like a crushed snow angel.

Terror sliced through my belly. He wasn't moving—wasn't jumping up with a laugh to dust the clumps of snow from his clothes.

"Kevin! Kevin!" My shriek fought past the strangled tightness of my throat. I fell to the ground beside him. "Kevin?"

He didn't answer.

Chapter Thirty-one

Blowing snow stung my cheeks. The air felt colder than the last time I had been here. I pulled the fur coat more tightly around my neck. It wasn't wrong to borrow the coat, was it? After all, we were still in the wardrobe—sort of.

"Let's go visit the faun," I suggested to my sister and brothers. His warm cave would be welcoming. The wind was moaning through the boughs of the pine forest. There was something sinister about the cold. Something unnatural. A cozy tea with the dear creature was exactly what we needed.

We trudged along, looking back at the lamppost occasionally to be sure we could find our way home.

"There!" I pointed. I'd begun to fear I wouldn't be able to find the faun's house. I wanted everyone to meet him.

We hurried toward his door, then pulled up short. The door hung askew. His furniture was tossed and broken like kindling. A grim sign informed us that he'd been arrested.

Fear bit into my heart, the way the cold was gnawing my skin. Was he dead? Was he frozen into a statue in a dismal courtyard? We had to find out. We had to save him. This was all my fault.

I pushed snow away from Kevin's face, afraid to move him. Afraid not to move him.

His head was turned toward the side. As soon as I dug away the snow, I pressed my ear against his lips, trying to hear or feel his breath. Wet snow continued to fall and sting my face.

"Kevin. Kevin, breathe. Please. You have to be okay."

I wanted to shake him, to do anything to end his frightening stillness. Tears drew hot trails on my skin, and I gasped a sob, sending a puff of steam into the air.

The air. I should be able to see Kevin's breath. Even if I couldn't see his ribs move under all the layers he was wearing, I should see his breath. It was as if he had turned to stone.

I shoved more snow away from the space around him and waited, holding my own breath. Was that a bit of vapor? He looked so white. "Kevin, wake up. Talk to me."

A throaty groan squeezed from him. The most beautiful sound in the universe.

"You're alive." The relief and wonder of it gave me a wave of vertigo. I sank back in the snow. "Don't move."

Another groan, then his free arm grappled the ground for leverage.

"Kevin, don't move."

He ignored me and pushed his body off his left arm, rolling over with a hiss of pain. Even though I could see his breath now, he still looked as pale as death.

"Sorry, hon," he gasped. "My arm. It's killing me."

"Okay, so you're off your arm. Now don't move until help gets here."

"Help? What help?" He squinted in my direction and struggled to sit up. "How long was I out?"

"Stop moving. You could have a broken neck."

He tilted his head from side to side. "Nah. I don't think so. But my shoulder—" He winced as he cradled his left arm with the other. "Can we discuss this inside?"

"I don't think you're supposed to move."

He gave me a level look, teeth clenched in obvious pain. "You want me to sit in a snow pile all day?"

Don't take this out on me, buster. You're the one who went crawling around on the roof.

How could I move from desperate terror to irritation so quickly? I struggled to my feet. Wet clumps of snow dropped from my sweater and pants. My hands were red with cold, and my wrists burned where snow had wedged in my cuffs.

I planted my cane between us. "Okay, move carefully. You could have a concussion."

Kevin shifted each leg, testing for injuries. When he reached for the cane, he gasped and cradled his bad arm again. His jaw clenched.

My adrenaline-induced crankiness left me in an instant. He was really hurting. "Wait. Let me help." I gently unwound his scarf and used it to create an impromptu sling.

With the arm somewhat immobile, he tried again and made it to his feet. He swayed and leaned forward. Eyes squeezed shut, he took several harsh breaths.

"Are you okay?"

He swallowed and shot me a glare. His skin looked grayish green.

"Feeling queasy? That could be a sign of concussion."

Another glare.

I decided to stop offering medical diagnoses. We made miserably slow progress toward the back door. Grandma Rose waited in the entry and helped guide Kevin inside and to a chair. The kids stood back, eyes intent, gauging whether their dad was okay.

Kevin seemed unaware of any of them. "Help me out of this coat."

"I don't know if that's a good idea. It hurts you to move it. . . ."

"I need to see it." His plea tugged me forward to help.

I suppose I'd feel the same way. I'd want to know how bad it was.

When Rose and I guided the coat a few inches off his shoulder, he let out a strangled moan. Micah ran to grab my leg. Kelsey gripped Dylan's hand, eyes wide. Children shouldn't hear their father in so much pain.

Grandma Rose noticed them, too. "Children, let's go in the living room and play a game while your mommy helps your daddy."

Three little ones sent me uncertain looks. I smiled. "Great idea. Daddy has a little owie, but Mommy will fix it. You go play." I peeled Micah off my leg and sent him toward his grandma with a light swat to his bottom. "Off you go."

Dylan tugged Kelsey's hand, and they followed Rose out of the room. When they all left the kitchen, I wanted to sink into a chair, bury my head in my arms, and have a good cry. Instead, I gave Kevin a nervous look.

He stared at a point on the wall. "Do it."

I managed to help him slip his good arm from his coat sleeve, although the contortions left Kevin panting for breath. When I untied the sling to free his left arm, he doubled forward with a whimpering sound that broke my heart. I pretended not to hear, because I knew he believed men didn't whimper.

"There's no way I can pull that off your arm. Besides, it's probably swollen." I rummaged through one of the kitchen drawers and pulled out a sewing shears. "This will do it."

His expression moved from bleary-eyed pain into alarm.

"Relax. I'm just going to cut open the seam."

Easier said than done. At first, I stopped every time he flinched with pain. Then I ground my molars together and forced myself to keep snipping, easing the fabric away from him.

One ruined coat and several shattered nerves later, I repeated the process on his flannel shirt. Slitting open the seam, I left the rest of his shirt in place. The fabric was matted to his arm with sweat. After one glance, I quickly sank back onto a chair and clamped a hand over my mouth, fighting the impulse to gag. Angry swelling surrounded his shoulder, where his arm wedged at an unnatural angle.

"Sorry." His voice was hoarse.

I looked away and took several deep breaths.

"Hon." He sounded weak. "I think I broke something."

"Kevin, we've got to get you to the emergency room."

"There's too much snow on the driveway."

"It's only going to get deeper if we wait." I stood up and reached into a cupboard for our first aid kit.

"Just call around to find a plow."

I rifled through the box. Flintstone Band-Aids and Bactine

weren't going to be much help. "Phones are out." I tore the wrapper from a gauze pad but wasn't sure where to put it on his arm. Eventually, I packed him with all the gauze in the box, and strapped his arm to his chest with an Ace bandage. "Let's go."

His eyes measured the distance to the door. Then he looked out the window to the shed, several dozen yards beyond. He moaned, obviously dreading the ordeal ahead. "Well, at least I got most of the snow off the roof."

I chose to ignore that comment. His eyes were glazing and his legs trembled against the chair. He was probably going into shock. If I didn't get him to the van fast, he might pass out and I'd have to carry him out.

That wasn't going to happen.

"All right. Stop stalling." I hobbled to the hook by the back door and grabbed the keys. "I know you'd rather drive, but I'm holding the keys." I kept my voice as light as I could, while inside I wanted to cry.

Using the back of the chair for support, he rose to his feet and wavered. I stepped closer. "That's it. You can wrap your right arm around my shoulder if it helps."

Keep it casual. Don't let him see how worried you are.

"Rose," I called. "I'm taking him to the ER. I'll call the phone company and the electric company from there and get someone to plow us out, okay?"

She stuck her head into the kitchen. Her gaze darted to the snow still falling fat and steady from the sky. Her forehead pinched with worry, but she took a cue from my confident tone. "That's nice. Don't worry about us. I'll watch the kids."

"Thanks."

Getting Kevin out to the shed was a major effort. Maneuvering with my cane in the deepening snow would have been difficult even without him leaning against me. Helping him into the passenger seat was another challenge. The strain of that effort washed the last remnants of color from his face, and I think he passed out for a moment or two.

I slid open the shed doors and grabbed a shovel. What I wouldn't do for an old-fashioned sleigh right now. Shoveling thick wet snow while leaning on a cane with one hand was quite a trick.

My plan was to clear enough space for the van to get traction—then gun it and try to push through the snow with enough momentum to reach the road.

The first part of the plan worked fine—except for the part where the engine roared. Kevin opened his eyes, planted his foot against an invisible brake, and yelled, "What are you doing? Trying to get us killed?"

Thankfully, that was all the energy he could spare, and he stopped shouting.

We went in the general direction of the road but then skidded sideways. That slowed us down. By the time we were pointing forward again, we had stalled out. I tested the accelerator, but the tires spun in place.

I glanced at Kevin. He had grabbed the door handle with his right hand while the van shimmied from side to side. Now he squeezed his eyes shut, breathing heavily.

I tried the old trick of rocking the van forward and back. I shifted from drive to reverse several times and succeeded only in packing the snow beneath us into ice. The jarring movements weren't doing Kevin any good. His head tilted back, and he moaned low in his chest. He was looking green again.

"No problem," I said brightly. "I'll get out and shovel some more. We're halfway to the road. Won't be long now."

He didn't answer.

His silence scared me so much I barely felt the cold as I plunged back out of the van. I had tossed the shovel into the back seat, so at least I didn't have to walk back to the shed. I shoveled another set of parallel ruts. My good leg shook with the effort of supporting my weight as I hefted snow and tossed it to the side. My bad leg screamed, shrieked, buckled, and finally realized it wasn't going to get my attention and went numb.

When I had several yards cleared, I pulled the floor mats out of the van and set them on the ground inches from the front tires. I needed traction to get us past this slick spot.

My first attempts didn't get us moving, even when I pressed my weight into the steering wheel, coaxing, "Come on, baby. Come on. You can do it."

Finally, I set the parking brake, shifted into neutral, and turned to Kevin. "Hon? I'm gonna need your help here."

He opened his eyes and stared at me as if he didn't know who I was.

"I'm going back to push. When you hear me yell, let go of the parking brake. I only need to push us a few inches."

He nodded weakly and reached across his body with his right arm, ready to release the brake.

"Don't faint again, okay?"

His lips twitched. "Faint? Real men don't faint. I was resting my eyes."

Good. He was still with me.

I climbed out, leaving the door open so he could hear me. The back of the van looked twice as wide and twice as tall as I remembered. I tried to find the best way to brace myself and settled for angling my shoulder into the tailgate, with my cane wedged behind me.

"Okay!" I yelled.

I leaned my full weight and pushed.

Nothing.

"I said you can release the brake!"

"I did," Kevin yelled back.

This is it, Becky. Dig deep. Kevin needs you. He seriously needs you. You can do this.

I tried again, straining with every ounce of strength in me. I felt a slight movement, but the van settled back as soon as I paused to breathe.

My nose began to run and tears broke free as anger expanded inside me. I shook with the intensity of my frustration.

Helpless.

I hated feeling helpless.

God, I need you. I need your strength. I love him.

Like a weight lifter, I took several breaths, then threw myself against the van with a guttural yell.

It rolled. Just a few feet, but that was all I needed.

I retrieved the mats and placed them in front of the tires again, and got in the car. This time the wheels grabbed, and we barreled forward into the snow. I punched the gas, and we fishtailed out onto the county road.

My loud whoop of triumph didn't rouse Kevin. He gritted his teeth, focusing inward on managing pain. I had probably looked that way when I was in labor and tuning out the rest of the world.

We were only ten minutes from the hospital. I knew he'd be all right now, but I couldn't stop the tears. My arms shook as I gripped the wheel.

"Thank you, God. Thank you, thank you." I wept, babbled, and strained to keep the car on the road.

Amazing clarity arrives at the most inconvenient moments. As I drove to the ER, I realized that I'd just done some remarkable things. Sacrificial, almost heroic things. All because I loved Kevin with everything inside me. I wasn't trying to impress him, win his gratitude, or score more points in the Good Spouse game. I loved him so much I *had* to help him.

I don't know why the insight arrived on a snowy road to the hospital, but it did. The adventure sealed my understanding of what I'd been doing wrong. Why marriage had become an unrewarding duty. Why we'd been drifting apart, sometimes close to going belly-up.

I'd been doing all the right things—for all the wrong reasons.

When I pulled up to the ER driveway, Kevin's eyes were closed. His lashes were dark against the pallor of his skin. I pressed a quick kiss against his cheek. "I love you. Stay here."

One of the least rational things I'd said during this crazy day. Where would he possibly go?

I limped into the lobby and asked for a wheelchair. An attendant listened to my garbled explanation and came out to the van with me. Kevin roused enough to help as the man assisted him into a chair. They took us straight back into a curtained room, and a nurse with a clipboard began asking questions. We had landed in a warm current of medical efficiency that would carry us smoothly along. The exhausting effort was over.

And that was when my bad leg decided it had had enough. Without warning, my knee buckled. I sank to the floor, unable to stop myself. My leg trembled with a sensation like a dozen jellyfish stings. That's what I got for teasing Kevin about fainting. I was going under.

Chapter Thirty-two

I helped my little friend from the van and raced to the bikes waiting at the playground. "We've got to get him to his spaceship. Otherwise the government guys will kill him again."

My brother's friends weren't used to taking me seriously, but this time they didn't argue.

"Let's go!" my brother shouted.

"Home." My friend's word was sad and hopeful at the same time.

"Yes, yes. I'll get you home."

Not an easy job when his family lived galaxies away. But he'd built some sort of alien telephone thingy, and his parents were coming to get him. All I had to do was get him to the clearing.

I placed my alien buddy in my bike basket and took off. I'd never pedaled harder.

Police cars screamed behind us. Suddenly, I saw a roadblock in front of us.

I didn't know what to do, so I kept pumping, followed by my brother and all his friends.

Somehow, when we reached the barrier, we just kept going . . . our bikes sailing into the sky. Even though I was scared and worried, it was a blast riding my bike over treetops.

We made it to the clearing and landed. The spaceship opened its door.

"Please stay." I couldn't stop myself from asking, even though I knew he couldn't.

My friend reached his hand toward me, his fingertip glowing.

Rose laid her gnarled hand on Kevin's knee. Her knuckles were swollen from arthritis. "I need my own home."

Kevin gathered her hands in his, an awkward move with his cast. "I'm sorry, Mom." I rarely heard his energetic voice this patient and tender. "I know this has been hard on you. But the doctors say you can't be on your own."

We were a sorry-looking group. I watched the discussion from a borrowed wheelchair, Kevin kept fidgeting with his sling, and Grandma Rose wore a nose tube attaching her to her oxygen on what we had dubbed "the golf cart."

My flush of victory from the snow adventure had carried me through the long day in the emergency room. The doctor had joked about a two-for-one special, but he was all business as he fixed Kevin's dislocated shoulder, set his forearm where he had a small fracture, and checked him for concussion. He'd also iced my knee, wrapped it, and told me to see my doctor as soon as possible.

A phone call to Heather brought us an eager ally. For a free-spirit type, she did an efficient job of contacting the phone and power companies, arranging for a plow for our driveway, and driving us both home. She and her daughter Grace even stayed overnight, getting the kids to bed and helping Grandma Rose.

Between our pain pills and sheer exhaustion, Kevin and I had slept through most of Sunday. Monday morning my doctor consigned me to staying off my leg for a couple of weeks, and after that, when the swelling eased, daily physical therapy at the clinic. He talked about surgical options, but I was too pain-fogged to pay attention. When I explained that I needed to go up the stairs to get to our bedrooms, and down the basement steps to do laundry, the doctor was unsympathetic.

"Maybe you should plan to move," he said.

I ignored that maddening advice. We couldn't lose the house now. Not after all of this. And not because of my stupid knee.

Or my stupidity in not taking better care of my leg all along.

Grandma Rose had been feeling stronger. Now, a few days after the blizzard, she had asked the children to go upstairs because the grown-ups needed to talk.

Her announcement wasn't a surprise, but Kevin didn't want to have this argument today. "You can't be on your own." He repeated the words and gave her his most caring big-brown-eyed, melting-caramel look.

She gently freed one hand and patted Kevin's cheek. "You are so sweet to worry. But I'll be fine. Harry said we could use his pickup. I'll be moving on January second."

Kevin sprang from the couch and rubbed the back of his neck. "No, you won't." He threw me a desperate look.

Yeah, pull me into this. If her darling son couldn't convince her, what was I supposed to do? I'd been trying for two months.

"Where did you find a place?" I asked. At least I knew not to issue ultimatums. If Kevin was going to play bad cop, I needed to play good cop.

She rewarded me with a smile. "Eldercare Estates." A bit of color rose across her face. "Harry put my name in when a place opened up."

Kevin gave a growl and paced away to stare out the window.

I wheeled closer to Rose. "What Kevin means"—I glanced at his tense back—"is that he's worried about how we will afford the assisted-living option that you need."

"Well, if he'd sit still for a minute, I could tell him."

Kevin spun to face us and rolled his eyes. Apparently, no matter how old the child, the eye roll remained the classic choice of response when exasperated. He walked back to the couch and sat down. "I'm listening."

Rose lifted her chin and looked at me. "This is private."

Her comments didn't sting me as much as they used to. Rose was Rose. With so little left in her domain, she had to control what she could.

I smiled at Kevin. "Sure. I need some coffee anyway."

I wheeled to the kitchen and studied the counters, wondering how to reach the coffee mugs.

Frankly, I wasn't pulling very hard for Rose to stay with us. With my gimpy leg, and our crazy on-the-go lifestyle, we weren't giving her much better care than she'd have on her own. I knew it was a matter of pride to Kevin, and some sort of payoff for old regrets, but I doubted he was going to win this.

He stormed into the kitchen a few minutes later.

"She had a secret account. She invested a little of every paycheck, and she even has enough money to cover extra services if she needs them."

"That's great. Good for her."

Kevin loomed over me. "Whose side are you on?"

Rose shuffled into the kitchen. "Becky, tell him he should be happy for me."

I threw my hands up, not wanting to get in the middle of this.

Rose turned on Kevin. "Why are you so upset?"

Kevin's emotions played across his face. Frustration, rejection. "Because I won't be able to take care of you." The truth broke out of him. "Just like I couldn't protect you back then."

The pain in his words, the vulnerable look on his face, made me catch my breath.

Rose stepped back, startled. Then she rolled her oxygen tank over toward Kevin, reached out, and hugged him. "It wasn't your job to protect me when . . . back then. You've been a wonderful son. Look at you. Good job, a nice wife, all those lively children, this house. I'm so proud of you." She pulled his head toward her, kissed his forehead, and released him. "Now, I need a nap." She frowned in my direction. "See if you can keep those children quiet for once."

Rose rattled off down the hall, pulling her oxygen beside her.

Kevin sank into a chair, a bit dazed. "What are we going to do?"

"We're going to have a lovely Christmas, then help her move to her new apartment. And you're going to stop trying to do things for her that she doesn't want done."

"But . . . she . . . and . . ."

I maneuvered my chair close to his and cut off his sputters with a kiss. "I love you, Mr. Miller. You're a pretty decent guy. Even if you are a little slow."

Kevin headed back to work the next day, and I tried to keep my church projects going from home. With the connections working again, my e-mail and the telephone became lifelines. Kevin dropped off the kids at school in the morning, and Harry volunteered to pick Kelsey and Micah up at lunchtime and bring them home. Then Harry spent the afternoon tearing things apart, trying to convince me he was fixing them.

How were we going to get the inspector to sign off on the house when Harry kept finding more things to work on? And should we even put any more effort into the house? According to the doctor, we should find a practical one-level home with a ramp up to the front steps.

Our "final" building inspection was scheduled for the next day. I'd lost track of how many inspections we'd had, but Kevin was sure this one would finally allow us to roll the high-interest construction loan into our conventional mortgage. If not, we'd have to surrender and plan to move.

When the big day arrived, Kevin was at work, so Harry came over to walk the man through the house. While we waited for him to arrive, Harry lumbered from one end of the house to the other, gnawing a hangnail and double-checking his work. My tension doubled as I watched the amiable giant acting so nervous.

When the inspector's car pulled up our driveway, Harry threw open our front door. "Smitty! Cold enough for ya?"

"Harry! How ya been? It's been too long." Smitty knocked the snow off his shoes and strode into the house.

Harry's jitters disappeared, and amid much backslapping and

insider gossip, he showed Smitty all the repairs on the house.

I chewed on my own hangnails and waited in the kitchen, praying nothing would explode, leak, or fall down during the inspection.

"Ya betcha," Harry's voice rumbled from the basement. "It's all up to code. Or close enough."

Apparently, old friendships went a long way, because Smitty signed off on our report.

The next day, we signed the papers for a new mortgage and celebrated with pizza. But the pepperoni was tasteless in my mouth. Would this success even matter? Sure, with a careful budget we could now afford to keep the house, but my leg wasn't cooperating. It was becoming clear that taking care of a household and chasing kids was too difficult if I couldn't navigate up and down stairs. I prayed that I'd have better news at my next doctor's appointment. That was all I could do for the moment.

The Christmas Tea was a huge success and brought in a lot of new women from the neighborhood around the church. Some of them signed up for our new members' class, which had Tom singing my praises instead of muttering about my lack of outreach zeal.

Judy called once to vent about the idiots she was working with, but from the energy in her voice I knew she was thriving on the challenge of taking over the new company and whipping it into shape. She casually dropped the nugget that she'd visited Greg's church. She said it was "even weirder" than mine, but she still thought she might check it out again soon. That was as much as I could get out of her, but the information made me smile.

Heather had the radical idea of holding our Thursday night Bible study at the mental health clinic where Lori was still a patient. Noah talked to Lori and her psychologist to make the arrangements. I secretly hoped the clinic wouldn't allow it. With movie images of *One Flew Over the Cuckoo's Nest* or *The Snake Pit,* my stomach was in knots when Doreen wheeled me up the sidewalk to the clinic doors. Heather and Sally were waiting in the lobby, and I glanced around, looking for the crazy people. It would be hard to make a quick getaway in a wheelchair. Doreen would probably leave me behind and make a run for it.

A nurse buzzed us back to a dayroom. The bland room held a few watercolor paintings that were probably meant to be soothing, and shelves with puzzles and games. An elderly man who needed a shave lounged in one corner, reading. Two teenage girls—one skinny as a rail and one with a cherubic face—chatted by the window. No straitjackets in sight.

Lori entered from a far door, glanced around the room, and beamed when she saw us. She looked so . . . normal. Her dark skin stood out against the pale walls. She was dressed in jeans and a sweater. Her lean form moved as gracefully as ever as she approached our huddle.

"It's so good to see you!"

We squealed and hugged, pulled up chairs, and forgot the surroundings. Lori brushed away our questions.

"Later. I want to hear about the real world." She grinned. "Heather, what have you heard from Ron?"

Sally pulled out her day-planner and took notes as Heather gave a praise report about how the mission project was progressing. As soon as Heather finished, Lori turned to Doreen. "Is work getting any better? How are the kids? Did they do okay on the trip?"

Doreen had driven to her parents' home out of state for Thanksgiving. "It was rough. I ended up yelling all those things I promised myself I'd never yell at my kids."

We all exchanged sheepish looks. "Like 'Because I said so!' Right?" Sally piped up.

Doreen winked. "Or 'If you don't settle down, I'm stopping the car right now.' Even though I was in the middle of the freeway."

"Oh, oh." I waved my hand. "And how about 'How many times have I told you not to . . . ?'"

"Throw the cat in the washing machine."

"Put beans in your ears."

"Hide ice cream in your closet."

We reviewed our crazy kids' conduct for a few more minutes, while I decided that by comparison, my household wasn't quite as messed up as I'd thought.

Finally, Sally tapped her pen. "Okay, so I'm adding parenting skills to our prayer list. We all need help to be gentle and encouraging in our words to our children."

Doreen smirked. "And we better also pray that our kids learn some common sense."

"Okay, Becky"—Lori gave me a warm smile—"what's the news on your leg?"

I shrugged. "I'm supposed to start physical therapy sessions after Christmas. I should get back on my feet pretty soon." I had chosen firm denial as my response to the doctor's recommendations about surgery. "But I'm not supposed to do stairs. And you've all seen our new house."

Sally giggled. "Just have Kevin carry you up and down. It would be romantic."

I gave her a pointed look. "He's in a cast, remember?"

Murmurs of sympathy flowed around the circle. "What will you do?"

"I don't know. Right now, I just want to get through Christmas. I don't have time to worry about my leg. After Grandma Rose moves out, Kevin and I will have a serious talk about everything."

"Well, you need to schedule the house blessing," Heather said.

"That's right." Lori lit up.

And before I could argue, my friends decided the first Saturday after the New Year would be the perfect day for this event.

"But, we might not be able to stay—"

"I'll bring some bars and cookies."

"Who else should we invite?"

"Who do we know that plays guitar? We need someone to lead the singing."

"Oooh, and I'll come and stay over on the Friday night before," said Heather. "That way you and Kevin can have a little romantic getaway. A night at a hotel before the big day."

I covered my face with my hands until they wound down. Clearly, I wasn't going to stop this juggernaut. When I popped up for air, I looked at Lori.

"So, how are you? Really? How is this place?"

"The food's not great. But I'm learning a lot."

Sally squirmed on her chair, her gaze darting around the room. "Well, I still don't understand why you're here."

Lori took a slow breath. "Partly because readjusting the meds can be tricky, and they needed to check my blood levels. Partly because I felt I was in danger."

I blanched at her frankness.

She pulled up her knees and hugged her shins. "It's ironic. My disorder makes me feel out of control. But one of the things I'm trying to learn is not to try so hard to control everything."

That sounded familiar.

Now Doreen squirmed. "What do you mean? I think it's great to be organized and efficient, to have focus and goals."

Lori nodded. "Yeah, but we can't do everything. Like Thanksgiving. I got all tense trying to impress Noah's parents and sisters. But I can't control what they think of me. It got me into a whole spiral of condemning myself."

"So it wasn't because you were helping us at the house?" I asked.

"Oh, get over yourself," she teased. "I was nutty long before I met you. A few paint fumes won't send me over the edge."

I heard it then. The tiny thread of sadness that hemmed her humor. How hard must it be to feel desperately sad and have so few people understand? Or have people judge her level of faith because of what she battled?

Empathy flooded me. "Let's have our prayer time, okay?" We all needed more help than what we could offer one another.

We pulled the chairs into a tighter circle, joining hands. Tears fell, petitions flew, and hearts swelled with gratitude as we turned our thoughts to the Keeper of our souls.

Before Doreen wheeled me back to her car that night, Lori knelt by my chair. "I'm so sorry about your leg. Don't be too discouraged about the house. God led you there for a reason."

I chewed my lip. "Yeah, but I thought it was so Grandma Rose could live with us, and she's not. And I thought it would help our family slow down and draw closer, and so far we've been more stressed than ever. And now with the thing about the stairs . . ."

She patted my knee. "Give it time."

"What hurts the most is that I figured fixing up the house would"—I dropped my voice—"fix my marriage. It's brought some issues to light, but we have a long way to go."

"You and Kevin love each other to pieces. When you clear some space in your lives, you'll have time to remember that."

I nodded, humbled that she was offering encouragement while wearing the plastic bracelet of a psych clinic on her wrist. It must be frightening, being in this alien environment. "And you get better and come home soon."

"Home," she sighed with longing.

I hugged her good-bye and watched her pass through the far door, back to a foreign world and a journey I couldn't fully understand.

Chapter Thirty-three

I ran along the streets of my small town. My precious, snow-covered, reliable hometown. Everything was back to the way it was supposed to be—the park, the five-and-dime, the trees.

My feet skidded on the snow as I rounded the corner to my street. There it was. My home. Restored. Right where it was supposed to be. Every droopy shutter, every weary shingle. It shimmered in the glow of light pouring from windows.

As I burst inside, my family gathered around me, worried about my absence. Worried about my state of mind. But losing the bank no longer terrified me. Even the threat of jail couldn't dim my gratitude.

That crazy old angel was right. My life was worthwhile. I hugged my children, kissed my husband, laughed with the delight of being alive.

And then a neighbor burst through the door. "I never repaid that loan. Here. This is to help the bank."

A friend followed on his heels. "I want to help."

More people crowded in behind.

A Christmas Eve miracle. I wrapped my arm around Kevin and lifted Micah to my shoulder.

"Look, Mommy." Micah pointed to our Christmas tree. A gust of wind from the open door tickled a branch, and a tiny bell jingled.

"Ooooh," Micah crooned, eyes wide. The tree by the church's altar was adorned with white crosses and doves, and now tiny lights flicked on, wrapping the tree in sparkle. The organist played the carillon, and the ushers finished lighting votive candles set around the sanctuary.

I'd expected to feel a bit disappointed at the Christmas Eve service.

After all, I was attending in a wheelchair—still on strict orders to rest my leg. And it was embarrassing to admit that my own choices had led me to this predicament. Overuse, neglecting my therapy and medication, and thinking it was noble to ignore my limitations had all been contributors.

And my leg wasn't the only thing still needing repair. Here at church, the building committee had hoped to have the work in the worship center completed in time for Christmas. Instead—as I'd learned during the never-ending work on our own house—delays and remodeling go together like angels and wings. The builders had apologized for the scaffolding that still surrounded the pews. But instead of diminishing the mood, the bare wood beams gave a rustic ambience that hinted at mangers and carpenters and crosses.

Dylan's class marched to the front and jostled into position on the steps. They had been asked to recite the second chapter of Luke. One by one, girls in velvet dresses and boys in crooked ties stepped up to the podium. When the narrative reached the story of the shepherds, Dylan walked forward and leaned in to the microphone. He spoke with conviction and a sweet earnestness and remembered each word. More important to me, he didn't shove any of his classmates the whole time the class was in front of the church. Things were looking up.

As Dylan came back up the aisle to sit with us, I decided Harry had been right. Spending purposeful time with Kevin had helped Dylan access a new level of patience and self-control.

During the sermon, Pastor Bob mentioned the unfinished construction, and compared it to God's ongoing work in our lives and in the world. Then he announced that the first stage of the project would be completed by the end of January, but instead of moving into the second stage, the church council was recommending the church wait before doing further expansion.

Pastor Bob smiled. "Growth in the size of our church is

wonderful. But we want to keep our focus on Jesus. Jesus who came to humble places, to small places, to broken people."

A weight eased in my heart. Maybe the relentless forward charge of our church could ease a bit, without deserting our desire for growth. Maybe the staff could find a healthier way to serve.

"We have a lot of great ideas for our church," he continued. "But not all great ideas are the right ideas. We want to spend more time in prayer before we make further decisions."

Although his words gave me optimism for the church, they also set me to mulling over our house, and what our family would do next. Despite the gals' insistent plans for a house blessing, I couldn't imagine a way that our dream house could still work out.

The overhead lights dimmed and brought to life the hundreds of small candles set on the wooden beams. Who cared about a little construction tape and bare joists? It was Christmas Eve. The congregation sang "Silent Night" with a tender, almost breathless tone. Micah snuggled against me in my wheelchair. Kevin reached over and squeezed my hand. On his other side, Kelsey leaned against him. Dylan sang along, looking up toward the cross, his jaw firm. Beyond him, Rose sat primly, relieved to be able to get along without her golf cart of oxygen. And on her other side, Harry fidgeted, tugging the collar of his best flannel shirt.

After the service, while I was still basking in the warmth of the closing hymn, Teresa scurried toward me. "Becky, I need to talk to you. In private." She grabbed the wheelchair handles and pushed me toward her office. I tried to find the brake lever, but it was too late. She wheeled me in, turned me around, and shut her door.

"I wanted you to know, even though we aren't telling anyone else yet." She giggled and played with the hem of her sweater.

"What?" Watching Teresa dither was unnerving. I was used to her hyper-focused style.

"And I really have you to thank. Well, not directly, but . . . you know."

"Know?"

Another shy giggle. "I'm pregnant."

I was too stunned to respond. And how exactly did she think I was responsible?

"We're going to have a baby." As if I didn't understand her the first time. "Me and Ben. Well, me. But you know what I mean."

My surprise was pushed aside by delight. "I'm so happy for you!"

"Don't tell anyone." She tugged her sweater down again. "I sure hope I can do this. I don't know if I'll be a good mom."

I opened my arms and she leaned down so I could hug her. I rested my cheek against hers and whispered into her ear. "You'll be fine. Everything will change. But it's the most amazing gift in the world."

After another warning not to tell anyone, she wheeled me back to the narthex.

After Christmas, Harry helped Rose move into Eldercare Estates. Kevin couldn't lift anything yet, and I was still in the wheelchair, so we weren't much help.

Suddenly, our house felt huge.

Keeping my New Year's resolution to take better care of myself, I faithfully made a follow-up appointment with my doctor. The soonest I could get in was on the first Saturday after the new year— the morning of the house blessing. Kevin and I were having our romantic getaway at a hotel the night before, but we had to check out by ten in the morning. I thought going to a doctor's appointment was an odd way to end our date, but Kevin convinced me it would be fine.

My friends wanted to set up refreshments for the house blessing and had ordered us not to come home until one in the afternoon.

I was grateful for the Saturday morning clinic hours that allowed Kevin to take me to the appointment. We were still a sorry-looking pair, but he was coping with one-handed driving pretty well.

Dr. Lorton was happy with how the enforced rest had helped

my knee and hip, and he said I was ready to use my cane again and begin physical therapy.

"How's the pain? Are you still taking the anti-inflammatory pills?"

"No, they bothered my stomach. And I think they damaged something, because it still doesn't feel right."

He asked me several more questions, nodding and frowning. "Could be an ulcer. Have you been under unusual stress lately?"

I thought of the past few months and sighed. "Yep. I guess you could say that."

"Let's run some tests before I give you a prescription for new meds, okay?" He scribbled on a sheet and handed it to me. "Take this to the lab. They'll do a few of them right now, so you can wait in the lobby. The rest of the results will take several days, so my office will call you when they're in."

Doctors sure love to run tests. I shuffled along to the lab and obediently offered my arm for blood, then detoured into the bathroom to fill a little jar for them. Then I settled into a lobby chair beside Kevin.

"Ready to go?" he asked.

"I'm supposed to wait for some tests."

He looked at his watch. "I hope they hurry. We don't want to be late for our own house blessing."

"Well, if the lab takes too long, we'll leave. I can call in for the results."

A toddler scooted around the room, careening into various patients while his mom ignored him and talked on a cell phone. A baby squawked and then worked up to a full-throated wail. Several children snuffled and coughed. I wished for earplugs.

Finally, a nurse called my name. She brought me back to the same exam room.

Dr. Lorton bustled in, seconds after me. He pulled up his stool and stared at the lab results. "Okay. This isn't what we were expecting. You're pregnant."

Waves roared in my ears. My head gave a shake of denial. "But we . . . but I . . . it's inconceivable."

He raised an eyebrow.

I giggled. "No pun intended." Hey, I was being clever. Giddy joy overwhelmed my confusion. Of course I was witty. I was amazing. I was carrying a new life. Delirium was a gift of my psyche that kept me from being overwhelmed by the news.

"You'll need to get serious about avoiding stairs. Your ligaments soften during pregnancy. That and the extra weight will be too hard on your knees unless you're scrupulously careful." Dr. Lorton began talking about vitamins, about the specialist he wanted me to see because of my damaged hip. He said he recommended a Cesarean when it came time for the delivery, to avoid undue stress on my pelvis. I'd have to be selective about pain management for my leg. His words were an annoying buzz in the distance.

Thoughts and images collided in my brain. The warm sweet skin of a newborn. The chubby hand splayed against my chest as he nursed. The torment of sleepless nights and endless diaper changes. Our budget. The big farmhouse, enriched by another child. Kevin rubbing my back and walking with me during labor.

Kevin!

"I need to tell my husband."

Dr. Lorton cut off midsentence, looking a bit affronted. Then he smiled. "All right. Go ahead and set up an appointment for next week, and see if he can come in with you. We'll talk more then."

I must have used my cane to make my way back to the waiting room, but it felt like I floated. Kevin stood up, already jangling his car keys. I surprised him with a hug. Then I surprised him even more with the test results I whispered in his ear.

I stepped back to watch the news sink in. First, his mouth gaped open. Then his skin paled a bit. Then small crinkles appeared at the sides of his eyes, and a smile broke across his face.

He squeezed me with his one good arm and whooped, drawing the gaze of everyone in the waiting room.

As we headed to the car, he kept shaking his head. "Wow. Imagine that. How did that happen? No, I mean . . ."

I giggled. "The kids are going to be so excited. And we can take Lamaze classes with Teresa and Ben. Won't that be fun?"

"A riot." Kevin opened my car door. "Hey!" He stopped short and whirled to face me. "I was wondering why God led us to our new place if my mom ended up somewhere else. Now I get it. Good thing we have such a big house, isn't it?"

He grinned all the way home, but my excitement dimmed a bit. The doctor insisted I needed to avoid stairs. I loved our new house. I loved the generous, uneven, imperfect spirit of it. We pulled into the driveway, and I stared at it with longing.

Lord, I can't help it. It hurts to think about giving up on this dream.

Cars cluttered the driveway and spilled over onto the packed snow around the shed. Our appointment had taken longer than we'd planned, and friends had already arrived. Good thing the gals had come over early to watch the kids and set up some snacks.

I still thought this house blessing was a weird idea, especially if we wouldn't be able to stay. Should I send them home? Tell them, "I'm sorry, but we can't keep the dream home, because I didn't do a good enough job taking care of my leg this past year."

Kevin led me to the porch and the front door. As we walked in a voice yelled, "Surprise!"

I shook my head at my goofy friends. They knew this wasn't a surprise party. My gaze skimmed the room. Noah with a protective arm around Lori, who looked tired but at ease. Heather, Ron, and their twins, happily reunited after the successful medical mission. Sally and Doreen, struggling to corral the kids. Some of Kevin's co-workers. Teresa and Ben—both wearing a secret glow. Grandma Rose, Harry.

They parted and created an aisle so I could see the staircase.

"What? What's that?" I hobbled forward, glancing at Kevin, who just kept grinning.

The room filled with laughter and chatter as I reached the steps.

A motorized chair rested on a rail set into the wall, and a glide followed the line of the wall up the stairs.

"Surprise!" everyone yelled again.

Confused, I looked at Kevin. "What is it?"

Doreen stepped forward. "It's a stair glide. It'll save a ton of wear and tear on your hip and knee. You sit down, press the toggle, and it carries you up."

"You mean . . . ?" Tears sprang to my eyes.

Kevin leaned in. "We can stay," he whispered. "We can make this work."

"We all chipped in," Sally said, her curls bouncing in her excitement.

"Ben and Noah installed it last night."

"I helped." Dylan jumped up and down.

Kevin laughed. "It was my job to keep you away, but considering how long it took at the doctor's, that wasn't hard."

Lori gave me a hug. "You can go up and down as many times a day as you want."

"And that's not all." Rose stepped forward. "Look what Harry did in the kitchen."

Kevin led me through the crowd, and I gasped when I saw the new arrangement. Along the ample wall near the sink, Harry had installed our washer and dryer.

"Now ya can do your clothes up here, missy," Harry said, tugging the strap of his overalls.

"And I can help," Kelsey piped up, twirling across the linoleum in her excitement.

I threw my arms around Harry and gave him a hug that turned him beet red. Then I turned to Kevin and buried my face in his good shoulder.

"Let's start this house blessing," Noah boomed.

So we did. Room by room, we thanked God and asked for His blessing on the activities that would take place within its walls.

When it was time to bless the upstairs rooms, I tried the new chair glide. It carried me smoothly up the stairs, with Micah sitting on my lap. Kevin winked at me when the group gathered in the spare bedroom, and Lori prayed that all guests who stayed there would draw close to God and find a safe haven.

I rested my hand against my stomach and smiled, looking forward to one particular guest who'd arrive in about eight months.

With songs, prayers, and laughter, we committed the house to God—as a place where our family could grow strong and where God could work in any way He might choose.

Later, over a piece of Heather's tofu cheesecake with wheat germ sprinkles, I rested my head against Kevin's shoulder and admired our living room. Dylan had his toolbox out and was asking Harry serious questions about one of the wrenches. Kelsey was showing a charm bracelet to Grandma Rose and telling her a long story about each piece. Micah leaned on the coffee table and was poking decorative holes into one of the desserts.

"Is this okay? What we did?" Kevin rested his chin against my hair, waiting for my answer.

"It's wonderful. I'm so happy we have this place."

His chest rumbled against my ear as he laughed. "Yep. Not so bad, now that we've got the plumbing fixed. We'll be tackling the wiring next."

I decided not to think about that. "I can't wait to plant a garden in the spring. And sit on the porch to watch the sunset. It's a happy ending."

Kevin squeezed me. "No. It's a happy beginning."

I looked at everyone milling around the living room. We truly had a wonderful life. "And isn't it sweet about your mom and Harry?"

"Huh? What about them?"

I patted his arm. "Never mind. I'll tell you later." The poor guy had enough news to adjust to for one day.

Appendix

Kevin and Becky have eclectic and diverse tastes in films. Did you recognize some of the movies they rented on their date nights that loosely inspired Becky's daydreams? Here's their chapter by chapter list. (Please note that this list doesn't necessarily indicate the author's recommendation or endorsement.)

1. The Bourne Identity
2. Gone With the Wind
3. An Affair to Remember
4. The Wizard of Oz
5. Casablanca
6. The Music Man
7. Star Wars Episode IV: A New Hope
8. The Secret Garden
9. Mary Poppins
10. Indiana Jones and the Raiders of the Lost Ark
11. Heidi
12. Gladiator
13. Sunset Boulevard
14. From Russia With Love
15. The Grapes of Wrath
16. Jurassic Park
17. Dracula
18. Titanic
19. Seabiscuit
20. Lord of the Rings: The Fellowship of the Ring
21. The African Queen
22. Snow White
23. The Fugitive
24. The Little Princess
25. Sabrina
26. Fiddler on the Roof
27. Braveheart
28. White Christmas
29. Jaws
30. March of the Penguins
31. The Lion, the Witch, and the Wardrobe
32. E.T.
33. It's a Wonderful Life

Book Group Discussion Questions

1. Remodeling From the Inside Out

Where have you noticed spiritual growth from God's renovation in your life? How has your life changed in the last ten years? Five years? Month? Share some ideas for cooperating with God's internal renovation work in your heart. (Romans 12:1–2)

2. Family Renovation

In addition to renovating our individual lives, God is at work in our family lives. Becky feels squeezed between serving her husband, children, mother-in-law, and sister. What family stresses do you face at this season in your life? (Matthew 22:35–40)

3. Church Reconstruction

Becky's church is experiencing growth. What challenges does this growth bring? What challenges does your home congregation face? How can you support and serve your local church community? (Ephesians 2:19–22, 4:11–16)

4. Subcontractors: The Support System

Who makes up your support system? Becky's small-group Bible study serves a vital role in her life. Are you part of a trusted small group for prayer, Bible study, and accountability? What steps could you take to find or create this sort of ongoing fellowship? If you are a part of such a group, what is working well? What could be improved? (Romans 12:3–13)

5. Power Tools: Getting a Little Assistance

Becky tries to ignore her physical limitations but learns that she has limits to her time, energy, and strength. Is this a copout or a wise discernment? Lori battles a chronic emotional health challenge that she has hidden from her friends. How do you make choices to nurture your physical, emotional, and spiritual health without becoming selfish? Has God been prompting you to make some changes? To slow down, cut back, care for yourself? Or to step out, try something new, and care for others? (2 Timothy 4:5–8; Psalm 127:1–2)

————————

For more information about this book and its author, please visit *www.bethanyhouse.com/renovatingbeckymiller* and *www.sharonhinck.com*.

Acknowledgments

It's been a delight to spend more time with Becky Miller and her family, so my first thanks go to the readers who embraced *The Secret Life of Becky Miller* and made this second book possible.

Thank you to all the marvelous co-laborers at Bethany House Publishers in every department. My special gratitude goes to Charlene Patterson and Ann Parrish. These dear editors are true servants of Christ with amazing insights into the challenges of fiction and the type of caring hearts and encouraging words that most authors only dream of.

I lean heavily on the support of my Book Buddies. Their prayer, interest, and ability to "buzz" about my books all keep me going through the inevitable days of doubt and fatigue. If you're interested in becoming one of my Book Buddies, visit *www.sharonhinck.com* and click on Contact Sharon.

St. Michael's Lutheran Church is a place of worship, truth, and support that amazes me week after week. In particular, I'm grateful to Family Fellowship and the "Church Ladies." You keep me real. Thank you for sharing your authentic hearts.

As a writer, I thrive on the wisdom of American Christian Fiction Writers, Writer's View, Minnesota Christian Writer's Guild, and the Mount Hermon Christian Writer's Conference. Thank you all for the generous sharing of knowledge.

Thank you to all the language arts and writing teachers I've had in grade school, high school, college, and grad school. Each word of support was planted in my heart, ready to sprout at the right time. Special thanks to Professor John Lawing, who red-penned my homework with one hand and guided me into magazine publication with the other.

Huge appreciation goes to my incredibly wise agent, Steve Laube. I'd have floundered into quicksand many times if not for you.

I also thank God daily for the dear author friends who share this path. The Christian community is richer because of you, and my soul is comforted by each of you who have reached out in fellowship and continue to set an example of dedication and courage.

Word Servants, my work as a novelist began in your tender care and continues to grow because of you. Thank you for honest feedback, patience with my whining, cyber chocolates for my disappointments, and Snoopy dances for each breakthrough.

Special thanks to Dr. Walter Hinck for medical insights. Any errors caused by my fictional interpretations are my own. Thank you as well to Julie Knollenberg for answering questions about mortgages, building loans, and refinancing. Again, if I got it wrong, it's not her fault.

Family and friends, you've shown love to me in a thousand ways during my work on this novel. You listened to plot threads without your eyes glazing over. You read early drafts. You coaxed me away for a meal when I forgot to eat. You sent me e-mail prayers. You took me for walks. You listened to my insecurities and consistently reminded me that God is in control of my life.

Mom, thank you for long phone conversations, and for laughing, caring, and praying. And thanks to Carl for his gentle kindness.

My deepest love goes to Ted, Joel, Jennelle, Kaeti, Josh, and Jenni. You amaze me with the ways you reflect the love of Christ in our family life.

To my Lord, thank you for loving me so much, even though I'm a "fixer-upper."

SHARON HINCK is a wife and mother of four children who generously provide her with material for her books. She has an M.A. in communications from Regent University and has served as the artistic director of a Christian performing arts group, a church youth worker, and a professional choreographer. She lives in Minnesota with her family. To learn more about her writing visit her Web site at *www.sharonhinck.com*.